SPELLS
LIKE
TEEN
SPIRIT

BOOKS BY KATE WILLIAMS

The Babysitters Coven

For Better or Cursed

Spells Like Teen Spirit

SPELLS LIKE TEEN SPIRIT

KATE WILLIAMS

DELACORTE PRESS

Text copyright © 2021 by Katharine Williams
Jacket art copyright © 2021 by Rik Lee

Visit us on the Web! GetUnderlined.com

Educators and librarians, for a variety of teaching tools, visit us at RHTeachersLibrarians.com

Library of Congress Cataloging-in-Publication Data
Names: Williams, Kate, author.
Title: Spells like teen spirit / Kate Williams.
Description: First edition. | New York: Delacorte Press, [2021] | Series: The babysitters coven; 3 | Audience: Ages 14+. | Audience: Grades 10–12. | Summary: Esme suspects that the trouble brewing in Spring River has something to do with a new band that reeks of Red Magic.
Identifiers: LCCN 2021001402 (print) | LCCN 2021001403 (ebook) | ISBN 978-0-593-30482-2 (hardcover) | ISBN 978-0-593-30483-9 (ebook)
Subjects: CYAC: Babysitters—Fiction. | Clubs—Fiction. | Witchcraft—Fiction. | Bands (Music)—Fiction.
Classification: LCC PZ7.1.W5465 Sp 2021 (print) | LCC PZ7.1.W5465 (ebook) | DDC [Fic]—dc23

The text of this book is set in 12-point Baskerville MT.
Interior design by Kenneth Crossland

Printed in the United States of America
10 9 8 7 6 5 4 3 2 1
First Edition

For Anthony, my second-favorite person

CHAPTER 1

I drummed my fingers nervously on the steering wheel. Even though the groundhog hadn't seen his shadow, the Riverbend Hotel parking lot was dotted with gray piles of snow and oil-slicked puddles, and spring still seemed a loooong way away, especially as the sun was going down. I shivered in spite of my puffiest jacket, my wooliest (rhinestone-encrusted) mittens, and a heater on full blast.

Cassandra and Janis were in the backseat, and I could tell by their silence that they were nervous too. I adjusted the rear-view mirror so that I could see Mom, who was sitting in between them. She looked really nice. I'd picked out her outfit for this occasion—a cream-colored wool suit with a silk shell underneath—and Janis had done her glam: a burgundy lip, a subtle cheek highlight, her dark hair swept to the side with a gold comb. She looked like a woman ready to celebrate her anniversary.

I smiled at her in the mirror. She didn't smile back and instead turned and stared out the window like she was ten million miles away. I wasn't offended. I was used to it. Mom was cursed. She had been besieged by a potent blast of magic that had left her distant, uncommunicative, and difficult for the better part of my life. Her behavior was what most people would call "crazy," and it wasn't until just a few months before that I'd learned why she was like this, and even more recently that I'd started to understand it. Even though she couldn't do anything to show it, Mom was totally aware of what was going on around her. She was paying attention, she was trying as hard as she could, and she was absolutely miserable.

Two weeks before, Dad and I had moved her out of the facility where she'd been living for years. Now she was living with us again, and so far it was going okay. We had to make sure she wasn't ever alone, since the curse meant that she wasn't in control of her actions and could easily hurt herself. We had a nurse who came during the day, and then the rest of the time we made sure either Dad or I was always with her. I could tell Dad was tired. But I could also tell that he was happier. We all were. Well, as happy as we could be, now that we were just a single-species family of three. Pig, our dog, was still gone.

"Esme, why are we listening to Christmas music?" Cassandra asked, leaning forward and snapping me back into the car and the present moment.

Of course, Janis had to pipe up too. "I mean, I like George Michael as much as the next girl," she said. "But every time I've been in the car with you, it's this same mix. I didn't even think you liked Christmas."

"Give me a break," I said. "I've been driving for, like, a week. I'm allowed to listen to whatever calms me down, okay?"

"Touché, Mrs. Claus," Cassandra said. "Tell me again how many medians you've hit?"

"Cassandra," I snapped back, "you know it was just that one, and it wasn't my fault, because it moved and—"

A tap at the window made me jump. I turned to see Dad outside the car, rubbing his hands together to keep them warm. "Okay," he said. "We're good to go." In the backseat, Janis and Cassandra were already unbuckling their seat belts and climbing out of the car. I popped the trunk, and then quickly followed them so that Dad and I could help Mom from the car. Dad looked nice too, in his best pleat-front Dockers and a navy blue blazer. My teeth were chattering in the damp cold.

"So, you said everything like we rehearsed?" I asked.

"Yep," he said, nodding as he took Mom's elbow and started walking with her to the door. "I told them that February eleventh was our anniversary, and my wife and I wanted to spend it in room 402, just like we did on our wedding night twenty years ago."

I groaned and pulled my coat tighter around me. "Dad," I said, "you got the date wrong. Today's the seventh!"

"Well, I'm sure no one noticed," he said. "Aren't husbands always forgetting anniversaries?" I sighed as he reached into the pocket of his khakis and pulled out a key. "So," he continued, "Mom and I will go in through the lobby, and you all will come up the back way?" I nodded and glanced at Cassandra and Janis, who were busy unloading bags from the trunk.

"You know where the back entrance is?" Dad asked.

"Trust me, Mr. Pearl," Janis answered, "we know just about every inch of this hotel. Even the roof."

This time it was Janis's words, and not the cold, that made me shiver. I'd been trying to put what had happened here at the Riverbend Hotel out of my mind, and even though we'd driven by this place a million times as we'd been planning for tonight, we'd never actually gone in. Now I was staring right at the hotel, and it was staring back at me, with its dead-eye windows and its bricklike acne-scarred skin.

This was the place where everything had fallen apart. Cassandra and I were Sitters, which meant we were trusted (or burdened, depending on the day and my mood when asked) with superpowers and spells to protect the innocent and keep the demons who prey on them in their own dimension. Back in December, we had come to this very hotel for a Summit, which was a gathering of Sitters from all over the country. We were supposed to have bonded, learned, and prepared, but all that had been put on pause in favor of stopping an apocalypse.

Sitters had an entire society—called the Sitterhood—and this was, or at least used to be, governed by a team of four called the Synod, über-powerful women who'd served as Sitters and were then chosen to stay on and guide the generations who came after them. Sounds awesome, right? Except it wasn't, at all.

Wanda, who'd been the head of the Synod, had revealed herself to be an eBay-addicted megalomaniac who would stop at nothing to get all the Beanie Babies she wanted. The magic that Sitters used was altruistic magic, meaning that it only worked so that we could help others. Sitters have found little ways to bend the rules here and there, of course, but that wasn't enough for Wanda, so she'd plunged headfirst into Red Magic. Red Magic = big bad magic. It was selfish, materialistic, and evil, and Wanda had gone all in in her pursuit of tiny plush animals. She'd even planned to destroy the entire Sitterhood by turning all of us Sitters into demon hors d'oeuvres, and she'd also tried to sacrifice Cassandra and me as part of an immortality ritual. (Because dead people couldn't place bids on eBay, I guess?) The rest of the Sitters had stopped her just in time.

And Pig too, of course. Pig had helped. She had saved me, but I'd been too late to save her. Wanda had thrown my dog off the top of a six-story building, and we hadn't seen Pig since. We hadn't seen Wanda since then either, but I couldn't give two effs about that. My anger had flushed her into the Portal, into the deepest depths of the Negative, and that was where I was hoping she would stay.

"Here." Janis's voice cut through my melancholic reverie, and she handed me a bag. "You take this one." It was surprisingly heavy, and I looked down to see that it was full of LaCroix and Amirah's Louboutins. Amirah was one of the Sitters that Cassandra and I had met at the Summit. She was from New York and had a fashion editor's wardrobe and a gossip columnist's knack for name-dropping. Amirah and I had gotten off to a bad start, but she'd turned out to be pretty okay. More than okay, actually—she had saved our butts. And it turned out that she was very generous with that wardrobe.

Janis, Cassandra, and I were back at the Riverbend now because we were trying to recreate a disaster. A very specific disaster. At the Summit, Cassandra and I had discovered that she had been cursed—another dollop of Wanda's Red Magic handiwork—but then, one morning, Cassandra's curse had disappeared, surprising the heck out of all of us. We were pretty sure some accidental combination of spells—a combo that included chickens, a dog, hotel food, lots of designer clothing, hot water, and a toilet—had come together to release her from the curse. So since then, we'd been listing like crazy and trying to remember every little thing we could about that moment so that we could recreate it for Mom. And that was what we were about to do.

Amirah had sent us everything of hers that we remembered had been in the room when Cassandra's curse had broken. It was several thousand dollars' worth of clothing, but she didn't blink an eye when we asked. "Donate it when you're done," she'd said. "I never wear that old stuff anymore." Needless to say, as soon as we were done with this experiment, it was definitely getting donated—to me and Janis. Amirah was coming back to Spring River in less than a week, and while I was excited to see her, I was also really excited to see her wardrobe and discover what new, totally incredible things she was done with.

And Amirah wasn't coming alone. In fact, it was going to be a little Summit reunion of sorts in the form of a Spring River staycation. Amirah's Sitter partner, Ji-A, was coming too. Ji-A was from New York, of course, and her wardrobe was just as amazing, and as expensive, as Amirah's. Though, sadly, Ji-A didn't seem to get bored with it as quickly as Amirah did.

Ruby, who was now Cassandra's girlfriend, and her Sitter partner, Mallory, were also coming from Miami, even though I was pretty sure that neither of them owned anything warmer than a windbreaker. I think they all found Kansas kind of exotic, in the same way some people get a ferret for a pet.

Janis, Cassandra, and I crossed the parking lot, stepping around slush piles and puddles, to make our way to the back entrance of the Riverbend. I set my bag down and raised my hand. All Sitters had a kinesis, which was a power they were born with, and mine was telekinesis, which I had to admit came in very handy for breaking and entering. I focused on the door and popped it open, then waved Cassandra in. She started the climb to the fourth floor, taking the steps two at a time. I followed her up, and Janis huffed and groaned as she brought up the rear.

"Hold up a minute," she said as we reached the third floor. "This isn't a sprint."

I turned back to look at her. Janis had been watching a lot of *Moesha* lately, which her outfit reflected—butternut-squash-soup-colored turtleneck, blazer that looked like it had been made from someone's mom's curtains, and a maroon miniskirt. The only part of her look that wasn't totally nineties-tastic was her shoes: a pair of Off-White black suede high-heeled sandals with red zip ties around the ankles, another one of Amirah's "donations." With open toes, I noticed for the first time. No wonder she was having trouble with the stairs.

"Janis," I sighed, "it's, like, negative fifty outside. Why'd you even wear those?"

"Chill out," she said, and started up the stairs again. "You sound like my dad. Besides, we're going to be inside, and my toes are really impervious to cold." Janis wobbled a bit as she climbed, and her bag squawked. I thought about offering to use my kinesis to carry her bags for her, but then, I liked those shoes, and they would have looked really cute with my own outfit. Which, if I do say so myself, was also pretty on point. I had dubbed it "straight Fs" for "Fran Fine Fashion," because I'd gone with an all-black base of turtleneck, opaque black tights, and flats, under a leopard-print denim minidress that had metal snaps down the front.

I took a step and danced a little jig. "Man, these shoes are so comfy!" I said to no one in particular. "I could climb the Empire State Building in these shoes." Behind me Janis grunted.

Cassandra was waiting for us when we reached the fourth floor, looking very bored. Cassandra thought fashion was wearing a shirt with no stains on it, and even then, she didn't always participate. She was holding the door open to a hallway I knew well, and now that we were back, it felt like I'd never left. The hotel gave me the creepies as I thought about all the guests curled up under comforters and wrapped in bathrobes, without a single clue that this hotel had been the site of a near-demonic implosion just a few short weeks before. It had taken some serious magic, and probably a lot of bleach, to clean up that mess.

At room 402, which had been my room, and eventually Cassandra's, Janis's, and Pig's, Cassandra knocked on the door. Dad opened it, looking nervous, and then stepped aside to let us in. The TV was on, turned to some home remodeling show that Dad never would have watched for two seconds if he'd really been paying attention. Mom was sitting on the bed, brushing her hair with a slipper. I set the bag down and then handed Dad back the key to the car.

"So, you'll text me?" he asked. I swallowed and nodded. I could feel my throat tightening up and my face starting to get hot, and I thought that if I tried to talk right then, I'd just cry.

He walked over and kissed Mom on the cheek. She stopped brushing her hair and looked at him like she understood, and like for one second, her body and mind were in agreement. Dad must have been about to cry too, because he turned quickly and walked over to give me a hug. "Good luck, kid," he said. "You can do it."

Up until the December disaster day, Dad hadn't known about the Sitterhood. I don't know why Mom had never told him, but I was sure she had her reasons, and so I had tried to keep it a secret too. The Sitterhood was adamant that no normies know about us, and most Sitters went around tossing out mind-erasing spells like they were Mardi Gras beads. So Dad and Janis, like everyone else in Spring River, had been zapped a few times—whenever it had seemed like their knowledge was too close for comfort. I'd never liked it, but I hadn't known I could do anything about it. Then Cassandra had discovered a spell that would make them immune to the occasional memory-erasing mind blast, so now they knew. I still worried about them, because their knowing about how I spent my free time was putting them in danger, but at least I didn't have to lie to my dad and my best friend anymore. Besides, Janis loved knowing about Sitters—she almost saw it as an extra-exclusive bite of cosmic gossip. Dad—well, I wouldn't say he relished it, but he was doing the best he could. I bit my lip as I hugged him back, then walked over and locked the door behind him when he left.

I turned around, and Janis and Cassandra had already done a number on the hotel room, trying to create the post-after-party atmosphere the room had been in when we'd somehow broken Cassandra's curse. Cassandra herself was on the phone with room service, ordering one of everything, and Janis had tossed Amirah's donations all over the room, stripped the sheets from the bed, and cracked a couple of LaCroix and tossed them onto the floor.

"A-holes," Cassandra said as she slammed the phone down onto the receiver so hard I could swear I heard the plastic crack.

"What's up?" I asked.

"They said they don't have ravioli on the menu, and they never had it," she explained. "And when I told them to just go to the store and get some, they got offended!" She huffed. "So we're getting pappardelle primavera. It seemed to be the closest." She paused for a second. "What is pappardelle primavera?"

"It's got peas in it!" Janis yelled from the bathroom, over the sound of the water that she was splashing onto the floor. Then she came out, drying her hands on a towel. "Well," she said, "should we let them out, so that they have some time to get used to the place?"

I swallowed as I thought of Dad's credit card, already pushing its limit, which had been used to make the room reservation. Then I looked at Mom, who was staring intently at the floor, where she was trying to get a hairbrush to fit onto her foot. "Sure," I said. "Let 'em out."

Janis was so excited that she actually jumped into the air and clapped her hands. Then she walked over to one of the bags and lifted out a wire cage with two chickens inside. "You were so good, and so quiet on the way up here!" she cooed at them. "What good chickadees you are!" She set the cage on the bed and opened the door. The brown-and-white one hopped out and immediately pecked Janis's finger. "Ouch!" she squealed, jumping back. "That's the mean one, right?"

"Nope," Cassandra said. "The brown-and-white one is the nice one, remember? It's the black one that's a little brat." Janis took a big step back from the bed as the black one stepped out of the cage and began pecking at the bedspread.

There had been two chickens present when Cassandra's curse had been accidentally removed, both of which Cassandra and I had conjured into existence during the Summit. Over the past couple of weeks, we'd tried as hard as we could to spell up a chicken, but the closest we'd gotten was a six-piece nugget. The original conjured chickens were now in New York with Amirah, and while she hadn't thought twice about parting with her clothes, the chickens were a different story. Especially since their @city_chicks account had fifty-three thousand followers, one of which was Ariana Grande. It turned out that Amirah was really good at making chicken-sized Balenciaga knockoffs, and that got a lot of likes.

We'd had to buy these foul birds, and as it had turned out, it wasn't all that easy for three teenage girls to buy two chickens, even in Kansas. We'd driven forty-five minutes outside of Spring River one day, only to get denied when Janis let it slip that we didn't have a coop. Another time, some woman called us a string of very nasty words when Cassandra said her chickens were "the wrong color." These two were the right colors, but they hadn't spent much time around humans. Fortunately, the farm supply store we'd bought them from had a forty-eight-hour return policy, and these two hens were headed right back at hour forty-seven.

Cassandra's phone dinged with a text. "Dion's here," she said, reading from it. "I'll be right back."

She disappeared out the door to go meet her brother. "I'm nervous," Janis said. The mean chicken pecked the alarm clock. Mom stood with her forehead pressed against the window, staring into the parking lot. I said nothing, and five minutes later, Cassandra was back with what I hoped, what we all hoped, was the final piece of the puzzle.

Her name was Petunia, and she was definitely a pit bull. She was white, her head was square, and I could tell the minute she walked in the door that she was a real good girl. "Yo," Cassandra said, shutting the door behind them and unclipping Petunia's leash. "She let one rip on the third floor, and I thought I was going to pass out. She's practically Pig!"

I bit my lip and nodded, thinking that there was Pig and not Pig, but probably no "practically Pig." Then I walked over so that I could scratch Practically Pig behind the ears. She was a little heavier than Pig. Her ears were cropped, which made my stomach turn a little bit, but she had big, sweet Oreo eyes and she licked my hand. "We've only got her for two hours," Cassandra added. "And apparently she likes these." She held up a big ziplock bag of what appeared to be dried sow ears.

"What did Dion tell his coworker we needed her for?" I asked.

"Well, I sent the texts for him," she said. "Because he can't be trusted, and I said we needed her to model a new line of dog perfume."

"And the guy bought that?" Janis asked.

"He thinks she's going to be internet famous," Cassandra said. "And I may have stretched the truth a bit and said that Khloé Kardashian was an investor."

"Isn't this guy going to want to see these pictures?" I asked, but Cassandra ignored me.

"Two hours," she said. "We'd better get cracking." As

Cassandra and I had been talking, Petunia's nose had started to twitch, and a confused, then focused, look crossed her face.

"Cass," I said, "maybe we should keep her leash on, because we don't know how she's going to do with the—"

Too late. Like a bolt of white lightning, Petunia leapt over one bed in a single bound and let out a window-shaking bark before snapping her jaw shut mere millimeters from the mean chicken's tail. Both chickens let out a torrent of panicked clucks and took to the air. They might have been smarter than they looked, because they split up. The nice one flapped furiously toward the closet, and the mean one shrieked its way to the bathroom. Janis shrieked too, and dove out of the way as the nice one almost took out an eye with her claw.

Petunia barked again, as she seemed to debate for a second which chicken would be the tastier prize. Then she bolted for the mean one, now perched on the shower curtain rod. Petunia jumped at it, and her front paws caught in the shower curtain, bringing the whole thing down with a crash that I was sure could be heard all the way in the lobby.

"Petunia! Stay! Down, girl!" I shouted, but Petunia was now locked in a furious battle with the shower curtain and did no such thing. Just as it appeared that the curtain might win, the dog managed to free herself, shaking it off triumphantly. Cassandra had grabbed the leash, and positioned herself inside the bathroom door, blocking Petunia's escape, but right as she bent down to clip the leash to Petunia's collar, the dog made another desperate lunge for the chicken. Her big block head plowed right into Cassandra's knee and knocked her off balance on the wet bathroom floor. Like a cartoon character who's stepped on a banana peel, Cassandra spun halfway around, running in place, before her feet slid right out from under her. She flew up in the air and came down on her back, water splashing up around her as she hit the floor, her head *thunk*ing like a gourd as it collided with the base of the toilet.

This was the exact, literal same thing that had happened the day Cassandra's curse had broken. It was déjà vu all over again. "You've got to be kidding me," Janis and I both said at the exact same time, and then we sprang into action.

In the commotion, Mom had hidden behind the drapes, so she was effectively out of the way as I held out my hands, grabbed Petunia with my powers, and lifted her up and away from the chickens, over Cassandra, still sprawled on the floor in a limp puddle, and out into the hotel room. The experience of flying through the air disoriented Petunia enough that she forgot about the chickens, and let out a little whimper as she looked at the ground passing underneath her. I set her down on one of the beds, then used my kinesis to grab the leash from the bathroom and zoom it to me. I ran over, looped it around one of the legs of the bed, and then clipped it to Petunia's collar.

Though, really, one look at her face told me that I didn't need to worry. In a matter of seconds, she'd gone from ferocious fowl fighter to trembling snowball, and she'd curled up as tight as a tortellini, facing the wall, with her nose stuffed between two pillows.

Fortunately, it didn't seem like Cassandra was seriously hurt, and Janis helped her up and over to the other bed while I set about the much harder task of catching the chickens. The relatively nice one was in the bathroom now too, and it sat on the closed toilet cover, while the mean one had settled down into a feathery fluff in the tub. I decided to get what would likely be the harder task over with first, and crept toward the tub, keeping my hands at my sides and planning to grab the bird and pin its wings, just like I'd practiced back at Cassandra's house.

But the chicken knew my game, and as soon as it saw me coming, instead of trying to get away from me, it flew out of the tub and sprinted straight toward me so fast that its scaly spaghetti legs became a blur. I jumped out of the way and collided with the bathroom door, sending it bouncing off the wall with a *crash*. Whoever was in the room next door was going to think that Mom and Dad were having one heck of an anniversary. Mom peeked her head out from behind the drapes, then darted right back in. I didn't blame her.

"Esme, get it!" Janis hissed. She and Cassandra barely had time to move their feet out of the way as the chicken barreled by the bed. I started to run after it again, then stopped. I was a powerful witch. Why was I chasing after a bird?

I held out my hand and, using my kinesis, scooped up the mean one, and held it hovering in the air. Keeping it in place, I walked over to the bathroom and used my kinesis to pluck the nice one off the toilet cover. They looked kind of funny, two no-fly chickens just floating there in the air, and then back into the cage they went.

Where, I had a feeling, they were going to stay.

"Come on, Mom," I said, walking over and unwrapping her from the heavy blackout fabric. "It's safe to come out now." I took her hand and walked us over to the bed. We sat down, and I leaned over and gave Petunia a quick pet. She'd stopped shivering, and scooted close to me and then dropped her big head onto my thigh.

"You okay?" I asked Cassandra, who was now holding a can of LaCroix to the back of her head.

"Yeah," she said. "I'm just soaked. And I can't believe it happened again. I never thought that my personal nemesis would be a hotel toilet. I ought to blow it up."

"Well, technically, the first time, it was your savior," Janis said. "It's just this time that it seemed like it wasn't on your side."

Cassandra took the can of LaCroix down from the back of her head, cracked it open, and took a sip. The chickens seemed like they were mad at each other. Janis looked at me, and even though she didn't say a word, I knew what she was thinking because I was thinking it too.

I reached over, took Mom's hand, and gave it a squeeze. "This isn't going to work," I said, feeling my nose start to itch as the tears seeped into my eyes. "There are just too many variables. Those are real chickens; this isn't Pig." Petunia grunted.

"We could still try?" Janis said, her face lifted hopefully. "Just to make sure?"

I shook my head. "I've never liked the idea of making Mom hit her head on the toilet anyway," I said.

"Honestly, that part's not that bad," Cassandra said. "It's just the being wet and cold afterward."

Suddenly I looked at Mom. She was still staring off at a corner of the room, where there was nothing, but I swear that I had just felt her squeeze my fingers, like she was trying to send me a message that it was okay.

There was a knock on the door. Instantly I hugged Petunia close to me.

"Who is it?" Janis called.

"Room service!" a voice called back.

I looked around quickly, at three teenagers, a grown woman, two chickens, and a dog that populated this hotel room. "Um, leave it in the hall," I called back, "and we'll get it in a minute."

"Someone needs to sign for it" was the response.

Crap.

"Can you slide the paper under the door?" I asked. Whoever was on the other side didn't answer, but then a second later, a small piece of paper poked through under the door. I grabbed it and winced when I saw the total. Poor Dad, poor Dad's credit card, but I added a tip and signed Mom's name anyway, realizing as I did that I'd never seen her do that herself, and I had zero idea what her signature looked like. Then I slid it back and looked out the peephole. I waited a few seconds for the employee to leave, then opened the door and wheeled the cart in.

Whatever pappardelle primavera was, it sure smelled good, and Petunia let out a long, low whine. Cassandra and Janis got up and started lifting lids and spreading the dishes out on the desk.

"Well," Janis said, stepping back and looking at everything, "at least we feast."

CHAPTER 2

For the next two hours, we put a serious dent in the room service dinner. Then we packed up any leftovers to take home to
Dad, and even let Petunia have a french fry. Okay, a few french
fries. When I texted Dad that he could come pick Mom back
up, he didn't even ask if it had worked. He just responded with
a thumbs-up emoji. I couldn't help but wonder if, deep down,
he'd known that it was the longest of long shots, and had just
gone along with it because at least it was something.

In my weaker moments, I had imagined grand reunions,
Mom and Dad sitting up late into the night, having the first
real conversation they'd had in decades, maybe even ever. Instead, when he came to pick her up, she grabbed one of the
drapes and tried to take it with her. I was able to pry it out of
her hands, but then she grabbed the bedspread and held on
to that for dear life too. We finally settled on a pillow, and she
held tight to it as they walked down the hall and waited for the
elevator.

I watched them go, and felt the life force melt out of me. As

Sitters, we were supposed to be powerful. We were supposed to be protecting the innocent. We were supposed to take care of our own, yet Mom had been cursed for almost my entire life, I couldn't do a dang thing about it, and the worst part was that no one seemed to care.

Wait, that wasn't totally true. Dad cared, and Brian—who was our Counsel, aka the adult charged with teaching me and Cassandra stuff—cared, and Cassandra and Janis of course, but that still only amounted to a few hours in a hotel room, spending a month's mortgage payment on room service, and hoping for a miracle. It wasn't fair, and I was mad, but that was pointless. My anger felt like a shotgun blast, shooting out of me in every direction with no particular target. I had discovered on Halloween that Mom was cursed, and I'd first thought this guy Erebus—aka Cassandra's deadbeat dad—was behind it. He was an all-around tool whose Red Magic practice had gotten him banished to the Negative, but not before he'd cursed Mom for ruining his Red Magic plans.

Or at least that was what we'd thought, before we'd found out that Wanda had really cursed Mom, and set Erebus up to take the blame. Wanda too was now in the Negative, where they both would stay. So, yeah, everyone who could be punished for Mom's state had been as punished as they were going to get, but she was still cursed.

More than anything or anyone else, though, I was mad at myself. Every day that went by where Mom stayed cursed felt like a fail. I was starting to see that I couldn't save her, no matter how hard I tried. And if I wasn't going to save Mom, then who would?

"Esme?" Janis said, coming up behind me. "You okay?

You've just been standing there with your hand on the door-knob." I shook myself out of it.

"Yeah," I said. "Just thinking. You guys ready to go?" Behind her, Cassandra was busy trying to get the chicken cage back into a bag, and was too busy cussing at the birds to answer my question, as the nice one kept trying to peck her fingers from between the bars.

Finally she succeeded and we filed out of the hotel room, then lugged everything down the hall, and down the stairs, Petunia following faithfully behind us. We left through the back door to the parking lot, where Dion was waiting for us in the van.

"How'd the photo shoot go?" he asked cheerfully as we loaded everything into the van. "Do you think Khloé's people will like it?" I shot a sidelong glance at Cassandra. Erebus had once manipulated Dion into being his accomplice, and Cassandra—rightfully so—still hadn't forgiven him. As his punishment, she'd cast spells on him that basically made him do her bidding, no questions asked—Dion had probably completed ten thousand late-night Twizzler runs at her request—but I think she'd grown tired of having a slave and wanted her brother back. Over the last few weeks, she'd softened a bit. She wasn't so mean to him anymore, and had started to trust him with bits and pieces of her real life.

But I'm pretty sure she just lied to him for fun sometimes.

"I think Khloé's people are going to love this dog perfume campaign," I said as Janis and I climbed into the back. The heater in Dion's van put out about as much heat as a flashlight, and as Janis and I sat on the floor, I saw her shift positions several times, trying to tuck her feet underneath her, and then trying to get Petunia to sit on them. As we pulled out of the parking lot, I looked back at the hotel, and realized I had zero desire to ever see it again. It could explode for all I cared. I mean, as long as no one was in it or got hurt or anything.

We dropped Janis off first, and as she ran up the front walk to her house, I resisted the urge to yell after her to put on some socks. Cassandra and I were going to go with Dion to return Petunia to her owner, but as we drove past a strip mall, I felt something, like being brushed with a leaf across the back of my neck. I scrambled to my knees to look out the window, and then looked at Cassandra, who was gripping her door handle.

"Stop the van, Dion," she said.

"I need to get gas anyway," he said. "There's a Quik—"

"Stop it now!" she shouted, causing Dion to slam on the brakes. The van screeched to a stop, and Cassandra and I jumped out. Or rather, she jumped out and then wrenched open the side door so that I could jump out too. As my flats hit the pavement, I was glad I'd resisted Janis's urge to dress for the occasion. I'd worn something I could run in.

"Where are you going? Do you want me to wait?" Dion asked, confused.

"Nope," Cassandra called back, already running into the parking lot. "See you at home."

I followed her, and the feeling on the back of my neck intensified from a tiny tickle to a full-on scratch. It was my Sitter sense. Cassandra's came on like a buzzing in her ears, and it was obvious that both of ours were firing at full strength right now. I stopped for a second and slowed my breathing so that I could look and listen. The strip mall had a hair salon, a water store, a children's consignment shop, and a pizza place, and everything was closed except for the pizza place. Which was good for us, because the fewer people around the better. Zapping people's memories, even if it was for their own good, was one of my least favorite parts of being a Sitter.

Cassandra stood beside me, and then slowly, without saying anything, we shifted so that we were back-to-back, and then began turning in a circle.

"Over there," Cassandra whispered. "By the U-Haul." I breathed a small sigh of relief—this was, thankfully, about as far away from the pizza place as we could get. "Okay, go!" Cassandra said, and we both took off at a sprint. One of our main jobs as Sitters was to capture escaped demons and Return them back to the Negative before they could do any harm. Cassandra and I had trained hard at Returns and were getting pretty good at them.

I caught a glimpse of this demon right before it ducked behind a side mirror. It looked like a lemon, though its yellow color was ghastly and pale, not cheerful at all. It was a Gamboge, and though it was petite in size, it was powerful. It had the ability to detonate itself, spraying a large area with the disaffecting funk of the Negative, and then reassemble after it had sufficiently sucked the joy from its victims. I'd never seen one IRL before, just in our study books, so this was almost exciting. Beside me, Cassandra had taken off her flannel and was tying the sleeves together. "I wish we had a net," she whispered, and then just like that, the Gamboge was off.

It couldn't fly, and it didn't run. It bounced like a tennis ball. And it was bouncing straight toward the pizza place. Cassandra went running after it, swinging her shirt, whereas I went to work with my kinesis. A Gamboge was tough to Return because there wasn't much surface area for me to grab on to—no fur, no tails. It was just small and oval and slippery. As it zoomed across the parking lot, I tried to catch it but just felt the rays of my kinesis close around air. On my second attempt, I still couldn't get ahold of it but did make enough contact to throw it off course, so it bounced into a big red pickup truck. Then the worst thing happened: I lost it. Frantic, I searched, standing on my toes and spinning as I squinted into the dark, trying to see around all the parked cars. But I couldn't see the Gamboge anywhere, and it was so small that it could hide behind, or below, anything. It could be perched on a radio antenna right now, pretending to be a tennis ball.

Out of the corner of my eye, I saw Cassandra raise her hands, and I shielded my face. Her kinesis was pyrokinesis, and the parking lot lit up as she shot out a spurt of fire like a flamethrower, but there were too many places for the Gamboge to hide.

A burst of laughter caught my attention, and I looked up to see a large group of teenagers, several of whom I recognized, spilling out of the pizza place. Crap, crap, crap. Cassandra and I would have to split up.

"I'll take them," she said, tossing me her shirt. "You got this." Then she took off running, and I had just heard her yell out "Hey!" to get their attention when I spotted the Gamboge again, bouncing around like this was Wimbledon.

This time, I lifted Cassandra's shirt in the air and sent it flying toward the yellow ball like I was trying to snag a butterfly. I managed to get the Gamboge tangled in a sleeve for a split second before it escaped. Then I decided that I was going to stop trying to grab it and start trying to slap it. Its bouncing accelerated, and it was making its way directly to the pizza place, where I knew Cassandra had cast a spell on our classmates to keep them from noticing anything. I reached out with my kinesis and whacked the Gamboge back in the opposite direction. It bounced off the side of a station wagon, and then I hit it again, this time sending it slamming into the door of a hatchback hard enough to make a dent. This seemed to put it in a daze, and it wobbled a little bit. I swung Cassandra's shirt at it, and caught it square in the middle, but to my surprise, it ripped right through the shirt, leaving a perfect Gamboge-shaped hole in the center of the fabric.

Cassandra's shirt fell to the pavement in a slushy puddle, and the Gamboge bounced on. I could feel my blood start to course with frustration and anger. I held up both my hands and focused my power. I hit the Gamboge as hard as I could into the U-Haul's window, cracking the glass into a spiderweb, and the demon dropped to the ground. That's when I felt a tug coming from the sky. I looked up to see that the Portal had arrived, which meant I must have been doing something right with the Gamboge. Now all it would take was one good whack to send its bright yellow butt back to the Negative.

Movement caught my eye—the Gamboge was up and at it again. I hit it down hard, and it made a *thud* when it hit the pavement. I realized I was smiling. And that this felt good. I smashed the Gamboge into the side of a van, then the pavement again, through a slushy puddle, and into the dumpster. With each new crash and bang, the Gamboge got a little slower, and a little shakier. In the distance, I could hear someone shouting my name. Cassandra, probably, but I couldn't stop to see. This was fun, and with each whack of the Gamboge, I felt a little better, a little less angry. I was totally focused, and then a screech stopped me in my tracks. Like nails on a chalkboard. Like a bird. A crow. I snapped my head up to look for it, but all I saw was black sky and light pollution. If there had been a bird, it was already gone.

Cassandra appeared, running forward with her hands out, and built a box of flame around the Gamboge, and then, with her actual hands, she bent down and scooped the demon up out of the fire box's center, shuddering a little bit as she did, and chucked it, as hard as she could, right into the middle of the Portal, which was swirling up above us like vomit in a blender. The Portal closed around the Gamboge, and then my ears rang with its signature flushing sound. Cassandra was standing in front of me, her eyes wide.

"Esme, what was that?" she asked. "You were in a zone. I was screaming your name, but you wouldn't stop. It seemed like you were going to kill it."

At her words, I looked down at my hands and realized I was shaking. Sitters weren't supposed to kill anything, even demons. It was one of our cardinal rules. Normally I didn't even like stepping on bugs, but right then I . . .

"I didn't mean to . . . ," I started, but then stopped myself, realizing that what I had been about to say wasn't quite true. "I didn't want to kill it," I said, and my chin started to quiver. Then the tears were coming, spilling hot drips down my cheeks. "I just wanted . . . I needed . . ." Behind us, the group of kids from our school laughed and joked as they made their way to their cars, totally unaware of what had just happened a few yards away. "I just wanted to do something," I said finally.

"You don't need to explain it to me," she said. "Trust me.

I get it." I looked at her for a second, then nodded without saying anything else. She wasn't just saying that. She did get it. Giving me a small smile, she turned and walked over to where her now-honey-colored shirt was lying in a puddle. She picked it up, and dirty water streamed off it.

"It gives new meaning to the word 'distressed,' doesn't it?" she asked.

I shrugged. "It doesn't look that different from what you normally wear," I said, "though maybe a little cleaner."

"Har-de-har-har," she said, then walked her dripping shirt over to the trash can and shoved it in. "Come on," she said. "I know what will cheer you up. I'll buy you a coffee."

Cassandra didn't drink coffee, which was probably a good thing for the rest of the world. But standing at Starbucks with her while she tried to figure out what to order was painful. The line behind us was growing longer and the customers more impatient as she asked about, and then dismissed, almost every drink on the menu. Some were too hot, some were too cold, some were too chocolatey, and some just sounded "disgusting." Finally she settled on a cup of whipped cream and a bottle of water. I got my usual iced Venti and sat down at a table by the window.

Raging out on the Gamboge had worked up a sweat, and I had a cold, clammy feeling in my armpits. I sipped my iced coffee while Cassandra alternated between a swig of water and a spoonful of whipped cream. She took me by surprise when she asked, "So, how you doing?"

"What do you mean?" I asked, shocked. Cassandra wasn't

one to talk about feelings, at all, ever, but over the past couple of months, it had seemed like she had changed. She had a girlfriend now, and that had softened her. She was happy, and she thought about other people. Maybe she was even getting in touch with her feelings and *wanted* to talk about stuff like emotions.

She licked some whipped cream off her spoon. "We don't have to talk about it if you don't want to," she continued, "but it seems like you're under a lot of stress. I mean, I know you're happy to have your mom home, but it can't be easy."

I sighed and leaned back in my chair. "It's not that," I said, twirling my straw and sending the ice spinning in the cup. "It's just . . ." I stopped and bit my lower lip. "I'm sick of this," I said finally.

" 'This' meaning . . . being a Sitter?" Cassandra asked.

I sat there for a second, processing the words that had just come out of my mouth. I hadn't even admitted this to myself before. I didn't look at Cassandra as I nodded. "Not totally, but yeah. I was okay before, you know?" I continued. "My life wasn't great, but it wasn't horrible, and I didn't know any better. Ever since Halloween, though, I know that there's a way out for Mom, and to know that, but not know what to do about it, that's somehow worse." I took another sip of my coffee. "I go to bed mad, and I wake up mad. And now Pig is gone, and it just seems like the Sitterhood is good for everyone except those who are in it. Like, we protect the world, but not ourselves."

To my surprise, Cassandra smiled. "Esme, you're talking to someone whose mom is missing and whose dad was so bad he's now in another dimension," she said, "so I have those same thoughts about ninety-eight times a day. But it's always like that for the heroes. I mean, haven't you seen Batman? His life blows."

I smiled, and snorted. "Did you just compare yourself to Batman?" I asked.

"Maybe." She smirked as she scraped the last of her whipped cream out of the cup. She had put her phone face-down on the table, and it had been buzzing nonstop since we'd sat down. She'd been ignoring it, but now that it started again, she flipped it over so that she could see the screen. Aside from Ruby's, which was saved under just one red heart emoji, Cassandra didn't save any numbers in her contacts, somehow keeping track of whose number was whose and just constantly hitting redial. I could see that the number that was calling now was local, and a look of concern crossed her face as she tapped accept.

"Hey," she said into it, "what's up?" She listened for a second, her brows knitting together. "Get out of there," she said. "Park the van down the street, lock the doors, and stay inside it. Watch the house. We're on our way."

She was out of her chair before she'd even hung up, and I was right behind her, painfully leaving my still-half-full iced coffee on the table. "Cass," I said, running after her, "who was that? Is everything okay?"

"Dion," she said, throwing the door open and breaking into a run. "We were robbed."

I had no choice but to follow. It had once taken me two class periods to complete the mile in gym, but since I'd started Sitting, I'd built up a stamina that was almost embarrassing. Even in my dress and flats, with my coat flapping in the wind,

I was able to pretty much keep up with Cassandra on the almost-mile back to her house as we dodged cars and leapt over puddles.

When we finally turned onto her street, I could see down the block that all the lights were on in their house. Dion's van was parked a little bit down the street, and he was sitting inside it in the dark, just as she had instructed. He climbed out when he saw us coming, and blabbered in disbelief. "The door was ajar when I came home, and the whole—the wh-whole p-place . . . ," he stammered. "I mean, you'll see it. Cass, it's freaking destroyed. The couch, the walls, everything. Your room . . ."

At these words, Cassandra turned and ran for the house. Dion and I were close behind, and I gasped when we entered the living room. Dion was right. There were no words to describe it. It was beyond destroyed. Couch cushions were ripped, and there were holes punched in the walls. The table was flipped and every shelf had been cleared off.

Plants had been pulled out of their pots and the roots shaken loose from the dirt. Even the insoles had been ripped from the shoes that hadn't made it into their owners' bedrooms. I carefully made my way to the kitchen, trying not to step on anything, and that room was even worse. The refrigerator door stood open, and everything had been dumped out, even the contents of the bottles and jars. There were globs of mayonnaise on the floor, mustard on the walls, pasta sprinkled everywhere like confetti, bags of flour ripped open and covering everything in white. Ice cream dripped from the freezer, and there were little puddles of water everywhere, from the ice trays being turned out onto the floor.

The back of my neck absolutely burned, so much so that I rubbed it, trying to dispel the physical sensation that was there to tell me that something *really* wasn't right.

"Esme." I spun around at the sound of Cassandra's voice. She was standing behind me, in the door to the kitchen, a look on her face that I'd never seen before. She was holding her hands out in front of her, cradling a bunch of black plastic. I took a step closer so that I could see what it was, and recognition shot through me like an electric shock.

It was the Magic 8 Ball, or at least what was left of it. It was in about a million pieces, the tiny answer orb now completely exposed, like a heart outside the body. Cassandra let the plastic bits fall to the floor, and held up the icosahedron between two fingers. "They broke it out of the ice, and then smashed it," she said, "like someone stomped on it."

I looked at Cassandra's face. Her irises were always as black as coffee, but now they were even darker, like the Portal itself. The 8 Ball wasn't just a toy. It was a communication device. It was the way she talked to Erebus. Erebus was hardly a candidate for Dad of the Year, but as Cassandra would say, he was the only dad she had, and they'd been talking, building a relationship bit by bit, triangle by triangle, ever since Halloween, even though she still kept the 8 Ball frozen in a block of ice just in case.

I got a chill just thinking about it. Though I trusted Cassandra, mostly, I still didn't trust Erebus. He'd gotten Dion to break him out of the Negative once before, and it seemed totally within his powers to manipulate someone into coming and trashing their house. "When was the last time you talked to Erebus?" I asked.

"Two days ago," she said. "It was just normal stuff."

"Did you leave the 8 Ball out afterward?"

She looked at me like she was pissed. "No, of course not. I froze it back up like I always do." She quickly shoved the icosahedron into her pocket as Dion walked into the kitchen, looking like he was about to cry or break something.

"I don't know what to do," he said, looking around, and then kicking a can of beans so that it rolled across the floor. He must not have realized it was open. The top had been cut off, and it left a trail of pintos behind it. "What the hell!" he said, his face turning red with rage. "They even opened our beans? We should call the cops."

"I don't want cops here," Cassandra said, and as with everything she said, Dion agreed immediately.

"I don't even think they took anything," he said. "It's like they just came in here and systematically destroyed every single thing we own."

"It almost seems like they were looking for something," I said, pointing to the couch cushions, every one of which bore a knife slash right down the middle. Every cell in my body was screaming that this was not your average break-in. This was all about magic.

"Maybe someone thought we had drugs or money hidden in here?" Dion suggested.

"I doubt it," Cassandra said. "Would we really still be working our jobs if we had thousands hidden in the walls?"

"Hey, I like my job," Dion said.

"Well, I hate mine," Cassandra said. "Frozen yogurt is for tools."

Cassandra and Dion started to bicker, and I tuned them

out as I exited the kitchen back into the living room. Whoever had trashed the house had done it methodically and left nothing unturned. "How long were you gone?" I called to Dion.

"Not even an hour?" he said, walking into the room. "Cass texted me that you guys were done, so I came to the hotel, dropped you guys off, got gas, then took Petunia back to Roger. We hung out for a little bit, and then I came back. I called Cass right as I came into the house."

"So, it was more than one person, then," I said. "Probably more than two, and they were thorough. They were probably watching the house to see when you were leaving." Suddenly something hit me. "Hey," I said to Dion, "you first found your dad's journal and the 8 Ball in the basement, right?" He nodded. "How hidden were they?" I asked.

"Not that hidden," he said, "just stuffed in between a couple of boards. I found them when I was down there looking for a breaker box."

Dion shook his head as he walked into his room, and I turned to Cassandra and lowered my voice. "Could that be what someone was looking for?"

"I was thinking that," she said. "But if they knew the 8 Ball was something special, wouldn't they have taken it? Instead of just destroying it and leaving the pieces here?"

"Where's your dad's journal?" I asked her.

"It's in my locker at school."

"What?" I was stunned. I had never even seen Cassandra go to her locker. In fact, I wasn't even sure she knew where it was.

"It's the perfect hiding place," she said. "No one ever keeps anything important in their lockers, just like homework and books and stuff."

"Sure," I said. Her reasoning was not totally unsound. Then something hit me. "Your mom?" I ventured.

We also knew, or at least suspected, that Cassandra's mom, Circe, was out there somewhere, and probably not all that far away. She and my mom had been Sitters together, and friends, but Circe had disappeared right around the time Erebus was banished and my mom got cursed. For a long time, everyone had thought Circe was dead, but we'd seen her, or at least someone that we really thought was her, at the Summit, but she'd disappeared again before we could really talk to her.

Cassandra started to nod, then shook her head definitively. "If she was looking for something," she said, "she wouldn't have trashed the place to do it. She loved this house, I know it, and that's why she left it to us."

"I know," I agreed.

Cassandra looked around, muttered a bad word, then said, "Well, let's clean it up."

Fortunately, one of the first spells that Cassandra and I had learned when we'd first discovered our powers was a cleaning spell, so she took the kitchen and I took the living room, and we both got to work. I held out my hands and uttered the spell, and cushions fused themselves together and books and board games returned to the shelves. Soil rose off the floor and molded itself around plant roots, which went back into their pots and stood upright. I put shoes back in pairs and piled them by the front door, sat chairs upright, and rehung jackets on the chair backs. A silver chain flew through the air and, not knowing what it was, I caught it in my hand. At first, I thought it was a dog collar, but when I got a closer look, it made me laugh.

"Hey," I called to Cassandra, "when did Dion get a wallet chain?"

"I have no idea what you're talking about," she called back. I wound it into a loop and set it on the table. I'd also found a can of something called Axe body spray for men. I pulled the top off, gave it a sniff, and gagged. It smelled like gas station incense. I couldn't believe I'd ever thought Dion was cute.

After that, all that was left was a bunch of papers. Opened and unopened mail, some stuff from school, coupons, catalogs, and notebook pages covered with Dion's scrawl and sketches. I wasn't sure where it all went, so I just stacked them into a pile and set them on the table next to the wallet chain, sure that neither Cass nor Dion would ever go through them.

As I turned to survey my work, a flyer for a band called Jacking Lanterns caught my eye—though, solely because the flyer, and the band itself, looked absolutely horrible. It was all male—of course—and their look was total hair gel, black eyeliner, and slightly-too-small T-shirts. It seemed like maybe it was a joke? Like maybe Jacking Lanterns was some sort of early 2000s butt-rock tribute band, but they were playing a show in Spring River on Tuesday night.

"Nice job in here," Cassandra said, coming up behind me. "It looks better than before."

"Thanks," I said, turning and holding out the flyer. "Where did this even come from? It's, like, the best worst thing I've ever seen." I was always grabbing things because they seemed hilariously bad, but Cassandra had no flair for irony, and also only listened to rap, so it was odd to me that she would have picked the flyer up.

"That's not mine," she said with a shrug. "It must be Dion's."

"What is mine?" Dion asked, appearing from the kitchen.

"This flyer," I said, waving it at him. "Where'd you get it?"

He crossed the room, took the flyer from me, looked at it for a second, and then handed it back.

"I've never seen that before in my life," he said, his face serious.

He sounded genuine, but out of curiosity, I pointed to the body spray and wallet chain.

"What about those?" I asked. He didn't say anything, just shook his head, his forehead wrinkling in confusion.

"I only wear Irish Spring," he said. "And is that a dog collar?" A small part of me was relieved.

Cassandra was next to me in an instant, yanking the flyer out of my hand. She studied it for a moment, then looked up at me, her eyes even more electric than usual.

"I think," she said with a smirk, "this is what you call a clue."

CHAPTER 3

Dion gave me a ride home, while Cassandra stayed behind, clearly worried about leaving the house empty. I normally hated Dion's guts for what he'd put Cassandra and me through the previous fall, but lately, that hatred had been shifting more toward a feeling of genuine sympathy. Cass and Dion had been on their own for most of their lives, and that couldn't have been easy. I totally understood why Cassandra wanted to share stuff with him, even after his earlier betrayal, but I still made sure I was careful around him. I didn't want to tell him anything that he didn't already know.

"So, do you think this break-in had something to do with you and Cassandra?" he asked.

"I don't know," I said. "Maybe."

"Where did that band flyer come from? Do you think the person who dropped it was planning to go to that show?"

"I don't know," I said again. "Maybe."

"Do you think you and Cass will find out who did it?"

"I don't know," I said. "Maybe."

"What is a wallet chain, anyway?"

That one, at least, I could answer.

"It's a chain that hooks your wallet to your pants," I explained.

"Why would anyone want that?" he asked, his eyes fixed on the road ahead. "Just don't lose your wallet."

I laughed. "I guess some people think it looks cool," I said.

When Dion pulled up in front of my house to drop me off, I felt a genuine desire to try to make him feel better. "Thanks for the ride," I said. "And sorry about your house. We'll figure it out."

"Yeah," he said. "I hope so."

Dion waited until I had opened the door and was inside the house before he drove away. Our house was dark, and when I pulled the front door shut behind me, I felt the momentary rush of expectant joy, followed by the harsh realization that it was misplaced. There was no dog coming to greet me, and I'd be the only one snoring in my bedroom tonight.

Dad was asleep on the couch, which was where he slept these days, and as I walked by the bedroom, I could see that the TV was still on. Mom was sitting up straight against a stack of pillows, the blue light flickering on her face. When I looked closer, though, I could see that she was asleep too, just still sitting up, so I went in and turned off the TV and tucked the blankets around her waist.

I brushed my teeth and did my skin care routine, and when I got into bed, all I could think about was the flyer, now magnetized to the middle of Cassandra and Dion's fridge. I couldn't help but think, or maybe hope, that it was a clue to something bigger than the break-in.

· · ·

I slept late into the morning and woke up to a bright sun and clear blue sky that seemed sneaky, since my widget said that it was only twenty-eight degrees outside. Janis and I had a Sunday-morning ritual that we followed religiously: Coffee. Doughnuts. Thrifting. We had big plans to take Amirah and Ji-A when they were in town the next weekend, and I hoped we hadn't oversold it, especially since they were both used to shopping at the kind of places where you had to make an appointment.

But what Spring River lacked in almost every other area, it made up for in thrifting, and Janis and I were like the empress and high priestess of the fantastical find. That is, we crushed it, and we had a battle uniform. I pulled on my hunter-green leggings, chartreuse socks, checkerboard slip-ons, lipstick-red bralette, an oversized men's tank top that fit almost like a minidress, and a red plaid Pendleton wool flannel that was a hand-me-down from Dad. This look didn't have a name, but it was highly functional and the best outfit for thrifting, since the shoes came off easily, and you could try on anything over a tank top and leggings, which was especially good, considering the thrift stores didn't have dressing rooms. Correction: the thrift stores didn't have dressing rooms that were anything more than a corner delineated by a shower curtain, and they were always damp, even when it hadn't rained in weeks.

I went downstairs to find Mom and Dad sitting at the kitchen table.

"Cosmo surname," he said when I walked in. "Six letters, first one *K*."

I looked over his shoulder at his crossword. "Kramer," I said, and he wrote it in.

"She's a smart one, Theresa," he said, looking up at Mom. "Thankfully, she got your brains and not mine. You want coffee, kid? There's still some left."

"Janis is on her way," I said, knowing she'd be there, like she was every week, to pick me up at eleven a.m. on the dot. I heard a car turn into the driveway almost as soon as the words were out of my mouth. I gave Dad and Mom both a kiss on the head, and then headed toward the door. Just before I opened it, I heard Dad asking Mom's advice on the next part of the puzzle that he couldn't solve.

It made me smile, but also made me want to choke back tears. I had sometimes wondered if Dad's devotion was something the Sitters had implanted in his brain, like all the false memories of his friendship with Brian. But no, it was real. Even before we'd known that Mom was cursed, even when we'd thought she was just destined to be like this for the rest of our lives, Dad had still been all in.

I pulled on my North Face puffer (Depop, thirty-five dollars) and headed out the door, all twenty-eight degrees slapping me in the face as I stepped onto the porch. I hurried to Janis's car and climbed inside, where she had both the heat and Ashanti blasting. Janis was dressed in basically the same outfit as me, though as per usual, hers was better: iridescent silver leggings, way oversized zip-up black hoodie, and a pair of Margiela slip-ons, inherited, of course, from Amirah.

"I forget," I said as I buckled my seat belt and she pulled out of the driveway. "Why did we decide that we were going to store all of Amirah's clothes at your house again?"

"Because, silly," Janis said, not meeting my eyes, "I have more closet space, remember?"

"Hmm," I said. "I don't. Did we do measurements or something? You're sure I was there?" Janis turned the music up, but a text from Cassandra distracted me anyway.

> **What are you doing?**
>
> Thrifting
>
> **Gross. Meet me after.**
>
> Will text when we're done. Meet us
> at the Perk.

"Who was that?" Janis asked.

"Cassandra," I said, and then filled her in on everything that had happened the night before.

"Jeez," Janis said as she pulled into the Donut Temple drive-through. "That sounds scary." Then the speaker crackled, and Janis said into it, "Can I get two strawberry cake doughnuts with sprinkles, one bear claw, a caramel Long John, a large hot coffee, and I know it's freezing out here, but a large iced coffee. Just dump ice into the drip if you have to. She doesn't mind."

I rolled my eyes. When it was winter, Janis always ordered my drink like she was asking for a can of chilled clam chowder with a straw. I handed her a five, and two minutes later she was handing me back my change and my breakfast.

By the time we pulled into the Goodwill parking lot, we were riding high on a wave of sugar sprinkles and caffeine and nineties R&B, yelling along to "The Boy Is Mine." It's such a funny song, because it's so obvious they should just ditch the dude and be best friends.

We waited until the song ended, and then ran across the parking lot and hit the door. Once inside, we each grabbed a shopping cart, and split. Janis went left, toward blazers and evening wear, while I went right, starting with men's button-downs before I moved on to women's pants and children's T-shirts. We shopped for each other, as that saved time, and now that Janis had her Depop store, we also shopped with an eye for what would be easy to style and sell. Forty-five minutes later, we met in the middle to survey our findings and deter-mine what was treasure and what was trash. If we hadn't been so busy chasing demons and trying to save the world, we could have filmed one heck of a YouTube haul series.

Today's trash: a crocheted cardigan with an unfortunate mustard stain that no amount of bleach would remove, vintage Levi's that were an implausible twenty-one-inch waist, and— much debated but eventually unanimous—an Ed Hardy bowling shirt. ("'Retro douchebag' is still douchebag," Janis reasoned.)

Today's treasure: a pair of Dickies engineer-stripe overalls; a magenta silk kimono with voluminous, purple-feather-edged sleeves; a *Rugrats* T-shirt; a near-perfect pair of high-waisted burgundy velvet leggings; and a nineties rayon floral baby-doll dress. Janis could easily make close to fifty dollars off the *Rugrats* T-shirt and the kimono alone. Provided she got around to shipping them out, of course. Between the two of us, our grand total came to $12.75, and Janis and I left the store feel-ing like queens.

The Park Perk was just a few minutes' drive from the Goodwill, and it was Spring River's anti-Starbucks. It was completely inefficient, probably hadn't made a profit since 2003, and had a sign at the register that said NO APPLE PAY AND BTW, CORPORATIONS ARE EVIL. Janis had an ongoing beef with the Perk because it smelled like ham, even though there wasn't a single pork product on the menu, but other than that, it was perfect. Even if you ordered nothing, you could camp out for hours with no risk of being kicked out.

It was always packed on the weekends, with college students doing homework, Ren Faire refugees wearing capes and playing D&D, and grizzled, black-leather-clad bikers who drank mochas with extra whipped cream. The Perk also always had live music on the weekends, which was most unfortunate. When Janis and I walked in, Cassandra had already nabbed us a booth, which happened to be right next to the stage, which was really just a carpet and a wooden stool. Cass was wearing her work polo and had an appalled look on her face that she made zero effort to hide. "Do you think he's going to do this all afternoon?" she asked loudly as a guy with an acoustic guitar finished up a song.

"Sadly, no," I said, gesturing at a guy in the corner, breaking out a flute.

"I'll go order," Janis said as we dropped our bags onto the booth bench. "Esme, I know you want your Antarctica special. Cassandra, what do you want?"

At this, Cass smiled. "I invented a new drink," she said. "It's hot water with whipped cream on top. I call it creamy water. I can come up if they need me to tell them how to make it."

Janis grimaced. "I'm sure they can figure it out," she said.

As per usual, the Perk took forever to make our drinks, and flute man was already on his second song when Janis came back. She handed me my iced coffee, and Cassandra her whipped cream and water. "It already melted," Janis said. "It kind of looks disgusting."

Cassandra just shrugged. "It's actually better this way."

Janis sat down and took a sip of her cappuccino. "I'm sorry to hear about your house, but let's see this flyer."

Cassandra pulled the flyer from her pocket and slid it across the table. As she seemed to do with almost everything, she had sealed it in a ziplock bag.

"Jacking Lanterns," Janis said, picking the baggie up and looking at it closely, before flipping it over to see the back side. "Interesting name choice. Seems a few months late, but okay." Cassandra and I were the magic muscle, but Janis was the brains in our three-person operation, and so we anxiously awaited her opinion on what the flyer could possibly mean.

"So, there are a few different scenarios here," she finally said. "One, whoever broke into your house is in this band. Two, whoever broke into your house is a fan of this band and will be at this show, or three, whoever broke into your house was chewing gum and was going to need something to put it in when they were done. My money's on one, or three, because judging by the looks of this flyer, I can't imagine that this band has many fans."

"Which one do you think it is?" I asked.

"There's only one way to find out," Janis said. "And you know what that is?"

"We go to this show," Cassandra said, a smile spreading across her face.

"Ding, ding, ding, ding," Janis said. "Right answer." Cassandra was now beaming, and Janis's smile matched hers. I leaned forward and got a closer look at the flyer.

"But it's at a bar," I pointed out. "How are we going to get in?"

Cassandra looked at me like I was as dense as a garden gnome. "The door," she said. "Duh."

"But we're underage?" I reminded her.

"Pshaw," Janis said, waving away my concern as though it were a fly. Now they had both leaned back in the booth and crossed their arms over their chests. The thing about a trio is that someone is usually outnumbered, and in our trio, that someone was usually me. I was getting used to it, but that didn't mean I liked it.

The flute guy at the Perk wasn't the worst musician I'd ever heard in my life, but he was far from the best. Cassandra drained the last of her creamy water, and we left right as he was asking the crowd if they liked hip-hop. Janis put her earmuffs on before we got to the door.

The van was parked outside, Dionless, awaiting Cass. She'd driven herself so she could go to her afternoon shift at the yogurt place after our meeting. "See you at school tomorrow?" I asked Cassandra as we crossed to it.

She was about to climb into the van, and she shook her head. "I'm staying home. Dion has to work tomorrow, and we're not leaving the house empty."

I nodded. At this point, Cassandra was going to end up being a junior again next year, but I didn't argue with her. She pulled the door shut behind her. Janis and I quickly walked to the Honda, and she put the heat on blast as soon as she started the car.

"This is exciting," Janis said. "We're going out this week. To a club."

"I don't think it's a club," I said. "It had the word 'grill' in the name."

"Whatever," she said, pulling out and nearly sideswiping a moped. "It's something new and different."

"I don't know," I said. "I'm kind of tired of new and different. I'd like more same and predictable, please."

"Ha," Janis answered. "Then you're in the wrong line of work. For both your jobs."

When Janis and I had first started our babysitters club several years before, we'd had four members and one burner phone. Then we'd dropped to two members, and after a couple of scary Erebus-and-Dion-related experiences last fall, even Janis had decided it was time to move on. Now we were down to one member, me, and the burner phone was long dead. (I'd lost the charger.) Besides, now with the Depop store, Janis could put "CEO of One in a Million Vintage" on her college applications.

I still babysat as much as I could, though. These days, between school and Sitting, that only amounted to about two times a week, but it was good money. Besides, I liked it, and unlike Cassandra's job, none of my clients had ever made me wear a polo shirt. I was babysitting that afternoon, and so instead of home, Janis dropped me at Kaitlyn's. Kaitlyn was almost three, and she had a promising future as a terrorist, a pro wrestler, or president of the United States of America. Babysitting Kaitlyn was like personally being in charge of a tornado, but I enjoyed the distraction.

I rang the doorbell and heard Kaitlyn's mom, Sharon, call to me to let myself in. Sharon was a real estate agent and had an open house that afternoon, and I found her in the kitchen with curlers in her hair, trying to remember where she'd put an air freshener. "It's birthday cake scent," she said, a note of panic creeping into her voice, "and it's good luck! Every time I use it, the house sells for at least five thousand over the asking price!" She slammed a drawer shut and started to paw through a backpack.

I left Sharon to it and followed the sounds of Daniel Tiger into the den. Kaitlyn was sitting with her back to me, but it seemed like she was licking a lollipop or something. "Hi, munchkin!" I said. "Ready to have some fun?"

"Mesme!" she squealed, but not before she shoved whatever she was licking between two couch cushions to hide it from me. I walked over and gave Kaitlyn a big hug, then ran my hand between the cushions.

"That's mine," Kaitlyn said as I pulled it out.

"I don't think so," I said. "Do you even know what this is?"

"Yes," she said with a scowl. "Candy."

"Sharon," I called out, standing up and walking toward the kitchen, "I found your air freshener!"

Kaitlyn and I had a pretty good time. We played dress-up, a game of which I thoroughly approved, especially since she had a box full of sparkly princess dresses and eschewed them all in favor of a rubber sword and a tube of brown fabric so that she could be a "killing hot dog."

By midafternoon, the sun had warmed things up enough that outside was tolerable if we kept moving, so we packed up some Cheddar Bunnies and apple slices and walked to the park. She made a little boy cry in the sandpit, so we moved to the swings. I made a big show of pretending that she was so heavy that I could barely push her, and she screamed and cackled, but then we evened out into a nice rhythm. I pushed Kaitlyn higher than I would have most kids her age, because I trusted her sense of self-preservation. She was a daredevil, but she held on tight.

She babbled and sang, and when she swung back toward me, I heard a snippet of her song, and it made me freeze. I caught her midswing. "Sweetie, what are you talking about?" I asked her.

"Higher, Mesme," she said. "More push!"

"Okay," I said, "but what were you singing?"

"A song about blackbirds," she said, which was exactly what I thought she'd been singing about.

"Like four and twenty baked in a pie?" I asked.

"No," she said. "That's silly. A song about Fred."

"Fred?" I asked. "Who's that?"

"He's a black bird," she said. "And he's my friend." I had my arm out, ready to push her, but when she swung back, I just stood still and she hit me in the chest.

"You mean you call all black birds 'Fred'?"

"No, I just call Fred 'Fred,'" she said, "because he's special."

"How do you know his name is Fred?" I asked.

"Because I named him," she said, kicking her feet.

"Is Fred here?" I asked.

"Yes," she said. "He followed us from home."

"Where is he now?" I asked.

She smiled, and pointed toward a tree near the slide. "Oh no," she said, her face falling, "He flew away."

"Come on, sweetie," I said, my eyes scanning the trees. "Time to go." Kaitlyn and I walked back to her house, and a few minutes later, her mom got home. She paid me, and as I left to walk home, I started to get that itchy feeling, the one that told me I was about to overthink something.

Sure, Kaitlyn was a kid with a psychedelic sense of reality, and maybe she had just picked a large black crow to be her not-entirely-imaginary friend, and then she'd named him "Fred."

Yeah, right.

The bird hadn't been an average, everyday, ordinary crow, and Kaitlyn had recognized that. And then she'd named him "Fred."

Burying things I didn't want to think about was one of my greatest talents. My mind had tons of rooms and other dark corners where I could file something away, slam the door, turn the key, and then throw the key into a trash can so that I never had to think again about what was in that room.

But lately, it seemed like my system wasn't working like it used to. I had picked a big drawer, nice and comfortable, for Adrian. It had taken quite a bit of shoving, and he hadn't wanted to go in, but eventually I'd gotten him in there, and thought that was the end of it. After all, he was a guy who'd flown away—like, he'd literally turned into a crow and taken off—from confrontation, and I had enough going on without a bird boy in my life. Or at least, that's what I kept telling myself.

But . . . he'd made me a mix CD. Not sent a link but burned an actual compact disc and left it on my front porch. Even with a million locks on the door, I was still going to think about that.

The afternoon sun had made the day seem warmer than it actually was, which I realized about halfway through my walk home, as the sun went down and I started to shiver. In a weird way, I appreciated the cold on my cheeks, and my breath puffing out in crystalline clouds, because it gave me something concrete, right in front of my face, to be angry at.

Adrian was in Spring River. That much was pretty obvious. So then why the heck wasn't he getting in touch with me?

CHAPTER 4

I was halfway home when Jim Halpert called me. Back when I'd been hiding everything Sitter-related from Dad, I had saved Brian's number under "Jim Halpert" in my phone. It still said that when Brian called me now. Not because I was trying to hide anything anymore, but because I thought it was funny.

"Hi, Jim," I said when I answered. "How's Pam?"

"I have no idea what you're talking about," Brian said. "Are you with Cassandra?"

"No," I said. "She's working the closing shift."

"Then I feel sorry for the openers," Brian said. "I'm calling because I have something that I think you will be interested in. When she gets off work, see if the two of you can come by my place."

"What is it?" I asked.

"Just come over," he said.

"I don't like surprises," I said, and he responded by hanging up. I texted Cassandra.

Brian has something he wants to show us.

Wut is it?

Dunno. He's being sneaky. Pick me up when you get off work?

I'll come now.

Aren't you closing?

Yeah, but I'll just close now.

I knew better than to argue with her, so I sent her a pin and blew on my hands to warm them while I waited. Somehow, Cassandra had managed to hold on to her Yogurt Haven job for almost three months, even though she was doing everything she could to drive the customers away. Like, for example, closing a couple of hours early or making up the most disgusting, off-season handle combos she could possibly think of. I wondered how she hadn't gotten fired yet.

Though, there was the fact that Cassandra looked how Cassandra looked, and the dude who ran Yogurt Haven was a dude. Oh yeah, *that's* why she hadn't gotten fired.

I found a nice tree to lean against, and less than ten minutes later, Cassandra pulled up. I opened the door and climbed in, knowing better than to ask about the large tub of fro-yo she had sitting on the dash. It only took us a few minutes to get to Brian's house, and Cassandra grabbed the yogurt before she got out of the van.

We walked up to Brian's front porch and rang the doorbell. Brian's cover for being our Counsel was that he was the head football coach at Spring River High School. In our town, being head high school football coach was basically like being a celebrity, but Brian's heart wasn't in it. He'd rather have been picking out throw pillows and comparing paint swatches. He was really an interior decorator, and the creative force behind what I was convinced was the most post-worthy fireplace in town. When he opened the door to let us in, I noticed that it was decked out with a tasteful arrangement of roses—red, pink, and white—for Valentine's Day. Brian loved a holiday like a cupcake mom loves a bake sale.

"Brought you something," Cassandra chirped, holding out the tub of frozen yogurt to Brian.

"Oh, thank you," Brian said with fear in his voice. "What flavor combo is it this time?"

"Pineapple jalapeño and peppermint chip," she said.

"Thank you," Brian said again, opening his freezer and popping it in. "I'll just, uh, save it for later."

"So, what's up?" I asked him, and he motioned for us to follow him. At the back of Brian's bedroom, through a closet full of nothing but tracksuits and maybe one turtleneck sweater, there was a door to his secret Sitter lair, and that was where he took us now.

Once the door shut behind us, he motioned for us to sit down in the chairs that were opposite his desk. He typed a few things out on his keyboard, and a giant electronic map of Spring River appeared on the wall behind his desk. It looked like a weather map, and I was pretty familiar with it, as it was sort of a demon Doppler that tracked Negative activity around town.

"Something's different," Cassandra said, pointing to it. "Where's all the green and yellow?" Normally the map showed green in places where a demon had just been Returned, and yellow in places where it seemed like one was about ready to show up. On the map, the demons themselves looked like tiny orange Tic Tacs, but now, the map was a blank slate.

"I've momentarily turned the Negative settings off," Brian explained. "I'll get to that in a minute. In my career as Counsel, I have previously encountered very little information about Red Magic. I came into the Sitterhood after Erebus was banished, as you know, which was a few years after Wanda had become the Premier," he continued. "But apparently, before Wanda's tenure, Sitters were quite familiar with Red Magic. Wanda, however, put a stop to that, no doubt because a general ignorance of Red Magic would better allow her to cloak her own use of it. But, if you're willing to do some digging and piece things together from multiple sources, there's a lot of information to be found. The basic gist is this: Red Magicians perform a ritual, which supercharges a talisman with powers. Those powers allow the magician to do all sorts of things that are outside the realm of Sitter magic. Things like curses, manipulation, increasing personal wealth, infringing upon another's will. You name it, Red Magic can do it."

"What's a talisman?" Cassandra asked.

"It can be any material object of the magician's choosing," Brian said. "Though, the more valuable the object is to the magician, the more powerful it will be."

"And people—I mean, Sitters—used to know all about this?" Cassandra asked.

"It appears so," Brian said.

"Every day, something new we've missed out on," Cassandra said, and Brian nodded.

"Not just you. Everyone," he said. "But that is changing

going forward, for all of us. Which brings me to this." Here he turned to look at the map, and even smiled a little. "With a few technological updates and a bit of reprogramming, we are now equipped with this." He hit a few more keys on the keyboard, and the map shifted.

Now several spots glowed red, like the map was dealing with a serious acne breakout.

I gasped. We didn't need Brian to explain what he'd done, because it was obvious he'd rigged the map to track places where Red Magic was being practiced.

"No friggin' way," Cassandra said.

"Way," Brian said, rolling back in his chair so that Cassandra and I could come around and get a closer look at the map.

Not that a closer look really told us anything, as the map was a cryptic thing—without any designated landmarks—that only Brian could interpret. He stood up from his chair and walked over to stand behind us.

"I've been able to pinpoint most of the red spots," he said, pointing to a blob of pale pink. "That's the Riverbend Hotel. It appears there's still a bit of residue surrounding the place, which probably accounts for the really bad Yelp reviews they've been getting lately."

"We should do something about that," Cassandra said. "The people are nice, and they make good pasta."

"I'll look into it," Brian said.

"What are all those tiny dots?" I asked, as parts of the map looked like they had been dusted with sugar sprinkles.

"Nothing major," he said, "just small bits of Red Magic being practiced by normal people. Someone with a voodoo doll of their ex, or someone trying to hex a rival." He tapped one of the dots with a finger, and as I looked at it, I could see that it glowed a smidge brighter than the rest. "I did a little investigating into this one," he said. "It's a dry cleaners, and a new dry cleaner opened up across the street. The owner has been trying to work up a curse but so far hasn't gotten further than a few pointed Google searches."

"And what's that one?" Cassandra asked, pointing at a red dot that was significantly larger than most.

Brian cleared his throat. "That's what I wanted you both to see," he said. "Cassandra, that's your house."

"Wh-what?" I stammered, and Cassandra's face went pale.

"I swear," she started, "I'm not doing anything other than the spells I cast on Dion. You know about those, and I've even been letting up lately because—"

"I know," Brian said, holding his hands up and stopping her. "It wasn't there yesterday morning. The first time I saw it was when I ran the program this afternoon."

"The break-in!" Cassandra and I said at the same time.

"The what?" Brian asked.

"We got robbed last night," Cassandra said.

"Oh Lord," Brian said. "I'm so sorry. What did they take?"

"That's the thing," Cassandra said. "Nothing." We filled Brian in on the details, and how we thought the burglars were looking for something, and he nodded as he listened.

"The whole thing just felt off," I said, "and my Sitter sense was firing the whole time. It almost seemed like it could have been just a super-destructive demon, but they left some clues."

At this, Cassandra pulled out her phone and showed Brian a picture of the body spray, the wallet chain, and the band flyer.

"Those clues definitely point to someone with bad taste," he said.

"And if this is right, then it was someone with bad taste who also practices Red Magic," I said, pointing at the screen. "And we all know someone who fits that description."

"Erebus," Brian said, and Cassandra nodded. "But that's not possible," he continued. "There's been no sign of Portal activity, which means he is still locked up."

Brian sat back down in his chair, picked up a stress ball, and started to squeeze it. "That's interesting that you think whoever broke into your house was looking for something," he said. "Do you have any idea what that would be?"

Cassandra and I both shook our heads, and Brian nodded. He had a far-off look on his face, and just kept abusing the stress ball. It looked like a duck, and its eyes bulged out of its head with every squeeze. "Interesting, interesting," he said.

"What?" Cassandra said. "Spill it, now."

"Wanda was looking for something too," he said. "We don't know what it was, but it appears it was very important to her, and it was stolen many years ago."

"Where'd you hear this?" I asked.

"I didn't hear it," he said. "I read it. We have been going through Wanda's grimoire. She was a cryptic record keeper, but it appears that she was trying to find a particular talisman. She believed she knew who stole it, but she still wasn't ever able to get it back. If this is true, and we have no reason to believe it's not, it's particularly unnerving because Red Magic talismans can be used by anyone who comes into possession of them. Most Red Magicians seem to start practicing with someone else's talismans before they begin to make their own."

"Wait," I said. "Who's 'we'?"

"Clarissa and myself," Brian said, and I swear I saw him blush. Clarissa was a fellow Counsel who Brian had met at the Summit. She was smart and attractive and had as much of a fondness for tracksuits as he did. As far as I could tell, it was a match made in leisure wear heaven.

"So this thing that Wanda was looking for," I said, "is still out there. So someone else could be looking for it as well."

"Yes," Brian said. "And it would be bad news if they found it. There is a small hope, of course, that whoever stole the talisman from Wanda in the first place was smart enough to just destroy it, but we don't know."

"Any suspects?" Cassandra asked.

Brian shook his head. "We don't know," he said. "But as long as it's out there, Wanda's work isn't finished." The three of us sat there in silence, looking at the map. I watched as the tiny red dot Brian had identified as the dry cleaner faded to black. Probably signing off the Google searches for the night.

"So, just brain vomiting out loud here," I said. "Last night, someone who practiced Red Magic, who appeared to be looking for something, similar to Wanda, and who had the taste level of Erebus broke into Cassandra's house, but both Wanda's and Erebus's whereabouts are accounted for."

"So, it's not option A or option B," Cassandra concluded. "It's option C, and at this point, option C is still unknown."

I raised an eyebrow at her. "The way you phrased that sounds like you've been paying attention in class," I said.

"Hardly," she scoffed. "I just watch a lot of game shows."

"There's also option D," Brian said.

"Who's that?" Cassandra asked.

"Adrian, Wanda's assistant," Brian said, and my heart started to pound. "No one has been able to find him since he flew away from the Summit."

"Do you think he had anything to do with it?" I asked, swallowing around the lump in my throat.

"We don't know," Brian said. "But everyone would like to speak with him, and the longer he stays hidden, the more guilty he looks."

My heart raced even faster. As much as I thought about Adrian, this conversation was the first time I'd heard his name spoken since the Summit, and the first time I had heard that he was now a wanted man.

"Esme," Brian said, clearing his throat, "I know you two were friendly. You haven't seen him, have you?"

"No," I said. "I mean, there are crows everywhere, and I see those all the time, but . . ." I trailed off, deciding then and there that I wasn't going to mention the mix CD. I hadn't told anyone, not even Janis, about it, and besides, Brian had asked if I had *seen* Adrian, and I definitely hadn't seen him.

Brian nodded. "If I am being frank with you, Adrian's situation is a complicated one," he said. "There are people who believe that his powers should be taken away. Not because he's presumed guilty but because he should never have had them in the first place. Wanda gave them to him when he was only seven, and it was a clear abuse of her power. Turning an innocent into a therianthrope is not the same as protecting them."

I could feel my face getting hot, and thankfully, Cassandra changed the subject.

"What about option E?" she said.

"And option E would be?" Brian asked.

"A member of the old Synod," she answered. "One of them could be out to finish what Wanda started, and they just left the flyer and other stuff to try to throw us off."

At this, Brian grimaced. "I don't think any of them would be capable of that at this point," he said. "They were all subject to mnemokinesis right after the Summit. In retrospect, it may have been a bit premature, but we didn't want to dilly-dally."

Cassandra nodded. "So, our best bet is C or D," she said.

"C!" I said sharply. Maybe too sharply. "Come on," I said, trying to cover my tracks. "Everyone knows that when you don't know the answer on a multiple-choice test, you just go with C."

"Okay, option C it is," Brian said. "I'd say, start with the clues."

If we were right, and I was pretty sure that we were, then there was a whole new person out there who'd grabbed the spoon and was stirring the magical pot. A new person who might have some answers. "Oh yeah," I told him. "We will find C, and they will pay." Cassandra and I locked eyes, and we both smiled. I knew my words were true. I mean, she'd dived into another dimension to save a kid, and I'd single-handedly flushed the leader of the magical world. Plus, we'd Returned an uncountable number of demons, and made it two-thirds of the way through our junior year of high school. So what couldn't we do?

Brian glanced at the clock and then stood up, signaling that it was time for us to go. It was getting late, and it was a school night for all of us. We made our way back through Brian's house and were just at the front door when Cassandra turned back to him.

"Hey, Coach B.," she said. "You remember at the Summit when you used a spell to make all those crappy party decorations look really awesome and amazing?"

"I do indeed remember that," he said, opening the door and ushering us out onto the porch.

"Can you use that same spell to, oh, I dunno, turn a business card into an ID?"

He gave her a look like he knew exactly where she was going with this. "What kind of ID, Miss Heaven?"

"Oh, you know, one that said I was twenty-one," she said.

"Good night," he said, and shut the door in our faces. But Cassandra wasn't done yet. She bent down and opened up his mail slot.

"You wouldn't happen to know where I could find a book that has that spell in it?" she called through the slot. "Or at least know what such a spell is called?"

Brian answered with his porch light, which he turned off, leaving us standing in the dark.

CHAPTER 5

When I got home, Dad and Mom were sitting on the couch, watching football. I sat down next to Mom and helped myself to the bowl of popcorn that she was holding in her lap. She didn't appear to be eating it so much as she was sorting the popped pieces by size. "This sport is still on?" I asked, and Dad shot me a look.

"This is the Super Bowl, Esme," he said.

"What's that?" I asked, tossing a piece up and catching it in my mouth.

"Well, you might know it as the 'halftime show,'" he said, "but what you might not realize is that the halftime show is sandwiched between the two halves of the biggest football game of the year. It's how the halftime show gets its name, actually."

"Interesting," I said. "Thanks for the etymology lesson, Professor. I'm gonna go microwave a burrito."

In the kitchen, I opened the freezer and pulled out a burrito, then popped it into the microwave. While it nuked, I pondered option C, an unknown villain searching for an unknown object. Being a Sitter meant that sometimes it felt like I was living in a movie, though without the getting ready, shopping, or makeover montages. Without the love interest either. At least, without a solid love interest. I looked out the window, at the bare, black branches of the trees silhouetted against the night sky. There were undoubtedly crows in those trees, and as much as I hated anything that felt like hope, I couldn't help but think that maybe one of those crows was also a boy.

The microwave dinged. I popped the door open and reached in, then immediately yanked my hand back. The plate was as hot as fire. I touched the burrito—it was still as cold as ice. I added a few more minutes to the timer and started the microwave again. I walked over to the sink to get a glass of water, and stepped around Pig's bowl, which still sat in the same spot because neither Dad nor I had the heart to move it. The metal clanged on the floor, and the sound made me want to cry. The microwave dinged again, and as was to be expected, the burrito was now way too hot, so I stuck it back in the freezer.

I walked to my room, changed out of my clothes, and pulled on my pajama pants, then checked on my burrito, which was now cold again. I sighed and grabbed it anyway, as I was kind of over the microwave thing by now and this was going to have to do. I took a bite as I headed to my room to blow through my homework and, more important, pick out what I was going to wear to school the next day.

I didn't feel like doing laundry, so all of today's thrifting finds would have to wait a while before they got into the rotation. I'd been burned too many times before by wearing unwashed clothes that started to smell halfway through the day. I sat down on the bed, took a bite of my burrito, and chewed. Nothing like cold beans to really get the appetite going. I looked around, taking in the clothes that were hanging in my closet, the ones that were strewn across the floor, and the stuff piled on a chair. I had a pair of black-and-white-check paper-bag-waisted jeans that I could pair with a lipstick-red sleeveless turtleneck crop top—the proportions balanced out nicely. A few weeks before, I'd thrifted a wide black leather belt that had a shiny green-and-red plastic apple for a buckle, so that would look supercool. I could throw on an oversized men's button-down for an extra layer, and thick, fuzzy black-and-white polka-dot socks would keep my feet warm inside my black high-top Chucks. **Black and white and left-on-read**, I texted Janis.

I planned to do all, or at least most, or maybe just some, of my chemistry homework, but the next thing I knew, I was startled awake with drool on my chin. My phone said it was eleven-thirty, so I turned off the light, shoved my books to the floor, and went to sleep for real.

The most notable thing about school on Monday was Janis's look. It was Olive Garden: an olive drab jumpsuit, floral head wrap, and breadstick earrings. We spent our lunch hour eating BBQ wings with ranch and planning our staycation weekend. Amirah and Ji-A were going to stay with Janis, and Mallory and Ruby were going to stay with Cassandra. I felt bad about not having anyone stay at my house, but with Dad sleeping on the couch, there wasn't a ton of extra room.

Janis had made a Google map of all the best thrifting spots, and I was in charge of entertainment. But aside from curating a list of nineties slasher flicks that we could watch, I was kind of drawing a blank. I'd made the mistake of mentioning that the Ford dealership had a karaoke machine—as a joke—and now Amirah wouldn't shut up about it. Improbably enough, "Any Man of Mine" was her song.

As if she could tell I was thinking about her, our group chat dinged with a text, and it was her sending yet another Shania Twain GIF.

Janis laughed. "She did say she bought cowboy boots."

"I know," I said. "She sent me a pic. They're Dsquared2." I turned to Cassandra. "What do you think Ruby will want to do this weekend?"

Cass shrugged. "I figured we'd just sneak into the gym." I nodded, though this was a totally foreign concept to me. If I ever found myself in a gym, I'd try to sneak out as quickly as I could.

One thing that we could all agree on was that the weekend couldn't come quickly enough.

The day went by in a blur. Usually, I counted the minutes to the final bell, but today, I felt myself getting more and more anxious as each class period came and went. Sneaking into a bar, even in the name of Sitting, was not part of the Esme Pearl playbook, and I wasn't exactly looking forward to it.

But time stops for no dread-filled girl, and after school, I headed home to relieve Mom's nurse for a few hours before Dad got off work and went to the gym. When I got home, Olivia was knitting and Mom was doing what she seemed to do almost 90 percent of the time: sitting and staring at the wall.

"How'd everything go today?" I asked Olivia as she was packing up her stuff.

"Just fine," she said. "She's a model patient. See you guys tomorrow."

I nodded and walked her out. The only reason that Mom needed round-the-clock care was to fix her meals and make sure she didn't just leave, though I had a feeling she wouldn't. Since she'd moved back in with us, she hadn't tried, even though it was something that had happened several times a week when she'd been at the facility. And really, who could blame her?

I wasn't meeting up with Cassandra and Janis until seven-thirty, so I had plenty of time to hang out. Mom and I worked on a puzzle for a while, and she actually seemed into it, though she *did* try to fit the same two pieces together for almost a half hour. Then I got up to make us some food. Dinner was a little specialty I liked to call spaghetti a la jarra—spaghetti with sauce from a jar—and then Mom and I went into my room so that I could get ready. Normally it didn't take me that long to get dressed, but I had no idea what to wear. It was a feeling I wasn't used to, but then, I'd never tried to sneak into a bar before.

"What do I wear to try to sneak into a bar?" I asked Mom, but she was too busy petting one of my pillows to answer. I texted Janis and Cassandra.

I don't know what to wear.

Look hot and older, Janis wrote back. NO FLAT SHOES.
Sumting slutty was Cassandra's response.

I was glad they were such good friends in all other areas, because they were zero help right then. "Slutty" I wasn't even going to justify with a second thought, but hot and older were two things that were not usually in my repertoire, so I was going to have to figure out how to interpret them.

For "older," I took that to mean no kitsch prints, cartoon characters, or jewelry that could double as a toy. "Hot" was confusing. For most people, "hot" meant looking just like everyone else, which was something that I always tried to avoid. I decided to go with basic black. I owned several "little black dresses," but none were basic. I had a black lace gothic Lolita dress; an asymmetrical, bilious black T-shirt dress; a floor-length black muumuu that Dad said made me look like the grim reaper; and a vintage eighties black sequined cocktail dress with shoulder pads. I had one bodycon, but it was printed like a tangerine, complete with leaves around the collar.

But black jeans I had, so I pulled those on. I also had a black, long-sleeved crop top. The sleeves were printed with pictures of Frida Kahlo, but I could hide those if I wore a jacket. I pulled out an oversized, black-on-black pinstripe blazer and shrugged it on. I added a silver necklace, made from hammered triangles overlapping like a snake's scales. Non-flat shoes were harder, as the only ones I had were made for warmer weather, and unlike Janis's claim regarding her own toes, mine did freeze. I had a cool pair of black platforms, so I decided to wear those, with a pair of silver socks. It actually looked pretty cute, and made the outfit seem a lot more me.

I put some styling creme in my hair and slicked it behind my ears with a sharp side part. I'd let Janis bleach it on New Year's Eve, and the dark roots were growing in in a grimy way that I liked. Then I added a whole lot of black eyeliner and layered on jammy lip stain until my lips were a deep berry. I wasn't sure I looked hot, or older, but I definitely looked different from how I normally looked. I kinda liked it.

When Dad got home from the gym, Mom and I were sitting at the table, basically just waiting for him. "Whoa," he said, opening the fridge and pulling out the spaghetti à la jarra leftovers. "You're all dressed up." He popped the container into the microwave and randomly punched buttons until it started. "Where exactly are you going, dressed like that on a school night?"

I stood up from the table, and in my platforms, I was looking Dad straight in the eye. "Sitter stuff," I said.

He looked down at my shoes. "You're going to chase down demons and fight them in those shoes and a bare stomach?" he asked.

"It's not that kind of Sitter business," I said. "It's more like an investigation." My phone dinged, telling me that Janis was outside.

"Sure," he said, "just as long as it's an investigation that ends by nine-forty-five."

"Huh?" I asked as I grabbed my keys. "Nine-forty-five?"

"So you can be home by ten."

"Dad—" I started, but he cut me off.

"Okay, nine-thirty, then, if you're going to argue," he said. "You may be in charge of protecting the innocent, but you're still a teenager, who lives in my house, and it's a Monday night."

"I haven't had a curfew in forever," I pointed out.

"I know," he said. "And if you were leaving the house in your combat boots with a backpack full of weapons and herbs,

I'd tell you to be safe and have a good night. But since you're leaving the house in heels, eye makeup, and a purse barely big enough to hold a strawberry, you've got a curfew."

My phone started to ring. Janis, no doubt wondering what was taking me so long. It wasn't that long ago that I would have stood there and argued with Dad just for the sake of arguing about whether or not I had a right to argue, but now I didn't have it in me. I had no idea what the night was going to hold, so figuring it was always easier to ask for forgiveness than permission, I nodded and then turned around and headed to the door.

Janis had picked up Cassandra before me, so when I got to the car, I climbed into the warmth and comfort of the backseat, which I had to share with about fifteen cardboard boxes, a disassembled garment rack, and two trash bags full of Janis's Depop merchandise.

"You can shove that stuff to one side," Janis said as I was trying, and failing, to do just that. "It'll be out of here in a minute anyway. I just need to swing by the post office and ship all those boxes."

"Janis, you're kidding, right?" I asked as I buckled my seat belt.

"Why would I kid about the post office?" she asked, pulling away from the curb.

"Because it's after seven," I said, "and the post office closes at five."

"You're kidding me," she huffed. "Is that right?" she asked Cassandra.

"As if I have ever mailed anything," Cassandra answered.

"I swear it's right," I said, and Janis gave a long, lingering sigh.

"Why can't they just have regular hours?" she said.

"I'm pretty sure closing at five is regular hours," I pointed out.

"The yogurt place doesn't close until ten," Cassandra said, as if that were relevant.

"See?" Janis said. "That makes sense. I needed to get these out today!"

"Why didn't you just go earlier?" I asked. "Like, after school?"

"Because I needed to get ready!" she said, the word "obviously" unspoken, yet still obvious, at the end. Pulling against my seat belt, I leaned forward so that I could get a good look at what Janis and Cassandra had decided to wear for a night out.

In the passenger seat, the person who had told me to dress "slutty" was wearing the exact same thing she'd been wearing the day before when we'd seen her at the Perk: a long-sleeved green T-shirt under a gray hoodie, and a pair of dirty, baggy jeans. "You sleep in those clothes last night?" I asked her.

"Yeah," she answered. "Why?"

I ignored that question and turned my attention to Janis, who had changed out of Olive Garden into something that— I had to give her credit—was spectacular. She too was wearing platforms, but they were thigh-high black suede boots, with black fishnets under a Romy and Michele–esque metallic-blue minidress, topped with a black velvet bolero that had long, tendril-like feathers tipping the edges of the sleeves. Honestly, only Janis could combine that many textures and not come out looking like a carpet catalog. Her braids were done up in several little Björk spiral buns, and she had on icy sky-blue lipstick, and silver highlights on her cheekbones, and I was 100 percent certain that she looked way too good for where we were going, which was a strip-mall bar sandwiched between a Jacuzzi store and a pet shop that sold tarantulas.

"You look good," I said.

"Thanks," she said. "So do you."

"So why do we have to be there so early?" I asked, thinking about my curfew and settling back into the seat.

"They go on at eight," Janis said, turning the corner.

"Isn't that early?" I asked, which was just a guess since I had never actually been to a show before.

"Yeah," Cassandra answered. "So, eight p.m. show on a Monday night. How good could they be?"

"Judging the band by their flyer," I said, "not good at all."

The strip-mall venue in question was close, and when Janis pulled in, the parking lot was pretty empty, yet she still parked about as far away from the bar as she could, a rhino-sized pile of gray, old snow in between her car and the building. "I hope no one steals my packages," she said as we got out and she locked the doors.

"Maybe they'll drop them off at the post office for you," I said. "Why'd you park so far away?"

"Because if they ask for ID, we can say we forgot them," she explained. "And they won't know we drove here."

"I didn't forget my ID," Cassandra said. "I have it right here."

"Is it fake?" Janis asked.

"No," Cassandra said, pulling it out of her pocket and giving it a flick. "See? It very materially exists."

Janis reached over and grabbed it from her, then sighed as

she handed it back. "That's your student ID," Janis said. "That says you're in high school."

"Hey," Cassandra said defensively, "I asked Brian to help us out, and he literally shut the door in our faces. So this is all I've got."

"I have my learner's permit in here somewhere," I said, opening my purse, which, contrary to what Dad had said, was actually more the size of a croissant sandwich than a strawberry.

"Both of you just keep your mouths shut," Janis said, stepping over a slush pile studded with Slushee cups, and leading the way. "Let me do the talking."

The bar was called Ray's Pool Bar and Hot Dog Grill, but as we got closer, I could see a sign on the door that said NO HOT DOGS! Good thing they'd cleared that up. Cassandra and I fell back and let Janis go first, as she had insisted. I had no idea what story she had worked up in her head as to why there were three of us here without our IDs, but I think she might have been a little excited to spin it, because she faltered a bit as soon as she stepped inside, since there was no one poised to stop us from waltzing right on in and sitting down wherever we wanted.

And we had our choice of seats. I had been worried that we would stand out because we were underage and overdressed. I hadn't thought that we'd stand out because, aside from three guys on the other side of the bar playing pool, we were the only ones in there. Janis picked out a random table in the middle of the space, and we followed her and sat down. We were all quiet, not sure what to do or where to look. Finally Cassandra pushed her chair back and stood up. "I'm starving," she said. "I'm going to go order a hot dog."

"There are no hot dogs," I hissed, reaching out and grabbing her arm to pull her back down into her chair. "Didn't you see the sign?"

"Yes," she said, shaking my hand off. "That's how I knew they have hot dogs."

"No, the other sign," I said. "Not the one that says 'hot dogs'! The one that says 'no hot dogs'!" My heart was beating fast, and I worried that we were already drawing attention to ourselves.

Then Janis shushed us. "Look," she said, tipping her head at the stage.

Jacking Lanterns was in the house.

It was the same four guys from the picture on the flyer, wearing the same amount of hair gel, and while they weren't wearing the same clothes, they might as well have been: ringer tees, ball-chain necklaces, and baggy jeans that were as frayed at the hems as Cassandra's. They were carrying drums and guitar cases onto the stage, and they all looked very serious. They had the vibe of guys who would watch YouTube videos about how to pick up women. Three of them were wearing bracelets, and two—that I could see—had barbed-wire tattoos.

A wallet chain wouldn't have looked out of place on any of them, and I would have taken the whole thing as a joke, except for how serious they seemed. I could see two of them arguing over what appeared to be the set list. There was nothing demonic about them, but as I watched them, the back of my neck started to feel like it was crawling with spiders. Something was off. Way, way off.

"Excuse me, ladies. I'm going to need to see some ID."
My head swiveled from the band to the bartender, who was

standing at our table, looking down on us with a tight smile. I looked from him to Janis. If she wanted us to keep quiet so that she could do the talking, I was more than happy to step aside and let her do just that.

Cassandra was looking at her too, and both of us were frozen. "Of course," Janis said, smiling up at the bartender and getting out her purse. She rifled through it, then looked up at him with a big smile. "Ugh, can you believe that I left my driver's license in my other bag?"

"I can absolutely believe that," he said, then turned to me. "And what about you?"

I swallowed, my tongue sticking to the roof of my mouth. "Me too," I said.

"Your ID is in her other bag?" he asked with a smile, and all I could do was nod. Now he turned to Cassandra, who just shrugged.

"I don't have a driver's license," she said.

The bartender pursed his lips and nodded. "All right, ladies, I'm real sorry, but we're a twenty-one-and-up establishment, and I'm going to have to ask you to leave." None of us moved an inch. "Now," he said.

"I feel so silly," Janis said. "It's crazy that we all three forgot our IDs on the same night, but can't we just stay for one song? I've heard these guys are really good." At the mention of the band, a weird look came across the bartender's face.

"Yeah, Phantom Limp really rocks," he said.

"Phantom Limp?" I asked. "I thought they were called Jacking Lanterns?"

The guy shook his head and looked at me like I'd just tried to order a Big Mac at Taco Bell. "They were Jacking Lanterns last week," he said. "This week they're Phantom Limp, and this place is gonna be packed."

"They go on in ten minutes," Cassandra said, a note of challenge in her voice. "And we're the only ones here."

"Yeah, we're gonna need this table, actually," the bartender said, either not hearing Cassandra or choosing to ignore her. "They've got a huge fan base. I got this T-shirt on their first tour, and at their last show, someone offered me three hundred bucks for it. I said, 'No way. I'm going to be buried in it.'"

All three of us looked at his T-shirt, and I saw the confusion flashing across Janis's face before she nodded and smiled. Unless Phantom Limp had once been known as "Star City Brewing, Colby, Colorado" (which did seem entirely possible), it was definitely not a band T-shirt.

Janis started to say something, probably more about how we didn't need to leave, but I tapped her with my foot under the table, and she shut her mouth. "So you've been a fan for a long time?" I asked, and he nodded vigorously. "What's your favorite song?" I asked.

"All of them," he said.

"Same," I said. "I was really looking forward to hearing them play all of their songs. What'd you think of the last album?"

"It rocked," he said. "Hard."

"You don't think it sounded a little overproduced?" I asked.

"Oh, no way," he said enthusiastically. "It was totally raw. These guys rock. If they keep going like this, I can see Hoobastank opening for them, and not the other way around."

"Do they ever play any covers at their live shows?" I asked.

"No way," he said. "All original."

"Totally," I said. Then I stood up, grabbing Janis's sleeve to pull her to her feet. Cassandra followed. "We're going to go get her bag with our IDs," I said to the bartender. "We'll be right back. Enjoy the show."

"Oh, I will," he said. "These guys rock."

As we were walking toward the door, I looked back and saw a member of Phantom Limp approaching the three guys at the pool table, carrying what appeared to be shots. For some reason, it made me shudder. I'd rather drink from a puddle in the parking lot outside than swallow anything that band had touched.

Outside the bar, it was frigid and silent. Janis was so cold, she broke into a run to get to the car, and we followed her. I managed to call shotgun, and as soon as we were inside, I turned the heat on full blast.

"What was that all about?" Janis asked. "We were making progress! He would have let us stay. I didn't even get to use my story. I was going to tell him that my cousin works in A and R and . . ."

Cassandra was shaking her head and looking back at the door to the bar. Cassandra was often quiet, but rarely speechless, and I got the distinct vibe that she didn't know what she wanted to say. "Something is seriously wrong with them," she said finally.

I nodded. "There was nobody there, but that bartender wasn't joking at all. He talked like he really did think this band was the next Led Zeppelin. And he really thought he was wearing their T-shirt."

"Yeah, that was really weird," Janis said. "What was the band he mentioned? Hoobastank? What the heck is a Hoobastank?"

"I think it's some sort of cleaning product," Cassandra said. "Like, something you use when your bong spills."

"The band didn't have a Negative vibe," I said, "but they weren't just your run-of-the-mill losers either. My Sitter sense was going off in there like fireworks."

"Same," Cassandra said, tugging at her ear.

"When that guy was talking about how great they were, it was like he was in a trance. Like he was a robot programmed to say certain things," Janis said. " 'They rock.' 'These guys rock.' He sounded like someone who gets their opinions on music from listening to the radio." She put the car in drive. "So what do you want to do now?" she said.

Cassandra's stomach answered with a growl. "Get pizza and go home," she said.

I agreed. I felt like we'd learned enough for one night, but I wasn't quite ready for pizza. With Janis and Cassandra, pizza had been a fight from day one. Well, at least from the day when Cassandra had ordered pineapple on it and Janis had said, "Oh, you're a pineapple person."

Cassandra had responded by calling Janis an "anti-pineapple activist," and the whole thing had devolved from there into an argument that had only been settled by me screaming "TASTE IS SUBJECTIVE!" at the top of my lungs and causing the whole restaurant to look at us.

Tonight Janis had thrown down the gauntlet early and said she would allow pineapple on half the pizza, to which Cassandra had responded, "But what if I want to eat more than half the pizza?"

"You're not eating more than half the pizza," Janis snapped.

"You're not even eating half of it. There are three of us, so the most you get is one-third."

"I'm not eating mushrooms," Cassandra said. "They grow on cow poop."

"They do not," Janis said, though I could tell that she faltered a little bit and this was probably something that she would look up as soon as she was alone. They finally settled on a pizza that was one half mushroom and pepperoni, one half pineapple. Janis would eat the pepperoni and mushroom third, Cassandra would eat the pineapple third, and I would be stuck with a slice of each. I was glad I'd already eaten.

Cassandra called the pizza in so that we could just pick it up, and as Janis drove, I looked out the window and went over everything in my head. In the brief time I'd been a Sitter, I'd met two people who were heavily involved in Red Magic: Erebus and Wanda. Erebus was a wannabe, and Wanda was in charge, but they were both petty, self-pitying, and power hungry. Two data points was not a lot of data points, but it seemed like that was enough to draw a rough sketch of a Red Magic user. Red Magic appealed to people who thought the world was holding out on them, people who thought they deserved more than what they had earned. I wondered if Phantom Limp fit the bill, and shuddered to think that we'd have to get closer to find out.

The more I thought about it, the more it seemed like everyone, and anyone, could be a Red Magic user. Who didn't want something that the world didn't want to give them? Cassandra certainly did, and I did too. Brian, Dad, Dion, Adrian . . . everyone I knew. Even Janis—who came from a stable family that had plenty of money—had life stacked against her in more ways than I could count. Maybe, if the circumstances were just right, any of us would be willing to hurt someone else, to bend the rules until they broke, to get what we wanted.

But if the band had something to do with Red Magic, how? The bartender that we'd talked to had truly believed all the crap he was saying. I had no doubt that magically inspiring that kind of devotion took more than a few bits of public domain Red Magic found on the internet. If they were the ones who had stolen Wanda's talisman all those years before, certainly she would have found them. I texted Brian.

U home?

The text had barely been sent when he wrote back.

School board meeting to discuss athletics funding.
Boorring. Wassup?

I shook my head. Brian really needed to stop spending so much time with teenagers.

Can you check the Red Magic monitor when
you get home? Wondering if anything new
shows up tonight.
Will do.

At some point, Janis and Cassandra had decided that we would go back to Cassandra's house, since apparently Janis had had a similar curfew argument with her parents and didn't want to let them win by getting home early. We pulled into the pizza place parking lot and pooled our money so that Cassandra could go in and pay. She was in and out and back in the backseat in a flash, pizza box balanced on the Depop boxes, slice in hand.

"Hey!" Janis said. "Driving up here! Hand me a napkin and give me a slice."

By the time we arrived at Cassandra's, we'd crushed the entire pizza. Dion was sitting on the couch, watching TV when we walked in, and he immediately perked up. "You got pizza?" he said, sitting forward on the couch.

"Sure did," Cassandra said, opening the box to show him that it now contained nothing but grease stains and that little plastic tripod. "It was delicious." Dion knew enough of his sister's ways to not complain too much, and he just sank back onto the couch only slightly more deflated than before.

"That's cool," he said. "I'll just eat some more peanut butter. Hey, why are you two all dressed up?"

"We tried to go out," I said.

"Yeah," Cassandra said, tossing the pizza box onto a mountain of recycling. "We tried to go to that show, the one from the flyer."

At that, Dion practically jumped up.

"The one that we found?" he asked, and Cassandra nodded. She went over and removed the flyer from the front of the fridge, where she'd stuck it, still in the same plastic bag.

"Why didn't you tell me?" Dion snapped. The force of his words took me by surprise, and I thought Cassandra was a little shocked too. She'd had him under pretty heavy spells since Halloween, and none of us were used to this kind of confrontation.

"If I find whoever broke into my house, they're going to regret that they ever even drove down this street," he said. Color had crept into his face, and I could see that one of his hands was clenched.

"We couldn't both go," Cassandra said, her voice exceedingly calm. "We decided that someone needed to always be here to watch the house, remember? Besides, we got kicked out right away anyway. It was twenty-one and up."

Dion scoffed. "Don't you guys have spells for that?" he asked. Cassandra looked up and caught my eye. In my nervousness at the bar, spelling the bartender had never crossed my mind, and I guess she hadn't thought of it either.

"Not tonight," she said. Janis sat down at the table and started to unzip her boots. I pulled out a chair and sat next to her, and Cassandra plopped down on the couch. Dion sat again, slowly, next to her. Shoes off, Janis tucked her feet under her, then pulled out her phone and was soon absorbed in it.

"So, what'd they sound like?" Dion asked.

"Dunno," Cassandra said. "We had to leave before it even started. They had drums and a guitar, though, and I'm assuming they were going to play them."

"What'd they look like?" Dion asked.

"Exactly the same as the photo on the flyer," Cassandra said. "Except they have a new name. They're 'Phantom Limp' now."

"Oh," Dion said. "That's kind of a dope name."

"No, it's not," Cassandra said with the same inflection of someone saying that the sky was blue.

"They had on jeans and T-shirts, and one of them was wearing a newsboy cap," I said. "Oh, and lots of jewelry, and two of them looked like they'd dyed their hair black and straightened their bangs. They might have been cool twenty years ago, but I doubt it."

"This is super weird," Janis said, looking up from her phone. "I tried to look them up yesterday, after you showed me the flyer, and didn't find anything."

"Same," I said. "I couldn't find any of their social media accounts when I looked, but if they keep changing their name, maybe their accounts are changing too?"

Janis nodded, looking back down at her phone. "Possible," she said. "But now I'm doing a deep dive on Jacking Lanterns and Phantom Limp, and I still can't find anything."

I watched Janis curiously. Cassandra and Dion didn't know Janis well enough to understand how weird it was that she couldn't find anything. Janis was a keyword queen. She could find any information online, and she was like a psychic at interpreting it. If Janis and Google had been around in 1996, we'd know who shot Tupac.

"You can't find *anything*?" I asked. She didn't answer, just shook her head, her thumbs a blur.

Then, all of a sudden, she dropped the phone like it was a too-hot Hot Pocket. "Holy crap," she yelped.

"What'd you find?" I asked, jumping to my feet and leaning in to look at the phone in her lap.

"Well, apparently they're not on Facebook, Instagram, Bandcamp, SoundCloud, TikTok, Snapchat, Twitter, or You-Tube," she said. "But they're still updating their Myspace page, where they were known as the Deltoids two weeks ago, before they were Jacking Lanterns or Phantom Limp."

"I know about deltoids," Cassandra said, joining us around the phone, "but I have no idea what Myspace is."

"There's no reason for you to," I said.

"They even have their flyer up for their show tonight," Janis said. "Though, they must have changed their name again after they posted it." She picked up her phone and started scrolling again, and we all watched her in silence for a minute. "There's a lot of stuff on this Myspace page, and it goes pretty far back." She paused and cleared her throat. "There are two super-weird things about this."

"Go on," Cassandra said, probably picking up on the fact that she was in the presence of a master.

"Well, the first one is the frequency of their posts," Janis explained. "They updated pretty regularly in the early 2000s, then took about a fifteen-year break." She peered at her phone again, and turned it sideways. "Then started to go hard again a little less than two months ago."

"The Summit was two months ago," I said.

"Yeah," Janis said. "And then there's this." She held her phone out, and I took it from her. "They apparently got some really bad band photos taken back in the day, and they must have been super proud of them," Janis continued as Cassandra came to look over my shoulder. "They've always used the same photos, even though it seems like they probably change their name more often than they change their underwear."

We leaned in to get a better look. There were several shots of the band standing on a train track, and some of them in a room, shot with a fish-eye lens. The whole thing was just . . . tragic. Janis clicked through to another picture, and I stared at it. It took me a second to realize what was different. This photo was a little bit older, it seemed, less professional, and there weren't four guys; there were five.

"Wait . . . ," I started.

"Holy crap," Cassandra said, grabbing the phone right out of my hand.

Holy crap was right.

The fifth band member wasn't just any guy.

It was Erebus.

Cassandra passed the phone back to me, and I held it close to my face to get a better look. "Don't lick it, Esme," Janis said. I'd only seen Erebus once, on Halloween, and Dion had one picture of him, but sure enough, this guy looked just like Erebus. It also jogged the thing in my brain, the red flag that had started waving as soon as I'd seen the band but that I couldn't quite place: they all dressed like Erebus.

"The page was archived almost fifteen years ago," Janis said, putting into words what we were all trying to process, "so that photo has to be at least that old, but they all look exactly the same."

"Is there a way to fake the archiving?" Cassandra asked.

"Probably," Janis said. "But it wouldn't be easy. And why would someone do that? Even if they wanted to, I doubt they'd know how, anyway. Judging from their online presence, or lack thereof, I don't think these guys are exactly tech savvy."

Cassandra, Janis, and I just stood there, none of us saying anything, all staring at Janis's phone. Dion had been listening, and now he got up and walked over to us. "Can I see?" he asked. Janis handed her phone to him, and he looked at it. "What's the big deal?" he said. "They're band photos." Then he did a double take. "Wait . . . ," he said, looking again in a way that made me think Dion probably needed glasses. "That's Dad." Then he looked up at us. "This was *his* band?"

"I guess so?" Cassandra said. "Unless he had more than one."
Dion shook his head. "I don't think so," he said.

"You didn't see them tonight," I told him, "but they all still look exactly the same. And so did your dad, on Halloween. But if he's in these photos, then that means they were taken over a decade ago. How old would your dad be?" I asked Cassandra.

"I don't know," she said, "but old. At least forty."

I nodded. "Though, bad fashion taste aside, when we saw him, he looked like he could have just graduated from high school a few years ago," I said. "And same with the band tonight. There are seniors at school who look older than they do. What do you know about them?" I asked Dion.

"Nothing, I swear," he said, and the frightened look on his face said that he was telling the truth. "He called the band 'Zeus Riot,' and all he ever said in his journal was that they rocked and they were going to get really big."

I sighed.

"Yeah, we've heard that before," Cassandra said.

"But if Erebus got banished, why are they still here?" Janis asked.

"I have no idea," Cassandra said, "but we're going to find out, that's for sure."

The three of us jumped when my phone rang. I pulled it out of my bag and put Jim Halpert on speaker phone. His voice sounded excited.

"You were right," he said. "There's a new red spot. It just showed up tonight, and it's bright. It's at"—he paused—"Twenty-First and West Street." We could hear him typing. "A place called . . ."

"Ray's Pool Bar and Hot Dog Grill," we all said in unison.

"Thanks, B.," I said. "We were just there and thought something was up."

"It's not too far from here," Brian said. "I'll swing by and let you know what I find."

"Sounds good," Cassandra said, and we all looked at each other as I hung up the phone. She ran her fingers through her hair, sighing as she shook her head. "I feel better now."

I looked at her, confused. "You feel better now?" I asked. "Now that you know that the one clue about who broke into your house points to four Red Magicians who have been the same age since 2005?"

"Of course," she said. "A normie breaks into your house, what are you going to do? Call the cops?"

"No," Janis said.

"Obviously," Cassandra said, "but this is magic. This is fun. This, Esme," she said, "is something we can handle."

I swallowed. Cassandra loved a challenge, but I wasn't so sure. A demon I could deal with in my sleep, but a band of four, full-grown male losers? *That* sounded exactly like the type of thing I would want to call the cops for.

Janis was still furiously typing on her phone. "Ugh," she moaned. "I hate doing serious research on my phone. None of these sites are optimized for mobile. You don't have a desktop around here, do you?" she asked.

"Yeah, the brand-new Mac is in the bedroom next to the Tesla keys and the Peloton bike," Cassandra said.

"Okay, point taken," Janis said. "But it's hard for me to keep digging on here. I'm going to go home and see what I can find." She stood up and started zipping her boots back on. "Even if they don't use the internet, the internet will use them."

Since my house was the opposite direction from Janis's, Cassandra borrowed Dion's van to give me a ride home and promised to stop at the gas station and buy him more cheese. We were a few blocks from her house when Brian called again. "I just drove by the bar," he said, "and it was empty. All the lights were off and the sign on the door said it was temporarily closed."

"What?" I asked. "We were just there and it was open." I thought back to the total dearth of customers. "At least, I think it was open. The lights were on."

"Well, it was all locked up," he said.

"Thanks for checking it out," I said, and hung up.

Cassandra was humming as she drove, something that I had never heard her do before. I gave her the side-eye. Cassandra was happy, and it wasn't just because of all the pizza. "So," I said when we were stopped at what seemed to be an exceptionally long light, "things must be going pretty good with Ruby, then, huh?"

"What do you mean?" she asked, drumming her fingers on the steering wheel.

"I mean, if she's coming for Valentine's Day," I said.

"Oh yeah, I guess," Cassandra said. "I mean, we didn't plan it that way. It was just the first long weekend. She didn't want to miss school."

"Really?" I asked, somewhat surprised, since Cassandra missed more school than she attended. "Why not?"

"She's got, like, perfect attendance or something, and she doesn't want to screw it up."

"Oh, wow," I said. "That's cool."

Cassandra nodded. "Yeah, we're really different like that."

"What do you mean?" I asked, surprised that Cass would make such an observation, and then go as far as to say it out loud.

"She's really got her stuff together, you know? Like, she's got a plan, and she knows what she wants to do with her life, and I just kinda got lucky." Right as she said the words "got lucky," the van died, and as Cassandra performed a complicated routine of gas, brake, gas, reverse, park, drive, gas, turn the key, I couldn't help but think that "lucky" wasn't exactly a word I would use to describe her.

"How so?" I asked, my words nearly drowned by the sound of the van roaring back to life.

"That I turned out to be a Sitter," Cassandra said. "Without that, I'd just be another crappy student with a bad attitude and no respect for authority. Now, at least, I'm a crappy student with a bad attitude and no respect for authority—who's protecting the innocent and saving the world in her spare time. I can see why Dion's jealous, because even if I have to grub my way through life, I've still got a thing, you know? A thing that makes me special. So I'm lucky, because most people don't have that. But Ruby's different. She'd be special even if she were totally normal."

Cassandra turned onto my street, and I glanced at her face

in the glow of the dashboard as the van ground to a halt in front of my house. Her face didn't betray anything other than the steely determination it always did, but that was the sweetest, most sensitive thing I'd ever heard her say.

"I think you're a good couple," I said as I got out of the van. "See you tomorrow. Thanks for the ride." I slammed the door, and as I walked up to my front path, I wondered if anyone would ever say anything like that about me. I listened hard for the sound of crows, but the night was silent.

In the house, Mom was already in her room, and Dad was spreading out his sheets and blankets on the couch. "Well, well, well," he said, "little miss I-fight-demons-and-don't-need-a-curfew is actually home early."

I rolled my eyes, though realized he couldn't see me in the dim light. "All we did was eat pizza and hang out at Cassandra's," I said. Dad must have picked up on something in my voice, because he didn't press the issue.

"Well, did the pizza like your outfit?" he asked.

"It did," I said, and I started to head down the hall to my room.

"Esme," he called out after me. "For what it's worth, I thought you looked really nice tonight." I paused, and smiled to myself.

"Thanks, Dad," I called back. I guess, when it came down to it, I was pretty lucky too.

CHAPTER 6

When I woke up on Tuesday morning, I was in a black mood. I tried to tell myself this was because the night before had felt like a failure, but myself knew better. It was Adrian. I felt ghosted, but then I wasn't even sure if that was right. We barely knew each other. We hadn't hooked up. We'd shared a few moments, that was all. I had no idea what he'd thought of me, and he might even be someone who I should be mad at, who I should vow to never speak to again for his role in Pig's disappearance. *If* he had a role in Pig's disappearance. After all, he was Wanda's gopher, not her right hand. There was always a chance he hadn't known anything about what she'd been planning.

And then, of course, there was the mix CD. Would a guy make a mix CD for a girl he was just going to forget? Probably not. Would a guy make a mix CD for a girl whose dog he had helped to vanish? Again, probably not. That'd be like giving a person a stick of gum when they had just said that they were starving, worse than not doing anything at all. I took a big breath, puffed my cheeks as I blew it out, and then threw off the covers and got out of bed.

I was determined to seize the day, and I knew of one thing, and one thing only, that was guaranteed to dispel one of my bad moods. And that was a really good outfit. I hadn't been Winona in a while, and today was as good a day as any. The week before last, I'd bought a lipstick-red skirt that completed an outfit I'd been mentally working on for a while, based on Kim Boggs from *Edward Scissorhands*. This was undoubtedly one of my favorite Winona movies—Young Johnny? Yes, please. Tim Burton? Double yes, please, yes, please—even if it was one of my least favorite Winona looks, since she had long, blond hair and that somehow felt like the opposite of what Winona was all about. But I got it—I mean, in the film she was supposed to be a popular girl with a jock jerk boyfriend, and those kinds of roles seemed to require long, blond hair.

I put on a long-sleeved white T-shirt and the red skirt. In the movie, it's warm, so Kim has bare legs, white socks, and bright red shoes, but since it was cold here, and also since this was an homage and an interpretation rather than a rec- reation, I pulled on white tights before pulling on white socks and my red-and-white saddle shoes. Then I put on the thing that had inspired my first glimmers of this outfit: a red-leather corset/harness/belt that fit like sexy suspenders that had been found deep, deep in the sale rack at Hot Topic. But when I looked in the mirror, I felt like something was still missing, and even with the post-fetish-accessorizing, the look was still a little saccharine. I walked over to my desk and picked up a pair of fabric shears, and made little horizontal cuts, evenly spaced, along the outside edge of both of my sleeves. Then I stepped back, looked again, and smiled. Perfection, and also realistic, as it would be impossible to fall in love with a guy with scissors for digits and not get at least a little cut in the process.

I picked up my phone, about to text Janis, This look is not complete, when I saw that she'd been texting me consistently since six a.m., the last text saying in all caps FORGET IT. I'M COMING TO PICK YOU UP NOW. I threw down my phone and had started to stuff all my school stuff into my backpack when I heard Dad calling my name.

"Esme!" he yelled. "Janis is out front, and it looks like she's threatening to honk the horn?"

"I'm coming!" I yelled.

"She's coming!" he yelled out the door.

"What's her rush?" he asked as I hurried down the hall. I rifled through the coat closet before finally just grabbing my black puffer since it was the most obvious and closest at hand.

"I have no idea," I said. I gave him a kiss on the cheek and then ran out the door. "Bye, Dad. Love you!"

"Love you too," he called after me, then paused. "Wait a minute—are you wearing a bra on the outside of your shirt?"

I didn't bother to answer, because as soon as I was barely inside Janis's car, she was already pulling out of the driveway. "What's the fire under your butt this morning?" I asked, struggling to buckle my seat belt.

"Can't tell you until we get Cassandra," she said.

"Can we get coffee before we get Cassandra?" I asked.

"Trust me," she said, "you won't need it! This will totally wake you up!"

"Sure," I said, and yawned. As she drove, I took in Janis's

look, which was unusually subdued: she just had on ripped jeans, combat boots, and a vintage A Tribe Called Quest T-shirt under an old red-and-black flannel that, even though I couldn't see the back of it, I knew had "Nevermind" painted on it in drippy silver letters. I was usually pretty good at picking up on Janis's fashion cues, but this one was kind of confusing, unless it was maybe some sort of nod to the fact that 1991 was such a good year for music that Tribe and Nirvana both released albums on the same day?

"What's this outfit called?" I asked, and Janis just huffed.

"There was no time for outfits this morning," she said. "And I was up super late last night. But trust me, it was all worth it."

"Yeah, yeah, I trust you, I trust you," I said as we pulled up outside Cassandra's house. To my surprise, Cass must have been watching and waiting for us, because Janis had barely stopped before Cassandra was out the door and jogging toward the car. She opened the back door, tossed a couple of boxes to the other side, and then climbed in.

"Okay," she said, "so what's this all about?"

"Well," Janis started, "when I got home last night, I figured I could just stay up and spend hours digging around on the internet trying to find out more about Phantom Limp, or I could just call the bar and see if I could get their info."

"So you called the bar?" I said.

She nodded.

"And what'd they say?" I asked.

"Nothing," she said.

"They wouldn't tell you?" Cassandra asked.

"No," Janis said. "There was no answer. They were closed."

"I know," I said. "Brian drove by and said the same thing."

"Weird," Cassandra said. "So, then, what'd you do?"

"I spent hours digging around on the internet, of course," Janis said. "And I found your dad's employment history. He did not pay a lot of taxes."

"What?" Cassandra said. "You can just look that stuff up?"

"We can't, but Janis can," I said, by way of explanation.

"So, guess where he worked?" Janis said. Cassandra and I just sat there.

"Big Lots?" Cassandra said finally.

"No," Janis said. "At the mall!"

"Wow," I said, "I never figured Erebus as the type to have a cool job."

"But it wasn't just anywhere at the mall," Janis continued. "He worked at Spill the Beanies!"

"What the hell is 'Spill the Beanies'?" Cassandra asked.

"A Beanie Baby kiosk!" Janis crowed triumphantly. Cassandra and I were quiet and let this information wash over us like sunlight at dawn.

"So that's how he met Wanda," I said finally.

"It has to be," Janis said. "He only made six dollars and fifteen cents an hour, but I bet he got an employee discount and access to new products before they hit the shelves."

"Which means he could have had something that Wanda wanted," Cassandra said.

"Wow," I said. "Who would have thought that the missing link was a cart on wheels?"

"Not just any cart," Janis clarified, "but the Spill the Beanies cart. And that's not it! There's more."

"What else?" Cassandra asked. "Did you get his Social Security number too?"

Janis shook her head and ignored the sarcasm. "No," she said. "Another number. A phone number."

"And so you called it and the phone booth outside your house started ringing?" I suggested.

"Well, no," Janis said. "I didn't call it at all. I mean, I'm not going to call it by myself! But here, look! It's a number to book Jacking Limbs, or whatever they're calling themselves this week."

"Whoa," I said. "Where'd you find that?"

"Well, that wasn't actually so hard," Janis said. "It was just on their Myspace page, front and center."

Cassandra whipped out her phone and started to dial.

"Wait!" Janis screeched. "At least turn off your caller ID first!"

Cassandra stopped dialing. "Okay, but how?"

Janis took her phone and, tapping around all the cracks in the screen, hit a few buttons, and then handed the phone back to Cassandra. I held Janis's phone so that Cassandra could see the number, and she dialed and then put it on speaker and held it out so that we could all hear. It rang, and rang, and then just as Cassandra was about to hit end, someone picked up. Or rather, a voice mail.

"Hey," said a gruff male voice, "you've reached Tom, Todd, Chad, and Brad, and we're too busy rockin' out to come to the phone right now." Insert earsplitting guitar riff here. "So leave your name and number, and we'll call you back. Maybe." Then there was a drum solo and someone howling into the mic. Then *BEEP.*

I couldn't help it. I burst out laughing. Janis looked at me with horror on her face, and Cassandra quickly pressed end.

"Well," I said, wiping my eyes, "at least we know it's the right number."

"They all share a cell phone?" Cassandra said, looking at her phone like it was covered in mucus.

"I bet it's a landline," I said.

"And we just left an anonymous giggling message for the people we're trying to stalk," Janis said.

"Come on," I said. "They want people to laugh, right? They can't be serious with that message. It has to be a joke."

"Esme," Janis said, "you saw them. They are totally, one hundred percent serious."

"They had a drum solo on their outgoing message," I started, looking at Cassandra for backup, but she was just nodding.

"Serious," she said.

"So, what now?" I asked.

"Well, fortunately, your Janis already figured that out," Janis said. "And through some reverse look-ups, I found out that the phone number belongs to a Tom Spano, and I got an address. I also found out that Tom Spano is forty-two, has lived in Spring River his entire life, and was most recently employed as the tile and linoleum manager at the Home Depot." With that, she put the car back into drive and pulled away from the curb. At the corner, I wasn't surprised when she turned in the opposite direction from school.

"So, we're going to go check it out, right?" Cassandra asked.

"Oh yeah," Janis said. "But first, coffee."

"Thank God," I said.

• • •

Janis got a hot mocha, I got my usual iced coffee, Cassandra got a Pepsi, and then we got two strawberry sprinkle doughnuts, a cinnamon bear claw, a chocolate twist with bacon sprinkles, and a hot pretzel. The pretzel was for Cassandra, of course, who somehow didn't like doughnuts but wanted a pretzel before eight a.m.

The address associated with the band's phone was on the south side of town, and as we drove, the sky was gray, and everything seemed pretty quiet. We'd pass the occasional car, but no one was walking and no kids were playing outside. In the parking lot of a gas station, someone had set up a card table selling Valentine's gifts: large stuffed bears with white fur holding hearts that looked damp in the gloomy morning, and dozens of red roses punctuated with baby's breath, all of which would certainly be wilted, if they were actually real, by the time Valentine's Day rolled around.

Janis turned onto the street and slowed the car to a crawl. "There it is," Cassandra said, pointing to a small, gray house with a couch on the front porch and a dark purple PT Cruiser parked in the driveway. I choked on my coffee when I saw the car. I'd always pegged Erebus as the kind of guy who would drive a PT Cruiser, and how right I was. I was going to have to start giving my car intuition a whole lot more credit. Janis sped up as we passed.

"What are you doing?" Cassandra asked. "Go back."

"I'm not going to just hang out outside their house," Janis said. "That would look super suspicious."

"Well, we need a plan to find out if they really do live there," Cassandra said. "Aside from just driving back and forth until someone comes out." She drank the last of her Pepsi, screwed the top back onto the empty bottle, and was about to drop it into the recycling bin that was the floor of Janis's car when something caught her eye. She leaned down and picked up a crumpled piece of paper. She put it on her knee and started to smooth it out. It was one of the many flyers I'd made for Pig. "Park the car," she said. "I'm going to go knock on the door and ask if they've seen my dog."

"It's barely eight a.m.," Janis said. "They had a show last night. They're not going to be awake by now."

"Their show was done by eight-forty-five," Cassandra said. "So even if they partied until ten-thirty, they're probably fine."

"True, true," Janis said, turning the corner and putting the car in park. "We can see you from here," she said, "so be careful, and scream if you need help."

"Will do," Cassandra said, "very loudly." She started to open the door.

"Cass, wait!" I said, stopping her. "What if they recognize you?"

"From last night, you mean?" she asked, and I shook my head.

"No, from your parents." Looking at her now, I was struck by something I'd noticed, but not really processed, when I'd seen Circe at the hotel. Even under the caked-on makeup, bad wig, and ill-fitting clothes, Circe had been a dead ringer for Cassandra. They had the same flawless skin, thick black hair, and full lips that Sephora would have loved to patent. "If they knew your dad, then they probably also knew your mom," I explained. "And you look just like her." I paused. I could see that Cassandra thought I had a point, even if she didn't exactly like it.

"You're right," Cassandra said. "So what now?"

"I'll go," I said, and grabbed the flyer from her hand and then jumped out of the car before she could stop me. As I was walking toward their house, their next-door neighbor's front door opened, and a woman came out carrying a bag of trash. If I was supposed to be canvassing the neighborhood for a lost dog, it would look weird if I wasn't talking to everyone.

"Excuse me, ma'am," I said, turning up her driveway. "I was wondering if you've seen this dog anywhere around here?" She hefted the bag of trash into the can and then walked toward me. I held the flyer out, and she looked at it, then shook her head.

"Sorry, sweetie," she said. "The dog chipped?"

"Yeah."

"Then she'll turn up. We'll keep an eye out too," she said.

"Okay, thank you so much." I'd started to walk to the band's house, when she called out to me.

"I wouldn't bother with next door." My ears perked up at her words.

"Oh yeah?" I said, turning back toward her. "Are they out of town?"

She glanced at the house, and a strange look crossed her face, a mixture of puzzlement and worry.

"No," she said, "they're there. I just don't like the idea of a young girl going up there alone."

"Really?" I said, deciding to play dumb to try to keep her talking as long as possible. "I think I've met the people who live there before. A redheaded woman with twins?"

The woman shook her head. "No," she said. "Used to be a bachelor lived there, but back in December he took off. Don't know where he went, but all of a sudden four young guys moved in. One of 'em told my husband he was Tom's nephew, but I don't know. My husband thought he was lying."

"Four young guys?" I said. "So probably lots of parties and stuff. People coming and going all the time?"

"No," she said, the look on her face serious, "that would be normal. But these guys never leave. I've hardly ever even see 'em. House is like a tomb, and they're always missing trash day." She scowled at their overflowing cans.

I felt a buzz with this new information. "Thanks for the heads-up," I said. "My friends are in the car, and I've got my pink mace." I held up my keys so that she could see I wasn't lying. "They probably won't even answer, so I'll leave the flyer in the mailbox."

"Okay," she said, still seeming skeptical of my plan. "Be careful."

"I will," I said, and headed next door. I turned back to see her hurrying inside.

The band's house didn't have a path leading up to the door, so I walked up the gravel driveway. As I passed the PT Cruiser, I noticed that it was that color of sparkly purple that looks green in certain light.

The closer I got to the house, the more the back of my neck started to prickle, and by the time I stepped onto the porch, my Sitter sense was overwhelmed. The house was dripping in magic. I could feel it snake around my ankles and up my legs, and run in rivulets down my arms. I hadn't felt anything like this before. It was more alive than the Negative vibes, so more creepy-crawly and gross. There were charms here working overtime, and I wondered what sort of manipulation they could possibly be doing, since the house remained an unimpressive dump.

The couch on the porch was cracked black vinyl with stuffing coming out in several places, and there were lots of empty cans of Natural Light and glass bottles of something called Zima, which I'd never heard of. Behind the couch was a big plate-glass picture window, but it was covered with a Pink Floyd tapestry on the other side. I gripped the flyer, took a deep breath, and rang the bell, my finger feeling like I had dipped it into a can of maggots when it made contact. I tried to control my shudder.

I stood there, waiting, but no one came, and I couldn't hear anything at all inside the house. I took another deep breath, rang again, and waited. I was just about to turn and walk away when I heard a cough from the other side of the Pink Floyd tapestry. Then footsteps, and the sound of the door being opened. The guy who answered it had dark circles under his eyes, and his skin was taut in an almost poreless, shiny way. Or at least the small amount of it that I could see was—he only opened the door about three inches.

"What are you doing here?" he said through the crack. Such a point-blank question threw me off, and I forgot my cover.

"Um . . ." I stood there, my mind a blank, and then . . . "Dog!" I blurted out, thrusting the flyer toward him. He didn't take it, and I turned it sideways to slide it through the crack. "I'm looking for my dog. She disappeared awhile back, and I was hoping that someone here might have seen her."

"No dogs around here," he said. He started to shut the door, and I held my foot out to stop it.

"Actually," I said, plastering a sheepish smile onto my face. "The dog was just an excuse. I really wanted to come here because I'm a fan. A fan of . . ." *Crap!* What was their most recent name? "Phantom Limp!"

Now I had his attention, and he opened the door a little more, though he still didn't smile. I wondered if he even could, and he was still completely blocking any view I might have had past him into the house. "You like that name?" he asked. "We were thinking about changing it."

"Oh yeah," I said, nodding like my head was going to detach. "It rocks."

He pulled the door open fully and stepped out onto the porch. He was wearing gray sweatpants, black slippers, and a camo T-shirt. He had a thick ball-chain necklace on, which looked a little dangerous to sleep in.

"Cool, cool," he said, running his hand through his hair, and he looked me up and down. "I always thought our demo was older, more sophisticated. But tweens have a lot of market spend, and labels like a fan base with disposable income. They buy a lot of CDs. How old are you anyway? Like, twelve?"

What the? He thought I was *twelve*? I tried not to think too much about the fact that a guy who thought twelve-year-olds still bought a lot of CDs thought that I was one of said twelve-year-olds. So instead I just smiled. "Actually, I'm seventeen."

"Cool, cool," he said. "Almost legal."

And almost throwing up in my mouth, thank you very much.

"So, what can I do for you? You want an autograph or something?" he asked.

"Yes!" I said, not having to fake the enthusiasm. "I wanted

you to, uh, sign my flyer!" He took it from me, and then looked at me expectantly.

"What do you want me to sign it with?"

"I, uh, don't have a pen," I said.

"Hold on," he said. He stepped back inside and shut the door. Two seconds later, the door reopened again. He had a purple marker, and he held it in one hand as he flattened the flyer against the doorjamb. "What's your name?"

"Es—" I started, and caught myself. "*Ter*. Esther." He nodded, then wrote "To Esther, Rock on." He scrawled his name with a signature that I was sure he'd practiced ten million times. "Thanks," I said, and looked down at what he'd written. His name was totally indecipherable. "Thanks. I'll see you around," I added.

"Yeah, yeah," he said. "Tell all your friends. And uh, tell them to tell their moms. Or, like, their older sisters. Unless their moms are MILFs, then tell them too." My grin stretched into a grimace, and then I turned and started to quickly walk back across the porch. I couldn't wait to get away from him, and that house.

I started down the gravel driveway, walking carefully because it was uneven and there were a couple of deep puddles. It was littered with bottle caps and cigarette butts and broken glass, and a small rectangular piece of plastic that caught my eye and made my heart start to pound. I glanced quickly back at the house. The door was closed and the Pink Floyd tapestry didn't look like it had been disturbed, but just in case, I bent down like I was tying my shoe. I scooped up the piece of plastic, and then stood up and ran back to the car.

Janis and Cassandra were waiting anxiously for me. I

opened the door and climbed in. I threw the flyer at Janis, and then turned around and handed what I'd picked up to Cassandra.

"What is this?" I heard Janis say. "It looks like an autograph. Though, I can't read it. Wait, yes, I can. Tom? You talked to Tom."

Cassandra was holding the piece of plastic in her hand. "Wait, are you serious?" she said. "You think this . . ."

"Cass, it has to be!" I said. "And that means she was there! Sometime right after we saw her!"

"Wait, what are you two looking at?" Janis asked, turning around. "A name tag? Who's Cybill?"

"It was my mom's," Cassandra said. The pin had broken off the back, the plastic was scratched, and the black paint that had filled in the engraved letters had all but worn off.

"Your mom's name is 'Circe,'" Janis said.

"Technically it's 'Cecilia,'" I said.

"Wait," Janis said. "I'm confused."

"My mom went by 'Circe,'" Cassandra explained, "but when we were staying at the hotel for the Summit and we saw her and she said she was going to help us remove my curse, she was going by 'Cybill.'"

Janis's eyes grew as wide as lily pads. "Whoa," she said. "And you just found that now?"

I nodded. "In the driveway," I said. "The neighbor I talked to said four young guys moved in here back in December. She said she thinks there's something weird going on, and they hardly leave the house."

"Goddess bless nosy neighbors," Janis said.

"The Summit was in December," Cassandra said. "These

guys started updating their Myspace page in December and moved here in December, and if that was my mom at the hotel during the Summit, she went missing in December." She shoved the name tag into her pocket. "Eff it," she said. "If my mom's in there, I'm going in." She grabbed the door handle and pushed the door open, and just as quickly I used my powers to pull it shut.

"Cass, stop!" I said.

"Esme," she said, throwing her weight against the door, "let me out of this car or I will set it on fire."

"Like hell you will!" Janis shrieked.

I clamped my kinesis down even harder on the door. "We can't just go back there and pound on the door and demand to see Circe! For all we know, she's not even there anymore."

Cassandra slumped back into the seat and crossed her arms over her chest. "When we saw her at the Summit, she told us she had something for us, but then she disappeared. She wouldn't do that unless someone made her," she said. "Unless *they* made her. She has to be there, because where else would she be?"

"Cass," I said, keeping my powers firmly locked on her door, "there are a million places she could be, but I know what you mean. I get it. I really do. For the past four months, all anyone has been telling me is that now is not the time to do anything about my mom. But honestly, now is not the time to do anything about your mom. If she is in there, we have to know for sure, because if you go busting in there now, and she's not there, then that might blow our chances of finding out where she really is."

Cassandra huffed and looked away from me, to stare out the window down the street, a sign that she was at least listening to me.

"Those guys aren't demons, so we can't just run in and flush them up a hole. Even if they're evil humans, they're still humans." I paused, and took my kinesis off her door, and it stayed shut.

"I know, I know," she said, uncrossing her arms and pulling a stick of gum out of her pocket, then jamming it into her mouth. "But what are we supposed to do? Just sit here!"

Janis hit the steering wheel with her palm. "That's exactly what we'll do!" she said.

"What do you mean?" Cassandra asked.

"We'll have a stakeout," she said. "We already have the coffee and doughnuts." She looked into the doughnut bag, which was empty. "Well, we already have the coffee, so we'll hang out here and see when they leave and where they go."

Cassandra started nodding. "Yeah," she said. "Then we'll know when the house is empty, so we can break in and see what we can find." Sitting in Janis's car and passively watching from a distance sounded like a good plan to me. What did not sound like a good plan was breaking and entering, but I figured I would just have to put out that fire once Cassandra had started it.

"We're going to need more than one car, though," Janis said, "because there are four of them, and if some of them leave, we can't stay here and watch the house and follow them at the same time."

"We can call Brian," I offered. "He won't be happy that

we're not at school, but he probably won't care about that once he knows that Circe is involved. I bet he can call in sick for the afternoon—"

But Cassandra already had her phone out. "No way," she said. "That'll take too long, and he'll just make us do something boring and stupid that doesn't break any rules. I'm calling Dion."

"Your brother?" I asked. "The same one who once kidnapped my babysitting charge?" She just nodded, so I tried another tactic. "Doesn't he have to work?"

"He won't go," she said. "He wants these guys to pay for what they did to our house just as much as I do." She paused for a second. "Look, Esme, my brother's not the best, we know that. But he's not the worst either. And besides, who else are we going to call?"

"Ghostbusters," I couldn't help but say, under my breath, and then Dion picked up on the second ring. I sipped my iced coffee and looked out the window. The gray sky had started to spit rain, and the drops that ran down Janis's window mirrored the drops of condensation on my cup. From what I could hear of the conversation, he was on his way to work, but readily agreed—and was even eager—to call in sick as soon as Cassandra explained to him what was going on.

I wasn't totally surprised that Cassandra wanted to rope him in on our plans. Brian and I had let her take the lead on deciding how to deal with Dion after the events of Halloween, and I trusted her evaluation of how much of a threat Dion actually was. The more time I spent around him lately, the more I was realizing that he wasn't really threatening, just maybe kind of confused.

"I'll send you a pin," I heard Cassandra say, and then she hung up her phone. Dion was on his way.

The truth was, I wasn't really worried about Dion doing anything that could compromise our investigation. It was just . . . I didn't really want to hang around him. I now had no doubt that Dion was an idiot, but he was an idiot I'd once had a crush on, and there'd even been a time when I didn't think he was an idiot. A time when he'd told me how he'd gotten a job in construction because he'd wanted to build buildings from the time he was a little kid; a time when he'd bemoaned his crappy tattoo, and told me about the not-crappy-at-all reason why he'd gotten it. And I'd taken such faux-confidences to heart, and dropped my guard, sharing info that I shouldn't have. Info that Dion had taken right to Erebus, and which no doubt had helped to get MacKenzie kidnapped. I hated thinking that I'd once just assumed that, yeah, of course, a guy who looked like Dion could totally be into a girl like me. The whole thing was just . . . embarrassing.

I pulled out my phone and looked at the time. First period had officially begun twenty-three minutes ago. I wondered if anyone would notice I was gone, and if so, would they call Dad?

"Do you think we'll get in trouble for skipping school?" I asked Janis, and she shook her head.

"I already sent an email from my mom's account, saying that I was staying home today because I had bad cramps," she said. I sometimes thought what a shame it was that it was me, and not Janis, who was the Sitter. As long as it didn't involve the post office, Janis was always at least two steps ahead of everyone else in the room.

"So, while we're all here together, I'm gonna share the

spreadsheet I made for this weekend," she continued, then tapped her phone a couple of times. My phone dinged, and I looked down to find a link to a Google doc called "Spring River V-Day Staycation."

"You made a spreadsheet?" I said, looking back up at Janis. "For what?"

"Well, we need a schedule," she said. "We don't want people to get bored. Esme, you can see the time frames I blocked off for you to fill in. I figured we'd spend all day Saturday thrifting. . . ." Cassandra pretended to snore, and Janis shot her a look. "But that still leaves Friday night, Saturday night, and all day Sunday." She looked at me expectantly.

"Uh, movies?" I asked.

Janis rolled her eyes.

"We can always get coffee," I said, to crickets. "A lot of coffee."

"Isn't there a school dance on Saturday night?" Cassandra asked. "Like, something for Valentine's Day?"

Janis's and my heads both swiveled to look at her. A Valentine's Day dance was the last thing I would ever imagine Cassandra even knowing about, much less caring about.

"As a matter of fact, there is," Janis said. "Are you suggesting that we go?" But before Cassandra could answer, a loud pop made us all jump, and sure enough, Dion's van was a few blocks down the street, backfiring its way toward us.

"Is this even going to work?" I asked. "That's not exactly a covert ops vehicle."

Dion pulled up across from Janis and rolled down the window. "So, which house is it?" he asked.

"That little gray one right there," Janis said, pointing down the block. "The one with the purple car in the driveway."

"Ha," Dion laughed. "That's their car? What a bunch of dweebs."

"Look who's talking," I said under my breath.

"So, what's the plan here?" he asked. "I brought my binoculars." He held them up through the open window, and Cassandra got out of the car, then walked over and snatched them out of his hand.

"Awesome," she said. "These will be great for Janis and me."

"Those are mine!" Dion said, at the same time I said, "What do you mean, you and Janis?"

"The whole reason we needed two cars was so that we could split up," she said. "Janis and I are going to stay here and watch the house, and whenever someone leaves, you and Dion are going to follow them and see where they go."

"Why not you and Dion and me and Janis?" I said, trying not to show how truly unhappy I was with this pairing.

"Because he's my brother," she said as if this were all the explanation that was needed.

"If you're taking my binos, do I at least get a walkie-talkie?" Dion asked.

I couldn't help but roll my eyes. "You sure do," I said. "It's called your phone."

"Oh, ha," he laughed. "You're right. I guess I can just put it on speaker and hold it like this." He grabbed it horizontally, and then held it up to his mouth while he made a bunch of beeps and crackly noises. In spite of myself, I smiled. "Come on, Es," he said. "Your chariot awaits."

"Here, I'll get your bag," Cassandra said, coming back to Janis's car and grabbing my bag through the open window. I took a long sip of my coffee while I sat there, stalling. Then I had no choice but to get out of the car and into the van. So I did.

Inside, the van smelled like Dion, which was a combo of alpine body wash and cinnamon gum. Like Cassandra, he didn't drink coffee, but downed pop like plastic bottles were biodegradable, and he had a large bottle of Mountain Dew in the cup holder, next to an open bag of powdered-sugar doughnuts. "Help yourself," he said, gesturing toward them. "I figured we couldn't have a stakeout without doughnuts."

"Thanks," I said, "but we got doughnuts on the way."

He nodded. "So, you really think my mom's in there?"

"That's one option," I said.

"What are the others?"

"Well, she was there at one point, and isn't anymore," I said, "and the other is that she was never there at all."

"But even if that's the case, you think these guys would know where she is?"

I thought for a minute, and then decided to level with him. After all, Circe was his mom too. "Maybe," I said. "We know they were connected to your dad, and we know that there's something weird going on with them. So I guess, right now, they're our best hope."

Dion nodded, then picked up the Mountain Dew, unscrewed the cap, took a big swig, and put it back. "You want to listen to music?" he asked. "The radio stopped working again, but we can play something from my phone. Do you like Maroon 5?"

"No, stop!" I said quickly, hoping to put an end to the Maroon 5 before he could cue it up. "No music. The silence is okay."

He nodded and put the phone into the cup holder. Then we both sat there quietly, looking out the window at the house down the street. The last time Dion and I had been alone together had been before Halloween, when we'd traded *Mean Girls* quips and I'd used magic to fix his tattoo. It was back to its original state now, with thick blurry lines and runny colors, and I wondered if Dion remembered it any other way. I wondered if he remembered hanging out with me. But like heck was I going to ask about either of those.

In Janis's Honda, I could see that Cassandra had reclined the seat so that she was barely visible above the window, and Janis was bobbing her head as she painted her nails. They were probably listening to something good. It definitely wasn't Maroon 5.

"So," Dion said finally. "When you say this band is your 'best hope,' you mean best hope for what?"

I thought for a minute. That was actually a pretty good question. "I guess for finding your mom," I said.

I was looking at Dion out of the corner of my eye, and I could see him swallow. "Why would she hide from us?" he asked. "I mean, we're her kids."

I felt a pang of sympathy for him. Being a spectator in your own family probably didn't feel great. "I doubt she's been gone all this time because that was what she wanted to do," I said. "It was probably just what she had to do."

"Do you think it's different now?" he said. "Now that Cass is what she is."

"A Sitter?" I asked.

He gave a little laugh. "Yeah," he said. "I just feel weird saying the word. I still don't really understand it."

"Ha," I said. "I don't either. But finding your mom, that would help us all understand."

"What don't you understand?" he asked.

"Why my mom is cursed," I said, fiddling with a peeling piece of plastic on the door, "or rather, why she's still cursed. Your mom and my mom were friends, and I think that Circe might care, and be able to tell me what to do about it. Every other adult I've tried to talk to basically just gives me the same story."

"Which is?" Dion asked.

"Oh, you know," I sighed. "All the typical adult BS—life isn't fair, learn to accept the things you cannot change, be grateful for what you do have. All those platitudes that are just different ways of saying 'do nothing.'"

I looked over at him, and he was holding out the doughnuts toward me.

"You sure you don't want?" he asked.

"Okay," I said. "Maybe one." Dion grinned as I reached into the bag.

"I know what you're saying," he said, a dusting of powdered sugar on his chin. "I mean, I know what it's like to want something to change so bad that you'll do anything to change it. I mean, I helped kidnap a kid because I thought it would make my life better." He looked out the window. "I should be in jail."

"Dion," I said, surprising myself with my genuine desire to make him feel better, "that was your dad."

"Yeah," he said, "but he was only able to use me like that because I let him. If I'd been a stronger person, it never would have gotten to that point. I would have smashed that stupid 8 Ball as soon as I'd found it. It would have saved us all a whole lot of trouble."

"I don't know," I said. "I mean, if that hadn't happened, then maybe I never would have— Oh crap! Look!" Someone had come out the front door of the house and was getting into the PT Cruiser. Two seconds later, they backed out of the driveway and started down the street. They all looked the same to me, though, so I couldn't tell if it was the same guy— Tom—I'd talked to earlier.

"All right!" Dion said, turning the key and starting the van. "It's showtime. At least a car like that won't be hard to tail." He let the purple Cruiser get to the end of the block and go around a corner before he pulled out. I shifted in my seat and gave a little wave to Janis and Cassandra, who was now sitting up.

"So, what do we know about these guys?" he asked.

"Well, they make terrible music, and they all live here together," I started. "We don't know if any of them have jobs, and we don't even know their last names. Their first names are Tom, Todd, Brad, and Chad. They just showed up here in December, though the house is owned by someone also named Tom, so maybe a relative?"

Dion nodded but kept his attention focused on the car in front of us. He never let it get too far ahead, and he always kept one or two cars in between us. He even cut through a gas station parking lot so we wouldn't get caught at a light after the purple PT made a right turn.

"I wonder where he's going," I said, then watched as the driver pulled into a Safeway parking lot. "Oh," I said. "Of course. The grocery store."

Dion parked a few rows away, and we watched the guy get out of the car. From this close, I was glad to see that it wasn't Tom. "Okay," Dion announced. "We're going in after him, just in case this Safeway's a front for magical drug running or something."

"That's ridiculous. I've been in this particular grocery store, like, twenty times," I said, then looked at Dion and realized he was joking. I made sure he could see me roll my eyes as I climbed out of the car.

"So, front and follow," he said as he locked the door. "And quick. We don't want him to hit produce before we get a good tail on him. It's like a jungle in there."

"Har-de-har-har," I said, following him across the parking lot. "What's 'front and follow'?"

"It's a complicated technique I studied for a long time," he said. "Just kidding. It's something I learned from watching TV. You start out and stay in front of him for a while, and I stay behind, and then I move up, and you fall behind, and we do this every few minutes. You won't exactly blend in with that outfit, though."

"Well, had I known my day was going to entail trailing one of your father's associates through the grocery store, I would have worn something different."

"Here," Dion said, and next thing I knew, he was taking off his flannel and holding it out to me. "Tie this around your waist. It'll help." The doors to the store opened, and we stepped in to see our dude doing his best to dislodge a stuck shopping cart.

Dion and I had been here before, at this shirt-sharing turning point, and I didn't really want to wear his flannel, but he did have a good argument about my outfit, so I did as he'd suggested.

"You first," he said. So, keeping one eye on the dude, I walked over to a display of boxes of chocolates and pretended to have a lot of trouble deciding between one that was shaped like a big red heart and one that was shaped like an even bigger red heart. I was able to get a look at not-Tom as he finally got his shopping cart dislodged, and I headed straight for the produce section.

It was actually kind of tough trying to stay ahead of him without losing him, and I meandered a lot, wondering if I looked suspicious or just like someone who couldn't remember what she'd come to the store for. My phone dinged, and I pulled it out of my pocket to read the text.

Cassandra:

> where'd he go?
>
> Safeway
>
> whats he doing there?
>
> Uh . . . shopping

He was currently browsing the avocados. So far, he'd carefully squeezed probably a dozen but hadn't put a single one into his cart. I watched him go through at least six more, and then more, and as I tried to watch him without appearing to watch him, I wanted to scream at him that if he wanted avocados in Kansas in February, then he'd better be prepared to take what he could get. Finally he found one that was satisfactory—one—and put it into the cart and walked away. I started walking in the direction I thought he was going, and then Dion was in front of me, so I fell back. I stifled a small laugh when I noticed that Dion was now carrying a pineapple and two potatoes, probably an attempt to blend in. I had to admit—I was almost having fun with Dion. The words we'd exchanged in the car had been almost a conversation, and he was starting to seem almost like a human to me. *Almost, almost, almost.*

Todd, Brad, or Chad had turned down an aisle by the pharmacy, and he walked past toothpaste, shampoo, and deodorant without picking anything up. Then he stopped, and I saw him pick up a large can, give it a shake, and then toss it into the basket. I'd seen that can—it was exactly the same can that we'd found in Cassandra and Dion's house. I guess when you accidentally drop your body spray while breaking and entering, you need to buy a replacement. I looked at Dion and could tell by the way he was crushing a box of granola to death that he'd seen it too. Then he met my eye and gave a subtle, quick nod, which I took as a cue that it was time to switch places again. As the guy wheeled his cart into the canned soup aisle, I moved forward and Dion fell back again.

From his previous selections, I had not-Tom pegged as a careful shopper, but now he was blowing my mind and seriously going HAM with the soup. Several cans of chicken noodle, beef stew, tomato, split pea, chili (ew, and double ew). So many cans of soup that I couldn't keep up, and I was having a hard time not staring. Accidentally I caught Dion's eye again, and the look of total disbelief on his face made it hard for me to keep a straight face myself. Finally, when Todd, Brad, or Chad must have had at least thirty cans in his cart, he was ready to move on. He made quick detours through paper products (a twelve-pack of toilet paper, not recycled), frozen foods (two cans of orange juice concentrate), and condiments (an economy-sized yellow mustard), and then headed for the checkout.

Dion ditched his potatoes and pineapple, and we headed out the door and back to the van. "Um, so, soup?" he said after we had climbed in, and I burst out laughing.

"What was that all about?" I said, then held up my hands. "Wait, I'm not sure I want to know. Every time I spend too much time thinking about what's in other people's carts, I end up depressed about the state of humanity."

"Cassandra and I buy all our food at 7-Eleven," he said. "You get in and out, and you can also get a Slurpee."

Our mark came out of the store and loaded everything into the PT Cruiser, and Dion started the van. We could tell by the direction not-Tom was headed and the turns he was taking that he was heading back home. I texted Cassandra.

> We're coming back
> You guys see anything?

nada. no one even opened the door.

When we got back to the house, Dion pulled to a stop next to Janis's car and rolled down his window. It was clear from the look on Janis's face that there was some tension in the car.

"Took you long enough," Janis said, scowling.

"What's up your butt?" I asked. "We were there exactly as long as he was."

"Janis has to pee," Cassandra said, explaining, "so I'm jumping in with you guys."

"There's a McDonald's just two blocks away," Janis said. "I'll be back in a sec." She was driving away before Cassandra was even fully out of the car. As Cass climbed in with us, I kept my eyes on the shopper. He was in the driveway unloading his groceries, and no one came out to help.

"Those definitely are the guys who broke into our house," Dion said. "We saw him buying Axe."

"What the hell is Axe?" Cassandra asked.

"It's body spray for men," Dion explained.

"Ew," Cassandra said. "Where do you spray it?"

"I don't know," Dion answered, then added, "Somewhere on your body?"

"It was the same stuff we found at your house," I pointed out, interrupting them.

"Oh," Cassandra said, nodding. Then, to my surprise, she gave a snort of a laugh. "Who brings their body spray with them when they're breaking into someone's house?"

I laughed too, and even Dion smiled.

"Seriously," Cassandra said, "we should just go kick the door in right now."

My smile faded, though, as I remembered the feeling I'd gotten stepping onto their front porch. "I don't think we want to kick the door down." Cassandra looked at me and arched an eyebrow. "At least not yet," I said.

• • •

We sat waiting in silence for Janis's return, but she was gone for a considerably longer time than it would take someone just to pee, and I scrolled my phone for a bit while Dion fell asleep and Cassandra just stared out the window. When Janis reappeared in the distance, I was relieved. As she pulled up next to us, I could see she was drinking a McFlurry.

"Ooh, my McGriddle!" Cassandra yelped, clambering out of the car.

"Thanks for asking if we wanted anything," Dion said with a scowl.

"Hey, you guys were just out and about. You had your chance," Janis called back.

"That was different," he said. "Who gets food at the grocery store?"

An hour passed, and nothing happened. More time and still nothing. "Maybe they're just taking naps?" Dion suggested.

The day dripped along, and then Janis rolled down her window. "Can you believe she's never seen *The Fresh Prince of Bel-Air*?" Janis called to me.

"One hundred percent," I said.

"Why would I watch a show that was on TV before I was even alive?" I heard Cassandra ask.

Janis turned back to her. "That's the whole point," she said. "Clothes were cooler then, people were cooler then, young Will Smith was a dream. Everything was better!"

"That show just sounds boring," Cassandra said.

"What about it sounds boring?"

"Does anyone go to prison?"

"No!" Janis said. "Just because it's a show about Black people doesn't mean that someone is going to go to prison!"

"I didn't say anything about Black people," Cassandra said. "I just like shows that are set in prison, where someone has to join a gang. . . ."

I checked my phone. It was only eleven in the morning.

At twelve-thirty, Dion and I were deputized to go to Taco Bell, which was good, because I really had to pee. When we got back, the Quesaritos momentarily revived everyone's spirts, but by midafternoon, we were bored out of our minds.

Cassandra and Janis went for snacks and to use the bathroom. Dion and I shared a bag of sunflower seeds, and cracking the shells at least gave us something to do. By five p.m., we were bored out of our skulls again.

The neighbor had not been exaggerating. These guys never left. I'd been to school assemblies that were more enthralling. Janis was ready to call it quits.

"My butt has been asleep for, like, the past two hours," she said, "and I need to go home and do homework." I needed to get home too. It was one of my nights to stay with Mom so that Dad could go sit in a crowded place somewhere and drink beer and yell at a TV screen.

Cassandra didn't seem quite ready to leave but finally gave in, as a day of inactivity was clearly getting to her. She cracked her neck and stretched her arms in a way that made me wince. "How do people sit all day?" she moaned. "I feel like I'm twenty-eight or something. I need to go home and do some push-ups." She looked back at the house. "I don't want to miss anything, though."

I nodded. This was the second day in a row that we had seen these guys and just left, but I wasn't sure what else we could do. "I'll text Brian," I said, "and have him switch the monitor to Red Magic. That way, if these guys do get up to anything tonight, we can save our butts and still be on top of it."

"Yeah, you're right," Cassandra said. Then she did one more elaborate stretch and climbed into Dion's van and they drove away.

I got in with Janis, and called Brian as she headed toward my house.

"Hey, you at home?" I asked.

"Yes," he said. "Just doing a bit of crafting. I noticed that the three of you weren't at school today, by the way."

"Ooh, yeah, that," I said. "We were doing a stakeout. Coffee, doughnuts, that whole thing. But don't worry, we studied the whole time."

"Of course," he said. "I'm sure you did. I know how much you hate to miss school."

"Hate it," I said. "Never want to miss school. Anyway, I need you to look up the address we were staking out on your Red Magic monitor thingy." I gave him the rundown of what we'd learned, and then read him the address. On the other end of the phone, I could hear him walking through his closet and then into the Batcave.

"One sec," he said, and I could hear him set the phone down and type. A short while later, he picked up again.

"Nothing," he said.

"Wait, really?" I said, kind of shocked. What I had felt when I'd stepped onto their porch was definitely Red Magic.

"Yeah," he said, "nothing shows up at that address, or even in that entire neighborhood."

"Weird," I said. "Okay, thanks anyway." As I hung up, Janis was turning onto my street, and I told her what Brian had said.

"Well, even if nothing registers on Brian's monitor, that band is up to something," she said as she stopped in front of my house, "and it's not just bad music."

CHAPTER 7

The next morning, I was digging through my locker when a "Hey" surprised me.

"Hey," I said back, turning to see Cassandra. "I didn't expect to see you here today."

She shrugged. "Someone cut off a finger, so Dion's jobsite shut down for insurance reasons."

"Ergh," I said, and grimaced. "Are they okay?"

She looked at me like it was a stupid question. "It's a finger, Esme. We don't need them to live. That's why we have ten of them."

"Of course," I said. "Silly me." I slammed my locker and started to walk to class. We were halfway down the hall when Janis turned the corner and fell into step beside us. Apparently, yesterday's *Fresh Prince* debate had inspired her look today, as she was wearing a navy blazer—turned inside out to show off the bright gold embroidered lining—with a striped tie, white oxford shirt, and backward 76ers cap.

"Janis," Cassandra said, "do you know your jacket's on inside out?"

"No," Janis said, and left it at that.

"So, I went back and watched the house again last night," Cassandra said.

"And what'd you see?"

"Nothing," she said around a yawn. "People on house arrest leave more often than those guys do."

"No crap," Janis said. "We'd have to set that place on fire to get them all out of there."

"I thought of that," Cassandra said. "But there might be something in there that we need. Not to mention, if my mom is in there, we don't want anything to happen to her."

"It's too bad we didn't know where they lived on Monday," Janis said, "as it seems like the only time they all go somewhere is when they have a show."

"That's it!" I said, the realization hitting me. "They need to have another show."

"I doubt that's going to happen anytime soon, considering their last one was at a bar that wasn't even aware they were playing there," Cassandra said.

We slowed at a traffic jam in the hallway, one that was created partly because two senior girls on ladders were trying to hang up a banner for the Valentine's Day dance in the middle of the passing period. It was the equivalent of hallway roadwork, made worse by the fact that one kept yelling at people not to bump the ladder, while the other was yelling not to walk under the banner, and this was effectively keeping them too busy to actually hang up the banner and get out of the way.

"What if we just pretend to book them for a show?" Janis

asked as we joined the bottleneck of students trying to squeeze around one of the ladders.

"I thought of that," Cassandra said, "but it doesn't give us that much time. I mean, they show up for sound check and get turned away at the door? Besides, I think we have to play it safe and assume that they are practicing Red Magic."

"They're definitely doing something," I said, "but I don't know how we're going to find out what. We can't just keep coming up with excuses to go knock on their door." I pressed forward when someone stepped on the back of my ankle. In this inexplicable hallway crush, I was starting to get annoyed. Not just with the ankle scraper but with school in general, and the upcoming dance, and school dances . . .

"We should just book them for the Valentine's Day dance," I said. "It's perfect. An apocalyptic scenario set to what will undoubtedly be horrible music, so Phantom Limp would be perfect. Ow. What the heck?" I spun around, about to unleash my own apocalypse on someone who clearly didn't know how to say "Excuse me," when I saw Cassandra grinning and realized that she was the one who had just punched me in the shoulder.

"Esme Pearl, you beautiful genius," she said. We were finally on the other side of the student crush, and I stopped.

"Wait," I said. "I was joking."

"So the dance is not an apocalyptic scenario with horrible music?" Janis asked.

"No," I said, "it most certainly is. But there's no way we can book Phantom Limp to play it. The dance is in, like, two days. I'm sure they already have some other horrible music booked and ready to go."

"I don't know," Janis said, her face scrunched up in that

thinking way, and I groaned. Cassandra's *Fresh Prince* transgressions were clearly being forgiven, and Janis and Cassandra were back on the same side again. "Even if that's true, it might not be too late to change."

"Oh really? Ya think so?" I said, wanting to smack myself on the forehead for ever daring to make a joke. "And how would we make that happen? Join the dance committee?"

"Exactly!" Janis said. She pulled out her phone, tapped a few numbers, and handed it to me. I didn't recognize the number it was calling, but I could hear a phone ringing.

"What do you want me to do with this?" I asked, but she didn't hear me because she had turned around and was fighting the crowd upstream to get back to where the two girls were hanging the banners.

"Kendra! Yoo-hoo!" she yelled, waving to one of the girls balanced on a ladder. "It's Janis from geometry." Whatever Kendra said back was swallowed up by the sound of the crowd and the ringing of the one-minute bell, and I had a sense of dread blooming in my belly. Just like the Jay-Z song, Janis could sell water to a well, so if she wanted to convince Kendra to let her join the dance committee two days before the dance, Kendra was probably going to let her join the dance committee two days before the dance.

The phone was still ringing, and then all of a sudden it stopped, and was replaced by a gruff male voice. Oh my gosh! It was Phantom Limp's answering machine. I hung up as quickly as I could.

And just as quickly, they called back. "Shoot," I said, looking up at Cassandra. "What do I do?" Wrong person to ask, obviously. As the phone was ringing, she wrenched it from my fingers, hit accept, and then passed it back to me.

I stood there, wanting to strangle her with my eyes and maybe a shoelace, if I'd had one handy. A male voice from the phone said, "Hello? Someone from this number just called?"

Cassandra stared at me expectantly, and then she stepped on my toe, hard. "Ouch! Shoot, uh, hi!" I said, putting on my I'm-just-a-responsible-babysitter voice. "My name is Esther, and I was calling because I'm interested in booking Phantom Limp for a dance at our school. I, uh, got this number off a Myspace page."

"Esther?" the voice said. "Are you that same kid who came by the house yesterday?"

Kid? "Uuuh, yes, that was me. Is this Tom?" He grunted in affirmation, and then it sounded like he blew his nose. "Well, like I said when we met, you guys have a huge teenage fan base. Like, everyone at my school is obsessed with you."

"Oh yeah," he said, then paused. "We're actually called 'Jump the Shark' now, but we could be down to play this dance. You guys buy a lot of CDs?"

"Tons," I said. "I buy, like, dozens a week, and so does everyone I know." I'd bought albums on vinyl before, but never on a CD and had no idea how much they cost. Maybe two bucks? I hoped that sounded right.

"Wow, crap," he said. "Bunch of rich kids, eh? That's cool, though."

Ugh, so maybe I was off. But how much could a CD cost? I decided to let it slide, and forged ahead.

"So, can I ask, why are you guys so into CDs?" I asked. "I

mean, obviously it's one of the many things I like about your band, but—"

"Who's not into CDs?" he said, cutting me off. "We don't just want radio play. We want our album blasting in every car and from every stereo system."

"Yeah, totally," I said, wishing there were someone else on the phone to witness this mind-boggling conversation. "So, anyway, our dance committee nominated me to call you and see if you guys would be interested in playing our school dance this Saturday night. I mean, I know it's a long shot, and I told them, no way, Phantom—er, Jump the Shark is probably way too booked to spend a Saturday night playing for hundreds of kids who all just love CDs."

"How much can you pay?" he asked.

Crap. I hadn't even thought of that. "Three hundred dollars," I guessed.

"Okay," Tom said. I guess I had guessed right? I decided to lean in.

"It will be really good exposure. You see, I would never ask Jump the Shark to play a show for just three hundred dollars, but the head of our dance committee, her dad does A and R for Universal Music Group, and he's going to be there on Saturday to chaperone, and we were brainstorming and we thought it would be really awesome to get you guys in front of him so that he can see, and hear of course, how good you are."

"Wow," he said. "Universal? So this A and R guy, he work with 3 Doors Down?"

Who the heck was that?

"Yes," I said enthusiastically, "all the time. Like, they're so close that the band even calls him the fourth Door." Cassandra was still staring at me, and a little smirk had crept onto her face, as she was clearly amused by the ever-growing amount of lies that I was pulling out of my butt here.

"All right, all right, all right," he said, now sounding more awake. "Let me talk to the guys and get back to you. Saturday night, you said? What time?"

Ergh, I had no idea what time a band would play at the dance. "I can text you all the details," I said, stalling.

"What?" he asked, sounding confused.

"I'll text you," I said.

"You'll do what?" he asked again.

I floundered. "Um, I can call back with details," I said. "Or you call me back, after you've checked with the guys."

"What's your number?" he asked.

"You can just call me on this one," I said.

"Yeah, but what is it?" he said, sounding annoyed, like I'd just asked him what toppings he wanted on his pepperoni pizza.

"The one on your caller ID," I said, since I didn't know Janis's number by heart.

"Listen, kid," he said, exasperated, "I ain't got all day here. Just tell me the best number to call you back on, and then I'm going to talk to my band and call you back on that number, that you're going to give me, and we're going to play your stupid high school dance so that we can get a record deal."

I didn't understand why he was treating me like I was the one who wasn't getting it, and I was glad that we weren't face to face, because I'm sure I would have been looking at him like he was something I'd stepped in at the dog park. "Of course, of course," I said, and recited my number. "I might be in class, so if I am, just leave a message and I'll check it when I get home."

"Cool, cool," he said. "Then you can call me back when you get my message, and if we're out playing a gig or something, then you can just leave a message for me and I'll call you back." I stifled a groan.

"Sure, sure," I said, then added, "Thanks, Tom. We're soooo excited." This was already shaping up to be more phone calls than I'd made in the past year. I couldn't imagine how much time people wasted actually talking to each other before texting.

I hung up the phone and thought for a second. Nothing about that interaction made sense. "Wait," I said, reaching out and grabbing on to Cassandra's sleeve. "Those photos of the band with your dad, when do you think those were taken again?"

"I'm not sure," she said. "Early 2000s, probably?"

"Oh my God," I said. "That's why they won't text and why they're obsessed with CDs!"

"What are you talking about?" Cassandra asked.

"What if they don't just look like they're living in 2002?" I said. "What if they actually are? What kind of spell does that?"

"One that did not work correctly, I bet," she said. She stopped for a second and grinned. "Now I'm even more excited about Saturday!"

"Stop smiling," I said to Cassandra. "We're all going straight to heck for what I just did. Even if Janis somehow pulls this off, it's not a good idea. We don't know anything about these guys. We could be putting the whole school in danger."

"Oh, come on, Esme," Cassandra said. "Like we can't protect a school." She was looking just over my shoulder, and I turned around to see Janis heading back toward us, a huge grin on her face.

"We're in," she said, walking up.

"What do you mean *we*?" I asked.

"You and me," she said. "We're on the dance committee."

"What about Cassandra?" I asked.

"She doesn't do school activities," she said at the same time that Cassandra said, "I don't do school activities."

I looked back at Janis. "And since when have I done school activities either?" I asked, but they both ignored my question.

"Kendra seemed really open to my ideas about the music," Janis said, seeming actually excited. "So now we just have to book the band."

"Esme just did," Cassandra said, reaching out and hitting me on the shoulder again. "And she was spectacular." Janis looked at me and raised an eyebrow.

I puffed out my cheeks in an exhale. "I told them that the head of the dance committee's dad did A and R for Universal, and that he was close with 3 Doors Down," I said.

"What's that?" Janis asked.

"Some band Tom likes," I said, and filled Janis in on my frozen-in-the-aughts theory.

"Wow," she said, whipping out her phone. She Googled something and then quickly scanned the results. Then she looked back up at me. "I think you're right," she said. "I just looked up 3 Doors Down, and Wikipedia says that they released their most popular album in 2000, and ewwww!" Her lip curled up in disgust. "They played Trump's inauguration! That seems just like the kind of band these losers would be into."

I nodded. "Anyway, it sounds like they're interested. We just have to call them back with details. Oh, and they're called 'Jump the Shark' now."

"Of course," Janis said, rolling her eyes. "This is totally going to work out!"

"I still don't think it's a good idea," I said.

"So what if it's a bad one?" Cassandra said. "It's our only idea."

"Dance committee meeting today in the library after school," Janis said with a smile. "Don't be late."

I watched my two best friends and co-conspirators head happily in opposite directions down the hall, and I groaned. Everything about tricking the band, the dance committee, and probably the entire student body, was wrong. It was breaking a million rules in the Sitter books, but as I made my way to class, weaving through the hallway throng like a salmon flopping its way upstream, I had to admit that I didn't really feel all that bad about it.

CHAPTER 8

School went by in a flash, and after the last bell I walked to the library and waited outside for Janis. I could spot her inside-out jacket from down the hall as she approached.

"I'm so excited," she said, grinning as she got close. "And this is perfect, because I've been needing to get a few more extracurriculars in anyway." It sounded like she thought we were actually joining the dance committee.

She pushed through the library doors, and I followed, buoying along in her wake. I'd never had a ton of interaction with my fellow students, but since I'd started Sitting, that had dropped to practically zero. Which, really, was fine with me. When it came to popularity, I'd never stood a chance, but Janis was different. Janis was better than popular. She was cool, and people knew it. It didn't seem totally out of whack for the Kendras of the world to think that having Janis Jackson on your dance committee, even if it was just for forty-eight hours, would make the dance better.

Over in the corner of the library, a group of students had

gathered, and Janis and I made our way to them and perched on a table just a few feet from the main group.

"So, what did you tell them about this band?" I asked her in a quiet voice.

"I told them that you were one of their biggest fans," she whispered back. "So you could explain it better than I could."

"Janis! Why would you do that?"

"You've met one of the members, and you got his autograph! You know way more about them than me," she said. "Besides, you're so much more articulate when it comes to talking about music."

I sighed. "I'm articulate when I talk about music that I've actually heard," I said. "We still have no idea what this band, whatever their name is this afternoon, sounds like."

"Maybe they're good," she said, and I was stopped from making a barfing sound by the sudden arrival of Kendra, who had appeared and was calling the meeting to order.

"Hey, gang," she said. "I hope you've all had a chance to check out the totally dope banner that Karen and I hung up in the hall this morning. It caused a big commotion because people were so excited. Karen painted it herself, and she killed it."

Kendra smiled over at Karen, her partner in ladder-jamming the hallway, and Karen grinned.

"Kendra, you're just being nice," she said with false modesty. "But yeah, it did turn out really dope. I wanted to go with something fresh and modern, to show people that this isn't just another traditional Valentine's Day dance."

Was Karen serious? The banner was pink paper covered with red hearts—what part of that was fresh or modern?

"And," Kendra went on, "we have a couple of new people joining the committee today. I know it's a little unorthodox to have people join so late in the game, but Janis and Emily"— with a start, I realized that I was the Emily to which she was referring—"saw Karen's totally dope banner and were so excited that they wanted to get involved with the dance, and Janis and I had a great convo this morning, and I thought she had some really great ideas and total passion for the dance, so I made an executive decision to let them join." Oh, jeez. This girl talked like we were supposed to lick her shoes in gratitude. "Janis, maybe you'd like to share some of your ideas about music with the group?"

"Sure thing, Kendra," Janis said, turning on a thousand-watt smile. "I think it would be totally dope if we hired a band." I had never before heard Janis say "dope," but when in Rome . . .

Kendra's smile faltered. "A band?" she said. "When you said you had ideas about the music, I thought you meant, like, a rapper or a DJ or something. . . ."

If they gave out Oscars for Best Performance in Pretending Not to Notice Casual Racism, Janis would win. Sadly, she had a lot of practice for the role.

"We already have a DJ," someone else on the committee pointed out.

"But a band is so much more interactive," Janis said before turning to me. "Esme, tell them about this band."

"Well—well, uh . . . ," I started, "they're called 'Jump the Shark,' and they make music, and there are four of them. There's a guitar, and some drums, and their music is best described as a sound. I mean, when they're playing, you definitely notice that there is noise . . . happening . . . and it's super different from when they're not playing." I cleared my throat. "They're totally dope," I said finally, summing it up.

"So, do they play covers?" asked a guy in a long-sleeved polo shirt so tight that you could see his nipples.

I shook my head. "No, it's all original songs," I said.

"So, the whole night we'd be listening to music that no one has ever heard of?" asked a girl in a hoodie and Uggs.

"Yeah, I guess," I said.

"You'd be totally introducing people to new music," Janis said. None of this seemed to be winning anyone over, and Kendra's morning hallway enthusiasm for Janis's ideas and participation seemed to be waning. The room was so quiet, I could hear the girl in Uggs chewing her gum. "Come on," Janis urged. "Do people really want to spend the Valentine's Day dance dancing to the same three songs they hear on the radio all day?"

"Yes!" Karen practically screeched. "That is exactly what people want to do at the school dance." She turned to Kendra. "Honestly, this is the worst idea that I've ever heard. Even if this band were the next Maroon 5—which I highly doubt they are—I don't understand why we're proposing changing our plan so last-minute!"

"I just really want to book this band to play the dance," Janis said plainly.

"And people in hell want Popsicles," Karen said, crossing her arms and staring Janis down.

"Okay, how about a vote?" Janis said, powering through. "Everyone in favor of ditching a predictable old DJ and hiring a groundbreaking band, raise your hand?" Janis and I raised our hands.

"Now," Karen said, "everyone in favor of sticking with our plan and not murdering our Valentine's Day dance by hiring an awful band that no one but two latecomers has ever heard of, raise your hand!" Everyone else raised their hands. Janis made a show of counting, but the vote was clearly eleven to two. Not surprising. Not surprising at all.

Kendra turned to us. "Thanks for coming," she said. "We appreciate hearing from the community."

"Well," Janis huffed, standing up. "It looks like the dance committee just wasn't for us."

"See you on Saturday," Karen called after us as we walked out of the library.

As soon as we were back in the hallway, I turned to Janis. "That was a total disaster," I moaned, but Janis just smiled.

"You didn't actually think I thought that would work, did you?" she asked.

"Uh, yeah, I did," I said, confused now. "Janis, we just made total fools out of ourselves in front of eleven of our fellow students. Not that I care, because they are a committee led by a racist and a *literal* Karen, but still, there are so many other things we could have been doing with those minutes of our lives." I started to walk out to the parking lot, but Janis caught me by the sleeve.

"I just figured it's always better to try the non-magical option first," she said, not letting go of my sleeve.

"Wait, so what's the magical option?" I said, shaking my arm loose. I didn't like being restrained by anyone, even my best friend.

"You go in there and spell them into thinking it's a great idea," she said, then snapped her fingers. "Even better! Make them think it's their idea!"

"Janis! I can't just go in there and cast a spell on eleven people," I said. "I'm supposed to be protecting the innocent and—"

"Ha," Janis scoffed. "Like anyone at this school is innocent."

She had a point there, and I racked my brain trying to think of someone . . .

"Nurse Beth," I said finally. "She's always been so sweet, and she let me go home that one time when all I had was a super-itchy mosquito bite—"

"The school nurse?" Janis asked. "Protecting the school nurse is why you think we can't make this happen. Esme, why would she even be at the dance?"

"You know someone's going to get alcohol poisoning," I said. "Every Spring River event guest stars at least one EMT."

"Exactly," Janis said. "There's no way that having Jump the Shark play is going to make this dance any worse than it is already destined to be. Besides, you've seen those dudes—no matter what magic they've got going on behind the scenes, they still present as a bunch of soup-hoarding homebodies. By the time the dance rolls around, you and Cassandra will have mad reinforcements—Ji-A, Amirah, Ruby, and Mallory will be here tomorrow."

Janis had a point. So far, the band seemed minimally threatening, and that was just with Cassandra and me, and tomorrow night, we'd triple our ranks. We'd be six on four. As I stood there, I took a deep breath, and two images flitted through my mind: First, Circe's eyes at the hotel, black with contacts to disguise them, and a constant stream of tears and mascara. I'd just assumed that the tears were because the contacts hurt, but maybe it was more than that. Maybe it was because she was face to face with her daughter for the first time in more than ten years.

And then, the look on Cassandra's face, in the backseat of Janis's car, when I'd found Cybill's name tag in the driveway. Cassandra wanted, desperately, to find her mother, and if spelling a bunch of my classmates was going to help her do it, then I was willing. The problem was I didn't know how.

I hadn't ever done a persuasion spell before, which meant that even after I found out what the ingredients were, I'd need to find them. I could use my kinesis at will, but Sitter spells required an incantation and, the first time you cast it, a specific set of ritual objects that ranged from throwaway and quotidian to valuable and esoteric. The spell I needed was probably in one of Brian's books, but I didn't have time for that. So I pulled out my phone. It was almost four in Kansas, which meant it was almost five in New York, and if I hurried, I could catch Amirah before she went to her private boxing lesson with a coach that, FYI, strongly resembled a young Keanu Reeves.

Hey, I wrote, do you know any persuasion spells off the top of your head? Asking for a friend.

Fortunately for me, except for the three times a week when she spent an hour getting sweaty with Olivier, Amirah was never not on her phone, and my text had barely gone through before I got a response.

How many people is UR FRIEND trying to persuade? she wrote.

Eleven, I said. Collective IQ around nineteen.

Off the top of my head, no, she wrote, but I do know popularis-kinesis, where you can manipulate popularity to make something popular. Then people will just persuade themselves.

Sounds good, I wrote. Hit me.

Friendship bracelet, rose quartz, a copy of Twilight, and pumpkin-spice something, she wrote. A latte works best, but cookies or, like, a candle will do in a pinch.

Got it, I wrote. I OWE YOU. Punch Olivier in the face for me.

She responded with the knockout and then the heart-eyes emoji.

I looked up from my phone and at Janis. "I can do it," I said. "But I need time. How long do you think that meeting will last?"

"I have no idea," Janis said. "Maybe fifteen more minutes?"

I shook my head. "I need more time than that," I said. "You're going to have to go in there and stall them. Don't let the meeting end until I come back."

"Got it," Janis said. "I mean, if there is anything that this school has taught me, it's how to waste someone else's time." With that, she turned and headed back into the library. Then I ran for my locker.

I wasn't one of those girls who carried around crystals, like "This one's for love, and this one's for protection, and this one's for inner peace." I was one of those girls who carried around crystals like "This one's to charm goldfish, this one's to control hail," and, in this case, "this one's to manipulate popularity." I fumbled with the lock and then threw my locker door open, grabbed my makeup bag, and started to rummage through it. I'd dropped it the week before and broken my blush into dust, so everything was coated with a fine film of rose gold. I had several almost-empty tubes of lip gloss, a concealer without a cap, two black eyeliners—pencil and felt tip—and obsidian, tiger's-eye, jade, a blue lace agate, a sunstone, and crap! Where the heck was my rose quartz? I was about to scream when I remembered I'd taken it out the week before when we'd tried a spell to cure Cassandra of her gum addiction, and I finally found it floating around solo in the bottom of my backpack.

So, 25 percent of the ingredients down, 75 percent still to go. A copy of *Twilight* would be easy, especially since the library stocked at least thirty of them, the result of an assistant librarian who wore fangs in her off-hours and who often had on a "Team Edward" T-shirt. I'd pick that up last, but where was I going to get a friendship bracelet? Someplace with a bunch of girls, obviously.

I turned and headed to the gym. Aside from people voting Republican and caring about cars, I couldn't think of anything I understood less than sports, especially because playing a sport seemed to involve spending a lot of extra time at school, but now, when I threw open the gym door, I hit the jackpot: the girls' basketball team was practicing.

Because they spent so much time traveling on buses and overnighting for tournaments, girls' teams shed friendship bracelets like snakes shed scales, and sure enough, I spotted two girls who had multicolored thread at least halfway up their forearms. One was a senior who was at least a head taller than me and could probably flick me out of the way with her fingernail, but one was a freshman I recognized from the time when she'd kindly tried, and failed, to explain "traveling" to me in gym. As she ran by me sweating, I quickly called out to her, "Hey, Michelle!"

She stopped and gave me a puzzled look. It clearly took her a minute to place me as the junior who was always getting in trouble for not complying with the regulation uniform in her freshman-year gym class. "Hey, Esme," she said, wiping her sweaty brow with the back of her hand, the very hand that wore the bracelets that I was about to try to buy off her. "What's up?"

"This is going to sound super weird, I know," I said, "but can I buy one of your friendship bracelets?"

Her eyebrows rose in surprise. "Sure, I guess," she said. "I've never sold them before, but I don't see why not." She looked back at her teammates, who were all still running and ball-bouncing around her. "Can we talk about this later, though? If you DM me what style you want, I can tell you what colors I have."

I shook my head. "Uh, that's the weird part," I said. "See, I need one right now. It doesn't matter what color."

"You want to buy one of the friendship bracelets that I've been wearing?" she asked, appropriately looking at me like I'd just offered to buy her used Kleenex. I nodded vehemently.

"It's for a project I need to turn in in fifteen minutes," I said.

"You need a used friendship bracelet for a project? For what class?"

"Performance art," I said, which was a class that Spring River most definitely did not offer, but I doubted that Michelle knew that. The basketball coach blew her whistle. "Salinger!" she yelled. "Stop loafing."

"Listen, I'll pay you. Twenty bucks." I was pleading now.

"For real?" she asked, and I nodded, whipping out my phone.

"I can Venmo you right now."

"Okaaaayyy," she said. Balancing the basketball on a hip with one hand, she held her other wrist up to her mouth, grabbed a friendship bracelet with her teeth, and ripped it off. Then she held it out to me. "It's sweaty," she said, "and spitty. But that'll be twenty bucks."

"Thanks," I said, reaching out to take it from her. It was, as promised, sweaty and spitty, and it also didn't smell all that great either. She had just enough time to tell me her user-name before the coach blasted her whistle again and threatened her with sprints. I was twenty dollars down, but now 75 percent toward persuasion. The clock was ticking, so I stuffed Michelle's bracelet into my pocket and raced back out into the hall. There were three vending machines at Spring River High, one on each floor. I passed by the ones on the first and second floors several times a day, and I knew their contents by heart.

But I hadn't been on the third floor in years, and half of those classrooms were barely even used. Maybe, just maybe, the vending machine up there hadn't been restocked since the fall. I took the stairs two at a time, and then when I got to the third floor, it felt like I'd entered into some sort of weird *Twilight Zone* high school. The sound of my steps echoed off the lockers as I ran down the hall, and the lights flickered like I was in an asylum for the cinematically insane. I ran almost the whole way down the hallway before realizing that I was going the wrong way, and by the time I did locate the vending machine, clear on the other side of the school, I was out of breath and as sweaty as Michelle's friendship bracelet.

I made a note to self to remember this particular vending machine on days when the lunch options were particularly dire, because it was pretty well stocked. There were Goldfish crackers, pretzel chips, mini Oreos, and Skittles, but the closest it had to pumpkin-spice anything was a gingerbread man, left from December, no doubt because his head had snapped off and was now trapped in the package down by his feet. I dug out a couple of bills and bought the G-man anyway. As I raced back down the stairs, my thoughts volleyed back and forth in my head: the gingerbread man would totally work; the gingerbread man would never work. Gingerbread and pumpkin spice were from two different seasons. They weren't even on the menu at the same time, and while one was beloved, one was merely tolerated, even if their ingredients were basically the same.

My feet, almost of their own accord, were heading to the gym. I pulled open the door again and kept my gaze down on the painted wood floor so that I wouldn't make eye contact with Michelle Salinger, who'd no doubt already told her teammates about her super-weird interaction with that one junior from her gym class. And honestly, I didn't blame her. It *was* weird. I was acting weird, and I was about to act weirder as I headed straight to the locker room. The guys' locker room.

As the athletic director and football coach, Brian had an office at the back of the guys' locker room. There was another way to get there, but it required going outside and taking the long way around, and I didn't have time for the long way right now. I braced myself, then pushed through the door and went for it. "Girl coming through!" I yelled as I headed toward Brian's office, holding my hands up around my eyes like blinders. "Total emergency! I'm not trying to see anything!" I heard some shouts and protests, but I let them go in one ear and out the other, not paying enough attention for any of the voices to register an identity. I was operating on the same principle as little kids when they close their eyes: I can't see you; you can't see me.

Thankfully, Brian was in his office, sitting at his laptop with another adult, deep in intense discussion. I couldn't see the screen, but as soon as I entered the office, I knew it was something football, by the sounds. They both looked up at me sharply, the assistant coach registering much more confusion than Brian.

"Brian—uh, I mean, Coach Davis," I said, "I need to speak to you in private, right now. It's an emergency."

"Did you walk through the locker room to get here?" the assistant coach asked. "There are people changing in there right now!"

"Gender is a construct," I said, before turning to Brian and trying to send him a message with my eyes. "It's a family emergency."

He definitely got my vibe. "Uh, yes, of course," he said, turning to his coworker. "Josh, can you give us a minute? Miss Pearl's father and mother are close friends."

Josh, whoever he was, had gone from startled to concerned, and he stood up quickly. "Sure thing, Coach," he said. "I need to track a new shipment of balls anyway. I'll check in with you later." Brian nodded as Josh gathered his things and left.

"What's going on, Esme?" Brian said as soon as we were alone. "Your entrance no doubt raised some eyebrows."

"I didn't see anything," I said. "I made sure of that." I threw the gingerbread man onto his desk.

"Oh, how nice," Brian said. "You brought me a snack."

"No," I said. "Don't eat it! It's for a spell, but first I need you to turn it into a pumpkin-spice latte."

"You need me to do what?"

"Like you did at the Summit," I said, "when you made all those cheap, cheesy decorations turn into a really classy après-ski theme." When begging, it never hurt to throw on a little flattery.

"I do remember that," he said. "Especially as you and Cassandra keep reminding me of it whenever you need anything. But why do you need me to turn this gingerbread man into a pumpkin-spice latte? Can't you wait until fall just like everyone else?"

"Brian, you know I only drink iced coffee, and unsweetened!" I said. "I need to do a spell, right now, and I need something pumpkin spice. It doesn't have to be a latte, if that's too hard; just make it a muffin or something."

Brian looked at me and nodded, then took out his phone and typed something into it. "Okay, so, pumpkin spice," he said, looking at me. "That means you're either trying to do popularis or gratiskinesis."

"What's gratiskinesis?" I asked, unintentionally taking the bait.

"A spell to host Thanksgiving dinner," he said, putting his phone into his pocket.

"What, do you have an app on there or something?" I asked.

"Counsel only," he said, avoiding my question and answering it at the same time. "So, since it's February and I know you prefer food that comes in plastic, or at least cardboard, I will assume that you are casting populariskinesis." He took my silence as assent. Then he sat down at his desk. "Esme, I never would have thought you cared about being popular," he said, flexing his fingers into that little triangle-house shape. "Is this about the Valentine's Day dance? Are you trying to get a date?"

I groaned. "Oh, jeez, Brian," I moaned. "I would rather barbecue my own foot than be popular at this school. It's Sitter related. The only way we're going to get Jump the Shark out of—"

"Wait, who is Jump the Shark?"

"The band we were staking out," I said.

"I thought they were called something else?"

"They were," I said, "but it doesn't matter what their name is. What does matter is that they literally never leave their house unless they have a gig, so with the Valentine's Day dance coming up . . ."

"You're kidding me, right?" he said. "You want to bring a bunch of suspected Red Magicians into this school? That's a dangerous operation, and we would need to get the Synod's sign-off—"

"Brian," I started as seriously as I could, "you know there's no real Synod right now, so where would we even start? And besides, the only thing that following the rules has ever gotten the three of us is almost killed." I paused, and I could tell from the look on his face that he was actually hearing me out. "Please, just trust me. Change the freakin' gingerbread man, and I promise that we will go over all these details."

Brian gave me one last look, then raised his palm over the

package and muttered an incantation, and just like that, a steaming latte was in the gingerbread man's place, pumpkin spice wafting into the air. "Thanks, B.," I said, swooping down to grab it, and then turning toward the door.

"Esme," Brian hissed after me, "don't spill it, or crumbled cookie will fall out!"

I nodded. Then, holding the cup up to help shield my eyes, I darted back into the locker room.

"Emergency! Girl coming through with a hot beverage," I yelled.

"I'm reporting you!" a male voice yelled after me.

"Title nine!" I yelled back.

"That doesn't mean you get to come into our locker room," he responded.

"Have you read it?" I shouted back, then pushed through the door into the hallway without waiting for a response.

Holding the latte carefully, I speed walked back to the library, and through the doors just in time to hear Janis say "But banning cell phones at the door would really encourage people to live in the moment."

"No one wants to live in the moment," snapped someone, probably Karen, "because then they'd realized that they got all dressed up to hang out in the gym." I snorted with a laugh, almost spilling the mirage latte, because I couldn't have spoken truer words myself.

"What if we put it to a vote?" Janis said.

"Oh my God," the same girl's voice screeched. "Is this a prank? Where's the camera? What are you doing here?"

I dipped through the young adult section, grabbed a copy of *Twilight* from the thirty that were still on the shelf—a block of black easily visible half a stack away—and then headed to where Janis was doing her valiant best to stall the dance committee.

"Oh my God," Karen said as soon as she saw me. "You're back now too? Please tell me that you're only here to retrieve your friend." She paused, and sniffed. "Wait, is that a PSL? How did you get a pumpkin-spice latte in February?"

I just smiled and set it down on the table. "Janis, you should leave now," I said, and she nodded quickly, then got up and started to run out of the library. The rest of the committee sat still, confusedly watching me as I lined up the latte, rose quartz, friendship bracelet, and the copy of *Twilight*.

"What are you doing? This isn't a yard sale," Karen snapped. Or maybe it was Kendra? Now I couldn't keep them straight, but I looked up, held my hands in the air, and addressed the committee as I chanted, "Populariskinesis, populariskinesis, populariskinesis." When I was done, I waited, hopeful. I had no idea if the spell had worked, since everyone still looked exactly the same.

"Jump the Shark is a really good band," I said, and Kendra, or Karen, practically swooned.

"Oh my God," she said, "I looooooovve them."

"Me too," said nipple boy.

"Don't they totally rock?" I asked him.

"They most definitely do," he said, nodding his assent.

"You should book them to play the dance this Saturday," I said, and the whole committee nodded like a bunch of bobblehead dogs.

"Can we?" a girl gushed. "I mean, that would be a dream."

"They might be touring right now," I said, "and selling out

stadiums, since they're so popular, but I have an in. Leave it to me. I'll take care of everything."

"Thank you so much, Emily," one of the Ks said. "You are the best."

I smiled broadly and started to gather up my spell ingredients to leave. Then, because I couldn't resist, I had to throw a few more concepts to the crowd. "Women's rights are human rights, and love is love," I said.

Nipple boy pumped his fist in the air. "I couldn't agree more!" he yelled.

My job here was done.

I was feeling pretty good about myself as I walked out of the library, and I spied Janis immediately at the end of the hallway. "Done and done," I said. "This is going to be the worst dance ever." She met my glee with a grimace, though, that was explained as soon as I fully turned the corner. She wasn't alone, and Brian was lounging against the wall, just a few lockers down from her.

"How was that latte?" he asked.

"Nice and crumbly," I answered as I tossed it into the trash.

"I said nothing," Janis said. "Even though he threatened me with torture."

"I threatened you with detention," he corrected. "Which is not the same thing."

"Depends on who you ask," Janis said.

"I'm not asking you," Brian said. Then he turned his attention back to me. "Esme, the more I think about this, the more it doesn't sit well with me, at all."

"Pun intended?" I asked, and he ignored me.

"By doing this, we are basically inviting four people, whom

we suspect of being Red Magic practitioners, and whom we know very little about, into a place where hundreds of teenagers are sitting ducks," he said, wiping his palms on the front of his tracksuit. "If you and Cassandra insist on doing this, we need to take extra precautions. I'm going to—"

I held up my hand to cut him off. "Brian," I said, "we got this. Mad reinforcements are on the way."

He crossed his arms. "Translation, please."

"Amirah, Ji-A, Ruby, and Mallory are all coming to town this weekend!" I said. "They'll be here to help."

"What?" he gasped, actually putting a hand on his chest like his heart was about to leap out of it. "You didn't tell me!"

"Well, it's not official Sitter business," I said. "They're just coming as friends."

"And we need something to do on Saturday night anyway," Janis added. "I can share the spreadsheet with you if you want. So far, we only have activities booked for Saturday afternoon."

Brain was staring down the hall, a faraway look in his eyes. "Good," he said. "Keep Saturday morning open, then."

"Okay," Janis said, "I'll update the Google Doc. But open for what?"

"I'm hosting brunch," he said.

I stared at him, dumbfounded. Two seconds before, he'd been ready to blow the whistle on this whole thing, and now he was talking about brunch? Sometimes I loved Brian so much, I wanted to hug him.

"Oh, cute," Janis said, excited, typing into her spreadsheet. "Consider it booked!"

CHAPTER 9

Janis dropped me at home just in time for dinner, which was Dad panini-pressing some chicken breasts on his George Foreman and heating up some steamed broccoli in the microwave. "Hey, kid," he said when I walked in the door. "You didn't eat already, did you?"

I grunted in the negative and plopped down into a chair. As he cooked, the little TV in the kitchen was on and Mom was engrossed in the Home Shopping Network.

"I tried to change it," Dad said. "But she got really upset. I wonder if there's something on here I should buy for her birthday." The item currently being shown was a fuzzy blanket with a matching eye mask.

"I mean, honestly, Dad," I said, "I kinda want that too. Cozy and chic!"

"Ta-da!" Dad said, wiping his hands on his jeans before turning around and setting plates down on the table in front of me and Mom. "The chicken might be a little burned and the broc still a little frozen," he said, "but it is dinner, and it is food!"

I looked over at Mom, and I swear I saw a little smile tugging at the edge of her lips. "Thanks, Dad," I said, picking up my fork. "It looks delicious."

After dinner, Mom and I watched some more HSN. Repeated calls to Dad to hand over his credit card number went unanswered, so we did not get to order the exfoliating pore extractor or the eighty-four pack of scratch-and-sniff washi tape, like we wanted. Then I helped Mom get ready for bed, and finally headed to my room. I hadn't looked at my phone in a while, so when I pulled it out, I had sixty-two unread messages in the group chat, seven of which were Shania Twain GIFs, and the rest seemed to be a discussion about whether or not Mallory should try to buy a coat tonight. I scrolled back a bit to see that she had asked, **What's the weather like there this weekend? Should I bring a jacket?** before getting roasted by everyone. It was currently eighty-two degrees in Miami, and thirty-one in Kansas. I went to send a GIF of the Ikea monkey as inspiration for what kind of coat Mallory should bring, then fell down a momentary GIF hole of monkeys on computers, many of which reminded me of myself doing my schoolwork.

When I finally pulled myself out, I saw another notification: a missed call and a voice mail. My stomach dropped as I looked at the transcript and realized the message was from Tom, confirming that the band did indeed want to play the school Valentine's Day dance, and now he wanted me to call him back with details.

It was now after nine, and I figured I could reasonably wait until tomorrow morning to call him back, and I sent Janis a quick text, asking her what time I should tell them to play.

We'll get with Kendra and Karen tomorrow, and get all the details, she wrote.

I'm already talking to the band, I wrote back. So can't you talk to Kendra and Karen?

No way, she replied. You're on the dance committee too. Don't shirk. A few seconds later, my phone dinged again. Harper Finkle makes a splash. I had to think about that one for a minute; then it came to me. My—and Janis's—favorite episode of *Wizards of Waverly Place* was the one where there was a fashion show, of course. Harper's outfits were always the epitome of inspirational (hello, Fruit Roll-Ups dress), and in this episode, she was wearing . . .

Rubber ducks? I wrote back.

Yep, she wrote. I had this all-denim look, but it was way too Britney-Justin, so I added some rubber duck earrings and a clear raincoat, and now it's totally magical.

Janis, you quack me up.

Since Amirah, Ji-A, Ruby, and Mallory were arriving tomorrow, I wanted to make sure my look was on point. I opened my closet and surveyed my options, and ultimately decided to lean into the Kansas thing: a sunflower-print bodysuit under a flowy, black oversized eighties high-waisted power suit. I could roll the legs of the suit up, and scrunch the sleeves, and then wear my black leather Sk8-His. I could tie a green-and-yellow scarf around my head, like eighties Madonna, and wear it with a single dangly earring—either the one that was a miniature watercolor palette with a real brush and paints, or one of the earrings that were made from Cheez-Its (sadly, plastic and not real). I couldn't decide between the earrings, so I figured I'd make a snap decision in the morning. It was a "flower power suit."

I got ready for bed, and then got out my books and looked at my homework. I liked to tell myself that my schoolwork was slipping because I was so busy being a Sitter, but tonight I couldn't lie to myself. Tonight my schoolwork was slipping because I'd spent too much time Home Shopping. I turned on my reading light, determined to stay awake long enough to do the bare minimum to get me through the next day.

Then a sound at my window made me freeze. It wasn't the sound of the wind whipping around a creaky old house or the sound of a branch scratching the glass. It was the sound of a tap. A deliberate tap.

I closed my book and looked at the window. The thick curtain was closed, so I couldn't see out, but that also meant that no one could see in. There were four people in the world who ever wanted to get ahold of me. One of them I lived with, and the other three—if for some reason they weren't able to call or text—would have just let themselves in the front door.

Maybe I was imagining it, or maybe it was the sound of something else, coming from somewhere else in the house. Or, maybe . . . my mind flashed to Tom, who now had my phone number. I had no doubt that Tom was stupid, and I had no doubt that he was also evil, but I'd take an evil genius over an evil moron any day, because at least a genius has a plan. A moron's likely to do something stupid, like show up at a teenage girl's house late on a school night.

Tap. Tap.

This time, there was no denying it, and my mind was most

definitely not playing tricks on me. Moving as quietly as I could, I set my book down and stood up. I raised my hand and concentrated, using my kinesis to feel through all the doors and windows in the house to make sure they were locked. The only one that wasn't was the window in Mom's room, which sent a chill down my spine, so I used my kinesis to lock it. I wasn't sure what to do next. I raised my hand toward the light switch, using my kinesis to flick it off. I took a deep breath and hoped that whatever creep lurked outside maybe thought I'd just gone to bed.

Now that I was sitting in my dark room, though, I realized just how not-dark my room was. There was the glowing light from my fan, and from my computer charger, and from my vintage Nickelodeon clock radio that I'd found at a garage sale, and from my lava lamp, and from— Another tap made me move quicker.

I walked to the window, and pulled the curtain back. It wasn't that dark outside either, and between the streetlamps and the light pollution, it was easy to see across the yard and into the night. There were no demons. No Tom. The yard was empty. Then I saw it, just a few feet away from my window. Darker than the night and seemingly designed to blend in with the shadows. A crow. My breath caught and my heart started to race.

For a second I felt frozen, not sure what to do. Then I snapped back and opened the window to let it in. It hopped over the sill and, with a few flaps of its wings, dropped down onto the middle of the rug. Then it turned into a boy.

It seemed like the process of turning from a human into

an animal, and vice versa, could be gross. Feathers tearing through skin, bones snapping, teeth morphing, and facial features stretching. Horror-movie stuff. This wasn't like that. It was just a snap, and there he was, not a feather to be found.

We stood there, not speaking, just looking at each other. I had a million things to say and a million emotions running through me. After all the time that I had spent thinking about him, all the interactions planned, I'd never imagined that he would come to my window. Never imagined that the first time I saw him again would be when he was standing in my room. I felt relieved and angry and concerned at the same time, especially because Adrian looked like crap.

Adrian was wearing the same clothes that he'd had on when I'd last seen him two months before, and they looked like he had been wearing them nonstop for those two months. His gray jeans were now tinted a grimy beige, and the neck of his black T-shirt was stretched out, with a large rip in the side. His hair, which had been a tight crop before, had now grown out so that just the tips were bleached, and he had bags under his eyes.

I wasn't sure what to say. Was I mad at him? Or did I want to run over and hug him? Finally he went first.

"Hi," he said, shifting back and forth on his feet. "Nice pajamas."

"Thanks," I said, looking down at the yummy-sushi flannel, bought in homage to Buffy. "I don't really eat sushi," I said, by way of explanation, "but I have yet to find a good microwave burrito print." A beat of silence. "Do you want to sit down? You look tired. Wait," I said as I pulled out my desk chair and moved the pile of magazines from the seat to the floor. "I know you're not supposed to say that to people, but you look like you . . . I don't know . . . Are you okay?"

He crossed over to the chair, and gratefully sank into it.

"Do you want me to take your coat? Do you want to take your shoes off?" I asked, feeling like I wanted to do something to make him feel more comfortable, but he just shook his head.

"I *am* tired. I'm exhausted," he said. "Sleeping in trees is for the birds. I mean, I don't know how to build a nest, so I just have to find a good branch and perch, so I'm waking up every few minutes feeling like I'm about to fall off and plummet to the ground."

I kept my eyes on him as I walked over to my bed and sat down on it, crossing my legs underneath me. "Can't you fly?" I asked, realizing that I had zero idea about how his power worked.

"Yeah, but not if I'm asleep," he said. "I need to be awake and focused. It's not instinctive. It takes concentration."

I nodded. "And sleeping on the ground is not an option?"

He shook his head, and ran his hand over his hair. "I tried, but man, those cats are killer." He looked at me, and smiled a little. "It's good to see you," he said. I swallowed and nodded.

"It's good to see you too," I said, looking down at my knee and tracing my finger over an illustration of a piece of sushi called "ikura," which looked absolutely disgusting. "Where have you been? Why are you here?" The questions came out quicker than I wanted them to.

Adrian's mouth moved like it wasn't sure which way to con-tort. "I've been around. I never left Spring River." He paused.

"I would have come earlier, but I wasn't sure you wanted to see me."

"Why'd you come now?" I said.

"Because I don't know how much longer I can stay out there," he said, "and I don't know where else to go. I'm scared to go home. I'm scared to go anywhere."

I swallowed. "I don't think you have a home anymore," I said. "Brian told me that Wanda's place was searched. He didn't say what happened after that, but . . . they're looking for you."

He nodded. "I know, and I'm not surprised," he said. "Esme, you have to believe me. I didn't know. I didn't know anything. If I had, I would never have let Wanda hurt anyone."

"If you didn't do anything, then why are you hiding?" I asked. "Just tell them."

He shook his head resolutely, and glanced at the window like he was about ready to fly right back out. "I wasn't born like this," he said, flapping his hands like a bird. "It's a power Wanda gave me because it would help her out. And if it can be given to me, then it can be taken away." He stopped, and swallowed. "I don't want that to happen."

"Then if they want to talk to you, tell them the truth," I said. "You're not going to get in trouble for something you didn't do."

"Yeah," he said, "but what if they believe me and still take my powers away?"

"I don't know," I said, not wanting to admit to him that this probably was a possibility. "Brian told me they're still trying to get a new Synod set up, so it sounds like they've got a lot going on these days. Once they talk to you, they might not even care about a . . ." I wasn't sure what to call him. "Bird boy," I said finally, though that sounded kind of like an insult. But I looked up, and Adrian was smiling.

"I like being a bird boy," he said. "And I'd like to stay this way."

"You really don't want it to be taken away?" I asked. He shook his head, and cracked his neck from side to side.

"I've been this way for a long time now," he said. "I've forgotten how to be a boy-boy, and if they take my power away, then I'm just back to being a nobody. As a bird boy, at least I'm something special."

"Adrian," I said, "not to sound like an inspirational post or anything, but you'll always be something special, even if you can't sprout feathers and fly away."

"Ha, thanks." He laughed, but he looked at me, and our eyes met for so long that I broke and looked away, standing up from the bed.

"I'm going to get a glass of water," I said. "Do you want anything?"

"Yeah." He swallowed. "Water's great."

I wasn't really thirsty, but it was a good excuse to get out of there and give myself a moment to think. Even covered in two months of bird grime, Adrian was still really cute, and I could tell by his eyes that he was telling the truth about Wanda. He was also telling the truth about being scared. But still— I hadn't heard from him in two months. And if he really had been in Spring River that whole time, he could have dropped by or given me a sign. Anything but a total ghosting.

In the kitchen, I got two glasses down from the cabinet and filled them at the tap, then turned around to head back to my room. I was startled to see Dad in the doorway, and he flipped on the light switch. "Have you seen my reading glasses?" he asked, glancing around at the counters.

"Um, no," I said. He looked at me, and took in the fact that I was now carrying two full glasses of water.

"What are you doing?" he said. "You're not going to drink all that before bed, are you?"

"No, of course not," I said. "I'm, uh, doing a hair mask." I started to walk past him, and he turned to watch me go down the hall.

"In your bedroom?" he called after me.

"It's complicated," I answered before opening my door just enough to squeeze in, which was hard to do without spilling. I set one glass down on my desk, and handed the other one to Adrian.

"Thanks," he said, and then drank it down in just a few gulps.

I sat on my bed, leaving my own water untouched. "So, have you been eating bugs and stuff?"

He laughed a little and shook his head. "No way," he said. "I have a Taco Bell gift card. But I only go there once a day, because I don't want anyone to see me."

"Who would see you?" I asked. He swallowed the last of his water and looked down, nudging a worn spot on my rug with the toe of his dirty sneaker.

"You," he said.

"Me?" I asked, surprised. "Why would you worry about me seeing you?"

"I thought maybe you'd turn me in," he said.

"Why would I do that?"

"Because out of everyone in the Sitterhood, you have the most reason to hate me," he said. "I mean, even if I didn't know what I was doing, I still helped Wanda, and Wanda . . ." His voice trailed off.

"Killed my dog," I supplied for him.

He nodded. "I'm really sorry, Esme," he said. "If I'd known what Wanda was planning, I never would have . . ." He trailed off again. "I understand if you hate me."

"Adrian, why would I hate you?" I said. "You . . ." There was a lot I could say, but I settled on "Made me a mix CD."

"Did you listen?" he asked, and I nodded. "Did you like it?"

"Yeah," I said. "I'm a scrooge no more. At least when it comes to music. But how did you make a mix CD if you were a bird living in trees?"

He looked kinda sheepish. "I actually made it for you when we were still at the Summit," he said. "When I still had a room to sleep in and stuff."

"You had a CD burner in your room?" I asked, incredulous.

"It was Wanda's," he said. "She kept trying to pawn it, but no one wants CDs anymore."

"So, why are you here?" I asked. "Not in Spring River but here, in my room?"

"I need help. I mean, I can't be a bird forever. I need a place to stay. I need a shower. I need to get out of these clothes." Hearing him say that statement made my cheeks start to get hot, and I looked away right as he realized what he'd just said. "Wait, I mean, I'm not suggesting that I do that here, or now. But I need you to help me. I was hoping that maybe you could ask around, find out what's going on, and see if the Synod do want to take my powers away."

So, that was it, huh? He'd gone from being worried that I hated him to asking me for help. Of course. But then he kept going. "And, if I'm being honest, I wanted to see you again. I mean, not just see you, because I've seen you, a lot, these past couple of months. I know that sounds creepy, but I didn't have a lot else to do during the day. I mean, you can only circle parking lots and look for dropped burger wrappers for so many hours before you start to crave a little more stimulation. I guess I just wanted to talk to you. I know we only knew each other for two days, and there was a lot going on, but I've missed you." He paused, and tried to drink the last drops of water from his glass. "It's a weird feeling, to miss someone before you even get to know them."

"I know," I said.

"You do?" he asked. I nodded, and he smiled. "If I had cleaner clothes," he said, "I would really like to come and sit closer to you." I looked at him and smiled back, thinking about what I wanted to say to that. It was crazy to think that all this time that I'd been thinking about him, he'd been thinking about me, and that the connection I'd felt at the Summit wasn't just in my head. It was real.

"Esme! Esme!" I jumped up off my bed. Dad was screaming my name. I looked at Adrian, whose eyes were wide. As quick as a blink, he was a crow again, those same wide eyes now round and as black as his feathers. We were both still as I waited for the sound of Dad's footsteps in the hall, and the inevitable pounding on the door.

But instead he just kept yelling my name, and Mom's. "Esme! Theresa! Come here, quick!"

"Stay here!" I whispered to bird-Adrian. "I don't think this is about you. I'll be right back." Then I let myself out of my room and went running down the hall. I passed Mom's room, where she was standing next to the bed, looking out the door but not moving. In the living room, Dad's blankets were spread out on the couch, and a cold blast of air from the open front door drew me into the entryway.

As soon as I saw Dad, my breath stopped cold and I couldn't move. "Oh my God," I said.

He was in his pajamas, kneeling down on the floor, tears streaming down his face as a wiggling, white mass with a ferociously wagging tail tried to lick them off.

"It's her. It's really her," Dad said, grabbing the sides of her face and mashing it from all directions. "She came back."

Suddenly I was aware of someone standing behind me, and I turned to see Mom. A tiny smile fought its way onto her lips. "Pig?" she said.

"Yeah, Momma, Pig," I said, and burst into tears.

At the sound of my voice, Pig bounded toward me, her tail wagging so fast, it was a blur. I dropped to my knees, and she was on me instantly, covering my face with kisses and almost knocking me over as she tried to get into my lap.

She was filthy and skinny, just like Adrian, but she was undoubtedly Pig, with the same tan spots and the same big, brown couldn't-hurt-a-caterpillar eyes. I was crying, but then I started to giggle, and I couldn't stop. I swear Pig's tail moved faster.

"Dad, where'd you find her? Where was she?" I asked.

"I have no idea," he said, wiping his own eyes with the back of his hand. "I was getting ready for bed, and I heard something at the door. I went to check on it, and there she was, sitting on the doormat like she'd just gone out to do her business and I'd forgotten to let her back in."

I stood up, and the three of us looked down at her. Like a good girl, she sat, and then cocked her head to one side, looking pleased with herself, like she always did whenever she knew she was the center of attention.

"I don't think she's hurt," Dad said, and he took a few steps, motioning for her to follow him. "Come on, girl," he said, and she trotted in his direction. There was a little bit of a limp in her back left leg, but nothing else different that would suggest it had been just two months since she'd taken a flying leap off a six-story building.

Dad knelt down and started to scratch her ears again, but she looked confused and let out a low whine. "Dad," I said, laughing, "she's disappointed. She thought you were heading toward the kitchen."

"Oh, Piggy," he said. "We don't have any dog food."

"That's okay," I said, pushing past him to the fridge. "She'll eat anything, because I bet you are a very hungry Pig right now." She whined in affirmation. I opened the fridge and pulled out the dinner leftovers. "Sorry, Dad," I said, opening up a Tupperware of boneless chicken breast. "I hope you weren't saving this for lunch." I put it down on the ground, and Pig ate it in two bites, then looked up at me for more. I opened the fridge again. There was no way I was giving her broccoli, even if she was starving, but I found some lunch meat of dubious origin, some half-wilted celery, and some baby carrots. I dumped them into her bowl, and then motioned for her to go ahead. Again, it was gone in two gulps.

"She's been eating," Dad said. "She's skinny but not emaciated. I'll go to the store first thing in the morning. Where could she have possibly been?" he asked, shaking his head as he stared at her in wonder. "And how did she get back here?"

"I don't know," I said, not able to take my eyes off her.

Dad was staring too. "Well," he said finally, "wherever she was, I'm happy she's home. I assume she'll sleep with you?"

I nodded. "Yeah, I'll be glad to have her back." Dad leaned down to give her ears a final scratch for the night. When he turned and headed back to bed, I gestured at Pig and patted my leg for her to follow me down the hall. Mom followed us too, and I couldn't help but notice that the look on her face was weirder than normal. Mom had met Pig twice. Once, we had tried to take Pig to the facility because I'd thought it would cheer us all up, but that had backfired and Pig had totally freaked out. The second time had been on Halloween, during the brief period of time when Mom's curse had been lifted. For those few moments, though, they'd gotten along swimmingly, and I wondered if that was what Mom was thinking about now. She kept squinting, her eyebrows furrowing together and then her forehead smoothing back out, like she was trying to solve a difficult equation.

"I'll be right back," I said to Mom, then walked quickly down the hall. I opened the door to my room and slid in, but of course, I needn't have worried about Dad, Mom, or even Pig discovering that there was someone in my room.

Because there wasn't. It was empty. He was gone. I wasn't surprised. It made sense that when you were a guy who had just snuck in a girl's window, the last thing you wanted to hear was her dad screaming. But just because I wasn't surprised didn't mean that I couldn't be disappointed.

When I got back, Pig and Mom were still in the hall, staring at each other, and I motioned for Pig to come with me. Before she did, she went over and pressed her big head against Mom's thigh. Mom was still slightly smiling, and gave Pig a nuzzle.

In my room, Pig sat down in the middle of the rug, almost exactly where crow-Adrian had landed just an hour before, and I could see her nostrils twitch with a sniff. I sat down on my bed and patted the pillows, trying to get her to come join me, but she didn't move. I fluffed the comforter and repeated my invitation, but she still just sat there. Finally I stood and gathered up all of my clothes that had been strewn across the floor, and dropped them into a pile. Pig got up, ambled over, nosed a sweatshirt around until the pile was just to her liking, and then plopped down. Within seconds, her snores were reverberating off the walls.

I slept better than I had in months.

CHAPTER 10

When my alarm went off on Friday morning, Pig was still snoring like a garbage truck, and she didn't even budge when I got out of bed. It had probably been a long time since she'd had a good night's sleep. Pig's return had given me a buoyancy that I hadn't felt in a long time. I was no longer made of sand and cement, but bubble gum and feathers.

Amirah, Ji-A, Mallory, and Ruby, an hour ahead of us, were already bombing the group chat with updates on their travel. I snapped a pic of Pig, then sent it with a text that said **happening now**. Almost immediately, six ellipses popped up on my screen. Then the texts came in a deluge.

> WKERWEIHFHGSHG WTFF!!!!
> SHE'S BACKKKKKKK???
> WHERE WAS SHE? HOW'D YOU FIND HER. I
> CANNOT WAIT TO SQUISH THAT FACE.
> [Inexplicable Shania Twain driving a race car GIF]
> She just showed up! Last night!

How is she?

OK? I think. Hungry? More later!

I got dressed, and then, no doubt sensing that breakfast was imminent, Pig woke up as I was about to leave the room, and she followed me to the kitchen. Dad had made coffee and was, as usual, sitting at the table working on his crossword puzzle, but I saw that he'd barely made any progress. He put his pencil down and came over and hugged Pig, tight and long. Dogs hated hugs, but Pig did a good job of tolerating this one, and she even licked his face in return.

I opened the fridge and pulled out some eggs, then some breakfast sausage from the freezer. "Breakfast today?" Dad asked, since I usually only drank coffee and ate doughnuts in the morning.

"Not for me," I said. "For her."

"I have to be in early today," Dad said, "but I'll stop and get some dog food on the way home."

"Get the kind that's cheeseburger flavored," I told him. "That's her favorite." Pig licked her lips as though she knew what we were talking about and watched me eagerly as I scrambled the eggs in the pan, and popped the sausage into the microwave.

"Where's Mom?" I asked as I scooped the eggs onto a plate and set them on the floor. They were gone in literally two seconds, so I picked the plate right back up and put it in the dishwasher.

"Her door's still closed," he said, looking over at it. "She must be sleeping late."

The microwave dinged. I pulled out the sausages, which

were only partly warm, and tossed them across the kitchen so that Pig could catch them in midair.

"Does she usually get up before you?" I asked Dad as he was putting on his coat.

"Yeah." He nodded. "She's usually sitting at the kitchen table when I walk in. But last night was a big night, so it would make sense if she was tired."

Suddenly I felt the back of my neck prickle, and in two steps, I was at Mom's bedroom door. I knocked and called out to her; then I tried the knob. It was locked. Then I pounded on the door, louder than before, and when I was met with nothing, I raised my hand and unlocked the door with my kinesis, and pushed it open so hard that it hit the wall with a thud and bounced back. The room was empty. Mom was gone.

Dad was right behind me. "Okay, I'm calling in," he said, with his phone out and already dialing. "She couldn't have gone far."

"Dad," I said, trying to keep my voice calm and steady, "we have no idea how long she's been gone. She could be anywhere." Beside me, Pig let out a whine, and then a pounding on the front door made me jump and run for it. I threw it open with a crash, and there was Janis, rubber duck earrings shaking with excitement.

"Where is she?!" Janis screamed. "Where is my stinky, squishy best friend?" Pig came bounding out of Mom's room and nearly knocked me over to get to Janis. Normally I would have raised a stink about the fact that Janis—who had once referred to Pig as a "vacuum bag of farts"—was now claiming my dog as her best friend, but right now I was freaking out. Janis picked up on it immediately. "Wait, Esme, what's wrong?"

"My mom," I said. "She's gone. She snuck out at some point last night." She'd probably unlocked the very window that I'd locked with my kinesis.

"Oh my God," Janis said. Dad came running to the porch, his car keys in his hand.

"I'm going to start circling," he said. "You stay here in case she comes back." I knew that was standard protocol for looking for a normie, but Mom wasn't a normie and neither was I, so we were going to pull out all the stops to find her. I stepped out into the yard and looked up at the trees.

"Hey!" I yelled. "If you're still here, don't just sit there. Help me." Dad, Janis, and Pig were all looking at me like I was seeing ghosts. "No one here is going to turn you in," I added. Across the yard, in the pear tree, there were three crows, and all of them eyed me warily. Then two flapped their wings and flew away. "Come on," I said to the one that remained. "You can change in the living room." Then it sailed down from the branch and flew through the open front door, sending Janis and Dad scrambling to get out of the way. Pig let out a little yelp.

"What the heck?" Janis said, flattening herself against the wall. Then her mouth fell open and her words stopped as the crow settled on the back of the couch, and turned into Adrian.

"It's you . . . ," Janis said, her words like the air slowly escaping from an inner tube.

"Adrian," I said, "this is Janis, who you already met, but I don't think you were formerly introduced. And this is my dad, Dave."

"Hi, uh, Mr. Pearl," Adrian said, sticking his hand out. Dad, still slightly in shock, just stood there and didn't take the offering. Then suddenly he realized his rudeness, and held out his hand.

"Esme," Dad said, "your mother . . ."

I turned back to Adrian. "My mom's missing," I said. "It looks like she snuck out her window. You didn't see anything, did you?"

His eyes got wider, and he shook his head. "I slept in a pine tree over by the Panda Sub," he said. "I just came back over here because I wanted to see if I could catch you on your way to school." I bit my lip and nodded. It sucked that he hadn't seen anything, but in a way it was a relief, as it would have been unforgivable if he'd seen Mom leave and just let it happen.

"Janis, looks like we're skipping school for the second time this week," I said to her, "because I need you to look too."

"Of course," Janis said.

"Wait," Dad said. "When was the first time you skipped school this week?"

"Dad," I said, "go." He jogged out to his car, and I turned to Adrian. "Can you look too?" I asked. "She's got dark hair, and the last time I saw her, she was wearing cloud pajamas and a pink robe."

"Of course," he said, and then immediately changed back into a bird. I walked over and opened the door for him, and he flew away. Then I stood there, looking at Janis and Pig while I tried to weigh my options. Just sitting there and waiting for Mom to come back wasn't really an option. If she stayed gone, then I'd call the police, but as always, that was my last resort. I grabbed my phone to call Brian.

Just as I was starting to dial, Adrian came back, a bird tapping furiously on a window at the front of the house. I opened the door and let him in, half-annoyed that he was wasting time, and wondering why he hadn't left yet, but as soon as he changed into himself, he said, "I found her."

"What?" I gasped. "Already?"

"She's in the backyard," he said, nodding. Instantly Janis and I turned and ran through the kitchen, Pig at our heels. I threw open the back door to an empty yard.

"She's back behind that tree," he said. I started toward it, and when Janis started after me, Adrian put out his arm. "Wait! Esme, I think maybe you should go alone." My stomach dropped as Janis stepped back. Still, I didn't hesitate for a second, and Pig hung back as well as I raced toward the tree where Adrian had pointed.

As soon as I could see the other side, I understood why I hadn't seen her earlier when I had looked out the window. She was sitting at the base of the tree, curled up in a ball, her arms wrapped tightly around her knees. She was shivering and didn't have her robe on anymore. "Momma," I said, dropping down to the ground and throwing my arms around her. "Come inside, come inside." Then I pulled back and got a better look at her.

She wasn't crying, but her face had that splotchy, puffy look of someone who had just stopped, and she looked exhausted. She was streaked with dirt from head to toe, her nails were caked with it, and the skin on her hands was raw and red, and even bleeding in some parts. Her chin trembled as I tried to pull her up, and then more tears started to spill from her eyes. She resisted, though, and the harder I pulled, the more she seemed to shrink back from me. "Mom," I pleaded, "you have to come inside. It's freezing out here and you've been here too long." Finally she took my hand and let me help her stand up, and then almost immediately, she bent back over and was pawing at the ground. The dirt was frozen, and it hurt me to see her battered fingers clawing at it, but the ground there was pocked with small holes just like the one she was now digging. There were dozens, more than I could count, and it was clear she'd been doing this for hours.

"Stop," I said, trying to grab her hands. "Whatever you're doing, stop it." She just pulled away from me and turned around, trying to dig in another spot. Now I wrapped my arms around her from behind, and physically tried to lift her off the ground. Her feet kicked at me, and then all of a sudden, I felt a sharp pain rip through my forearm, startling me into letting go. She'd bit me.

In all my life, I'd never seen Mom like this. She'd escaped from her facility several times, but every time someone had brought her back, she'd always seemed the same. Sad, but docile, even if she'd just been wily. Now, though, she seemed possessed, frantic and digging, crying again. And I was crying too. "Momma, stop it!" I said. "Stop it. You're hurting yourself. What's wrong? Please come inside."

I looked away from her and across the yard, where Janis and Adrian were both standing there, frozen, not knowing what to do. Pig, sensing pain as she always did, jingled across to us. I was rubbing my arm, and Mom had bent back down to dig at a spot right by the roots of the tree. Pig went straight to her and licked her face, then tried to squeeze under her arms.

It was something I'd never seen her do before, and then understanding clicked: she was trying to put herself between Mom and the dirt. She was trying to make Mom stop.

It was like Mom realized it too, and before I even knew what was happening, she stood up and kicked Pig, hard, right in the side. I didn't even have time to think about it. Instinctively I raised my palms and grabbed Mom with my kinesis, forming a straitjacket, clamping her arms down at her sides and her legs together. She let out a scream that could only be described as a howl. Pig was whimpering and cowering against the tree. "Are you okay, girlie?" I asked her, and she wagged her tail a bit to let me know that she was.

"Come help me," I called, and Janis and Adrian ran quickly to join me as Mom continued to scream, even though the only part of her body that could thrash now was her head. "We have to get around her," I said when they were standing next to me. "I can carry her inside, but I'm sure the neighbors are looking by now, and they can't see her floating through the air. We have to pretend like you're helping."

Janis moved to stand next to me on one side, and Adrian positioned himself opposite us. Pig was close at our heels. "Hold your arms out," I said, and they followed my directions. Mom was still making awful noises. I didn't want to do it, but I had to, and I used my kinesis to clamp her mouth shut. She fought as hard as any demon I'd ever encountered, as though her strength were supernatural. Pig was whining, and I could see that tears were streaming down Janis's face. I felt frozen, stunned, not able to believe what was happening.

Janis, Adrian, and I worked well together, Pig a few steps

behind, letting out whimpers. At the back door, Adrian kept one arm on Mom for show, while he stepped forward and opened the door. Once we were in the house, I took my kinesis off Mom's mouth and was relieved when she didn't start screaming again. Janis stepped back, and I could see that Mom was shaking. I didn't know what to do, so I carried her into the living room and put her down right in front of the couch, someplace soft where she wouldn't hurt herself if she fell over. Thankfully, she just stood there, kind of limp. I couldn't see where Adrian and Janis had gone, but I figured that they were probably making themselves as small as possible somewhere in the background.

I felt a warm weight on my leg, and looked down. Pig had come and sat down next to me, and was leaning against my shin. I leaned down and put my palm on her skull, realizing how much I had missed her presence. Pig always made you feel not alone. It made me choke up to think how grateful I was that she was there now.

Mom dropped onto the couch, and Pig walked over and started to lick some of the dirt and blood from her hand. I took a couple of steps toward her. "Come on, Momma," I said. "We're going to get you a nice warm bath, and then you can go to bed. You must be tired, and you need to sleep. . . ." She was looking at me, and then her face twisted and she lashed out with a kick, her foot hitting me hard in my kneecap and sending me crumbling to the carpet in pain. Then she elbowed Pig in the face, and Pig scampered to my side, looking back at Mom with confusion and hurt in her eyes.

Instinctively I wrapped Mom in my kinesis again and didn't

let go until I'd backed away, far across the room and out of her reach. The shock I'd had a few minutes before had worn off, and now I was openly crying. I didn't like the thought of treating my own mother like something I was about to flush, but I had no idea what to do. "Janis," I managed to sniff through my tears, "call my dad and tell him to come home." Janis nodded, and then ducked into the kitchen. I stood up, and winced when I put weight on my leg. Instantly Adrian was by my side, helping to hold me up.

"Are you okay?" he asked, and I nodded.

"My knee will be fine," I told him. He seemed to accept that as an answer, and I was glad that he didn't ask about the rest of me.

"Your dad will be home in two minutes," Janis said, coming back into the living room. "He was just around the corner."

"Great," I said, and swallowed. "Thanks." I didn't know what to do. Mom was just sitting there, her arms down by her sides, a blank look of inescapable sadness on her face, but she seemed calm. I wanted to get her out of those dirty clothes, fix her some breakfast, get her to take a nap, but now I was scared to even take two steps toward her. I could handle a kick, a punch, or whatever it was that she wanted to throw my way. That was no big deal. But it seemed like it hurt her more than it hurt me, and I swear, in all the years that she had been cursed and living at the facility, I'd never seen her look as miserable as she looked now.

I heard tires crunch in the driveway, and a door slam. Dad burst through the front door, breathless. "Oh thank God," he said. "Where was she?"

"Just in the backyard," I said, "behind the tree, so we couldn't see her when we looked out the window." Dad ran over and knelt down beside Mom, taking her hand in his as I loosened my kinetic grip on her.

"Theresa," he started, "you scared us to death. You can't do tha—" The words were barely out of his mouth before she yanked her hand away from him and swung at his face, clawing his cheek with her dirty and broken nails. Dad stepped back and spun so that he was facing me.

"What happened?" he said.

"I don't know," I told him. "She just . . ." Then I started sobbing.

Adrian cleared his throat and spoke for me. "Esme had to carry her inside," he said. "She kicked Esme, and the dog. She just . . ." He faltered. "Seems really pissed."

I sniffed, swallowed, and managed to pull myself together enough to speak.

"You guys should go," I said, turning to Janis and Adrian. They both nodded, but Janis seemed hesitant.

"Are you sure?" she said, and I nodded. "I can pick you up after school if you want to go to the airport with me and . . ."

"No," Dad's voice broke in behind me. "Esme, you're going to school."

"Dad," I protested, "I can't. We don't know what's going on here. Mom's clearly upset and . . ."

He shook his head. "And I can handle it," he said. "I may not have magic powers, but I am still the adult here."

"But what if—" He held up a hand and cut me off.

"It's not up for debate," he said.

"Dad! I'm not even going to be able to concentrate. I'm just going to be worried about—"

"That's understandable," he said. "But her nurse will be here soon, and I will keep you updated. If we're always waiting for a normal day around here, we're going to be waiting a long time. Go to school and just be a high school junior." He paused, and we both just looked at each other. "Esme," he said, "it's not a request. It's an order. Go with your friends, now."

"Okay," I said, looking back and forth between him and Mom, who was still sitting in the same place on the couch. "Okay," I said again. I picked up my backpack and started to walk through the door, then turned and went back to give Pig a hug.

"Dog food," I said as I gave Dad a hug. "Don't forget dog food."

"I won't," he said. "She won't let me." I turned to leave, got a few steps, and then turned and walked back toward Dad, lowering my voice.

"Uh, this is weird, but if you happen to talk to Brian, don't mention Adrian."

"The bird?" he asked, and I nodded. "Why?"

"Just don't, please?" I said. "Trust me."

"Okay," Dad said, and nodded. I fought back tears as I walked outside, and Adrian and Janis kept a respectful distance behind me. I wiped my eyes with the back of my hand, and then turned toward them when we got to Janis's car.

"Sorry," I said, "that you had to see that."

"Pshaw," Janis said, waving it away, and Adrian smiled.

"You're doing it again," he said.

"Doing what?" I asked.

"Apologizing for something that's not your fault."

"Ha," I said. "Okay, sorry." I looked back at the house. "I don't like leaving my dad alone."

"I don't think you have a choice," Janis said. Then she turned to Adrian. "We've got to bounce if we're going to make it to second period, but do you need a ride? We could drop you somewhere."

Adrian shook his head. "Thanks," he said. "I'm cool." As Janis was getting in, I turned to him.

"Thanks for your help," I said.

"No problem," he said. "You gonna be okay?"

"Yeah, I'll be fine," I said. "I'm just worried about my mom. She's been seeming really happy lately, so I don't know what happened."

"Yeah." He nodded. I waited for him to say something else, and then was kind of relieved when he didn't offer any platitudes about how she'd be fine or how everything was going to be okay, because it clearly wouldn't. "I'll catch up with you later," he said finally.

I nodded, then got into the car, and he shut the door for me. I buckled my seat belt as Janis drove away, and when I looked in the rearview mirror, he was still standing on the sidewalk watching us.

"What do you think happened?" Janis said, her voice cracking on the last word. "You don't think anyone re-upped her curse, do you?"

I felt completely deflated. I was starting to think that nothing good could happen in my life without something bad happening at the same time. "I don't know," I said, and felt the tears come again. I tipped my head back so that I was looking up at the ceiling, rested my head against the headrest, and closed my eyes. The thought of trying to figure out what was going on with Mom was exhausting. I could tell Brian, but he wouldn't know, so he'd have to ask someone else, and it would be more of the same. An endless round of kick-the-can as everyone tried to pretend that they weren't really as helpless or as ignorant as they seemed to be. Janis's and my phones dinged, and I checked to see that Ruby and Mallory's flight had been delayed.

Ruby! Of course! If there was one person in my life who was going to have answers, it wouldn't be an adult. Ruby knew more about curses than anyone else I'd ever met, and she was on her way to Kansas, right now. The tiniest sliver of a silver lining.

"Soooooo," Janis said, and I could tell by her tone that she was trying to change the subject and lighten the mood. "He's cute. His overall vibe is a little derelict, but I can see why you dig him."

"He's been sleeping in trees ever since the Summit," I said. "He normally smells really nice." I paused and reconsidered. "I mean, the only two days that I've ever hung out with him before, he smelled really nice."

Janis nodded and pursed her lips. "So tell me about him. . . ."

"He's funny," I said. "And he likes coffee, and has good taste in music, and . . ."

"He's a bird," Janis said.

"Well, I mean, he's not a bird," I said. "He just has the

power to turn into a bird, and when he exercises that power, then yeah, I guess he is a bird. But Wanda gave it to him, and now the Sitterhood might take it away. That's why he's hiding."

"He's hiding?" she asked. I groaned and leaned my forehead against the passenger-side window.

"Yeah," I said. "Just don't mention him, okay? To Brian or any of the other girls?"

"So you're keeping this on the DL?"

"Janis . . ."

"Sorry," she said, quickly recanting. "Too soon for jokes. I get it." Janis pulled into the school lot and, as usual, wedged her car into her spot at about a forty-five-degree angle. "Man, if there ever was a morning for coffee and doughnuts, then this would be it," she said.

I just sat there, staring out the windshield, not able to get the image of Mom's torn-up, dirt-encrusted hands out of my head. Janis looked at me.

"Esme, if you want to spend the rest of the morning sitting in my car, I do not blame you," she said. "There are a million empty water bottles in the backseat if you need to pee."

In spite of myself, I let out a little laugh as I reached for my backpack. "No, I'll come in. It'll be a distraction at least, and Dad seemed really serious about it." I climbed out of the car, and then walked around so that I was standing next to Janis. "It just seemed like we were making progress, you know? I think Mom liked being at home, and Dad and I liked having here there. But this morning, I've never seen her like that. It was worse than ever before. I'm supposed to be helping her, and if I'm failing at that, I can deal. But what if I'm actually hurting her?" Janis put her arm around me in a side hug as we started walking toward the school.

"You're not," she said, "and your mom is not going to be cursed forever. It's something that I just know, just like I know you're my best friend and Pig's a good dog. But right now you're doing all that you know how to do, and when you learn how to do something else, you'll do that too. Besides, this weekend is gonna be awesome, one way or another."

"Crap," I said, reaching for my phone. "I was supposed to call Tom back and tell him what time the band is supposed to play on Saturday. I need to talk to Kendra and Karen." Interacting with the KKs, even when they were bespelled, was not exactly something I was looking forward to.

"Don't worry," Janis said, "I'm happy to do the honors. And I've also been coordinating with Cassandra and Amirah about when everyone gets in. Cassandra's going to borrow Dion's van so we can pick them up at the airport."

I gave a little laugh. "Amirah is going to looove Dion's van," I said.

"Oh yeah," Janis said. "It's going to be epic. If we're lucky, it'll die and everyone will have to get out and push." Janis squeezed me again. "We've got everything else under control, so I want you to listen to your dad, and pretend that this is just a normal school day."

"You mean stare out the window and count the minutes to lunch?" I asked.

"Exactly," she said.

"Got it," I said. "I'll try my best."

• • •

I made it through English, and then French, where Mademoi-selle Ferguson subjected us to a long lecture on the history of the baguette. I was walking to biology when Dad texted. **Mom okay,** he wrote. **You free for lunch?**

Sure, I wrote back. **I'm done at 12:15. I'll meet you outside.** Biology was actually kind of interesting, since we were study-ing plant life cycles and I was hoping to pick up some tips on how to keep my ficus from dying a slow, miserable death. As soon as the bell rang for lunch, I texted Janis that I'd meet up with her later, and walked outside to wait for Dad. He was right on time, and when I got into the car, I noticed some new scratches on his neck and that one side of his lower lip was swollen.

"So," he said, drumming on the steering wheel, "I think we should go someplace nice. TGI Fridays or Ruby Tuesday?"

"Um," I said, "Ruby Tuesday, I guess? It's a Friday, so TGI's is probably packed."

"Smart thinking," he said. "Too bad there's not a Manic Monday's or a Hell, Yeah, It's Humpday's."

I snorted. "I would not eat at either of those restaurants," I said. "Can you imagine the service at Manic Monday's? No one would be able to concentrate long enough to take your order."

Dad laughed, and then we drove in silence for a few blocks.

"So, how did this morning go?" I asked finally as we were pulling into the parking lot. Dad turned the car off, and touched his lip gently.

"Not great," he said. He unbuckled his seat belt and leaned back against the seat for a second.

"What happened when the nurse got there?" I asked.

He shook his head. "It was the weirdest thing," he said. "When she got there, Mom seemed fine, so we thought maybe it was just an isolated incident, but then I went over to say goodbye and she lashed out at me again." We both opened our doors and got out. "Same with Pig," he said as we started a cold walk across the parking lot. "She doesn't like the dog getting anywhere near her. But she was just fine with Olivia helping her." The parking lot was nearly empty, and we walked up the ramp to the glass doors. Dad pulled one open and held it for me. The inside of the restaurant was dark and quiet, and the hostess led us over to a booth by the window.

Dad and I sat down, and he pulled a menu over to him, opened it without reading anything, and then looked back up at me. "Kid, so the reason I wanted to take you to lunch . . . ," he said, and paused.

"Was so you could buy me a lot of mozzarella sticks?" I asked, trying to delay what I knew in the pit of my stomach he was going to say next.

"Well, that too," he said. "But Olivia and I were talking this morning, and I think Mom has to go back to the facility, at least for a while. It just seems like something changed, and she's just too unpredictable right now. I don't want you to get hurt, and I don't want her to get hurt."

The waitress appeared at our table, and hovered for a sec. Dad flipped the menu closed and ordered the crispy shrimp platter.

"I'll have a double order of mozzarella sticks," I said, and she nodded.

"That it?" she asked.

"And a large iced coffee," I added.

"Uh, we don't have iced coffee," she said. "We have hot coffee?"

I nodded. "That's fine," I said. "And can I get a cup of ice?"

"*Okaaay,* sure," she said, and walked away. I turned back to Dad, who was fiddling with a corner of his place mat.

"You don't think we can just hire someone else to help?" I asked, even though I felt like I knew the answer. "In addition to Olivia?"

"That's the thing," he said, "and I know this sounds weird, and"—he paused, and gave an ironic smile—"and particularly awful, but I don't think it's about just anyone. She was totally fine with Olivia. I think it's only me, and you, and Pig. It's like something happened between last night and this morning, and she's mad at us or has some sort of emotion toward us that she can't express in any other way."

"It's so fast," I said. "I mean, she has one bad day, and we send her back?"

Dad sighed. "I know, Esme, I know," he said. "But I'm trying to think preemptively here. If she stays with us, and something really bad happens, then . . ." He trailed off, and I nodded. He didn't need to finish, because I knew what he was thinking—something really bad was any one of several things that could take Mom away for good.

The waitress was back, and she set a very small cup of coffee and a very large glass of ice down in front of me. "Thanks," I said, and proceeded to pour one into the other. The ice melted almost instantly, but I unwrapped my straw anyway and took a long slurp. Not exactly coffee, but definitely coffee water. "I'm sorry," I said to Dad.

"It's not your fault, Esme," he said.

"I know," I said. "And everyone keeps telling me that, but I can still feel sorry about stuff that's out of my control. Like, this sucks. I can describe it a million different ways, but it all comes back to that: it just sucks."

The waitress appeared out of nowhere and set Dad's shrimp platter down in front of him, and my double order of mozzarella sticks. Dad and I both stared at my plate.

"Wow," he said finally. "That is a lot of fried cheese."

"Yeah," I agreed. "At least something's going right today."

I picked one up, dipped it into the sauce, and took a big bite. It was scalding hot, and almost against my own will, I spit it back out, and then took a gulp of my coffee water to try to soothe my soon-to-blister tongue. For some reason, the too-hot cheese tipped me over the edge, and I could feel the tears start to come again. "It's just . . . it's not fair," I said, my mouth full of ice. "It's not fair to me, but I'm a Sitter. But you . . . you've got a wife who's so cursed you can't even go near her, and you've got a daughter who'll probably never do anything normal ever again."

Dad smiled, then reached over and took a mozzarella stick off my plate. He broke it in half, blew on it, and then popped one half into my mouth. "Esme, I hate to break it to you, but you've never been normal, not even before you knew you were a Sitter. Remember first grade?"

I chewed and swallowed. "What happened in first grade?" I asked.

"Well, you wore a life jacket and a 'Happy New Year' crown to school every day for at least two months," he said.

"Fashion, Dad. You wouldn't understand." I smiled and looked down at my plate. "I guess I'm just feeling sorry for myself right now," I said. "Even if I do have all this cheese."

"That's okay," Dad said, taking a bite of his shrimp. "Cheese or no cheese, that's allowed."

"Like, sometimes I just find myself wishing I didn't know that Mom was cursed," I said. "Because knowing that there's a way out, and that I just don't know what it is, only makes things more difficult."

Dad nodded and chewed. "Esme," he said, "you want to know the scariest day of my life?"

"Sure," I said.

"The day you were born," he said. "I loved you so much that it terrified me. I took one look at you and knew I would do anything I could to protect you, and I knew that I had no idea how. I still feel like that, and knowing what you do as a Sitter scares the crap out of me. Do I sometimes wish I didn't know you were out there chasing demons? On a superficial level, maybe. But deep down, I'm glad I know, because that means I get to know the real you. I get to see you be your true self and live the life that was meant for you. Sometimes people choose to live a lie, or believe one, because that's easier. But I'm not like that, and neither are you. We can handle the truth." He gave a little laugh, then made his face serious. "We can handle the truth!" he said, his voice all weird.

"What was that?" I asked.

"Sorry, my Jack Nicholson impression. *A Few Good Men*? Tom Cruise?"

I shook my head. "No idea," I said.

"Never mind," he said. "Anyway, what I've learned in my

decades on this planet is that as life gets bigger, the hurts hit harder. The only way to not get hurt is to not care, and that's not how we do things, you and me. That's not how your mom does things either."

"Thanks," I said, smiling at him. "You give one heck of a motivational speech, Dad."

"Thanks," he said. "It all depends on having a good audience."

"I don't really wish I didn't know," I went on. "It's just . . . a lot sometimes."

"Of course it is," Dad said. "Protecting the innocent is no small task, but you're up for it. And I don't want you to think that Mom's never going to be able to live with us again. This is just a rough patch. We'll get through it."

"Our whole life has kinda been a rough patch," I said, smiling at Dad.

"That's not true!" he said. "Remember when the Chiefs won the Super Bowl a couple of years ago?"

"That's that big tennis tournament that's held in England every year?" I asked.

"Har-de-har-har," he said. "And also, need I remind you that our dog came back last night? That's pretty darn lucky, if you ask me."

I smiled, thinking about Pig. "I don't think Pig is a dog," I said, and Dad cocked an eyebrow at me.

"You mean she's an intergalactic being sent here to teach us about love?" he asked.

I smiled. "Yeah, something like that." Sometimes Dad really did get it.

Dad and I each made dents in our lunch, and then the

waitress was back, looking down at my plate. "You want me to get you a box for that?" she asked. "I can see if we have one big enough." I nodded, and she swooped the plate away, and then reappeared a few moments later and dropped my doggy bag onto the table with a thud before handing Dad the check. He slipped a couple of bills onto the table, I hefted my leftovers, and then we got up and made our way to the door.

"So," he said as we were walking back into the parking lot, "this bird. You guys just friends?"

"Dad," I groaned. "Not today, okay?"

CHAPTER 11

Dad dropped me back at school, and Cassandra was waiting for me at my locker. She stepped aside so that I could open it, and then I saw her nostrils crinkle. "What smells like mozzarella sticks?" she asked.

I lifted my lunch leftovers into view. "That would be this bag of mozzarella sticks," I said.

"I'll give you three bucks for it," she said.

I handed it over to her. "I'm feeling generous today," I said. "You can have it for free." She grinned, and dug in, eating a stick in two bites.

"So, Janis told me about this morning," she said after she swallowed.

"Yeah," I said as I shut my locker. "It sucked."

"What are you guys going to do?" she asked.

I started walking to class, and she followed, making fast work of the mozz.

"My dad is moving her back into the facility this afternoon," I said. "I guess it seems like she's okay with other people, just not us?" At those words, I could feel my eyes get hot again, so I quickly tried to think about candy and baby kangaroos, because I didn't want to cry at school.

"You should talk to Ruby," she said.

"I know," I said. "I was planning on doing that." Ruby's grandmother had been somewhat of a scholar on curses, and Ruby had picked up a lot from her.

"She and Mallory's flight gets in at four," she said. "And Amirah and Ji-A get in before that. You're coming with me and Janis to pick them up, right?"

I thought about it for a second. That was what I'd always planned on, but now I wasn't so sure. I knew I should go check on Mom, or go home to be with Dad, since I thought he'd probably taken the whole day off work.

"You should come," Cassandra said, pulling me out of my thoughts. "You can go check on your mom tomorrow. Esme, this weekend is going to be really fun. You need to have some fun." She chewed and swallowed another bite. "We need to have some fun."

"You're right," I said, realizing she was right as I said it. "I'll come."

Cassandra looked into the bag and scowled. It was apparently empty, which meant that she had eaten approximately eleven mozzarella sticks in the time that it had taken to walk to my government class. She crumpled the bag and tossed it, arcing it into the trash can across the hall.

"Hey," I said, "maybe Mallory should stay with me this weekend? That way you and Ruby can just hang out."

A smile flashed across Cassandra's face, and it lingered in her eyes. "Yeah," she said, "that'd be great."

"So, I'll meet you at the van after school?" I asked.

Cassandra flashed me a thumbs-up as she walked away, headed toward the door that was in the opposite direction from any of her classes. I went into class thinking that maybe Dad was right and I wasn't so unlucky after all. I did have pretty great friends.

I made it through government without getting into an argument with Mr. Sutton about his thinly veiled libertarian beliefs. One would think that the fact that he and I were on opposite ends of the political spectrum would work against me, but I actually think I was one of Mr. Sutton's favorite students, owing to the fact that I was awake most of the time and could correctly identify the vice president. Or, for that matter, the president. I will never forget the look on Mr. Sutton's face when Liz O'Reilly gave a presentation on the forty-fourth president of the United States with a picture of Jordan Peele glued to her poster board.

My last class of the day was pottery, another class in which I was a standout student, considering that we were now more than a month into the semester and I had yet to make a bong and try to pass it off as a bud vase. In that class, I was working on Janis's birthday present—which was a legit bud vase, in the shape of Grace Jones's head—and I had to say, it was coming along nicely. I was especially pleased with my vase's cheekbones.

When the final bell rang, I scrubbed the clay from under my nails and hurried out to the parking lot. Janis and Cassandra were already waiting by the van, and when Janis saw me, she gave me a big hug. "How are you doing?" she asked when she finally pulled away.

"Good, I think," I said, and I heaved the van's sliding door open and started to climb in. "It is what it is, and I'm happy to have this distraction." Janis shut the door after me, since the inside had no door handle, and then she climbed into the passenger seat. Cassandra got into the driver's seat and turned the key, causing all three of us to hold our breaths for a second, as an ill-timed backfire could send the entire parking lot ducking for cover. Fortunately, the van just gave a few sputters before we were on our way.

The Spring River airport was, as was to be expected, small, with just one terminal and only, it seemed, direct flights to places that you could easily drive to. We were halfway there when Janis's phone dinged. "Ji-A and Amirah got in early," she told us, "so I guess they're getting something to eat." She turned around in her seat and gave me a frightened look. I met her gaze with a grimace. There was only one restaurant at the airport, and that restaurant was Panda Sub. The last, and only other, time she'd been in Spring River, Amirah had bemoaned the lack of uni, so I couldn't imagine what she was going to order at a place that served General Tso's chicken on an Asiago bagel.

"Should we warn them?" I asked Janis.

"I think it's too late," she said as her phone dinged again. "Ji-A just sent me a picture of her teriyaki iced tea."

When Cassandra pulled up outside the airport and stopped at the arrivals door, I noticed the security guard eyeing the van warily, no doubt half-worried that we were there to bomb the place. But then Janis jumped out and pulled open the sliding door, and happy screams filled the air as Amirah and Ji-A came bursting through the revolving door, rolling suitcases clattering on the ground behind them.

Amirah and Ji-A were both dressed in travel-uniform sweat suits. But, of course, as soon as they got close, I could tell that these weren't just any sweat suits. Ji-A's hoodie and joggers were oversized to the point of almost swallowing her up, and they were matching monochrome, in a color that I could only describe as a beautifully depressed rose. "Oh my God," I gushed, gesturing to her look, "I love that."

"Thanks!" she squealed as she threw her arms around me in a hug. "It's all organic and dyed from flowers. I can send you the pre-order code for their next drop!"

"Yeah, awesome," I said, knowing that her hoodie alone probably cost as much as Dad's car. On her feet were bright green Balenciaga sneakers, the color of a tree frog, and she had a black Carhartt bucket hat on her head. Lots of people in Spring River wore Carhartt, but none of them looked anything like Ji-A. She had finished this look with an ever-practical black denim Off-White cross-body bag with a bright yellow logo strap, and a brushed aluminum suitcase that looked like something James Bond would use to smash someone in the face and knock them out the side of an airplane.

Whereas Ji-A had gone for a swimming-in-sweats look, Amirah's sweat suit was sleek, fitted, and all black. She had on a cropped Palm Angels hoodie with a cutout at the neck, slim-fit Dsquared2 joggers, and black Balenciaga speed sneakers. Her suitcase, like Ji-A's, looked like it was built to survive an explosion, and her bag was an architectural black backpack from the Row. I saw a woman trying to sneakily take Amirah's picture, no doubt convinced that she was in the presence of a celebrity. Amirah didn't notice, though, as she and Janis were engaged in a mutual hug-and-squeal fest as they complimented each other's outfits, and when they finally broke it off, Amirah turned toward me and I got a good glimpse of the front of her baseball cap. It wasn't Rick Owens, or Gucci, or Burberry, or any of the other brands I would expect from Amirah.

It was from Panda Sub.

Amirah was a hugger, and she gripped me hard, picked me up off the ground, and spun me around. "I am so glad we're here!" she said as she set me down. "New York has been a total borefest lately, and if I had to go to one more fashion week party, I was gonna barf into my bucket bag."

I stifled a laugh, as the mere thought of fashion week parties made me sweaty with jealousy. "Sounds awful," I said. "Hey, is that an employee hat?" Amirah turned from side to side, grinning with pride as she modeled it.

"Yeah," Ji-A said. "She paid some dude named Larry fifty bucks for it."

Fifty was probably more than Larry made in a shift.

"Why didn't you guys tell me about Panda Sub when we were here last?" Amirah asked, looking at me, Janis, and Cassandra accusingly.

"I'm sorry," Cassandra said. "We woulda warned you, but—" Amirah wasn't listening, and cut Cass off.

"OMG, it is amazing!" she said. "I mean, if you ask anyone who knows me, they will tell you that my favorite foods are Chinese and Italian." She looked at Ji-A. "Right, Ji-A?"

"Totally," Ji-A said, and I swear I could see a hint of amusement on her face.

"So a place that combines the two, and I am in heaven," Amirah continued. "I mean, have you tried their Bolognese egg rolls? To die for. Literally. Like, I might be dead now. Wait," she said, stopping her five-star review of Panda Sub to point at the van. "What is that?"

"It's your ride," Cassandra said, tugging open the sliding door.

"Oh," Amirah said. "Cute." And then she threw her suitcase in. I'd never seen her in such a good mood. Ji-A followed suit, and Janis and I climbed in after them.

"This is cool," Ji-A said. "I've never been in a van without seats before." She stopped and thought for a minute. "I don't even know if I've been in a van before."

"Me either," Amirah said. "Unless a limo counts?"

"It does not," I said.

Amirah dug into her purse, and then held something out. "You want a mint?" she asked. "They're the same ones I always have. You know, those seaweed ones from Japan? But now these have THC."

"Uh, no thanks," I said. If I remembered correctly, Amirah's mints tasted like the underside of a toad, and I was willing to bet that the amount of THC they contained meant that a lightweight like me could probably get high just by looking at them.

"Suit yourself," Amirah said. She shook three into her hand and then popped them into her mouth.

Cassandra stayed outside, leaning against the van, and out of the corner of my eye, I watched her for a second. I couldn't see her legs, but I was sure her foot was bouncing, and she was chewing the heck out of her thumbnail, two classic signs that

Cassandra was nervous. I guessed I would be too if my IRL reunion with the person I'd been texting with nonstop was going to happen in the presence of basically everyone I knew.

All of our phones dinged at the same time. "Looks like they just landed," Ji-A said. Outside the van, Cassandra stood up straighter and took her hand out of her mouth.

Another ding. "They're off the plane," Janis read.

Ding. "Stopping so Ruby can pee," Amirah said.

Ding. "Oh no," I said. "Mallory's starving, so they're stopping at Panda Sub to grab a snack."

"Should I ask her to bring me something for later?" Amirah asked.

"There are Panda Subs everywhere," I assured her.

"Oh good," she said.

Ding. "Ruby left her phone on the plane," Janis read.

Two minutes passed and another ding. "She got it," Ji-A said.

Two more minutes. *Ding.* "I guess Mallory checked her laptop and it hasn't shown up yet?" Amirah read.

Ding. "Never mind," I said. "Laptop was in her carry-on."

"Checked bag still not here," Ji-A read. A few beats, then another ding.

"Bags are here," Janis read. Jeez. This was shaping up to be the most anticipated arrival in Spring River since that time Britney Spears's private plane ran out of gas and had to do an emergency landing.

Then, no more dings, and there they were, coming out of the revolving doors with smiles on their faces and Panda Sub cups in their hands. Janis, Amirah, Ji-A, and I tumbled back out of the van and surrounded Mallory. Out of the corner of my eye, I saw Cassandra step toward Ruby kind of awkwardly, and I turned away, wanting to give them as much privacy as possible, and climbed into the van.

"So," I asked Mallory as we all climbed back in and tried to get comfortable on the floor, "did you find anything you liked at Panda Sub?" Mallory was an insanely picky eater whose tastes ran toward bland and breakfast, but to my surprise, she nodded and grinned.

"Oh my God, it's so good!" she said. "That broccoli-parm rangoon with the sweet-and-sour dipping sauce? Like, it may be my new favorite food."

"Ooh," Amirah said, nodding in agreement. "I'll have to try that next time. Esme assures me that Panda Sub is every-where in Spring River."

"Yay, what a relief," Mallory said, "because I was just think-ing that it would be super silly to come all the way back to the airport just to get breakfast, but I was totally down to do it."

"It's Spring River," I said, "so 'all the way back to the air-port' is, like, a five-minute drive, but there's one that's even closer to my house. So, how was your flight?"

"Flights," Mallory said. "We flew from Miami to Memphis to St. Louis, and then here, but they were all fine. Ruby got a little freaked out on that last flight, and said she didn't want to go down like Aaliyah."

"No joke," Ji-A said. "Those planes are almost as small as flying private, but way scarier."

"Did it not remind you of that one we took in Saint-Tropez?" Amirah said to Ji-A. "I mean, except for the fact that that flight was over turquoise crystal waters and this one was over . . ." She turned to me. "So, what do you call this kind of landscape anyway?" she asked. "Is there a word for when something is all brown and flat with nothing on it?"

"The plains," I said. "It's called the plains."

"That makes sense," Amirah said, looking very serious as she nodded.

Ruby and Cassandra must have finished getting re-acquainted, at least for now, because the next thing I knew, Ruby was screaming "Helllooo" and launching herself into the back of the van, tossing the rest of us into a dog pile. There was another round of hugs and squeals, and then Ruby climbed back up into the passenger seat. Even when she wasn't flying, Ruby's look was very "pop star on a coffee run," and it was equal parts comfy and glam. Today she had on a cream-colored Adidas tracksuit with a cropped tank top underneath, and then everything else about her was gold, from her hoop earrings to her layered necklaces, her backpack, her high-shine lip gloss, and the highlighter dusted across her cheeks. She looked like human sunshine, and I realized she must really be into Cassandra to come here, where the only beach was at a man-made lake and riddled with copperheads.

"Wait," I said as she took a sip from a cup. "What did you get at Panda Sub?" Ruby was the healthiest eater I'd ever met. She even ate fruit for dessert.

"Water with lemon," she said, and took a sip, then looked around. "Cass, I like this van."

"Yeah, it's real incognito," Cassandra said as she pushed it into gear and started to drive away. "We blend right in with all the pervs and weirdos."

"So, what are we doing this weekend?" Mallory asked.

"Right now I'm going to take everyone to drop your stuff

off, and change or whatever," Cassandra said, and I was super impressed that she was acknowledging the fact that sometimes people had to change their clothes. Janis gave everyone a rundown on brunch at Brian's—"Cute," squealed Amirah, which was apparently how she described everything these days, and Ruby asked if he needed us to bring anything—and then said that we would go thrifting in the afternoon.

"So, 'thrifting,'" Ruby started. "You mean, like, buying dead people's clothes?"

"They're not all from dead people—" I started, but Cassandra interrupted.

"The great thing about thrifting is that you can buy a pair of used jeans, and only maybe someone died in them, but they definitely farted in them," she said.

"Don't listen to her," I assured Amirah. "I've found Halston on the racks before."

"We can always skip out and go to the gym," Cassandra assured Ruby.

"That sounds like a great idea!" I said enthusiastically. I'd taken Cassandra thrifting before, and it had not been pretty. She managed to break a VCR, and I will never forget her screams when she happened to find some pornographic Polaroids wedged into a copy of a Mother Goose book. Plus, she was obsessed with the fact that someone might have (okay, probably had) farted in the pants.

"Then, tomorrow night, there's a school dance," Janis said. "And Esme booked the band."

"Wait," Mallory said, "what are we doing Sitter-wise? I mean, the last time we were here, we pretty much helped overthrow the government, and Cassandra's also the only Sitter

I've ever known who went to the Negative after summoning the Portal in an abandoned mall. You two are like the most epic Sitters in the whole Sitterhood right now. I didn't come all this way just to eat brunch and go shopping."

I watched Mallory, and my jaw almost dropped. The Mallory I had met two months before had been a meek little thing who'd lived off protein bars. This Mallory was dipping broccoli-parm rangoon and looking to stir up trouble. I certainly wasn't the only one who noticed a change, because everyone else went quiet as well, and then Ruby's laughter broke in from the front seat.

"Have you met the new Mal?" she asked. "She's quite assertive."

I looked back at Mallory, who smiled and shrugged. "I started listening to these empowerment podcasts," she said, "and I realized a couple of things. One, I am definitely a feminist, and two, I'm really tired of doing stuff I don't want to do."

"Heck yeah," Amirah said, reaching over to give her a fist bump.

"But anyway," Janis continued. "The school dance *is* Sitter stuff. Esme, tell them about Jump the Shark."

"Is that like cow tipping?" Ruby asked. "I think that sounds mean." I shook my head, and started at the beginning. It turned out that Cassandra had already told Ruby about the break-in, our main suspects, the band, and the possibility that her mom was being held captive in their house. Cass just hadn't mentioned the band's name because she couldn't keep up with what it was. So now Janis and I filled everyone else in.

"Tomorrow night we'll split up," I finished. "Half of us will go to the dance, and the other half will do a little B and E, I guess."

"Team B and E," Ruby called out, shooting her hand into the air.

"Good," I said. "Their house is dripping in spells, so it might not be as easy as breaking a window."

"Or kicking down a door," Cassandra said.

"Yeah, uh, that either," I said.

"Maybe we could go tonight and do some recon?" Ruby said, turning to Cassandra. "We might need to gather some stuff to break the spells we run into."

Cassandra nodded.

"I can go with you tomorrow night," Mallory said. "If Cassandra's mom is there—and I hope it doesn't come to this—she might need my help." Mallory had a healing kinesis, which had come in very handy the last time she'd been here, when so many Sitters had gotten hurt at the Summit. Cassandra nodded again, and from where I was sitting, I could see her jaw tighten.

"Thanks," she said.

"So we're team dance, then," Ji-A said. "I'm cool with that. Maybe I can find something to wear when we go thrifting?"

"Sounds good," I said, and then sat back in awe. It seemed nuts, but we had reinforcements and a plan. Maybe this would work out after all?

As Cassandra drove, everyone chattered, catching up on everything that had happened in the past two months. Ruby and Mallory had been dealing with a rash of Cloak demons at the beach, which were tricky things, able to take on the guise of whatever was around them. "It's crazy," Ruby said. "They'll just look like sand, or a beach towel, or sometimes even just people in the distance, so if we're not careful, people walk right into a Cloak and don't even know what's hit them."

"I've actually had to use my powers a lot lately," Mallory said. "So I end up telling people that they were stung by a jellyfish and that my dad's a marine biologist, and I know just what to do."

"And people buy that?" Janis asked, and Mallory nodded vigorously.

"They don't ask a ton of questions," she said. "They're just happy they're not getting peed on."

"In New York, we've had problems with the subways," Ji-A said. "Have you guys ever heard of a Noxious demon?"

Mallory and I shook our heads.

"It literally has no form," she continued. "It's just like a cloud of bad smell. Which on the subway, that could be anything, you know? It's wasted so much of our time these past few weeks. Last Tuesday, Amirah and I spent almost an hour tracking what turned out to be just a tub of sauerkraut on someone's long commute. It's very frustrating."

"Wait," I said. "So if you guys are here, who's watching the subways and beaches while you're gone?"

"It's V-Day weekend, remember?" Mallory said. "Demons hate romance, so at most, they'll cause a couple of fights or eat all the good ones out of a box of chocolate, but nothing that would prevent us from having this much needed vacay."

Ji-A nodded in agreement, and I sat back, kind of amazed. Almost four months of Sitting and one Summit under my belt, and I still had so much to learn.

"Wait!" Amirah said, leaning over and slapping my knee. "Tell us about Pig!"

"I don't know." I shrugged. "She just came back? It's crazy."

"You're sure it's the same dog?" Ji-A asked.

"Yeah," I said. "It's definitely her, except . . ." I trailed off.

"Is she okay?" Mallory asked. "Was she hurt?"

"She seems fine," I said. "She's skinny, and limping a little, and hungrier than normal, but she's very happy to be back."

"I can't wait to see her!" Amirah said.

"Where do you think she was?" Ji-A asked.

"We have no idea," I said. "It seems like maybe someone else was taking care of her?"

Ruby nodded. "My grandma had a cat that came back once after eight months," she said. "It turns out, some other family thought they had adopted him."

I nodded. "Maybe . . ." As always, though, whenever I thought about Pig, nothing added up. But we were about to see her in a minute, because Cassandra had pulled up in front of my house. "This is us," I said to Mallory, and grabbed her bags to help her with them.

"Hang at my house later?" Cassandra called as we climbed out of the van.

"We'll pick you up in a couple of hours," Janis yelled, before I could answer, and then Ruby slammed the door shut and they drove off.

Looking up at my house, I felt insanely grateful for my van full of friends, and for the fact that Mallory was staying with me this weekend. Pig might have been back, but the house was still going to feel very empty with Mom gone, and it would be nice to have someone there as a distraction.

CHAPTER 12

Mallory dropped her stuff off in my room, and I tried—bravely and valiantly—to clean it up while she showered. Pig was close at my heels the whole time, and definitely grunted some disapproval as I picked up the piles of clothes from the floor. I managed to make some space where Mallory could keep her suitcase, and cleared off the back of my chair in case she wanted to hang up some of her clothes. I found a clean towel for her, which was too late for this shower but might come in handy in the morning, and sheets to make up a bed on the couch.

I realized I hadn't told Dad that I would be having anyone over tonight, but when I texted him, he responded with a thumbs-up. It turned out he was still at Mom's facility getting things settled there, but he seemed happy that I was hanging out with "friends" and doing "normal" things for the night.

After the shower, Mallory blow-dried her hair and got dressed, and we hung out in my room. I hadn't gotten to know her that well at the Summit—because I hadn't gotten to know anyone that well—but I liked Mallory. She was funny, into books, and a sharp observer. She was also besotted with Pig, and I told her the whole story, about how Pig had just appeared to us one day like a vision in a parking lot and had never left.

"She's helped in rituals before too," I said. "And she was really good at it, because she knows how to sit and stay. But Brian did some research, and hasn't been able to find any other examples of when a ritual worked with an animal. So . . ." Pig scratched an ear, and then chewed an itch. "It's almost like she's not a dog?"

"Yeah, weird," Mallory said, getting up and moving over toward her, and Pig looked up as Mallory raised her hands. Mallory started at Pig's ears, and then slowly moved her hands down, staying just a few inches away. Pig whimpered a few times, and when Mallory stepped back, she had a puzzled look on her face.

"What?" I asked her.

"She had a few fractures that were almost healed," Mallory said, "so I helped those along. And she's still really hungry, but other than that, she's in pretty good shape." Mallory looked at Pig again. "I mean, I'm no veterinarian, but I'd say she's in excellent shape for a dog that flew off a building just two months ago." Pig lay down with a contented sigh.

"I know," I agreed. "It's a miracle."

"It sure is," Mallory said, still looking at Pig. Even without her saying anything, I knew what she was thinking, because I was thinking it too. In the Sitterverse, much like coincidences, miracles didn't exist. Mallory held her hands out again, and frowned.

"There is one weird thing, though," she said. "How old is Pig?"

"We're not sure," I said, "but probably seven or eight."

"The only thing I'm picking up is that she's much older."

"Like, ten?"

Mallory shook her head. "Like, seventies?"

"Dog years, maybe?"

"I guess," Mallory said as Pig settled down with a snort.

Soon Janis was texting from outside; she'd come to pick us up to hang out at Cassandra's. I fed Pig, giving her so much food that it spilled out the top of the bowl and onto the floor, and then we left. As we climbed into the car, my phone dinged, and I checked it to see a text from Brian for me and Cassandra. As was to be totally expected, he was spinning out about brunch, and wanted to know what we thought about a "build-your-own-bagel bar." The text was to Cassandra and me, but I figured that she probably wouldn't respond.

> I'm not sure what that is.
>
> You get bagels, cream cheese, onions, everything. And you go down the line and add whatever you want to your bagel yourself.
>
> So it's like Subway? Do we get visors?
>
> Nvrmnd. I'll think of something else.

I didn't want Brian to feel too dejected, because it was sweet that he was trying to do something for all of us. In Janis's car, Amirah had shotgun, so Mallory and I squeezed into the back with Ji-A.

"Hey," I said to them, "Brian needs more specifics about

brunch. In an ideal world, what would you guys want to eat?"
Everyone answered at the same time.

"Cinnamon Toast Crunch," Mallory said.

"Macaroons," replied Ji-A.

"Chocolate croissants," Amirah said.

"Lucky Charms," Janis said.

I myself would prefer doughnuts.

> I just did an informal poll. And pastries and
> sugar cereals are the clear winners. I can't
> ask them, because I'm not with them, but I'm
> sure Ruby will want some green juice, and
> Cassandra's been really into hot dogs lately.

The dancing ellipsis popped up, then disappeared, then popped up again.

> I think I'm just going to go online and get some
> ideas.

Poor Brian. At least Pinterest never let him down.

Janis pulled up to Cassandra's and parked at the curb. We all piled out of the car, crossed the yard, and walked in without knocking, like Janis and I always did, but I grimaced as soon as I saw Cassandra and Ruby, both flushed, sitting on the couch. I made a mental note that no-knock entries should be saved for singletons like me. They didn't seem to mind too much, though, and soon everyone was discussing what kind of pizza to order.

"Oooh," Amirah gasped. "Can we get Panda Sub delivered?"

Mallory nodded vigorously, and thank God Janis jumped in.

"Their delivery area is really weird," she said in such a convincing way that I started to wonder if maybe she was telling the truth. "And I don't think they'll come here." Eventually we settled on four pizzas—including a whole one with pineapple, because apparently Ruby liked it too—two orders of breadsticks, two two-liters of Coke, and one green salad, for you know who. Amirah even used her credit card to buy everyone dinner. When Janis passed the phone to her so that she could give the pizza place the number, I thought I was going to die when Amirah said, "So, you guys do take black cards, don't you? . . . No, it's not a Discover . . ."

I was kind of impressed with how much Cassandra had cleaned up, or with how many cleaning spells she had used, because the house looked good and almost homey. It still didn't have anything that signified an adult lived there—like dish soap or paper towels—but there was a bowl of fresh fruit on the counter, something that I had never seen in her house before, ever.

"Where's Dion?" I asked her.

"He's taking a shower," she said, then paused. "I figured I'd let him hang out. If he wants." There was a tone in her voice that I'd never heard before, and with a shock, I realized what it was—Cassandra was asking permission.

"Yeah, sure," I said. "Your call."

She nodded. "He's been pretty okay lately."

Then my phone started to buzz because Dad was calling, and I hurried out to the front porch and answered it. "Hey," I said, holding my breath a little bit.

"Hey, kid," he said, his voice weary. "How's it going?"

"Good," I said. "I'm over at Cassandra's. We're getting pizza and going to watch some movies and stuff."

"That sounds fun," he said.

"How's Mom?"

"Well, I just left the facility," he said, "and she seemed pretty settled." He paused, and I braced myself for whatever he was going to say next. "I hope this isn't too hard to hear," he continued, "but it almost seems like she was happy to go back. She didn't lash out at anyone there, and let them help her quite a bit."

"How was she to you?" I asked, and he gave a sardonic little laugh.

"Let's just say I will be applying lots of that arnica gel as soon as I get home," he answered. "I never thought I'd need it for this. Kinda breaks my heart, if I'm being honest."

"Yeah, mine too," I said, thinking of our first aid supplies, left over from Dad's failed one-week attempt to make Muay Thai his thing. We were quiet, I think probably both worried that if we delved too deeply into the subject right then, we wouldn't be able to pull ourselves back out.

"Mallory and I won't be home too late," I said.

"Sounds good," he said. "I'll be happy to meet her. And your other friend? Where is he tonight?"

I looked up at the trees. "I don't know," I said.

"I'm sorry," Dad said, surprising me.

"Yeah, me too," I said, then added, "All right. Love you. Don't wait up."

"Love you too," he said. "And I won't."

I hung up and stood there for a moment, listening as hard as I could. No bird sounds, though. Just branches and tires. I heard the door open behind me. I turned, expecting it to be Janis or Cassandra coming to check up on me, but it was Ruby.

"Hey," I said.

"Hey," she said, then sat down on the porch swing and wrapped her arms around her knees. "Jeez, it is so cold here. I'm like a lizard. I need a warm rock."

"You should come back in the summer," I told her. "It's so hot and humid that stepping outside feels like going for a swim in the bathtub."

"That sounds divine," she said with a smile. She looked away, then looked back at me. "Hey, I don't mean to pry, but Cass told me something kind of gnarly happened with your mom this morning. We definitely do not have to talk about this if you don't want to."

I sat down next to her on the swing, and the metal chain gave a plaintive creak. "No, it's cool," I said. "I want to talk about it, especially with you."

"So, what happened?" she asked, and I told her about the digging, and the biting, and the kicking.

"She's never been like that before," I said. "And she was happy at our house, I know it. I wasn't just projecting that on her. It felt like we were a family again. We were learning how to be broken and whole at the same time."

Ruby nodded. "So, Pig came back the night before?"

"Yeah," I said. "And then the next morning, Mom just flipped." I could see Ruby working something out in her head. "What would your grandma say?" I asked.

"She was too happy," Ruby answered finally.

"Your grandma?"

She shook her head. "No, your mom," she said. "I think that you were probably right. She was really happy being at home with you and your dad, but something about Pig coming home made her too happy."

I sniffed. "Is there even such a thing?"

"With curses, yeah," she said. "The whole point of a curse is a punishment, right? And how do we punish people?"

"I don't know," I said.

"Yeah, you do," she said. "You're a babysitter, so I'm sure that you have to punish people all the time."

"Well, you take stuff away from them," I said. "Like, you take away their video games or make them go to their room and don't let them play outside. But it has to be something they care about. Otherwise it won't make an impact."

"Exactly," Ruby said. "You take away what makes them happy. So, your mom's curse will take away what makes her happy, which is her family. So if she gets too happy, her curse will activate to remove whatever caused the happiness."

I sat there, looking out into the dark of Cassandra's street, and let Ruby's words sink in. "So, as long as she's cursed, Mom will never be able to experience true happiness?"

"I don't know for sure," Ruby answered. "I mean, I'm just guessing, based on what I've read in my grandma's papers. Oh, yay, the pizza's here." I looked at her, confused, as there was no pizza in sight. Then a second later, a car turned the corner, drove down the street, and parked in front of Cassandra's. Ruby's kinesis was that she was psychic, but she only saw about five seconds into the future. It made her a fierce fighter, but otherwise her power was so subtle that I sometimes forgot about it. The driver got out, unloaded a bunch of pizzas from the backseat, and then started walking toward the house. He spied us, and called out.

"I've got an order for Mariah," he said.

Ruby smiled and stood up. "I'll get her," she said, disappearing inside.

I'd never been one to ignore a pizza guy, but all I could think about was Mom. Her curse was a prison. A horrible, unfair prison, and I was going to smash it, no matter what it took.

The door slapped open, making me jump as Amirah swished out to sign for the pizza. Cassandra was right behind her, and took the food and headed back inside. "Seriously?" Amirah said, looking up from the receipt. "This has to be wrong, right? All these pizzas cannot be this cheap!"

She held up the receipt for the delivery guy, who looked back at her, confused. Clearly no customer had ever accused him of not charging enough before.

"No, uh, ma'am," he said. "That's correct."

"I love it here," Amirah said, adding a tip and signing with a flourish. "It's so . . . affordable! It's like monopoly money!" She handed the receipt back to the delivery guy, and I could see his eyebrows rise as he took in the amount.

"Wow, thanks," he said, looking back up at her, but Amirah had already turned around and was headed toward me.

"Esme, come on," she said, grabbing my arm. "Come eat! And tell me everything. Are you going to make Pig an account? She could get so many followers! It's too bad the chickens are back in New York. If they were all in one place, they could do cameos on each other's feeds and that would be huge. . . ."

I let her pull me back into the house, where Cassandra and Ruby were spreading out the food and plates and cups on the table. Janis and Mallory were talking about feminism. Dion sat on the couch, trying to follow along as Ji-A explained something about astrology and did calculations on a piece of paper.

I looked around, wanting to feel happy. I was surrounded by people who knew, and apparently liked, me for exactly who I was. I wasn't lying to my dad or my best friend anymore. I still didn't know what to think about Adrian, but I knew he hadn't ghosted me. And my dog had come home. But as long as Mom couldn't be happy, then I couldn't either.

We demolished the pizzas and did the kind of getting-to-know-you that we hadn't done at the Summit. I mostly hung back, listening to people tell stories, and I found myself in a position I had rarely been in before, one where the more I learned about people, the more I liked them, and not the other way around.

Ruby talked about how hard it had been for her to quit boxing, even though she knew it was the right thing to do because her kinesis gave her an unfair advantage. But now she was working at the gym as a coach, and her youngest trainee was an eight-year-old girl. "I swear," Ruby said, her always-radiant face beaming even more, "she's going to win a gold medal someday. I've never met anyone else with such focus. Well, almost anyone else." At this, her eyes glanced toward Cass, who'd been watching her rapturously but now quickly shifted her gaze down to the floor.

"I got in a fight once," Mallory said, causing everyone's head to swivel toward her.

"What?" Ruby squealed. "You never told me that!"

Mallory rolled her eyes and grimaced. "It's kind of embarrassing," she said. "It was at my Jewish summer camp when I was ten. I got really mad when this girl from Tampa hung her towel on my hook, so I pulled her hair and hit her."

"Mal!" Ruby gasped. "That does not sound like you, at all!"

"Well," Cassandra said with a grin, "who won?"

"Me, I think," Mallory said, slowly starting to smile. "But I felt so bad that I cried."

"Now, that does sound like you," Ruby said.

I was also shocked to find out that neither Ji-A nor Amirah had their driver's licenses. What was more, they had no desire to drive, and had never even been behind the wheel of a car.

"Not even a go-kart?" Cassandra asked.

Ji-A shook her head while Amirah asked, "What's a go-kart?"

"It's like a small car," Cassandra said, "that goes—"

"Sounds boring," Amirah said. "I just don't understand why anyone would drive when you could just have someone else do it for you."

Ji-A rolled her eyes, then looked at me. "Seriously, though, Esme," she said, "don't bother with your license. Just move to New York."

Eventually Cassandra got up and got the Jacking Lanterns flyer, and passed it around so that everyone could see.

"Is this one of those things where it's so bad that it goes back to good?" Ji-A said, taking a long look at it before she handed it over to Amirah.

"I don't think so," Janis said. "As Enid Coleslaw would say, it's so bad, it's gone past good and back to bad again."

"Who's that?" Ruby asked. "Someone you go to school with?"

"Never mind," Janis said quickly. "So, I called Tom today—from the band—and told them to be there tomorrow night at seven, and that they go on at eight. Esme, you and I should be there to meet them, and I'm assuming that Karen and Kendra will be there too, now that they're, like, in looove with this band."

"Wait," Ji-A said. "So people at your school actually like this band?"

Cassandra gave a snort. "No," she said. "Esme cast a little spell to convince the dance committee."

"Well done," Ruby said, smiling.

"Oh!" Amirah said. "So that's what you needed the popularis spell for. I was wondering."

"Yeah," I said. "Trust me, I'm not trying to win prom queen."

"You'd look really cute in a crown," Ji-A said.

"Totally," Amirah agreed. "Like one of those little yellow diamond ones from Tiffany! You would look just like a petite pixie princess!"

"Thanks," I said. "I'll look into that."

"The dance is at the school?" Ji-A asked.

"In the school gym," I said. "I know, it's like the lamest—"

But Amirah interrupted me by clapping her hands. "We get to go to a dance! In a gym!" she said with a squeal. "This is going to be the best weekend ever!"

"You don't have dances in New York?" Janis asked.

"Oh no, we do," she said. "But our school's gym is an Equi-nox, and there's no way we could have a dance there, so they were always someplace boring. Like the Met."

"How awful," I said, unable to keep myself from smiling.

"It is," Amirah agreed. "Like, I already have to go there once a year for the Met Ball, so just have it someplace else, right?"

"So, you want to go by the house to scope it out tonight?" Ruby asked, looking between me and Cassandra. "That way, we have plenty of time to get anything we might need."

Cassandra nodded. "I don't think we should all go, though," she said. "Since we're trying to be inconspicuous."

"That's okay!" Janis said. "Amirah, Ji-A, and I will just go back to my house and try on their clothes. Wait—I mean, hang out."

Cassandra turned to me and Mallory and said, "You guys come with us, and I can drop you back at Esme's on the way home."

Everyone agreed with the plan, and we started to gather up our stuff.

"Cassandra," Janis said, "if you can pick up Esme and Mallory in the morning, I can go directly to Brian's and we can all meet there."

Ruby nodded happily. "Maybe we can grab some flowers or something," she suggested. "It'd be nice to take him a host gift."

I smiled. "Brian would fall over dead," I said, and Ruby looked at me quizzically. "I mean, he would love that," I clarified. Janis offered to share the spreadsheet with the out-of-towners if they had any questions about the weekend's schedule, and only looked slightly disappointed when everyone declined. Then we headed toward the van, and before I could stop her, Ruby opened the sliding door and climbed into the back.

"Esme, you take shotgun," she said as Mallory got in with her.

"Are you sure?" I asked, climbing in as Cassandra started the van.

"Oh yeah. I want to stretch out on the floor," she responded, then contorted herself into a yoga pose that I'd previously only seen in illustrations.

"Wow," I said as we started to pull away from the curb. "I didn't even know that was possible in a moving vehicle."

"Anyone can do it," she said, her voice not even strained from being upside down. "It just takes balance."

"Do you do yoga?" I asked Mallory.

"Only Savasana," she answered. "And only right before bed."

"Same," I said, laughing. "Same."

CHAPTER 13

It was only a ten-minute drive to the band's house. A streetlamp was out on their block, and the darkness made everything seem even quieter. Cassandra drove past the house, and in the back of the van, Ruby and Mallory got on their knees so they could look out the window.

"Which one is it?" Mallory asked.

"That one right there," Cassandra said, pointing.

"With the purple car?" Mallory asked, her nose and forehead crunched in disbelief, or maybe it was confusion.

"I know, right?" I said.

At the next intersection, Cassandra did a U-turn and then parked the van on the opposite side of the street. I told Mallory and Ruby about how Brian had modified the doppler to track Red Magic, but that nothing had showed up here at all. "Only, as soon as you get close, you can feel something," I said. "There's definitely magic."

"You two stay here," Cassandra said. "Ruby and I will go check it out."

"No way." I was already opening my door. "Cass, we've talked about this before. You look exactly like your mom, so if anyone catches you snooping around, it will be hard to be casual, even with those guys." She stared straight ahead, drumming her fingers on the steering wheel. I could tell that she didn't like the idea of staying behind, even for what was just a recon mission, but she also knew that I had a point. "Besides, they know me," I added. "Or, at least Tom does, so if Ruby and I get caught, I can make up some stupid excuse about how I lost his number and needed to talk to him about the dance."

Cass sucked in a deep breath through her nose. "Okay," she said. "But if you so much as stub your toe, then scream or something."

"Don't worry," Ruby said, leaning forward and squeezing her shoulders from behind. "We'll be fine."

I got out and slid the door open for Ruby. Then we made our way down the street to the house. Even without speaking to each other, I could tell that Ruby and I were on the same page, both walking like we had every right to be there. As we turned into the driveway of Jump the Shark's house, I suddenly felt sick, like I was going to barf, and I stifled a gag. The first time I had been here, it had felt gross, but now that feeling was amped up to awful.

Ruby's step faltered, and I heard her say "Ew" under her breath.

"Right?" I whispered back, and she nodded. We kept walking past the car, and up to the side of the house. Ruby was sucking in air like she'd just finished a triathlon, and she kept rubbing her arms.

"Crap," she whispered. "I've got goose bumps everywhere and I feel a headache coming on. My Sitter sense is screaming." I nodded silently, my own head starting to throb, and I followed her as she crouched behind a bush. Then she crept toward the band's house and laid one hand on the side door, then moved over a few feet and laid the other one against a window. She waited for a few seconds, and shook her head.

I motioned for us to go around back. When we'd come to the house for our stakeout before, I hadn't seen anything beyond the driveway and the front porch, but as I circled to the other side, I got a good look at the peeling paint on the window frames, the missing shingles on the roof, and the backyard. The *dead* backyard. It was big and open, with an old clothesline stretching across it, a couple of broken lawn chairs, and nothing else. I glanced around for cover, but there really wasn't anywhere for us to hide, and Ruby and I stood there, frozen in the shadow of the house. Then a sound ripped through the air.

A guitar solo. Coming from the garage. We swiveled our necks so that Ruby and I were looking at each other, and she raised her eyebrow at me. Now we knew where the band was, and we practically sauntered over to the garage to get a better look. There was one window, which was covered with a thick cloth, but light seeped out around the edges. I tried to peek in, but I couldn't see much. What I heard, though, surprised me.

The guitar solo was good. Like, Jimi Hendrix good. Then suddenly it stopped. Not like the person playing it had stopped, but like the power had been cut. There was a few seconds of silence, and then someone started yelling.

"What the hell, man? I was just getting going, and I was shredding it! Shredding!"

"That sounded really good, dude!"

"Of course it sounded good! It sounded too freaking good! I thought we talked about this! We don't need them for our music, because that already rocks!"

"I know, but . . ."

"No buts, dude! That's what we all decided. We're trying to be conservative here until we find the big one, but you go and use one to shred during practice?"

The big one? What were they talking about? Now someone was saying something that I couldn't quite hear, and as I tried to get closer, Ruby grabbed me. "Esme, no!" she hissed.

But too late. My foot hit a pile of boards leaning up against the garage. I held out my hands, ready to stop them with my kinesis, but Ruby grabbed me and started to run, pulling me along behind her down the driveway. We were just past the car when the pile tumbled down with a crash.

We got to the street, and Ruby held her hands up. Every streetlamp on the block blinked and went out. In the darkness, we slowed to a stroll, once again acting like we were just out for a walk. I glanced back for a split second, but it was long enough to see that a light had come on, and the band members were standing in the driveway, all looking in different directions. I gasped as the magic from the house wore off and I started to feel normal again. Ruby and I didn't speak to each other until we had turned the corner. Her breathing had slowed, and my headache was subsiding.

"You feel okay?" she asked me.

"Now I do," I said. "Back there, I felt like I was about to barf all over their car."

"Yeah, same," she said. "Now I just feel like I need a kombucha and a shower."

"Did you hear what they said?" I asked her. "Right before I ruined everything?"

Ruby laughed. "You didn't ruin everything," she said. "You just cut our spying short."

Cassandra came around the corner, and slowed the van so that Ruby and I could climb in. I told Mallory and Cassandra what we'd heard, and how we'd felt.

"So wait," Mallory said. "This band is good?"

"I don't think so," I said. "But I do think they have access to a trick or two that makes them sound good."

"I guess we'll find out tomorrow," Ruby said. "There was definitely Red Magic at work there. All around the house."

"They're hiding something," Cassandra said, "and it could be my mom."

"They definitely don't want people coming around there," I said. "I just don't understand why it's not showing up on Brian's monitor."

"Oh!" Mallory said. "It could be a protection spell, right?" She looked toward Ruby.

"Yeah, I guess so," Ruby said.

"And then the spell would prevent the house from showing up on the monitor because it's protecting it," Mallory explained. "It might be keeping the normies away too, to stop people from snooping around."

My mind flashed back a couple of days to when I'd grabbed Pig's flyer and gone up on the porch. If there were protection spells, they hadn't been that bad then, but Tom had seemed extra cautious, and almost surprised, to find me standing on their porch. "Oh God," I said. "What if me showing up there alerted them to something?"

"That's possible," Ruby said, "but regardless, if we are going to come back tomorrow night, and actually try to break into the house, we need to be prepared."

"We'll have to layer up, then," Mallory said. "And use protection spells to protect *us* from the protection spells. If I remember correctly, black plastic is really effective."

"Well, I know where we can get some trash bags," Cassandra said.

"Really? Where?" I asked. We had just pulled up to a stop sign, and Cassandra turned around and fixed me with a look.

"The store," she said.

"Oh, duh," I said. "I think maybe I should get some sleep."

Ruby yawned luxuriously. "We all should," she said. "Big day tomorrow, and I want to go for a run before brunch."

Beside me, Mallory pretended to gag, and she and I burst into giggles. Cassandra dropped us off, with plans to pick us back up in the morning, and when Mallory and I walked into the house, Dad was still up. I felt a pang when I saw that he'd already made the couch up for Mallory. He came out of his room—which had been Mom's room as recently as this morning—to introduce himself to Mallory and ask her a few questions about her trip.

"Well," he said with a sigh, "I tried to make your bed up for you. And those sheets are, or were, clean."

I heard a snort, and I walked over to look down at the couch. Sure enough, Pig was luxuriously lounging, her head on the pillow and her legs stretched out to their full length.

"Get off!" I said, starting to shove her. "Not everything soft is meant for you."

"That's okay," Mallory said, laughing. "Dogs are, like, the one thing I'm not allergic to. I'm happy to share the couch."

"Are you sure?" I asked. "She snores. A lot. When she's awake, and when she's asleep."

"That's okay," she said. "I'm a very heavy sleeper."

I let Mallory use the bathroom first, and then I brushed my teeth and washed my face, and went back into the living room to make sure she had everything she needed. Pig had moved over a few inches, leaving Mallory barely enough room to fit on the couch.

"I should feel betrayed," I said, giving Pig a pat. "Your second night back, and you've already ditched me for someone new."

A sound from outside made me look up sharply toward the window. The wind had picked up, and I could see the silhouettes of the bare tree branches whipping around in the cold. It couldn't be pleasant for any species to sleep out there tonight.

"So, I heard that the Sitterhood is still looking for Adrian, Wanda's assistant," I said, turning back to Mallory, who was now cuddled up with Pig. "How well do you know him?"

"Not well," she said. "We know who each other are, of course, but whenever the Sitterhood has had family weekends and everyone got together, it was a lot of people, so it wasn't like we all hung out together. And Adrian was always off by himself anyway. I think some people thought it was because he was snobby, and that he thought he was better than everyone because he worked for Wanda, but I always just thought he was shy."

"What do you mean?" I asked, eager to keep talking with

someone who had known Adrian, if not better, then at least longer, than I had.

She stroked one of Pig's ears. "He was different and he knew it," she said. "A lot of people said giving him powers was an abuse of Wanda's magic. She shut that down pretty fast, but I'm sure Adrian still heard about it."

"What was Wanda like?" I asked.

Pig gave a *harumph*, apparently unhappy that we were disturbing her snooze with our yapping. Or maybe it was because we were discussing the person who'd tried to kill her without giving it a second thought.

"I didn't know her that well personally," Mallory said, "but from what I heard, she wasn't very tolerant of anyone disagreeing with her. Like, when she gave Adrian his powers, I heard that one of the members of the Synod at that time was really against it. Well, Wanda did it anyway, and a few months later that woman quit the Sitterhood to open her own nail salon. She kept saying it was her lifelong dream, but there was some gossip about how no one had ever heard her mention it before, and people said they'd never even seen her with a manicure."

I nodded. "So Wanda could have used some sort of magic to get the woman to quit so she'd be out of the way?"

Mallory nodded. "Or just forced her out the old-fashioned normie way," she said, "through a mix of bullying and gaslighting." Both of those sounded like tools Wanda definitely would have had in her toolbox.

"So, was Wanda the only Sitter to get caught using Red Magic?" I asked.

"I don't know," she said. "I'm sure she wasn't, but I bet every other time someone got caught, the Synod was able to keep it under wraps. Wanda's just the first person to get caught with a full-scale plot to destroy the entire Sitterhood." Mallory stopped, and shivered. "Also, she *was* the Synod. Honestly, Esme, you're a hero. It gives me chills to think about what could have happened if she'd succeeded."

"I don't feel like a hero at all," I said.

Pig's breathing had mellowed, a sign that she was moving from falling asleep into completely asleep. I envied her, because now that my encounter with Jump the Shark's protection spells had worn off, I was totally wired. "Are you tired?" I asked Mallory.

She thought for a second, and then shook her head. "Not really," she said. "Do you want to watch a movie?"

Those were seven of my favorite words in the English language. "Yeah," I said, jumping up to get the remote. "Anything in particular?" I asked as I flipped on the TV.

"Well, if we're going to a school dance tomorrow, I feel like we should probably watch *Prom Night*."

I spun around and stared at Mallory, because it was like she had read my mind. She misinterpreted my look, though, and quickly backpedaled. "I mean, if you like scary movies," she said. "I know some people don't like horror."

"No," I said enthusiastically, "I love it. *Rosemary's Baby* is my comfort movie. And *Prom Night* is an excellent choice. But do you mean the original or the remake?"

"The original, obviously," she said. "If you can find it streaming somewhere, of course."

"Oh, don't worry," I said, queuing it up. "I already own it." I muscled Pig over a few inches so that I could curl up on the couch, and then pressed play. The original *Prom Night* had all the elements of a classic—a killer disco soundtrack (pun intended), mysterious phone calls, and a young Jamie Lee Curtis in a role that helped establish her as the scream-queen-final-girl prototype.

"You know," Mallory said as the movie started, "I've never actually been to a school dance, probably because horror movies totally scared me away from them. Actually, not just horror movies, all movies. I feel like there's no way anything good is going to happen at a dance. You're either going to get drenched in pig's blood"—she paused and covered Pig's ears—"hacked to death in a locker room, or all your friends are going to end up making out with someone and you're going to end up standing by the punch bowl making small talk with a math teacher who feels sorry for you. I think I fear the third scenario the most."

"Same," I said, giving an involuntary shudder. "I went to one dance freshman year, before I knew better, and came dangerously close to that exact situation, though it was a health teacher. Also, teachers love dances. All adults do, and I can't help but think that whenever adults are telling you how important and special something is going to be, it's probably just going to be mediocre and forgettable."

Mallory nodded as the sound of children playing hide-and-seek came from the television, and we watched in silence for a few moments. Eventually our girl, Jamie Lee, came on the screen, playing a high school student, but dressed like she was about to approve someone's home loan. "I don't think it's a coincidence that Sitters are teenage girls," Mallory said as she jammed down the pillows to make herself more comfortable. "It's the same reason why the final girls survive—because no one expects anything of us, and the only way you can carry the weight of the world on your shoulders is if you're not already lugging around a bunch of expectations."

"Yeah," I said. "I never really thought about it that way before, but you're totally right."

"So, what do you think is going to go down at this dance tomorrow night, anyway?" Mallory asked. "Will there be pig's blood?" Again, she covered Pig's ears as she said it.

"God, I hope not," I said, thinking of K and K. "I think that would give the dance committee an aneurism. What I hope is that we're all just subjected to some horrible music for a while, Cassandra finds Circe, and then we go get ice cream. What I think is going to happen . . . well, I have no idea. I'm glad you all are here, though."

"Me too," Mallory said. "Sitters stick together."

We both fell silent as the movie picked up, and about fifteen minutes later, I heard a little snore. Mallory had fallen asleep, for real this time. It was after midnight, and since I'd already seen the movie a million times, I turned it off and headed to bed.

Back in my room, I climbed into bed and pulled the covers up, my mind spinning like a Tilt-A-Whirl as I went over everything that had happened these last few days, and tried to prepare for everything that was going to happen in the next. It was overwhelming, but I felt strangely calm. Mallory was right—Sitters did stick together, and no matter what happened, I wasn't alone.

CHAPTER 14

In the morning, Mallory and I got up and got dressed to go to Brian's. Since we had an afternoon of thrifting after, I kept it casual with leggings and a flannel, and when I turned around, Mallory was looking at me.

"You're good at getting dressed," she said. "I never knew that was a skill before. I always just figured clothes were a thing that kept spilled soup from getting on your skin."

"Thanks," I said. "I like getting dressed up. It makes things more exciting." I paused. "Wait, I mean, they're pretty exciting now, no matter what I wear, but before I knew I was a Sitter, clothes were about the only thing that got me out of bed in the morning. You can borrow something if you want?"

"Really?" Mallory said, her eyebrows shooting up her forehead. "Thanks!" She jumped off the bed and headed to the closet.

"Uh, most of the good stuff's on the floor," I said, "and it may or may not be clean." She nodded, and started to pick through the pile that had been Pig's bed less than an hour before. A few layers in, she found something that she liked, and turned around holding it up: an oversized hand-knit sweater, black with a white hand that displayed pointy red nails as it proudly raised a middle finger. Janis and I had spent a lot of time musing on the origins of this sweater, and finally had decided that it was probably made by a grandma going through a divorce.

"Can I borrow this?" she asked, and I nodded. "I feel like it really goes with my new personality," she said as she pulled it over her head, causing her red hair to be filled with static and fly out into a halo.

We walked into the kitchen, where Dad was sitting at the kitchen table doing the crossword puzzle.

"Sleep well?" he said, looking up, "Aw, I see that Esme has let you borrow what I lovingly refer to as her 'positive attitude' sweater."

"Yeah," Mallory said, smiling. "This sweater is super warm, and that couch is super comfy. Pig is kind of like having a white-noise machine and a space heater, all rolled into one fur ball." Pig was currently lying on Dad's feet, and she gave a sigh at hearing herself talked about.

Dad gave her a little shove, and then stood up. He was dressed in his gym clothes. "I thought I'd hit the gym this morning," he said with a little half-hearted smile. No doubt it was a bittersweet freedom, because when Mom had been living with us, Dad and I had had to carefully coordinate our schedules to make sure she wasn't left home alone. "You need me to drop you off anywhere?"

"Yeah, actually, that'd be great," I said. "We're just going to Brian's." I could see Dad give a little pause, but then he just nodded and grabbed his keys. It was a relief to have things out in the open now, but I'm sure it still seemed weird to him that Brian, who he'd thought for years was an old football buddy, was my Counsel. And that Brian did things like host brunches.

Mallory and I gave Pig a few goodbye pets, and I sent Cass a text telling her we didn't need a ride. Pig looked mournful at being left behind. "I'd let you come to brunch, girlie," I said, "but white dog hair and Brian's indigo couch do not mix." We followed Dad out to his car, and I let Mallory have the front seat. As Dad drove, he played tour guide and pointed out notable Spring River attractions. "That used to be a great little record store," he said, nodding toward an H&R Block. "Esme would have loved it." A few blocks later. "You see that McDonald's? Well, two summers ago, someone drove right through the drive-thru, and took the whole thing out." I couldn't tell if Mallory was genuinely entertained or if she was just playing along, but she laughed a lot and asked a few questions. She was also incredibly surprised at how quickly we arrived.

"Wait, so this is across town?" she asked as she unbuckled her seat belt. "It only took five minutes!"

"Perks of small-town life," Dad said. "Shorter commutes mean more time to watch TV!"

"Do you want to come in and say hi?" I asked Dad as I followed Mallory out of the car. "I'm sure Brian would love to see you."

"That's okay," Dad said, forcing himself to smile. "I'm sure you guys have lots of official business to go over, and I'd better get to the gym. That stationary bike isn't going to ride itself."

"Speaking of rides," Mallory said, "thanks for this one."

"No problem," he replied. "Es, you'll call me if you need me to come pick you up?" I nodded. "All right, have fun," he said, "and stay out of trouble." He gave the horn a little beep as he drove away.

"Your dad is really nice," she said.

"Yeah," I agreed, nodding, not wanting to spend too much time thinking about how Dad's life was pretty much in the blender these days. "Now let's go get some brunch. Fingers crossed that Brian made French toast."

We were headed up the walk to Brian's front door when I heard a distinctively terrible sound and turned to see Dion's van round the corner, Cassandra driving and Ruby waving at us from the passenger seat. From the other direction, a totally different sound—that of squealing tires—announced that Janis, Ji-A, and Amirah were arriving too. Cassandra parked across the street, and Janis parked right in front of Brian's house, so close to the curb that one of her back wheels was on it. As the three of them tumbled out of the car, I could tell from their outfits that everyone had dressed for thrifting, and it was leggings all around. Amirah's were—of course—black leather, and Ji-A's slip-ons were limited-edition Nikes. I guess they were as ready as they were ever going to be for digging through piles of used pajamas.

My phone started to ring, and when I looked down, I recognized Tom's number. "Janis!" I said, waving her over, then holding out the phone. "It's Tom! From . . ." My mind blanked on their name. "The band!" My heart started to pound. After last night, I was now paranoid that me showing up on their front porch had tipped them off to something, and I was even less looking forward to having them at the dance.

The phone kept ringing, and Janis looked at me like she was waiting for me to do something. "Esme! Answer it!"

Oh yeah. Of course. I hit the button. "Hello?"

"Yeah, Esther?" he said.

"This is Esme," I said. "I mean, Esther Whatever."

"Yeah, I wanted to get your fax number so we can send over our rider."

"You want to fax over your rider," I repeated, to make sure Janis could hear, and raised my eyebrows at her in question.

"Fax is broken," she mouthed at me, and then dug into her purse and pulled out a pen and piece of paper.

"Uh, our fax machine is down," I said to Tom, "but you can just tell me, and uh, we'll make sure we have it."

"You got something to write it down?"

"Yeah," I said. "I've got a pen."

"Okay," he said. "We want chicken noodle soup."

"Chicken noodle soup," I repeated. "Got it." Janis looked at me like this was nuts, but then she wrote it down.

"Three bottles of ranch dressing," Tom said, and I repeated that too. "And it has to be Hidden Valley," he added. "None of that generic ranch."

"Oh, Tom," I said, "we would never do generic ranch." Janis sputtered and sprayed spittle onto the paper she was writing on, which seemed appropriate.

"Tomato soup," Tom continued, "veggie chili, cream of mushroom, and beef stew." I snorted, and tried to cover it with a cough, then repeated the latest demands. Janis was bent over the hood of her car, scrawling everything I said.

"Grape juice and root beer," he said. "Any brand of root beer is fine."

"Noted," I said, and waited, but Tom was silent. It appeared that after listing several types of soup, brand-name ranch dressing, and two very mediocre beverages, he was done.

I couldn't help myself. "You guys don't want any chips, candy, or cheese and crackers?" I asked. "A bag of baby carrots?"

"No way," Tom said, suddenly sounding stern. "And if any of that junk is in the green room, we will lose our crap and won't play."

"Got it," I said. "Not even a single baby carrot." I shook my head at myself, since I could not believe the words coming out of my mouth. "So, I will see you tonight."

"Oh," he said, stopping me, "one more thing. A blender. A nice one. High-speed. Sharp blades. Very powerful."

I mean, good God? Who were these people? "Got it," I said. "High-speed, powerful, sharp blender." Janis looked at me like I was the weirdo, but she wrote it down.

"Yeah," he said. "And who's gonna help us load in?"

Load in? What did that mean? "Uh, yeah," I said, "me and my friend Janis."

"You?" Tom scoffed. "You're scrawny."

"Looks can be deceiving," I said. "I'm very strong, and so is Janis." Tom's manners were to be expected, and all he did was grunt again and hang up the phone. I stood there confused. Was I scared of these guys? In almost every way, they were just pathetic. Except they might have kidnapped Circe, and their house was dripping in Red Magic that made me want to ralph. I sighed, and tucked my phone away.

Amirah had hung back to wait with us, and she raised her eyebrows at me. "Honestly, that is the weirdest rider I have ever heard of," she said. "And when Harry Styles played my sweet sixteen, all he asked for was three kinds of lip balm and frozen raspberries."

I looked over Janis's shoulder at the list. "I guess we can just go to the store later?" I said.

"Nice blenders are expensive," Janis said. "My mom treats our Vitamix like it's her third born."

I sighed, and started toward Brian's house.

"So, what do you think is up with these guys anyway?" Amirah said. "They seem lame."

"They are lame," I said, "but also evil." I told her and Janis about how Ruby and I had felt walking up to their house.

"I hope they don't bring that with them," Janis said. "I am suddenly having second thoughts about inviting these guys into our school."

"I've been saying that from the . . ." I trailed off as I caught sight of Brian standing at the door and motioning for us to hurry up and get inside. No doubt not wanting to have to explain to his neighbors why he had seven teenage girls descending on his house on a Saturday morning. Maybe we could whip up some awards for Girl Scout Troop Leader of the Year and display them prominently in his window?

At the Summit, the rest of the girls had been introduced to Brian's aesthetic prowess when he'd put together the closing event. Until Wanda had hijacked it to try to simultaneously end the Sitterhood and give herself eternal youth, the party had been a tasteful après-ski-themed soiree, complete with fondue fountains, sleigh-ride photo ops, and lots of cozy sweaters. But still, that had hardly prepared them for what was waiting for us inside his front door. First off, the place smelled like bacon, maple syrup, and freshly ground coffee, and Brian had indeed made French toast. Or, rather, he had made tiny, star-shaped pieces of French toast for dipping into tiny pots of syrup. There was also a bagel board, with plain and everything, and different kinds of cream cheese, fresh herbs, red onions, and smoked salmon, something that had always sounded disgusting to me, but I had to admit it was really pretty.

There was asparagus and eggs baked into puff pastries, silver-dollar pancakes topped with whipped cream, chocolate chips, and fresh berries. There were muffins, croissants, omelets, and coffee. So much coffee. Brian had even set out a carafe of iced, probably just for me. It melted my heart a little bit, because nothing says "I see you" like cold brew in February.

"What?" Cassandra asked, putting her hands on her hips and looking around. "No beans on toast?" Brian started to sputter, but then she just smiled as she grabbed a piece of bacon. "I'm kidding. This looks great!" Ji-A, Janis, and Mallory had already whipped out their phones and were food-porning away, while Ruby was asking Brian if there was anything she could do to help, and Amirah was cooing over Brian's house.

"You know what?" she said. "This totally reminds me of Laura Dern's place. You guys have very similar style. You know Laura Dern, right? The Oscar-winning actress?" Brian was nodding and offered Amirah a mimosa.

"It's virgin, of course," he said. "Fresh-squeezed OJ and sparkling apple cider."

"That's perfect," Amirah said, "because I don't drink." Then she popped a couple of her THC mints into her mouth and took the glass from Brian.

Everyone filled their plates—and Brian made a special

green-ginger juice for Ruby—and then we sat down around his table, which had a totes adorbs desert-themed terrarium full of terra-cotta-colored rocks and tiny succulents.

As we ate, we told everyone what had happened the night before at the band's house, and everyone offered their theories for what the "big one" was. Ji-A guessed demon, while Brian suggested guitar teacher. Janis thought it could be a favored T-shirt. Mallory guessed a lucky rabbit's foot, and that was when a light bulb came on for me.

"It's the talisman!" I said. "Maybe even the same one that Wanda was looking for! That could be what they were looking for when they broke into Cassandra's house, because they are worried about the one they have now running out."

Brian nodded. "If they somehow came into possession of a talisman recently, that could explain why they are just now coming across our radar," he said.

"We'll look for a talisman when we go back to the house tonight," Ruby said, and Brian turned toward her.

"I thought you already tried to look in and all the windows were covered," Brian said, looking at her suspiciously.

"Oh yeah," she said. "I meant we'll look in the yard and stuff. Again."

"Sure," he said. "Sure you will." Then Brian turned toward me, and I clenched up in anticipation of whatever was coming next. "So," he said, "what is your plan for the dance?"

"Janis and I will meet the band there at seven p.m., and they go on at eight," I said.

"And?" he said.

"I'll try my best to pretend like I'm exactly what I said I am," I added, "a super fan."

"What's the rest of the plan?" he said.

"That *is* the plan," I said, not quite sure what else he wanted.

Brian shook his head, and then said the four worst words in the adult human language. "I'm disappointed in you."

I grabbed a mini quiche and stuffed it into my mouth. It was ham. I hated ham. Who liked ham? I forced it down and then stifled a sigh. "Crossing your fingers and hoping for the best is hardly a plan, much less protecting the innocent," Brian continued. I could feel everyone's eyes on me. The silence was uncomfortable, and when I swallowed, it practically echoed.

I was used to being the passenger, and being along for the ride, but Brian was right. Cassandra was focused on finding Circe, as she should have been, and if I was going to the school with Janis, Amirah, and Ji-A in tow, then I was going to have to take charge, since I was the only one of us who knew the school and was also a Sitter. But the more I thought about it, the more I realized that no plan WAS my plan.

"Okay, so here's what we know about them," I said. "They're four white guys who have an awful band that they think is really good. Nothing unusual there, at all. But we know that they were associates of Erebus, and from the spells around their house, we know that they are practicing Red Magic." I paused and took a sip of coffee. "We also know their band took a fifteen-year break and only recently started playing again, and that none of them have aged a bit in that time. Hence, more evidence in favor of the idea that they recently came into possession of a talisman and were looking for another one when they broke into Cassandra's house. But while we can assume that they are indeed evil, we are still not sure just how powerful they are, considering they, uh, all share one purple car, and that signs point to the fact that they think it is actually still 2002. So, as much as I hate to admit it, I think we have to try to keep whatever-their-name-is-this-week happy as long as possible, and hopefully for the entire time they're at the dance. We need them to think that it's a regular dance, and that everyone really loves them, at least until we know for sure what's going on at their house. We might even"—I swallowed again—"have to buy some CDs."

"So, if they have all of these powers from Red Magic," Ji-A said, looking up from her plate, where she'd been arranging blueberries in what looked like a constellation, "how do we take the powers away?"

A loud, gaseous sound ripped through the air. All eyes at the table swiveled to Cassandra, who was in the midst of throttling a ketchup bottle that was protesting with all of its flatulent might as it squirted onto her plate. I saw Ruby watching her with an unreadable look in her eyes, and I wondered if we were all witnessing the moment when she discovered that her girlfriend was one of those people who put ketchup on everything. Cassandra, feeling everyone watching her, looked up and focused her gaze on Amirah. "You want?" she asked, holding out the bottle.

"Thanks," Amirah said. "I'm good."

"If Esme's right, and they do have a talisman," Ruby said, "then all we have to do is find it and take it away. Their powers will only work if they have access to it."

"What does this talisman look like?" Amirah asked.

"We don't know," Brian said. "A talisman can be anything, and they could have more than one. So, if that is the case, then we have no idea what exactly it is you will be looking for."

"We're looking for my mom," Cassandra said. "When we find her, she might know what the talisman is."

We all nodded, and Ji-A cleared her throat. "From what I understand, in the past when Sitters were caught using Red Magic, their memories were stripped and they were exiled," she said. "Can't we just do that with these guys? Then, even if we didn't find the talisman they were looking for, they wouldn't remember that it existed."

"Maybe we can just flush 'em all?" I said. "They can get the old band back together in the netherworld. Rock out with their . . ." I caught myself before I went too far. "Shirts off."

"I mean, that is my idea of hell," Janis said. "But I'd kinda feel bad for the demons who are already in the Negative."

Brian stood up and started clearing dishes, and Ji-A and Ruby stood up to join him. "I'll make some calls this afternoon to see what I can find out," he said, taking my plate from me. "But regardless, all of your attention tonight needs to be focused on making sure nothing goes wrong at that dance." Ji-A went to grab Cassandra's plate, but Cass snatched it back, apparently planning on going back for thirds. Or maybe it was fourths?

I sighed. "I know," I said, then held up my hands. "B., I know you're not going to like this, but hear me out." He stood there, holding dirty dishes and staring at me. "I think I need to spell the entire student body."

"Hahaha," he said. "That's a funny joke. Wait, tell me you are joking."

I shook my head. "I wish I were," I said, "but the band will know something is up if everyone hates their music, and the students will riot if they're subjected to music that isn't the same three songs they hear on the radio."

"But the band will be happy if the crowd is really into them," Janis said, "and if they buy a lot of CDs." She paused, her eyes getting bigger. "But no one buys CDs. How do we keep the students happy? I don't know—give them lots of treats? I hear the football team likes Snausages."

Mallory snorted, then grabbed a napkin to dab at the orange juice that had just come out of her nose.

Brian rolled his eyes. "We'll have to use populariskinesis again," I said. "And on everyone this time. If the students really love—or at least feel like they really love—the band, then that will keep the band happy. Our priorities here are keeping everyone safe and finding out if these guys really do have anything to do with Circe's disappearance. If they do, we want to keep them, and their brains, intact long enough to get her back." I glanced over at Cassandra, who had finally finished eating, and saw her looking back at me, that kind of set look that I saw in her eyes every time we were about to do a Return—steely determination with more than a sprinkle of come-at-me-bro. "After that," I said, looking back at Brian, "we can figure out what to do with the band. But we'll keep you updated and—"

He cut me off. "You won't have to keep me updated," he said. "I'll be there."

"You will?" I asked, surprised, and he nodded.

"I have to chaperone," he explained, "and it is one of the worst parts of my job, as everything about the decor of a high school gymnasium made to look 'special' offends me on a cellular level. And, as I was informed yesterday, since I am the athletic director, it falls on me to make sure all the ball closets, and any other dark, semi-private spaces in and around the gym, remain locked and inaccessible through the evening, lest we have another homecoming repeat with . . ." He stopped himself and headed into the kitchen.

"Coach, wait!" Janis called after him. "What happened at the last dance? I'd been taking a break from my gossip podcast, but I could always bring it back if you've got something really juicy for me."

"I can't hear you over the sound of the dishwasher," he called back, though from where I was sitting, I could see that he was just standing at the sink, turning the faucet off and on and banging some plates together. Janis popped the last bite of a chocolate croissant into her mouth, and then looked at her phone.

"Crap!" she said. "It's already after two. We have to hurry!" She grabbed my hand and pulled me up with her.

"Hurry?" I said. "We're not meeting the band until seven."

"Yeah," she said. "But we have to go shopping for soup, and we need plenty of time to get ready! And we promised Ji-A and Amirah that we'd take them thrifting."

I groaned. The thrifting was awesome, but I wasn't sure which of the other two sounded less appealing: being a lackey soup shopper or getting ready for the school dance. Normally I loved nothing more than putting together a special-occasion outfit, but going to school on a Saturday night could ruin even that. Everyone else was getting ready to leave, and Brian walked us to the front door. Then Cassandra surprised me by speaking first. "Thanks, B.," she said. "That was delicious, and fun."

"Ohhh my God," Amirah groaned, "I am going to be dreaming about those French toast stars for weeks. Honestly, I would never tell her this, but I think they're better than Chrissy Teigen's French toast casserole. The last time she made it for me, it was a little dry and—" Ji-A grabbed her by the sleeve and pulled her out the door as Brian nodded and accepted thanks from everyone else.

As I turned to thank him, I spotted something in his kitchen. "Brian," I said, "I hate to do this, but we're going to need to borrow your blender."

CHAPTER 15

Janis and I were not the kind of girls to break a promise, so a-thrifting we did go. Ruby and Cassandra were, of course, uninterested, so they took off to do their own thing, but Mallory decided to tag along.

"I'm not much of a shopper," she said, "but they have a books section, right?"

We assured her that they did. Amirah and Ji-A were very enthusiastic, but I started to worry as soon as we pulled into the parking lot of the thrift store.

"Ooh, DAV," Amirah said. "What's that stand for? 'Designer American Vintage'?"

"Um, no," Janis said. "'Disabled American Veterans.'"

"Oh," Ji-A said, "that sounds less cute."

Inside, things didn't exactly go as planned. Amirah kept asking Randy—the bleached-mullet guy who worked there—if they had any other sizes in the back, and Ji-A just kind of wandered around, bouncing from T-shirts to pantsuits to nightgowns, like she was a transfer student on the first day of school.

To my surprise, though, they both ended up buying something. Amirah got a perfectly distressed plain black T-shirt, and Ji-A got a dress that she planned to wear to the dance. It was a teal stretch-jersey with one sleeve and an asymmetrical hem, and looked really cool. Contrary to our advice, she refused to try it on. "It's, like, two dollars," she said. "I'm just going to buy it."

Mallory got a vintage Joan Didion book with a very cool cover. Janis got a black secretary blouse woven through with rainbow metallic threads, and she had the find of the day, which, because Janis is the Patron Saint of Thrift-Store Generosity, she actually found for me. It was an eighties prom dress, petal-pink, with an off-the-shoulder bow top and a frilly skirt. The dress was very *Welcome Home, Roxy Carmichael* and it fit like a three-dollar dream.

We had decided that we'd get ready at my house, so on the way there after thrifting, we stopped at the store to buy everything Tom had listed for their rider.

"Wow, this grocery store," Ji-A said, looking around as she trailed after me. "There are so many chips."

As Janis and I filled the cart with soup, Amirah disappeared and reappeared a few minutes later, carrying a vanilla sheet cake. "You're getting a cake?" I asked.

"I was looking for poke, but the woman behind the counter said they didn't have it?"

"Yeah," I said. "Probably not?"

"Anyway," she said. "This cake costs less than a latte."

Ji-A was very interested in the ranch dressing, as it turned out she had somehow never had it. "So, what does ranch taste like?" she asked.

"Um," Janis said, struggling. "I don't know? It just tastes like ranch?"

"So, like grass?" Ji-A asked.

Janis looked at me, but I just shrugged. "I guess?" she said. "Creamy grass with hints of buttermilk?"

"Fried chicken?" Ji-A asked, and Janis gave up.

"We'll just let you taste it later," she said. "There's no way they'll eat all of this."

The ranch was the last thing on the list, so we checked out and paid—chump change for Amirah—and then headed to my house. We were going to my house partly because it was a place where we wouldn't have to hide anything or watch what we said (Janis's little brother was a notorious eavesdropper), but mainly because everyone wanted to hang with Pig. On the way, we stopped at Cassandra's to drop off Mallory.

"Frequent text updates, please," I said to her as she climbed out of the car. "Cassandra barely knows how to work her phone, so you and Ruby let us know what is happening every step of the way. I figure you've got at least two hours, but let us know if we need to stall them so you can have more."

"Aye, aye, captain," she said. "We won't go dark." Janis honked, and we all waved as we drove away.

When we got to my house, Dad was sitting on the couch reading a James Patterson novel with Pig's head in his lap. I told him Mallory was at Cassandra's and introduced him to Ji-A and Amirah. "You girls moving in?" he asked, taking in the garment bags that they were carrying, and the rolling suitcase that Janis was currently wrestling through our very narrow door.

"We have to get ready for the dance," I explained. "And we need options."

I had to admit, I had started salivating as soon as I had seen Ji-A's and Amirah's bags. I mean, I wasn't shallow enough to be friends with someone just because they had a good wardrobe, but I was definitely shallow enough to take advantage of my friends' good wardrobes. Janis bumped her suitcase down the hall to my room, and Amirah and Ji-A followed, cooing over Pig. "Can I give her some beef jerky?" Amirah asked.

"Sure," I said, "but where are you going to get beef jerky?"

Amirah dug around in her The Row backpack and pulled out a ziplock bag. "Oh, I always have beef jerky," she said. She tossed a piece into the air, and Pig caught it with a snap, and I truly had no idea what to say.

In my room, everyone dumped their bags onto my bed.

"Esme, I like your room!" Amirah said. "It's so cozy." "Cozy," of course, meant "small." "Everything I brought is really boring," Amirah continued. "I'm sick of black. It's so New York. I want something fun, like a bright color or a cute print."

True, almost everything she'd brought was black, but it was still the kind of clothing that I wanted to lock up behind glass so that nothing ever happened to it. A classic Versace square-neck double-breasted minidress with iconic gold buttons—black. An off-the-shoulder, sweetheart neckline Alexander McQueen fit-and-flare silhouette with a flounce hem—black with a pink lining. A velvet, long-sleeved Saint Laurent body-con with a crystal collar and a crystal-edged heart cutout in the back. Black, too. I stared at it for a few seconds and then had to remind myself to breathe.

Amirah tossed it toward a pile on the floor, and I dove after it, picked it up, and glared at Pig, who I could tell had already been eyeing it as potential bedding. "Beef jerky and YSL do not mix," I whispered to her, though I guess that, in Amirah's case, they did.

"Amirah, this is possibly one of the most badass dresses I have ever seen in my life," I said, standing back up and holding it out to her. "Definitely the most badass dress I have ever actually touched. Are you sure you don't want to wear it?"

"Yeah," she said, shaking her head. "It's too serious. It makes me look like I'm going to a premiere or something."

"And that's a bad thing?" I asked.

She nodded. "I just want to dress like you and Janis," she said. "You guys always look like you're going to do something fun, like hanging out in a parking lot or going to Panda Sub." Had anyone else ever told me that I looked like I was about to go hang out in a Panda Sub parking lot, I would have clawed their eyes out, but now that I was getting to really know Amirah, I was starting to understand her. The more offensive something sounded, the more she meant it as a compliment.

Ji-A had already pulled off her shoes and stripped down, and was now trying on the teal dress she'd bought at the thrift store. "What do you think?" she asked when she finally had it on. She was facing us, away from the mirror, and I tried to keep the look on my face as neutral as possible. The best way to describe how the dress looked on Ji-A was that it made her resemble a piece of blue raspberry saltwater taffy. There were bulges where there shouldn't have been bulges, and extra fabric where there shouldn't have been extra fabric, and then it was also weirdly short in the front.

"Um," Amirah said, trying to be diplomatic, "did you pack any shapewear?"

Ji-A spun around to look in the mirror, and her face fell. "Ugh," she said. "I look like a Slurpee someone has dropped on the ground." She yanked it back over her head and threw it onto the pile of Amirah's LBDs. "I should have tried it on at the store." She bent down and rifled through the clothes she had brought, and then stood back up. "I might wear this," she said, and I turned around to see her holding up a rain-forest-green Valentino dress with pleats from top to bottom and drapey, full-length epaulets that looked like superhero techno parrot wings.

"That dress . . . ," I started, but didn't finish because I had no words.

"Is it too much?" she asked.

"Yes," Janis said. "Way too much, and if you do not wear it, then we cannot be friends anymore. Sorry, bye."

Ji-A laughed. "Okay, I will definitely wear it. But I don't have the right shoes. Esme, can I look through your closet?"

"Yeah, sure," I said, shocked and flattered that she would want to borrow anything from me.

Amirah sighed dramatically. "I hate my clothes," she said.

"Here," I said, picking up the teal dress that Ji-A had just discarded. "You should try it on."

"You saw it on Ji-A," she said. "It made her look like a puddle."

"Yeah, but it might look different on you," I said. Amirah reached out and took it from me, and her eyes looked like she was really considering it.

"They dry-clean everything before it goes on the racks, right?" she said.

"Sometimes," I said, which had to be almost true, and did not tell her about the time Janis found a tooth in a shirt pocket.

"Esme, can I wear these?" Ji-A asked. I turned around to see her holding up my cowboy boots, the black ones with the red roses and blue sparrows stitched into the leather.

"Sure," I said. She sat down, pulled one onto a foot, and then gave a little yelp.

"Yay, they fit perfectly," she said.

"So," Janis said, standing by the bed, looking at Amirah's discards, "if you wear that thrifted old rag—I mean, the teal cocktail gown!—does that mean the Versace is up for grabs?"

"What'd you say?" Amirah asked, her head caught in the stretch teal fabric as she fumbled with the zipper before finally freeing herself and yanking in down.

"Can I borrow this?" Janis asked again, holding up the Versace.

"Go for it," Amirah said, then turned to look at herself in my mirror. She zipped the zipper, adjusted the sleeve, and pulled down the hem, and holy crap, she looked amazing!

"Wow," she said, taking in her reflection. "This is kinda awesome."

I nodded enthusiastically. "Opposite of puddle," I said.

"Esme," Janis said. "I think you should try the Saint Laurent." I walked over and picked up the dress, but as much as it was a work of art, it didn't feel like *me*.

"I think I'm going to stick with my Roxy Carmichael dress," I said, pulling the pink fluff out of the bag and yanking off the tags. Unlike Amirah, I had no illusions about the Goodwill and dry-cleaning, but the dress was too perfect not to risk a case of scabies. The look needed boots, though—specifically black boots, like Winona's character, Dinky Bosetti, wore, which she tied up with hot-pink laces. I always had my Docs, but those were my everyday black combat boots, and I needed some dress-up black combat boots. Then I spotted a bit of sparkle amid Ji-A's stuff. I bent down and unearthed combat boots. Black glitter combat boots by Alexander McQueen.

"Can I borrow these?"

"Of course," Ji-A said. I pulled on the dress, and the boots, and they were perfect.

"How does this look?" Janis asked. Everyone swiveled to see her. She had on the Versace minidress with shoulder-grazing gold ankh earrings, a piece of hot-pink-and-yellow wax-print fabric as a head wrap around her braids, and these flat black sandals that she'd bought in Greece and that tied up her calves all the way to her knees. She looked freaking incredible.

"I would compliment your outfit right now," I said, "but I can't, because I'm dead."

"So dead," Amirah said.

"Absolutely deceased," Ji-A added.

"Good," Janis said. "I just need to keep these on until we get there." Then she pulled a giant pair of tube socks on up and over her sandals.

"I thought your toes didn't get cold," I said.

"I thought so too," she said. "But I was wrong."

We did our hair and makeup. Or, rather, Janis did everyone's hair and makeup, and then we were ready to go. Pig, who had been watching quietly from the corner, to her credit farting only minimally, now let out a long whine. It was like she knew she was being left.

"We'll be back soon, girlie," I said, walking over and

bending down to scratch her ears. She wrinkled her nose, and then sniffed my dress. She apparently liked what she smelled, because she went in again. It wasn't exactly confidence boosting.

"She's so cuuute," cooed Amirah, the one who hated dogs. "Can't she come with us?"

"I don't think so," I said.

"We can just say she's my date," Amirah said.

"Each student is only allowed one guest," I said. "And so you're already my date."

"Yeah," Amirah said, "but the rules don't apply to me, because I'm not a student, so Pig can be my date."

"Yeah," I said, "but you see, that means I'm bringing two guests."

"No you're not," she said. "You're bringing one guest, and I'm bringing one guest."

"Yes, but you're my guest," I said, though I could tell from Amirah's face that I was getting nowhere. I think she was used to saying "Yeah, but the rules don't apply to me," so I changed course. "Pig could come, but she doesn't have anything to wear."

"Oh, yes she does!" Janis said, then sock-footed it across my room to dig through one of my drawers. "She can wear this!" Janis was triumphantly brandishing my tuxedo T-shirt. Pig sat obediently while Janis jammed it down over her head, and then put her front paws through the sleeves. The shirt dragged on the ground, so I secured the back with a ponytail holder. Really, they were right, and I don't know why I ever resisted. Pig looked so sophisticated in black tie.

The five of us made our way to the living room, where

Dad had taken a break from his James Patterson novel and appeared to be shopping for socks on Amazon. "Wow!" he said. "It's been a long time since I've been to a high school dance, but they must have gotten a lot fancier since my day." Then he got a glimpse of Janis's socks.

"Hey," he said, "nice tubes. They look like they've got good circulation support. Where'd you get those?"

"Sam's Club twelve-pack," Janis said, and Dad wrote it down like it was a hot tip.

Then he lined us up to take some awkward photos in front of a background that included the trash can and the Swiffer. When he passed my phone back to me, I could tell there wasn't a single photo where at least one of us didn't look like she had just accidentally swallowed a slug. "Don't worry," Janis whispered, "I'll pick the best faces and photoshop them all together." Dad waved us out the door, and then we piled into Janis's car. Spring River High School Valentine's Day dance, watch out. Cuz we weren't the only ones on our way.

CHAPTER 16

So, yeah, the thing about populariskinesis was that it worked. Really well.

We were early, so most of the other students hadn't arrived yet, but the dance committee was in full swing. And they were very, very hyped. "We've been waiting for you!" Kendra said, rushing over as soon as she spotted Janis and me. "Are they here yet? They're still coming, right? I can't believe we got Jump the Shark to play our Valentine's Day dance. I mean, they're *huge*! They're so popular. They sell out stadiums! Everyone loves them."

None of this was true, but I nodded, also happy that she had just reminded me of what their most recent name was. "Yeah, it's crazy, right?" I shifted the bag of groceries I was carrying from one arm to the other.

"What is that?" Kendra asked.

"Uh, Jump the Shark's rider," I told her. "It's what they want in the green room."

Kendra's eyes widened, and she peeked in the top of the

bag. "Oh my God," she said, "Jump the Shark loves soup. *I love soup.*" She clasped her hands in front of her and wrung her fingers. "I can't believe we have so much in common."

Nipple boy, whose name I had forgotten, if I had ever known it, came up to us. Now, instead of a polo shirt, he was wearing a button-down oxford, but the nipples were still visible through that. I guess he'd never heard of undershirts?

"That stuff is for the band?" he asked, reaching out to take Janis's bag from her, which had the blender sticking out of the top, balanced on yet more cans of soup. "Here, allow me." His shirt sleeves were rolled up, and I could see a big, dark Jump the Shark tattoo snaking down his forearm.

I swallowed. "Is that real?" I asked, my mouth going sour with fear.

Nipple boy sighed and shook his head, and I relaxed.

"No, my mom would kill me," he said, "so I just drew it on for tonight. Do you think they'll like it?"

"I think they'll love it," Janis said, and he beamed.

Yeah, I was pretty powerful, all right.

Karen came walking over at a clip, legit holding a clipboard. "Ryan, I need you back on balloon duty," she said. "And, Kendra, that punch isn't going to make itself."

"I know," Kendra said, a smile plastered onto her face, "but Esme and Janis were just telling us that Jump the Shark are on their way."

Karen's expression softened, and she actually smiled. "I still can't believe I got them to play a high school dance," she said. My spell had worked so well that now Karen thought this whole debacle had been her idea. I stifled a giggle by turning it into a cough. "People are going to remember this dance forever. I hope they play . . ." Karen trailed off. "What's the name of their big song again?"

"Oh, you'll know it when you hear it," Janis said.

The fangirl glow on Karen's face had faded, though, and now her eyes were fixed behind us. Ji-A, Amirah, and Pig had followed us in, and were standing about ten feet behind us, watching this whole scene.

"Hi," Karen said, smiling a smile that did not extend to her eyes. "Can I help you?"

"We're Esme's and Janis's dates," Ji-A said.

"Well, you're certainly dressed up," she said, "but no dogs allowed. Someone brought a dog to last year's homecoming, and let's just say that the papier-mâché decorations were not, uh, treated with respect. The dog will have to wait outside." No one moved.

"She's my date," Amirah said with a smile.

"But you're already a date," Karen said. "So it can wait outside."

"I know," Amirah said. "And the dog is my date, and she is not an *it*. Her name is 'Pig.'"

"You can't have a dog in here unless it's a support animal," Karen began. It didn't surprise me one bit that Amirah was not used to being denied, and now a look crossed her face. I could see a gleam in her eye, and she smiled, a little smirk as sharp as an ice skate, and then she started to open her mouth.

"It's Jump the Shark's dog!" I blurted out. As much as I would have loved to see Karen obliterated into a million pieces that needed to be Dyson-ed up off the floor, we already had enough drama on the books for one night. "They really wanted her to come and see the show!" Ji-A started to laugh and then faked a coughing fit.

"She'll need to be in the front row too," Amirah said, "or else they might mess up your favorite song."

Karen's mouth twitched, but her normal disapproving stance was no match for my populariskinesis. "Does she need a chair?" she asked. I started to say no, but Amirah beat me to it, nodding gravely.

"With a cushion," she said. Now Janis was the one seized by a coughing fit, and Karen eyed her like she had the plague.

"Come on," I said, hefting my bag, "we have to go set up. Where's the green room?" I asked Karen.

"The teachers' lounge," Karen said. "It's the best room in the school, and I wanted to make sure they liked it."

I raised my eyebrows at her. "Great," I said, "but where are the teachers going to lounge?"

"Honestly, I couldn't care less," Karen said. "But I made it nice in there, so don't mess it up." A sound like a balloon popping echoed through the hallway and made Karen jump. "Jeez!" she screamed. "We only have five hundred of those! Who keeps popping the freaking balloons?" Then she stormed off down the hallway.

The school was still far from crowded, but people were starting to stream in, and I could see that a lot of them were going to great pains to not stare at Amirah and Ji-A. And honestly, I didn't blame them. Amirah and Ji-A looked like they could have come straight out of a fashion video, and Amirah had a pit bull in a tuxedo shirt.

"So," Ji-A said as we walked, the heels of her—my—cowboy boots echoing on the floor and her dress flowing out behind her like a cape, "this is your school, huh? It's crazy. It looks like something out of a TV show. There are lockers and everything." She stopped, and stood up on her toes so that she could peer into a closed classroom through the small glass window in the door.

"Your school doesn't have lockers?" I asked, and she shook her head.

"I'm homeschooled," she said, "so mostly the teachers just come to me, and then we go on field trips."

"What kind of field trips?" I asked.

"Oh, you know," she said, "historical sites. Like the Great Wall."

"Of China?" I asked. She nodded, like a field trip to China was the most natural thing in the world.

"What's your school like?" I asked Amirah, who just shrugged.

"Normal," she said. "A lot like this one. Only everyone's rich, and some of them are famous."

We'd reached the teachers' lounge, and Janis pulled the door open. "Wow," she said. "They really took the concept of the green room literally." We followed her in. I set my bag of groceries down on a table and glanced around. It looked like Kendra and Karen had skipped V-Day all together and gone straight for St. Patty's. I had no idea what the teachers' lounge looked like on a regular basis, but now it held a couch with green pillows, a long table covered with a green paper table-cloth, and a big banner that said, in big green glitter letters, WE 💚 JUMP THE SHARK. Ji-A's dress fit right in.

Janis was unpacking the soup, and I was looking for an

outlet to plug in the blender when my phone buzzed. A text from Cassandra.

"The band just left their house," I said, reading from it, "so they should be here in a few minutes."

"Ooh, that's exciting," Ji-A said. "I can't wait to lay eyes on these guys and see if they're as disappointing as you make them out to be."

"Oh, I bet they're even more disappointing!" Janis said, and I turned to see that she had arranged the cans into a pyramid.

"That looks very . . . grocery store?" I said, and she shrugged.

"I wasn't sure how else to do it?" she said. "How do you take a bunch of cans and make it look sexy?"

"So," Amirah said, plopping down on the couch and propping her feet up on Pig, "what time is dinner served? I'm starving."

"What do you mean?" I asked.

"This is an event," she said. "So, I'm assuming there's food?"

"Uh, no . . . ," I said.

"May I interest you in a can of"—Janis grabbed the top one from the pyramid and read off the label—"beef stew? I assume there's a microwave around here somewhere."

"Gross," Amirah said. "But there really isn't a dinner? Usually when you buy a table for—"

I interrupted her. "This is just a school dance," I said. "No one buys tables. It's free." I could sense that I wasn't getting through, and that she was legitimately expecting there to be shrimp cocktail or something. "But you know what? There is a Panda Sub just, like, two blocks away," I offered.

She was on her feet like her butt had just been electrocuted. "Really?" she said. "Do we have time to go?"

"Of course," I said. "We'll be here all night." I gave Amirah and Ji-A directions, and they assured me that even though they didn't have jackets, they wouldn't be cold.

"We've got spells for that," Ji-A said, and then they headed out the door. I wasn't totally sad to see them go, because I was starting to get more and more nervous. I had every reason to suspect that the members of Jump the Shark were not the brightest crayons in the box, but I imagined that even for them, Amirah and Ji-A wouldn't necessarily look like they were regulars at Spring River High School, where half the students wore athleisure even to a dance.

My phone started to buzz again, and I looked down to see that Brian had texted me. "Brian wants to see us in his office," I said to Janis, who was busy trying to get Pig to pose in front of the soup pyramid. Pig just kept looking at the soup like she wanted to eat it, which she probably did. I grabbed her leash, and the three of us left the teachers' lounge and headed to Brian's office, cutting through the gym on the way. Pink, white, and red streamers dangled from the ceiling and the basketball hoops, and balloons in the same color scheme bounced around, gathering in the corners, and a few helium ones floated through the air. I had to hand it to the Ks, they had made this place look pretty okay for a gym.

I held Pig's leash, and Janis followed after me, and as with taking Pig anywhere, it felt like being a bodyguard to a celebrity. A celebrity who was very easily distracted by anything that might hold the promise of a tasty nibble. I turned down photo ops and laughed at dumb dog jokes all the way across the gym, then took a deep breath before I pushed open the door to the boys' locker room, though I doubted there was anyone in there at this time of night, or Brian wouldn't have asked us to come.

"Wow," Janis said, "so this is where the patriarchy is built, huh?"

"Yeah," I laughed. "Everything you expected?"

"Nah," she said, shaking her head. "I expected more. I mean, where are all the phallic symbols and monuments to capitalism?"

"What about that?" I asked, motioning to a freestanding punching bag in a corner, and she curled her lip.

I knocked on Brian's door, and he called for us to come in. He did a double take as soon as he saw Pig, and when she saw him, she made a break for it, and the leash went flying out of my hand. Brian crouched down to the floor, and soon she was covering him with kisses as he covered her with pets. Whenever he'd come over to our house, I'd never seen Brian give Pig more than a passing pet, and she'd never seemed to care much about him.

But now, when he finally stood up, his eyes were glistening. "She looks good," he said, with a sniff. "Same old Pig. Any idea where she was all this time?"

I shook my head. "None," I said. "Wherever it was, she's not telling." Now Brian was silent for a second as he looked at her, and I wondered if he was thinking the same thing that I was: Pig was not just a dog. But that was a discussion topic for another time, and Brian shook his head briefly and went back to what he'd been doing. Normally when I went into Brian's office, he was doing something like watching football, or drawing about football with a bunch of *X*s and *O*s on a big whiteboard. Now he was, I kid not, ironing a tracksuit, while wearing a tracksuit. Both were exactly the same.

"What are you doing?" I sputtered.

"Ironing," he said, holding up the iron. "This is an iron. You have seen an iron before, right?"

"I know what an iron is, Brian," I said. "I just choose not to use them." I paused. "Doesn't nylon melt?"

"Not if you know which heat setting to use," Brian said, laying the freshly ironed track jacket on the ironing board, and unzipping the track jacket he had on. "Anyway, I wanted to check in and make sure everything was set for tonight." He then took off the un-ironed track jacket and replaced it with the one he had just finished working on. He zipped it up over his T-shirt, and I swear on frozen pizza he looked exactly the same.

"Well," I said, "the band is on their way, and I don't mean to pat myself on the back, but my populariskinesis spell worked really well, and the dance committee seems to think that Jump the Shark are the best thing to happen to music since Nirvana."

"And where are the other girls?" Brian asked.

"Well, Amirah and Ji-A are getting Panda Sub right now, and Ruby, Cassandra, and Mallory are at Jump the Shark's house, ready to see what they can find." As if on cue, my phone dinged, and I looked down to see a text from Ruby.

"Wait," I said, reading the text. "Apparently they're waiting, because the next-door neighbors are barbecuing, so there are a whole bunch of people in the neighbor's backyard? They're going to wait to see if they go inside soon. If they don't, Ruby will spell them."

"Barbecuing?" Brian said. "In Kansas in February?"

"I don't know!" I said, shrugging. "People like to grill?"

"Cassandra sent that text?" Brian asked, and I shook my head.

"Ruby," I said. "She's in charge of the updates, since Cassandra . . . you know."

Brian nodded, because he did know. "Well, that's good," he said. "At least she'll keep us in the loop." Then my phone started ringing, a local number I didn't recognize.

I tapped accept and was met by a voice practically screaming at me. "Where the heck are you? The band is here, and there's no can opener!"

"Karen?" I asked.

"No, Kendra!"

"How'd you get my number?"

"Who cares?" she screamed back. "How are they supposed to eat this chili?"

I hung up and turned to Janis. "That was Kendra," I said. "The band is here, and apparently they are freaking out because there's no way to open all that soup."

"Oh crap," Janis said, then dug into her bag and pulled out a can opener. "I brought this."

"Well, we'd better get back there before someone has a meltdown," I said. We started to head out the door, and Brian stopped me.

"Esme, before you go, what's your plan for casting popularis-kinesis on everyone?"

"I don't know," I said. "I was just going to cast it on everyone."

He shook his head. "Do it in sections," he said. "You'll have more control that way. And please do not let the teachers get caught in the cross fire. If they think the band is awful, that just makes it more believable."

I nodded. That was a good point. "Thanks for the tip, B.," I said. "See you on the other side." Then Janis and I went back through the locker room, Pig trotting after us, and booked it through the gym to the teachers' lounge.

I pulled open the door, and the smell of dollar-store cologne hit me in the face. Farther into the room, I could see that the four members of Jump the Shark were sitting on the couch, somewhat packed in there, and that Kendra, Karen, Ryan, and a few other members of the dance committee were standing there, awkwardly, right in front of them. I could hear a girl whose name I didn't know babbling about how she loved all their songs, even though she didn't refer to a single one by name.

On the end of her leash, Pig started to whimper and plant. "Come on, girl," I whispered, giving her a tug into the teachers' lounge. "We have to do this." Her claws scraped on the ground as I pulled her over the threshold, and I didn't blame her for the resistance, because looking at the band made me want to do the exact same thing. Once we were in the room and the door had closed behind us, I took off her leash, and she headed straight to a corner. Fortunately, the Ks were too enamored of the band to know that the band's own dog didn't want anything to do with them.

I had to force myself to swallow. I had to be extra cautious tonight. I didn't want to give the band any more reason to think that there was anything strange about me—or about this dance. I could still feel how the magic around their house had made my stomach roil, but I steeled myself to act "normal" and walk toward them. In my experience, the best way to distract someone was flattery. Lots and lots of flattery. So that was what I was going to do.

They were all dressed almost exactly the same as the first time we'd seen them at the bar, but this was the first time I was seeing them all together this close up. They all looked kind of the same, and now I couldn't tell the difference between the one that Dion and I had followed through the grocery store, and the one I'd talked to on the front porch. Maybe I could just say his name, and see which one of them would stand up, but then I worried that might out me as not knowing the names of the members of my favorite band, so . . .

"Look what I brought!" Janis said from behind me, and instantly all four members of Jump the Shark were up and off the couch. I turned to see Janis brandishing the can opener like it was the keys to a Lamborghini.

The four of them responded like it was keys to a Lamborghini, and one of them snatched it out of her hand almost immediately. Kendra and Karen were shooting her death daggers too, since she had effectively stolen their thunder and the band was now totally focused on the soup pyramid in front of them. I took this as my cue, and stepped over to Karen.

"I think you guys should get out of here," I said. "No offense, but they don't like to have a lot of hangers-on around, you know, hangin' on." The look on Karen's face was priceless. "They need to be able to concentrate before their set. We don't want to harsh their mojo." I had no idea what I was talking about, but no matter how much Karen might have hated me in that moment, she still loved Jump the Shark and didn't want to do anything that would prevent them from having the best show ever.

She nodded. "I'll get everyone out of here." She started to turn away, then turned back to me and lowered her voice. "Do you think they like the banner?" She gestured at the green glitter one, and now that I was looking at it closely, I could see that it said "I love you—Karen" in the corner of the *K*.

"I'm sure they love it," I said, and then motioned for her to leave. The rest of the dance committee grumbled about leaving, but they followed Karen out, and soon, Janis and I were alone in the green room with Tom, Todd, Brad, and Chad. I made eye contact with Janis. "Which one's the one you talked to?" she whispered. I grimaced and shrugged. She pointed to a filing cabinet, and I looked over to see that she was pointing at a Sharpie and a stack of "Hello, my name is . . ." stickers.

"Great idea!" I mouthed back. I grabbed one, wrote down "Esther," and stuck it onto the front of my dress. I wrote "Janet" on another one and stuck it onto Janis. She narrowed her eyes at me—she's a little sensitive about the whole Janis/Janet Jackson thing—but I think she got that it just seemed better if Jump the Shark didn't know our real names.

"So," I said loudly, turning back to the band. "I'm Esther and this is Janet, and we got these name tags so that you wouldn't have to remember our names, because I am sure that you guys meet people all the time, and I thought it would be great if everyone wore one." I held the name tags and the marker out toward them. "You know, for solidarity." Finally one of them took them from me and wrote "Todd" in big block letters, and stuck the sticker to the front of his T-shirt. The others followed suit, and I was once again thankful for Janis's genius, because the one I had been betting on to be Tom was actually Brad.

I wondered what kind of vibes Janis was picking up from them, because my Sitter sense was firing away. The back of my neck felt like it was crawling with ants, and the overall drippy, gross feeling that surrounded their house surrounded the band as well. The air was dense, and I was starting to feel slightly nauseous.

I was going to do my best to hide it, though. I turned to the one who actually was Tom, and smiled. "It's so good to see you again!" I said, making my voice sound extra perky. "So, we are here for you! Please let me and Janis—I mean, Janet—know if you need anything."

"Yeah, there's one thing you should know," he said, his face and voice very serious. "We're not Jump the Shark anymore. We're Superfood."

"Like, blueberries?" I asked. Surely he had to be joking, but he just nodded.

"With an umlaut over the *U*," he added.

"So, Süperfood?" Janis said, drawing out the "oo" sound in "super."

"No," Tom said, shaking his head. "Over the *U* in 'food.' 'Superfüd.'"

"There is no *U* in—" Janis started, but I kicked her ankle and she stopped.

"Great name," I said. "I love it." He looked at me like he was waiting for me to say more. "It rocks," I added.

"Yeah, so that banner's gonna have to come down," he said, pointing at Karen's love letter.

"Sure," Janis said, walking over to the banner. We all watched as she pulled it off the wall, wadded it into a ball, and stuffed it into the nearest trash can.

"Cool, cool," Tom said when she was done. "This is a cool soup pyramid."

"Thanks, yeah, Janet made it," I said.

"Cool," Tom said, and I doubted that he had aced vocab tests in high school, whenever that was.

Behind Tom, the rest of Superfüd were making quick work with the can opener, and each member of the band had opened their own can of soup.

"Do you need a microwave?" Janis asked.

"Nah, we're cool," Brad said as he pried open the lid on the can of chili and then dumped the contents into the blender. He hit pulse a few times, then took the lid off and peered into the top. Next to me, Janis made a weird noise, and I could tell she was stifling a gag.

Apparently, what Brad saw wasn't to his liking, so he put the top back and pulsed the blender a few more times. Then he took the pitcher off the blender base and dumped the now liquified chili into one of the Styrofoam cups that Janis had set out for the drinks. I felt like I was watching a YouTube video where stoners decide to add strawberry jelly to their nachos— because next he took a bottle of ranch dressing, popped the foil seal, and then squeezed a whole bunch onto the chili, and then sat down and began to sip it. It was still cold. I looked away before I threw up in my mouth. Janis started to hum, clearly trying to distract herself from the scene in front of us.

When Chad stepped up to the blender with a can of

chicken noodle I had to turn away again. They didn't rinse the blender out between soups. Fortunately, Tom didn't seem to be hungry, and just sat at the end of the couch, sipping a glass of grape juice.

Steeling my stomach and mentally telling my gag reflex to take the night off, I went over and sat down on the arm of the couch. "So," I said, "how long have you guys been playing together?" Tom looked up at me, his teeth already stained purple, and I could see his eyes narrow a little bit. "I mean, I know, of course, because I know everything about you. But I want to hear the Superfüd story from Superfüd themselves."

I would have bet all my babysitting money that I was the only person to ask Tom about Superfüd in maybe all of history, but he still had the weariness of a musician who'd been doing interviews all day with journalists who clearly hadn't listened to the album.

"Well," he started, taking a sip of grape juice and savoring it like it was thirty-year-old Scotch. "Only a couple of years now," he said.

I tried to keep my face neutral, and just nodded. "You ever take any breaks?" I asked. "I bet it's tough being in a band, and sometimes you just want to chill out for a while. Like a week, or fifteen years, maybe?"

"No," he said, looking up at me. Crap. Maybe I was being paranoid, but I thought I could see something in his eyes that hinted at him being onto me.

I changed tactics. "So, tell me about your influences. Who, in your opinion, is really rocking right now?"

This was a question that Tom could answer, and he sat up

a little straighter. "Puddle of Mudd, for sure," he said. "Those guys are super inspirational. They're from Kansas City, you know, so it's cool to see another Midwestern band make it big." I nodded enthusiastically.

"Mud puddle, yeah, I love them." I had never heard of this band. "So, you guys used to be a five-piece, right?" Tom nodded and gave a little grunt. I decided to take that as a sign of encouragement and run with it. "What happened to the fifth guy?"

"He died." His bluntness kind of shocked me, especially since he said this with all the emotion of an exterminator delivering news on the fate of a rat.

"Oh," I said. "I didn't know that. I'm sorry."

He just shrugged and sipped his grape juice.

"So," I said, "what do you do when you're not playing music? Any hobbies? I've got tons of hobbies. Lately I've been really into flooring, especially the waterproof kind. Like, tile and linoleum . . ."

Maybe it was a good thing, but my words had no effect on Tom. "Music only," he said. He certainly had the mute-rock-star thing down.

I glanced at the clock. I had a few more minutes before I needed to excuse myself to go spell the school. Not that I was going to tell Tom that, of course. "Here," I said, standing up, "let me refill your drink." He passed the cup to me, and I shivered as our fingers touched just slightly. He had all the life and humanity of a dead frog soaked in antifreeze.

"Make it root beer this time," he said. Across the room, Janis had been making small talk with Brad and Chad, which left Todd sitting by himself reading a comic book. As I walked across the teachers' lounge to get Tom some root beer, Janis came sidling up to me.

"Ummmm . . . ," she said, her voice barely a whisper, "so Chad thinks that George W. Bush is the president, and Brad just said that he's the band's webmaster, so he's in charge of their Myspace page."

I nodded as I poured Tom's root beer. "They're definitely frozen in time," I whispered back. "I couldn't get anything out of Tom about them taking a break or about him working at the Home Depot. Did you get any insight into the soup?"

"No," she said, "but we had a long conversation about ranch dressing, and they are very impressed with the blender. When do they go on? I'm running out of aughts references."

I glanced across the room at the clock on the wall. "Fifteen minutes," I said under my breath. I turned away from the soup table and surveyed the room. Pig was still in her corner, and instead of settling in and curling up into a ball like she normally did, she was still sitting upright, very still. As I watched, Brad got up and started to walk over to her, but when he was a few feet away, Pig started to growl. In a split second, I was across the room, spilling Tom's root beer in the process, but putting myself between Pig and Brad.

"She's, uh, not super friendly," I said. "Best not to pet her right now." It felt wrong to slander Pig in such a way, but I didn't want there to be any dustups before the show.

Brad scowled. "Why is there an unfriendly pit bull in our green room?" he asked. "Seems like a liability. We will sue."

"I know, I know," I said, turning him back toward the couch. "It's the principal's dog. It's a long story." I smiled, though I'm sure it looked like a grimace, but Brad took me at my word, and walked back over and sat down on the couch next to Tom. I walked with him, and handed Tom his root beer. He took a sip of it, and then licked the foam from his lip. All I could think about was how much I hated root beer. It was like the creepy old uncle of soda.

"We want to go scope out the venue," he said, "and get our merch set up." Tom stood up and turned to Todd, handing me his half-drunk root beer like I was a waiter. "You have the backpack?" he asked, and Todd nodded. Janis came over to join us, looking relieved at the fact that Superfüd seemed to be leaving.

"They want to check out the venue," I said to her, and she nodded.

"Cool," she said. "We can show you the gym, and the stage."

"You got somebody to help with the equipment?" Brad asked. "It's out in the car." Just then, Kendra's and nipple boy's heads appeared in the window to the teachers' lounge, I assumed because they were trying to get a glimpse of the band.

"We do, actually," Janis said. "And they just arrived." She opened the door, and they started to scurry away, but Janis called them back. "Superfüd needs help unloading their equipment."

"Superfüd?" Kendra asked, and I couldn't help it. My masochistic side came out.

"That's their name now," I said sternly, "so don't call them anything else."

"Oh c-crap," nipple boy stammered as he started frantically trying to rub off his tattoo. "Obviously, of course. We can help them unload. It'd be an honor." Beside him, Kendra was nodding so furiously that I worried her head might detach.

"Their instruments are outside in their van," Janis said.

"Sports car," Brad corrected. "Sports car."

Janis opened her mouth like she was going to say something, but then she closed it again. Fortunately, she didn't have to say anything else.

"Well, heck, let's go get it, then!" nipple boy said. "You lead the way."

Brad, Chad, Kendra, and nipple boy headed toward the parking lot, which left me and Janis standing there with Tom and Todd. I redid Pig's leash, and again pulled her across the floor to join the others. The fur on her back was in a telltale ridge, and if I hadn't already known that these guys were trouble, Pig's reaction alone would have alerted me.

"So, there will be drinks, right?" Todd said as we started walking toward the gym.

"Of course," Janis said. "I mean, not alcoholic, because we're in a high school. But there's punch."

"Cool, cool," Todd said. "Don't want people getting thirsty."

"Yeah, sure," Janis said, pulling the door open to the gym. "Whatever."

I had to give it to the Kendras and the Karens of the world, or at least of Spring River High—they really tried. They had given the gym transformation their best, complete with a shiny metallic photo wall that quivered in the breeze of a very deliberately placed fan. There was also a giant pink-and-white balloon arch in the shape of a heart, and a junior DJing from his phone in the corner. He was working hard to crank out some beats to a dance floor that was populated solely by one art teacher and a sophomore who looked to be on some sort of combination of MDMA and taurine.

Various groups had assembled on the sidelines so that they could stare at the other groups assembled on the sidelines. If I was going to do what Brian had said to do, and cast populariskinesis on small groups, then everyone was making it easy for me, as they were already clumped together in little tufts no bigger than eight or nine people. If I worked quickly, I could get everyone done in less than twenty minutes, probably.

"Let's see this drink table," Tom said. Janis steered him in that direction, and I followed. Up close, I could see that the punch was a pure Red #40 and had little heart-shaped pieces of pineapple floating in it. The keeper of the punch was none other than Karen herself, who was doling it out one cup at a time.

"One per person," she said sharply to a girl.

"But he just got two!" the girl said, pointing to a guy who was walking away with a cup in each hand.

"Yeah," Karen said, "because he got one for his date. You don't have a date, as evidenced by the fact that you're here right now, getting your own drink, so one cup for you."

Ouch, Karen, ouch.

At the punch table, Todd dropped to his knees and started to dig through his backpack, and as he did, a dime and a tube of lip balm rolled out of a hole that he had apparently tried to fix with a piece of duct tape. I picked them up and handed them back to him, and he grunted a thanks. I suddenly understood how someone could drop their body spray, wallet chain, and totally identifying band flyer while they were trying to do something secret.

"Where do I put these?" Todd said, standing up with a stack of CDs in his hand. "We've got some tees too." Karen was still under my spell to think that Superfüd was an insanely popular band, but even with that, she wasn't totally stoked on having them crash her drink table.

"Um, I didn't really plan space for that," she said to Todd, who ignored her.

"Here's our price list," he said, handing her a piece of cardboard with black Sharpie letters.

Her face looked like he was trying to hand her his old gym socks. "Um, had I known you were going to be selling stuff, I would have made a special sign that went with the color scheme," she said.

Todd dropped the CDs onto the table, and then started to move cups out of the way to make room for the T-shirts. I bent to get a closer look, and saw that the CD cover had the same band photo as their Myspace page, and that the name "Superfüd" was written on yet another piece of duct tape on each.

"Let me help you with that," Karen said, the smile on her face stretched as tight as a ponytail holder about to break. I watched her try to aesthetically arrange Superfüd's ringer tees, which had their new band name made to look like it had been stenciled onto the side of a metal garbage can. I had no idea how they'd gotten the T-shirts made in time, but I couldn't have designed the band a better logo myself.

"You're folding them all wrong!" Tom said. At first I thought he was talking to Todd, but then I realized he was talking to Karen. She realized it too.

"Excuse me?" she said. "I spent two summers working at the Gap. I think I know how to fold a T-shirt."

"One horizontal fold only!" Tom said, taking a shirt to demonstrate. "When you fold it in thirds, you can't see the logo!"

"Oh, who cares!" Todd interrupted, grabbing the T-shirts from both Tom and Karen and dropping them into a pile on the table. "These are so cool that they'll sell out no matter how they're folded." He looked at me and Janis like he expected us to say something.

"Haha," Janis said finally. "Maybe I'll just buy them all myself."

"That'd be cool too," Todd said, and then he and Tom went to help their bandmates set up.

CHAPTER 17

"Hey, Janis, cool dog." Bode Chase was standing in front of us. Bode Chase was a senior, and looked exactly like you would expect someone named "Bode Chase" to look. He had shaggy blond hair, blue eyes, and, somehow, a tan even in Kansas in February.

I didn't know much about him, except that he was a star soccer player, girls practically fainted when he walked through the hallway, and he wasn't really from Spring River, but had just appeared at school one day the year before. He was popular but still kind of a loner and didn't really hang out with anyone other than a few of his soccer teammates, and I'd seen him reading books before.

Ugh, so maybe I did know a lot about Bode Chase, but I did not know what he was doing here, now, holding two cups of punch.

"Thanks," Janis said. "She's Esme's. Her name's 'Pig.'"

"Nice, that's awesome." Bode kept standing there, not even looking at Pig. Just looking at Janis.

"I like your earrings too," he continued. "Did you know that the ankh symbolizes both eternal and mortal life?" he asked. "And that differing theories posit that the loop and cross construction of the ankh was taken either from the form of the Egyptian sandal or from the belt buckle of Isis?" He sipped his punch. "The goddess, not the Islamic state," he added.

Janis just stood there, looking at him. "Wow," she said finally. "I did not know that."

Bode nodded. "My mom's an Egyptology professor," he said. "We moved here last year because she got a job at the university."

"No way," Janis said. "Both my parents teach at the university."

"I think I heard you mention that once," Bode said. "What department?"

"Nothing as cool as Egyptology," Janis said, and Bode smiled a toothpaste smile, then held out a cup of punch.

"Hey, you want some punch?" he offered. "I haven't drunk out of this one."

"Sure," Janis said. She handed me Pig's leash so that she could take the cup from him, and now it seemed like, in spite of using my dog as a conversation entry point, he was just now noticing me.

"Hey, Esme," he said. "You want me to get you some too?"

"No thanks," I said. "I'm allergic to pineapple."

"Whoa," he said. "I've never heard of anyone being allergic to pineapple before."

I just nodded.

"Yeah, it's crazy," Janis said. "Last time she ate some, her lips swelled up so much, she looked like one of those women who get addicted to plastic surgery."

Thanks, Janis. Thanks a lot.

"That sucks," Bode said, still staring at Janis. "Would you like to dance?"

"Not really," she said. Bode nodded, and took a sip of his punch. Janis took a sip of her punch too.

"So," Bode started, "I was watching this documentary about André Leon Talley—"

"Oh!" Janis said, perking up. "He's one of my heroes!"

"Yeah," Bode said. "My mom saw him in the airport in Paris once and . . ." Honestly, was this for real? If I had used a spell to create the perfect guy for Janis, it would not have created someone half as good as what was standing in front of us right now. I knew a third wheel when I was one, so I decided that now was the time for me to take my leave. Besides, I had work to do.

"Come on, girlie," I said, giving Pig a tug so she'd move closer to me. "Hey, Bode," I said, "I hate to interrupt, but . . ." I stepped between him and Janis and pushed her behind me. Holding my hand up and moving it in a semicircle so that I got Bode and a whole spray of people behind him, I muttered the spell and set my intentions.

As I was walking away, I heard him say, "So, I hear that people really love this band. They're pretty good, aren't they?"

Janis responded with, "Oh yeah, I love them." Goddess bless Janis—she was really good at playing along, and I hoped that a sincere, even if artificially induced, love for Superfüd wouldn't be enough to sever any genuine connection that might, right now, against all odds, be blossoming in this gym that still smelled, if you took a deep enough breath, like sweaty socks.

By now the dance was finally picking up. There were a few more people on the dance floor, and the groups that lined the walls were breaking up and intermingling. Pig trailing behind me, I wove my way through the crowd, my palms up, casting the spell on anyone who crossed my path. I figured I might miss a few here or there, but that would just make it more realistic. I'm sure that even Fleetwood Mac had a few haters in the crowd every once in a while, and Superfüd was no Fleetwood Mac. If anyone thought I was doing anything weird, no one gave me a second look. With Pig, it was extra easy, as people came to me, squealing and giggling and taking about a million pictures. One sophomore got so excited that she dropped her punch onto the ground, and then filmed it as Pig slurped up the puddle.

From the other side of the gym, I could see that Bode and Janis were still talking, and that Bode was saying something that had made Janis lean forward with laughter. When she stood back up, she was dabbing at her nose, which told me the giggles where real. When Janis really laughed, something always squirted out of her nose.

I checked my phone. It had been awhile since I'd heard anything from Team Circe, so I sent them a quick text. **Band about to go on,** I wrote. **What's happening over there?** My work here was done, at least for right now, so I decided to duck outside for a second to see if Pig needed to use the facilities. We headed down the hall and out the front door. Outside, it was freezing, and a damp wind had picked up, but Pig was being extra particular about which blade of grass she would turn into her toilet.

"Oh, come on," I said, giving her leash a yank. "Pick a spot already so we can go back inside." I heard a strange rustle of leaves behind me, and spun on my heel, hand raised and palm out, ready to blast any demon sneaking up on me. It wasn't a demon, though, and the rustle hadn't come from leaves. It'd come from feathers.

Adrian was standing there with his hands up and an apologetic look already on his face. "Sorry, sorry," he said. "I didn't mean to scare you."

"So, as long as you're on the run, you're never going to just knock on a door or send a text or anything?" I asked.

"Doors seem too risky," he said. "And my phone died back in January. I was charging it at a T-Mobile store for a while, but I think they were starting to catch on to me, and then my service got shut off, so I just gave up."

The wind picked up a little, and ruffled the tulle on my dress. Then I burst out laughing.

"I'm sorry, I know I shouldn't laugh," I said, dabbing my eyes with the back of my wrist, carefully, so that I wouldn't mess up my makeup. "It's just, like, I don't know, it's kind of pathetic." A smile flicked across Adrian's face, and I giggled again. "I mean, you're falling out of trees and charging your phone at a T-Mobile store. Don't get me wrong. I know I'm no better. Look at me—I'm at a dance with my dog. We're like a couple of characters in a YA novel who think we're outcasts, but really we're just losers." Now that flicker of a smile burst into a grin.

"Speak for yourself," he said. "Maybe I like brushing my teeth in the Pizza Hut bathroom."

"I apologize," I said. "Maybe you do."

"Nah," he said. "I really don't." Adrian smiled at me, and I felt my soul turn into moths and start fluttering all around inside my body. Pig had stopped sniffing and was looking back and forth between us.

"So, why are you here?" I asked finally.

"I wanted to check on you," he said. "How's your mom doing? How are you doing?"

I sighed. "I'm okay," I said. "She's okay." I filled him in on everything that had happened, and how she was back in the facility, and he listened and nodded.

"I'm sorry," he said. "And I'm not trying to apologize for something that is not my fault. I just feel genuine empathy for your situation right now."

"Thanks," I said. "It is what it is."

"So are you just here tonight having fun?" he asked, and I laughed.

"No way," I said, and gave him the short version of the Superfüd and Circe situation. "They should be going on soon," I said, pulling out my phone. My last text still sat there. It hadn't gone through. "But I haven't heard anything from Cassandra, Ruby, and Mallory in a while. I'm starting to get worried, but I can't leave."

"If you want, I can fly over there and check on them," Adrian offered.

"Really?" I said, feeling a rush of relief. "That would be a major help."

He nodded. "Yeah, no problem," he said. "There are some perks to being a bird boy, and to having a bird boy as a friend."

I told him where the band lived. "It's probably less than ten minutes," I said, "as the crow flies."

He smiled. "As the crow flies," he said. A gust of wind blew up, sending the few late winter leaves swirling around our feet. I shivered in my dress, and Adrian shoved his hands deeper into his pockets. Pig let out a little whimper, as her tuxedo shirt wasn't much of a windbreaker.

"I should get back inside," I said, and Adrian nodded. Neither of us moved, though. Finally I gathered up Pig's leash and started to turn to go.

"Esme," Adrian said, and I stopped and looked up at him. "You look really nice tonight," he said. "And I wish that I could have been your date for the dance."

"Thanks," I said, smiling. Then, so quick that I didn't even have time to realize what was about to happen and make it awkward, he kissed me.

He pulled back, smiled, and said, "Okay, gotta go." Then, with another rustle of feathers, he flew away. I stood there, slightly stunned, and then a sound made me look down. Pig had finally picked a spot to pee.

When she was finished, we went back inside, and I was pretty sure it wasn't just the glitter Alexander McQueen boots on my feet that made me feel like I was walking on air.

We'd just walked back into the gym when someone tapped me on the shoulder. I spun around to see Ji-A and Amirah standing there, Amirah looking significantly less happy than she had when she'd left. "Why are you grinning?" she said, cocking an eyebrow. "Something good happened. Spill. What was it?"

I wiped the smile off my face. "Nothing," I said. "I was just thinking about a meme I saw. But hey, how was Panda Sub?"

"I don't think it sat well with me this time," she said, and then burped. "I mean, those Bolognese egg rolls were just as good as they were last night, but now I feel, I don't know, all bloated." She held out her hand, and her fingers looked like they'd been inflated.

"Uh, yeah," I said, feeling bad for not warning her. "I can't eat Panda Sub because there's too much sodium in it. And I'm someone who mostly eats things that come wrapped in plastic." She burped again and tried to stifle it, and I could tell by the look on her face that it came out her nose.

"I'm going to go get us something to drink," Ji-A said. "Maybe that will make us feel better. Esme, you want some punch?"

"I'm allergic to pineapple," I said.

"That's weird," Amirah said. "What happens when you eat it?"

"I swell up like a—" I stopped as a note of feedback pierced through the gym. Superfüd's show was about to start, and the full weight of what Brian had warned us of hit me. Like he'd pointed out—over and over—by inviting Superfüd to play, we were putting all of the students at risk. But also, we were ruining their night. Anxiety and guilt washed over me. Sure, they'd all gotten dressed up to come hang out in the gym, but some of them would have had fun. I tried to console myself by thinking maybe they'd all go home thinking that they'd at least seen their favorite band, but that just made me feel worse. I'd have to station myself at the door, and get Ji-A and Amirah to help, so that we could reverse the spell on everyone on their way out.

Ji-A reappeared with two glasses of punch. Amirah took one from her, gulped it, and then burped again. "Any word from Cassandra?" she asked.

"Not in a while," I said, pulling out my phone to see that I still hadn't gotten a response. "The last I heard, they were waiting for the neighbors to go inside."

"How long ago was that?" Ji-A asked, taking a sip of her punch.

"Over an hour ago," I said.

"I wonder if we should go check on them?" Ji-A said, looking at Amirah. "We could just call an Uber and go by?"

"Yeah, totally," Amirah said.

"That would be great," I said. Having Adrian check on them was one thing, but if they were in trouble, he wouldn't be able to do anything about it.

"On it," Ji-A said, tipping her glass back and draining the last of her punch. "You know, it's too bad you can't have pineapple. This is really good."

"I'll pass your compliments on to Karen," I said.

"Okay, let's go," Amirah said, and then a guitar chord rang out, and Superfüd launched into their first song.

There are two types of bad music: obvi bad, and sneaky bad. Obvi bad is like a polka band playing Snoop Dogg covers. You recognize it immediately, but sneaky-bad music tricks you. Like, when you're scanning through the radio and stop on what you think is a new pop song, only to have the chorus be about how all us sinners are going to hell. Or like one of Dad's favorite bands, Pearl Jam.

Superfüd was sneaky bad.

The crowd was rapt, though, and everyone was watching when Todd stepped up to the mic and said, "Hi, we're the band formerly known as 'Jump the Shark,' but we're 'Superfüd' now." Nipple boy howled like a werewolf, one fist raised in the air as he started to headbang.

"Thanks for having us," Tom added, then started to strum a few chords on the guitar. Brad kicked in with the drums, and Todd started singing. The first few chords struck me as okay, not quite as bad as I had expected, but then I really started to pay attention. On bass, Chad stomped back and forth across the stage like he was on his way to dispute a parking ticket. Todd's voice was smooth enough, it didn't crack, and I listened to the lyrics, which sounded like they were about camping. When the chorus hit, I no longer had any doubt. It was definitely a song about camping. "I hope you brought a taarrrrrrp," Todd crooned, "cuz it looks like rain."

"Raaaaaaiinnn," sang Brad on backup.

"This tent only holds one," Todd sang, and then Tom interjected with a little spoken word.

"Take your double sleeping bag and go sleep in the car!"

That was when I lost it. "Oh my God," I said, turning to Amirah and Ji-A. "This is even worse than I expected. I'm jealous you guys get to leave." But they didn't answer. Nor did it look like they were going anywhere.

Both of them were staring straight ahead, at the band, totally enraptured. Amirah was clutching her empty punch cup to her chest like it was a rose from *The Bachelor*, and her fingers twisted it. "I. Love. Superfüd."

"What? You can't be serious?" I stared at her, waiting for her to start cracking up, but she didn't even look at me. She was totally focused on the band. I turned to Ji-A. "She can't be serious."

But Ji-A barely even noticed I was there. She just swayed back and forth slightly, singing along. "I hope you brought a tarrrrrrp," she said, her eyes half closed in ecstasy.

"Ji-A," I said, snapping my fingers at her, "you're from Manhattan. Do you even know what a tarp is?"

"It's gonna rain," she sang, getting the words wrong but still singing along. I stood there for a second, and then felt a cold panic wash over me. Something was wrong. Something was *really* wrong.

"Come with me," I said, grabbing Ji-A. "We have to find Janis." She yanked her arm away.

"I'll share your sleeping bag!" she yelled at the stage.

"Amirah! Please! We need to go," I pleaded, turning to her. "This isn't right. We need to find Brian and fix it." Amirah had tears pouring from her eyes, and the cup that she still held in her hands was now totally shredded, ripped to pieces. Her mouth was moving, but no sound was coming out. I stared at her lips for a second and could just make out that she was saying. "Superfüd is the best band in the entire universe. Superfüd is the best band in the entire universe."

Crap, crap, crap. I had to find Janis. I grabbed Pig's leash and turned to run, but Pig had planted. I pulled again, and she didn't budge.

"Not now, Pig," I said. "We need to go."

But she retained her anvil pose, and what was worse, she too was staring straight ahead. At the stage, at the band, and suddenly she began to howl. "Rorrr-rorrro-rrrrorr-rrrooorrr!" she crooned. She was singing along!

I had to make a split-second decision. I grabbed Amirah's hand and wrapped Pig's leash around it several times. "Stay here!" I yelled at all three of them. "Don't go anywhere!" Then I turned and ran, pushing my way through the crowd. Several people shoved me back, angry that I'd disrupted their view of the band for even one second. When a sophomore tried to shoulder me out of the way, I shoved him back, hard, with my kinesis.

"Ouch!" he yelped.

"Mosh pit, dude," I said. "Toughen up." Finally I spotted Janis. Or rather, I spotted Bode, and Janis was standing right next to him. Bode had a fist raised in the air and was pumping it and banging his head back and forth to the beat.

"Esme!" Janis cried when she saw me, grabbing me by the shoulders.

"Oh, thank God!" I yelled, trying to get her to hear me over the crowd. "Ji-A and Amirah and Pig were somehow affected by my spell. They think Superfüd is the best band in the world." My words did not have the jolt-into-action effect I had hoped for.

"I agree!" Janis shouted, jumping up and down. "Superfüd is the best band in the world!"

Oh no.

Someone near the front of the crowd had started a chant, and Janis joined in. "Pitch the tent! Pitch the tent!" she yelled.

"Janis!" I screamed at her, grabbing her shoulders and trying to get her to look me in the face. "You despise camping for what it does to your hair!"

"Let's make s'mores!" she yelled.

I dropped my hands and took a step back. What the heck was going on here? Slowly I started to turn around, and everywhere I looked, every person I saw was 100 percent, completely, and totally focused on Superfüd. People were singing along. Girls were crying. The few stoners who hadn't switched to vape were holding lighters in the air. So was the art teacher. Everyone loved it.

My spell was good, but there was no way it was this good. Superfüd had done something. But when? How? I'd been with them from the time they'd gotten here, and I hadn't seen them do anything. Unless . . . Oh God. The punch.

They had been really interested in the punch, and I'd just assumed it was because they were obvious weirdos when it came to food and drink. But what if they'd spiked it? Right under my nose when they were making such a fuss about their CDs and ringer tees? I was supposed to protect the people at this school. How could I have let this happen? Even Pig had drunk the punch!

Suddenly a deep voice broke through the crowd. "Booooooo! Boooooo! You suck! Get off the stage!"

I spun, frantically, trying to locate the sound of the only other sane person in the entire gymnasium. Then I saw who it was: Stacey Wasser, hands cupped around her mouth as she yelled at Todd and told him to do something very obscene with his microphone.

"Stacey! Stacey!" I said, running over to her. "You hate this band!"

"Eff yeah," she said. "These guys blow!"

"When did you get here?" I asked her.

"I dunno," she said. "Five minutes ago. Long enough ago to know that these guys are posers!" She yelled this last part over the crowd.

"Did you drink any punch?"

She took a break from her heckling to give me a weird look. "No way," she said. "I only drink milk."

"Come with me, please," I pleaded, grabbing her hand. "My dog is here, and I want you to meet her." Now I had her attention.

"The dog you lost?" she asked, following me back through the crowd.

"Yes, but she came back this week." We cleared a crowd of sophomores, and I was relieved to see Pig, Amirah, and Ji-A standing right where I had left them. "See?" I said to Stacey, pointing at Pig. "There she is!"

"That's a good-looking dog," Stacey said.

"I know, right?" I said, grabbing Pig's leash from Amirah and thrusting it at Stacey. "Could you just watch her for a minute? You can still yell at the band from here, but I, uh, need to go to the bathroom." Stacey reached out and took the leash from me, and I could see her giving Ji-A and Amirah a strange look.

"Sure," she said. "But what's wrong with your friends?"

I looked back at them. They now had their eyes closed, and their arms around each other, swaying along to the music. "They're drunk," I said, going for the most believable lie.

"No," Stacey said, "I mean their clothes. What's wrong with their clothes?" Stacy herself was wearing a pixelated camouflage long-sleeved sweat-wicking T-shirt, army-green sweatpants, and SpongeBob Crocs with socks.

"They're from New York," I offered, and she nodded. Then, apparently satisfied with my answer, she turned her attention back to heckling the band. I started to weave my way through the crowd, and when I looked back, Stacey was still gripping Pig's leash tightly.

On one side of the gym, a fountain of screams erupted as two girls started clawing at each other and pulling hair, desperately fighting over what appeared to be the last Superfüd T-shirt. Karen jumped up onto the punch table, and for a brief second, I expected her to try to break up the fight. Then she lifted the punch bowl over her head and threw it, pineapples and all, onto the two fighting girls. Momentarily stunned, they stopped fighting, and in that second, Karen jumped off the table, grabbed the T-shirt, and took off at a sprint.

I hadn't seen Brian since he'd been ironing his tracksuit, and I hoped, prayed, crossed my fingers that if he'd gotten thirsty, he'd just drunk from the drinking fountain like a teacher should. I tore through the guys' locker room, but Brian's office was empty. I ran back out and stopped, peering up and down the dark hallway.

There was a light at the end of the tunnel, literally, and it looked like someone was in the principal's office. I sprinted toward it, the sound of Superfüd and their rioting throng of superfans growing muffled behind me. I crashed through the door, and as soon as I did, I could hear Brian's voice.

"Brian!" I yelled, running toward his voice. I skidded to a

stop at the assistant principal's door, and saw not only her and Brian but also two very stoned-looking freshman who didn't know where to look: at their teachers, at me, or at the three-foot glass bong that was sitting in the middle of the desk.

"Esme," Brian said, looking concerned as he stood up and came toward me. "Is everything okay?"

"Not at all," I said. "It's an emergency."

"Oh dear!" the assistant principal said, glancing at the freshmen and their bong. "It's not the toilet again, is it? I told the janitorial department that those pipes couldn't take another dance."

"No! You stay here!" I said, too forcefully. "I mean, it's a family emergency."

Brian was already halfway across the office. "We're practically family," he called back. "Gayle, you follow protocol, and I'll be right back." Then we both speed walked out of the office, and when we got to the hall, the sounds of cheering and screaming hit us.

"Is that the dance?" he said, moving faster toward the gym door. "How many spells did you cast?"

"Just one," I said, starting to break into a run and motioning for him to come with me. "But I think the band cast one too. Everyone is freaking out! Even Janis and Amirah and Ji-A! Even Pig!" As we got closer to the gym, the sound got louder and louder, the screaming crowd totally drowning out the band. Brian pulled open the gym doors, and the wall of sound hit us in the face.

"Holy . . ." Brian's words were lost in the screams. Fights had broken out everywhere, some people fighting over CDs, some for a spot at the front of the crowd, and some just because.

Several of the guys had taken their shirts off, and a few of the girls had as well. Someone had pulled the climbing rope down and scaled it almost to the ceiling and was now holding on for dear life as a few people on the ground swung it wildly back and forth. All of Kendra and Karen's decorations had been torn down and destroyed, and right in the middle of the gym, there was a pile of bodies. People, lying on the ground, and on top of each other, not dead but sobbing their lungs out with love for Superfüd.

Now that we were in the gym, I could make out a few of the lyrics. Was this still the same song? I listened for a second. No, the chord progressions were different, and it was in a different key, but the lyrics . . . Yes, I was right. Superfüd had moved on to their second song about camping, and the crowd no longer wanted to pitch a tent. They wanted to . . .

"Build a fire! Build a fire!"

I looked over at Brian, and saw his nose wrinkle at the same time that an acrid smell hit my nostrils. He was looking behind me, and I spun around as soon as I saw his eyes widen. Some freshmen had taken the chant to heart, and the wall of streamers was going up in flames.

"Stop the band and get them out of here," Brian said. "I'll handle the crowd." Then he ran toward the wall and yanked the fire alarm. The gym filled with flashing lights and an ear-splitting bell, and then, probably triggered by the flames creeping toward the balloon arch, the sprinklers came on, filling the gym with a soft spring rain.

The rioting crowd barely noticed the water, and Brian didn't miss a beat as he rammed his tracksuited elbow through the glass door of the fire extinguisher. He grabbed it, pulled the pin, and immediately turned it on two girls who were in a rolling tangle on the floor, pulling each other's hair and fighting, it seemed, about who got to be Todd's girlfriend. The foam covered them from their hair-sprayed updos to the hems of their dresses, and they both started sputtering. One then rolled onto her back and started to wail. Not from pain but from unrequited love for Todd and hatred for the harpy next to her.

"Dance is over!" Brian attempted to yell over the chaos, brandishing the fire extinguisher. "Leave the gym now or you're all getting detention! I repeat, the dance is over!" He started to move through the crowd, blasting a few puffs of white foam at anyone who looked like they might challenge him.

"Jock! Fascist! Jock fascist!" someone screamed at him. It was the art teacher. Brian shot some foam into her face and kept going. I had never seen this side of Brian before, and I could have grabbed some popcorn and watched all night, but Superfüd's second camping song had ended, and I needed to stop them before they launched into a third.

I ran for the stage but slipped in one of the pools of water that was forming on the floor. I slid but didn't fall, and pressed on, careful not to eat it. The Spring River students had gone full-on Woodstock now, wet hair plastered to their faces, dresses torn and ragged, and blue oxford shirts and khakis soaked through. A guy I had never seen before stopped me, grabbed me by the shoulders, and gave me a strong shake, yelling, "I love this band!" I used my kinesis to pry him off and give him a shove, sending him tumbling into a nearby group of people, who quickly hoisted him onto their shoulders to crowd-surf.

My mascara and glittery pink eyeshadow, which Janis had carefully applied just a couple of hours earlier, were now melting in the water from the sprinklers, and running into my eyes. I tried to wipe it away with the backs of my hands, but that just made it worse. The crowd around me was now chanting "Superfüd! Superfüd!" and it seemed like they were trying to deliberately keep me from getting to the stage, by tumbling in front of me, by pushing me off course, or, in the case of one senior girl in a black one-shouldered gown, by literally picking me up and spinning me around before setting me back down facing the opposite direction.

I stopped and stood in place momentarily, then raised my hands above the crowd in the direction of the stage and used my kinesis to pull the plugs on all of Superfüd's equipment. Like a car screeching to a halt, the music stopped, the sudden absence of it drawing a huge wail from the crowd. I figured I had no more than a few seconds to get to the band, and I had no idea what the students would do next. I sprinted toward the stage, being careful not to step on any of the people who were now sprawled out on the floor. At the front of the crowd, I could see the band standing there, looking out at everyone, maybe a bit concerned that all their instruments had just gone out, but ultimately looking pretty happy. I leapt and then scrambled onto the stage.

"Tom! That show was incredible!" I said, trying to get his attention. Crap! It looked like Brad and Chad were looking around now, and it was only a matter of seconds before they would realize that their instruments had just been unplugged. Fudge. I splayed my hands behind me, muttering "Oscurokinesis," and plunged the room into darkness. "People loved the show so much, they set a fire!" I yelled. "And it seems to have blown a fuse!" I didn't know what a fuse was, but I blew one almost every time I used a hair dryer, and Dad was always griping about it. "I'm so sorry, but I think we'll have to shut down early tonight," I added.

Brian must have gotten the fire put out, and my eyes were adjusting to the darkness, a little light streaming in from the windows at the top of the bleachers. I could see the four figures on the stage, stepping around their instruments. Then one of the guys was standing in front of me, a lighter sparked, and his face flickered into view. Tom. But what I had seen in the split second before that had made my heart stutter. His eyes, in the darkness, had been glowing red. Not brightly like coals but a deep raspberry. It had been barely there. But it had been there.

I swallowed, my mouth dry. "Time to pack it up and go home," I said, hoping he didn't notice that my voice cracked. "Told you everyone here loved you! Maybe a little too much. Hahaha. You sold out of CDs!"

Tom shrugged, and the lighter went out. Again that glow in his eyes that turned my blood to concrete. "We sold out of CDs?" he asked.

"Yeah," I said. "They're all gone." This part was true, though I had no idea if anyone had actually paid for them.

"Should we stick around and sign some autographs or something?" he asked, and I shook my head violently.

"No, no, no," I said, scrambling to think of an excuse. Then I didn't have to. Behind me, the crowd had grown accustomed to the darkness and had pinpointed the location of their favorite band, and they were coming in this direction.

"Guitar player! Guitar player!" a girl yelled, scrambling to get onstage. "I want to marry you!" She was soaking wet, and in her crazed state, she looked like a zombie trying to climb out of the grave. I wasn't worried about the band's safety, but I did want to minimize their interaction with the students, so I used my kinesis to give her a little shove and send her tumbling backward.

"Whoops," I said to Tom. "She slipped." But almost instantly, three more Superfüd zombies were trying to take the stage.

"Sign my arm!" one guy yelled. "If you sign my arm, I'll never wash it again."

"Whoa," Tom said, actually taking a step back. "Wow. This is the most nuts show we've ever played. The crowd usually goes crazy, but not like this." I grimaced, and used my kinesis to knock the new round of zombies down.

"Whoops!" I said again. "They slipped too!" I could see Tom's glowing eyes watching me. Superfüd was a bunch of idiots and egoists, but it was clear that at least Tom's curiosity was piqued, and there was no way I could keep this up.

Then a towering figure leapt onto the stage, shook a fire extinguisher, and blasted the next round of incoming Superfüd zombies. It blasted them again, and let out a roaring laugh. "Go cry in your cars, losers! This dance is over!"

I had never been so happy to see Stacey Wasser in my entire life.

"Stacey!" I screamed. "Where's my dog?"

"I traded her for this!" she said, brandishing the fire extinguisher. "To the gym teacher!" So she wasn't the best dog sitter ever, but at least Pig was in good hands now. I wondered if Brian had deputized Stacey, or if she had just taken it upon herself to crowd control her classmates. I suspected it was the second option. "Your band sucks!" she said, turning to snarl at Tom.

"See!" I said to Tom, forcing myself to laugh. "Every crowd's gotta have a hater. But I don't know how long she can fend them off. You guys should get packed up and get out of here."

"Yeah, yeah," Tom said, "but we still gotta get paid."

"Oh yes!" I said. "We can Venmo you."

"Huh?" Tom said.

Crap. I'd forgotten. "Check?" I offered.

"Cash only," he said.

"Got it," I said. "I'll meet you in the parking lot by your car."

"Sports car," he said, and I nodded.

"Sports car," I repeated. "And you should hurry. That fire extinguisher is going to run out eventually." I plunged back into the crowd, the sound of Stacey's laughter at my back as she blasted it again. She had quite the future as a mall cop or prison guard.

On the gym floor, the assistant principal, who apparently hadn't drunk any of the punch either, was trying her best to herd who she could through the door, and at the other door, the school security guard was doing the same. The Superfüd fervor seemed to have dissolved into a lot of crying and confusion, just like a slumber party where everyone gets drunk for the first time. I pulled out my phone and quickly sent a voice-to-text to Ruby, Mallory, and Cassandra, who I could see still hadn't responded to me from earlier.

"The show ended early. Bad news. Will explain later, but Superfüd is on their way home! Get out of there." Brian was nowhere to be seen, so I called him.

He answered after three rings, and I could hear him talking, almost shouting, to someone. "Jackson, get back in the car! Stop dancing! Ji-A, that is *not* a microphone." Then something muffled. "Teachers' parking lot," he said into the phone. "My car. Get here. Fast." I heard him grunt. "This dog is strong, and I don't have any treats." As I hung up, I heard him yelling, "Sit! Stay!" He could have been talking to any of them.

I turned and started to run toward the teachers' parking lot, cutting back through the gym, where the assistant principal and security guard where now being helped by a couple of cops, who seemed totally flummoxed by what to do with a bawling girl who'd wrapped herself in singed streamers.

I ran out of the building and cut across the lawn, my breath billowing out in white clouds in front of me as I headed to where I kept seeing flashes of green. Ji-A's Valentino dress. As I got closer, I could see that she was on her knees, on the hood of Brian's Ford Explorer, using his radio antenna as her fake microphone. "I hope you brought a tarp," she sang in a voice that was actually not bad.

On the other side of the car, Amirah and Janis pounded on the hood and cheered her on, while Brian was trying to coax her off. "Off the car, now!" Brian yelled. "Or you're getting detention for a week!" He was holding on to Pig's leash, and she kept leaping at Ji-A, trying to join in the fun.

"You can't give her detention," Janis yelled at him. "She doesn't even go here!" I noticed that one of her earrings was missing, and her head wrap had come undone. Her eyebrows shot up and her face broke into a grin as soon as she saw me. "Esme! Did you see that show?" she said. "It was incredible. It was like Patti Smith at CBGB, or N.W.A. in Detroit!"

"Janis," I said, "it was like neither. It was a bunch of guys in bad T-shirts singing about sleeping bags." At the mention of sleeping bags, she closed her eyes and started to dance a little groove. "Janis," I said, grabbing her by the shoulders to hold her still. "How much punch did you have?" She ignored me, continuing to dance as she chanted "Superfüd" under her breath. It sounded like she was a waitress, asking "Soup or food? Soup or food?" over and over again.

"I don't know what to do," Brian said, walking over to me and handing me a water bottle. "I thought that the water from the sprinkler system would have broken the spell, but maybe that only works when the water is thrown by a Sitter."

Realizing what he wanted me to do, I twisted the cap. "Sorry, Amirah," I said, and splashed it into her face. She blinked a few times, drops dripping off her nose, and I had no idea if it had done anything.

"What's your favorite band?" I asked.

"Well," she started, "most people don't know this, but 'Sade' is actually the name of the singer and the entire band. I know this because they played the pre-party for my dad's fortieth birthday, and for a long time I thought they were my favorite band." Okay, this was surprising. Maybe a little Fiji in her face had broken the spell? I was relieved, and also surprised that Amirah had such good taste in music. "But after tonight," she continued, "I love Superfüd always and forever."

Okay, never mind.

Behind me, Brian sighed. "Where is the band now?" he asked. "Did you convince them to go home?"

I nodded. "It didn't take much convincing," I said. "But they're still waiting to get paid."

"How much do you owe them?" he asked.

"Three hundred dollars." Brian's eyebrows shot up. "I don't know if that's a lot or a little for a band," I said.

"I don't either," he said. "But I do know that it's about two hundred and ninety-nine dollars too much." I laughed. "But let's just pay them and get out of here."

"I know," I said, "but they need to be paid in cash. How much do you have on you?" Brian reached into his pocket, pulled out his wallet, and flipped it open.

"Eleven," he said after he'd counted it.

"How do you only have eleven dollars?" I said.

"How much cash do you have?" he shot back at me.

"None," I said, "but I'm a teenager. You're a grown-up. One of the few things grown-ups are good for is cash."

"Just send them money with whatever that app is that you kids use to pay your drug dealers."

"Brian," I said. "It's called 'Venmo,' and I use it for babysitting."

"The nearest ATM is two blocks away at the Panda Sub," he said. "It'll take too long to get there and back." At the mention of Panda Sub, I had an idea and turned to Amirah.

"Amirah, can I borrow some cash?" I said. "We'll pay you back."

"Esme, I totally would," she said. "But I didn't bring my wallet, so all I have is my emergency money." She reached into her bra and pulled out a bill that had been folded into a tiny square. When she handed it to me, the money was wet and sweaty in my palm. I unfolded it to see that it was a five-hundred-dollar bill. "How much do you need?" she asked. "Is that enough?"

"Thanks, Amirah," I said. "This is great." Amirah turned back to Ji-A and Janis, and I could hear them start to discuss which Superfüd song was their favorite—that one song about camping or that other song about camping.

Pig lunged at Brian's car again, almost pulling him off his feet. "Sit!" I hissed at her. "No punch ever again! Bad Pig!" She sat down with a whimper. "I guess Superfüd is getting a big tip tonight," I said to Brian. "Not that they deserve it. But I guess I'll run over and give this to them, then meet you guys back here. I still haven't heard from Cassandra."

Illuminated in the parking lot lights, I could see Brian's nostrils flare as he sucked in air. "I don't like the idea of you meeting up with them alone. Where is their car?"

"In the student parking lot," I said. "You can't miss it. It's a purple PT Cruiser."

"Let's get these four into the car, and we'll drive you over there to meet them," he said. "And from there, we can go straight to their house, and hopefully intercept Cassandra before they get home."

"I think we should split up," I argued. "You head to their house now, and I'll try to stall the guys in the parking lot. Then I'll meet up with you later."

"But we only have one car," Brian said.

"Janis drove us here," I said.

"Janis isn't driving anywhere right now," Brian said, his voice going all teachery.

"I can drive her car," I said, and one of his eyebrows shot up. "I'll be fine," I assured him, not quite sure myself. "I have my permit."

"I heard about the median," he said.

"Stop!" I said, starting to grow frantic. "We're wasting time!" I turned to Janis. "Janis! I need your keys! And, everyone, get into Brian's car so he can take you to the after-party!"

Janis held out her keys but looked at me suspiciously. "And where are you going?" she asked.

"To get more soup, obviously," I said. "I offered to do it since I knew you wouldn't want to be late."

"Oooh," she said as I took her keys. "Get more beef stew. That's their favorite. Extra chunky."

"Will do," I said. Then I gave Brian a quick wave and started to run, not wanting to waste another second.

The school grounds were dotted with people in various stages of comedown—climbing trees, cars, and anything else they could find, or else lying on the ground, sobbing like Amirah. Word must have spread that the dance had shut down early, and I could see a few confused parents starting to appear, plus a fire engine and two cop cars. I was scanning for the band when the PT Cruiser pulled up right in front of me.

Brad was driving, and Tom was in the front passenger seat. He got out and started walking toward me. "I've got your money," I said. "The dance committee got together and decided to up your fee because it was such a good show and everyone clearly loved it so much." I held out the bill, and Tom reached for it as he came toward me. Instinctively I let go, right as he grabbed it, not wanting our fingers to touch. Out of the corner of my eye, I saw a dark shape coming toward me.

"What the?" I said, starting to turn toward it. Then I heard a crow squawk, and everything went black.

CHAPTER 18

I came to with something sharp poking into my side, and my head jammed up against something hard. I couldn't move, or even blink, and realized that my eyes had been open the whole time, but I was just now returning to consciousness. I was halfway on my side, twisted and contorted into an awkward position and crammed into a space where I didn't really fit. As my vision came into focus, I could see just enough to know that the sharp poke in my side was a drumstick, and the hard thing currently pressed against my forehead was a guitar case. I was staring straight up at the ceiling of the car, and out of the corner of my right eye, I could see part of a cymbal, gently jiggling. Everything was moving, except me. I couldn't move a muscle. I couldn't even blink.

I was in the back of a car. Specially, Superfüd's car, and they were currently occupying the front and backseats, and arguing about it.

"Dude! How long have I been saying we needed a van?

There's not enough room for the four of us and our equipment in this car. We look like tools all jammed in here!"

"Shut up." I recognized that voice as Tom's. "Everyone agreed this was the car for us when we bought it, so bite me. We've got bigger things to think about right now."

"Yeah, no crap! You just freaking kidnapped a teenager from a school dance! We've been lying low this whole time, and now every cop in the county is going to be looking for us!"

"I had no choice! Trust me on this. Her people don't call the cops. Now shut up and give me time to think."

"Dozens of people saw us do it!"

"No one's going to say anything. All those kids think we're gods. Besides, what part of 'shut up' do you not understand?"

"I'm not going to shut up! I shut up two months ago! We all did! We went along with your plan then, and where did that get us?"

"Where did that get us? Where did that get us? When was the last time you looked in the mirror? Because where it got us is written all over your face. And were you asleep for that show we just played? People freaking love us!"

Whoever was driving drove like Janis, and each time the car turned a corner or came to a stop, some part of some instrument rammed into some part of my body, and I couldn't move a millimeter to readjust or get out of the way. The cymbal rang out like a wind chime in a hurricane.

"I'm not arguing with that! I'm just saying that I signed up to be a rock star! Not a kidnapper two times over!"

If I could have broken out in goose bumps, then I'm sure I would have at that. Two kidnappings? Obviously I was one of them, and then the other . . . it had to be Circe. It just had to be.

"The kidnapping was what made us into rock stars!" Tom's voice was now screeching.

"Now, let's all be reasonable here," a third voice spoke up in a tone of measured calm. "I think we can all agree that we like being rock stars, but I also think it's okay to acknowledge that some of us don't enjoy breaking and entering or kidnapping. Those who feel that way—"

"Chad, shut the hell up. . . ."

Okay, so now they had just copped to breaking and entering too? If I hadn't been in fear of being decapitated by a cymbal the next time we went around a corner, I might even have gone so far as to say that getting myself kidnapped had been a stroke of genius.

"Tom, you know I don't like it when you take that tone of voice with me," Chad said. "And even you have to admit that breaking into that house was a risk that was not worth it. We barely got out of there before that guy came home, and we found nothing."

"It also lead this girl right to our door." At hearing that, I felt a jolt go through my entire body. Ugh. So my showing up at their door had tipped them off to something?

"Well, maybe that wouldn't have happened if *someone*— Todd!—hadn't had a hole in his backpack and basically left a trail of clues, including a flyer with our freakin' picture on it!"

"Hey! I fixed that hole!"

I could hear someone give a loud, theatrical sigh.

"That backpack is butt ugly too. It makes you look like

you're excited about your first day of third grade. Also, I friggin' hate the name 'Superfüd.' It makes us sound like we're a smoothie."

"Well, let's all just air our grievances right now. Todd, your dandruff is disgusting."

"What the? I'm not even a part of this argument!"

" 'Superfüd' is a rad name! It makes us sound like we're an über-version of something everyone loves!"

"We should have gone with 'Shredding Chicken.' That's the perfect name."

"Are you friggin' kidding me? That sounds like you're getting prepped for Taco Tuesday!"

"I am so tired of arguing about names! You think Nickelback got where they are by changing their name all the time? No! They picked one name, and they stuck with it!"

"Shut up! All of you! Can we just focus for a minute? We just kidnapped a teenage girl from a school parking lot, so what the hell are we going to do with her?"

"We'll put her with the other one," Tom said.

"Then what?"

"Then I'll take some time to think, and I'll come up with a plan, since I seem to be the only one who cares about this band!"

"I don't want to do this anymore," someone whined. "I don't care about being famous. I just want to go back to being normal. I can't take these side effects anymore. I'm sick of soup! Do you know what I would do to eat a non-pureed sandwich? Or some freaking chips and salsa? I miss crunch, man! I would kill for some crunch."

Okay, so I guess it wasn't just outsiders who found Superfüd's eating habits a little odd. Apparently it was out of necessity rather than preference.

"Me too, Todd! You think I eat split pea because I like it? I don't! No one likes split pea! We made this decision—together—that we were going to do whatever it took to make it! That we were going to be bigger than 3 Doors, bigger than Puddle, bigger than Hooba, even! And now you guys just want to give up? When we're finally on our way?"

"You yourself said that those things don't last forever! What if it runs out before we get famous and we're just stuck like this forever?"

"Well, Chad, that's why we kidnapped this girl, remember?" Tom's voice now was a low hiss. "So we can trade her for the big one."

"If Circe couldn't find it, what makes you think this girl can?"

"Positive thinking, Chad!" Tom snapped. "No one gets anywhere by being a downer!" My mind was racing. So they were looking for the talisman, the big one, and they planned to try to trade me for it. That meant . . .

"Shit! Watch out for that bird." Then there was the sound of squealing tires as the car swerved wildly. The cymbal crashed into the window, and my useless body crumpled into a corner. Bird. I desperately wanted to know what kind of bird, but Superfüd didn't elaborate.

"Freaking hell, Brad!" someone yelled. "When will you ever learn to load a drum kit? Fix that cymbal, or the next time it makes a noise, I'm going to throw it out the window." There was some grumbling, and then all of a sudden, a face appeared above me, and an arm to mash the cymbal into different positions, now making ten times as much noise as it had been. Then the face—Todd's, I think—glanced down at me, and then looked back again, alarmed, his eyebrows knitting together.

"Her eyes are open!" he screeched. "I knew it wouldn't work!" A horrible smell filled the car. Then all I saw was darkness, and just like that, I was out again.

I could smell the coffee, and I needed it today. I was bone-tired, and as I shifted slightly in bed, my body protested the effort, but my mind was electrified with the realization that I could move again. The coffee smell was strong as I pushed myself up into a sitting position.

My vision was blurry, and I could just make out shapes ringed with rainbows, and I felt like I couldn't breathe. The coffee wouldn't let me breath. It felt like it was in my nostrils.

Then I realized, it was in my nostrils. Literally, my nose was full of coffee grounds, so full that I couldn't breathe. I launched into a sneezing fit, sputtering, puffing air out of my nose and sending coffee grounds spraying. There was a crash as something jumped out of the way of my olfactory spittle.

I pawed at my face, trying to dislodge the remaining grounds, and managed to inhale some of them, sucking them up through my nose until I could feel a drip down the back of my throat. I launched into another fit, coughing this time.

Finally they were gone, at least to the point where I could breathe unobstructed, and that was when my eyes finally focused and I saw where I was. It was a small room, with no windows, cinder-block walls on three sides and a corrugated metal door on the fourth. It was dark, the only light coming from an orange lava lamp that glowed in one corner. There were cardboard boxes stacked halfway to the ceiling, plus a weight bench, a pair of Rollerblades, a beach umbrella, and all kinds of other junk.

And I wasn't alone. There was someone else in here, who had jumped out of my way. I squinted, trying to see them better. It was a woman, and she had dark hair, and was dressed like she was going to work, in ill-fitting pants and a blazer and—

"Oh my God," I said. "Circe!" And then I started to sneeze again.

She laughed. "Yes. I wish we were meeting under better circumstances. Here." She walked over and held something out to me. "I found this old bandana you can use to blow your nose. It's been in here for ages, so any germs it once had are petrified now."

"Thanks," I said, taking it from her and giving my nose a few honks. Circe was wearing the same outfit she'd had on two months before, when we'd seen her at the hotel, but her helmet-shaped wig and the pancake makeup were gone, and she looked prettier now. Like an older version of Cassandra, basically.

"Sorry about the coffee," she said, sitting down on the weight bench. "It was the closest I could find to smelling salts."

I used the bandana to dig the last of the coffee grounds out of my nose. "What did they do to me?"

"They knocked you out," she said. "With magic at first, I think, but then it seemed like that didn't work, so they just used ether."

I nodded, and my head throbbed. "Coffee," I said. "I like coffee." I rolled my neck back and forth, and every nerve ending whined like Dion's van. "Who just carries around ether?" I asked. "Does that mean it was premeditated?"

"With them, who knows," she said. "Though I get the feeling that they don't have much of a plan."

"Where are we?" I asked. "This looks like a . . ."

"Storage unit," she said. "It's the band's storage unit. Those," she said, pointing at the Rollerblades, "are Tom's. Before he decided he wanted to be a rock star, he thought he was going to go pro."

"A professional Rollerblader?"

"'Blader,' as he called it," she said, shaking her head. "Honestly, and maybe this is just my ego talking, but the thing that bothers me the most about being kidnapped is that I was kidnapped by such a bunch of idiots." She stood up from the weight bench and walked over to a large Styrofoam cooler. "Do you want anything to drink?" She opened the lid to reveal several bottles of a generic sports drink, ranging in flavor from PT Cruiser purple to the same blue as Amirah's thrifted dress.

"Sure," I said, "I'll take a purple." She pulled it out and brought it over to me, twisting the cap off before she handed it over. I took a sip. It was cold and electrolyte-y, and it did a little bit to wash the taste of coffee grounds from the back of my throat. I took another sip. My brain was grinding as I tried to take everything in. It was a lot, the biggest being Circe. She was here, right in front of me, alive and well. I had ten million questions, but the first one came out as a statement.

"You're alive."

She sat back down and smiled. "Yes, I am."

"Then where the heck have you been?" My words came out a little accusatory, and I opened my mouth to backtrack, but then shut it again. I wasn't sorry. Cassandra and Dion had grown up thinking their mother was dead.

"Well, for the past month I've been in this storage unit," she said. "Before that, I was in their garage, but then they decided to turn it into a 'totally rocking practice space.' Their words, not mine." She gave a little smile. "But I'm sure you mean before that." I took another sip of my purple drink and nodded. "How much do you know about what happened, all those years ago?"

"On a scale of one to ten, ten being everything and one being nothing," I said, "I'd say I'm at about a negative three."

Circe laughed. "I'm glad to see you have Theresa's sense of humor," she said. "She could always make me laugh, even in the worst of circumstances."

I sat up a little straighter, feeling kind of proud, as I always did, whenever anyone compared me to Mom.

"So, Erebus was—or still is—my husband, as you know," she said, "and he was in a band, who you've met. Cassandra was just a baby and Dion wasn't much older. My Sitting days were over by then, but I was still babysitting, and watching other people's children while I watched my own. Erebus was working at the Beanie Baby kiosk at the mall, and we were barely getting by." She paused and looked away from me, up into a dark corner of the storage unit, and I could hear her sigh. "I'm not proud of this, but when he started dabbling in Red Magic, I looked the other way. I believed, or I wanted to believe, that he was doing it for us."

"What do you mean?" I asked.

"This is where his band comes in," she said. "He told me that everything he was doing with Red Magic was so that the band would be successful so that he could take care of our family. It seems so far-fetched and stupid now, but back then I wanted to believe. The band wasn't the best band I'd ever heard, but it wasn't the worst either. Erebus was a decent song-writer, and I just thought that if Frog Injection—"

"Frog Injection?"

"That was what they were called back then," she said. "Have they changed their name?"

"Yeah," I said. "A lot. But not important. Go on."

"I was distracted," she said, nodding, "with two small children, and maybe also a little willfully naive. I didn't put it all together, and figure out that Erebus wasn't just playing with bits of Red Magic that he found here and there, until it was too late."

"What do you mean?" I asked.

"Erebus had always hated his job," she said. "I mean, it was Beanie Babies. But suddenly he was all about it. He was in Beanie forums all the time, and collectors were always calling the house. You would have thought he was trading stocks or something from how seriously he took it. I started to get suspicious. One day UPS delivered this box to our house while he was gone. I didn't open it, but Cassandra started playing with it, and she drew all over it with marker. Just the outside. But when Erebus got home, he went ballistic. I'd never seen him so mad, and he yelled at the baby, saying she had almost ruined everything. Then I knew for sure, and when he left the house the next day, with the box, I had a friend follow him. She saw him meet Wanda in a park, and do some sort of a trade."

"How'd your friend know the person he was meeting was Wanda?" I asked.

"Well, that friend was your mom," Circe said with a little smile. "You were probably with her at the time."

"Oh," I said, sitting there, stunned. Not from the spell, but from the first real bits of information I'd ever been given.

"From there, it didn't take us long to piece together what was going on," she said. "Erebus was trading Beanie Babies for Red Magic talismans."

"What?" I said, not really believing that I had heard her right. "That's insane. If Wanda wanted the Beanies so badly, why didn't she use the Red Magic to just get them herself?"

"The hard-core Beanie Baby enthusiasts are pretty committed," she said, "and are not easily swayed, even by magic."

I sat there for a second, letting Circe's words sink in. "What did you do?" I asked. "You and my mom?"

"We did everything wrong," she said. "We confronted Wanda, who denied everything and placed all the blame on Erebus, and we believed her. I sent Cassandra and Dion to stay with some family, and then prepared to confront Erebus, but that never happened."

"Why not?" I asked. I took another sip of purple, and swished it around in my mouth, nodding at Circe to urge her to keep going.

"Wanda and two other members of the Synod showed up at my house, and the way Wanda was acting made me think I was going crazy. She had turned everything around and was now accusing me of practicing with my husband." Circe stopped. "Even after your Sitter powers go away, your Sitter sense remains," she said, "and I will never forget the feeling I got when I opened the door to find them standing there. I felt like I had been plunged into cold water. I let them in, though, and was polite and played dumb. They kept talking about how if I confessed, they'd work with me." She shuddered. "But I knew they were lying. Why would I trust anything that Wanda said? And I knew better than to confess to something I didn't do. So I excused myself to go to the bathroom, and I ran."

"You what?" I was still groggy but feeling much more awake now.

"I ran," she repeated. "I literally climbed out the bathroom window and ran."

If it hadn't been so dark in the storage unit, she'd have been able to see how shocked I was. "But there were three members of the Synod sitting in your living room," I said. "How come they didn't just find you in, like, three seconds?"

"On my way out the window, I stole Erebus's Red Magic talismans," she said. "By then, I knew what they were, since they were things he had traded for, and I grabbed every one I could find. I'm not proud, but they served me well. I never thought I'd be gone so long, but I have been using them ever since. At least, up until two months ago."

"When you got kidnapped," I said.

"Yeah," she said, shaking her head. Her voice sounded weary. "After I ran, Wanda blacklisted me and let it be known that if I was ever found, my memory would be stripped." She gulped. "That would have meant I wouldn't even remember my own children. I didn't want that. I never went far. I wanted to be able to come back and check on my kids whenever I could, and this year, when I saw that Cassandra had been cursed, I knew I had to take the risk and intervene."

I wondered how Cassandra and Dion would feel if they knew that their mom had been close by this whole time, all those years when they had just assumed they were totally on their own. Relieved, maybe? Or angry? Or, most likely, a little bit of both? My mind was starting to spin.

"Intervene how?" I asked.

"After I was blacklisted, your mother and I kept in touch by leaving each other messages on the bathroom wall at the Perk."

"You did what?" I wanted her to repeat it, and she did. The Perk's bathroom, in keeping with its overall grimy vibe, was covered floor to ceiling with graffiti. Sometimes it seemed like poetry to me, and I'd spent many a pee searching the words for hidden meanings or important messages. Now hearing this blew my mind.

"Theresa stole one of Wanda's talismans, one of the most powerful ones Wanda had ever created, and planned to use it to reveal Wanda's true nature to the Sitterhood," Circe said. "But that never happened, and the writing on the wall stopped. I knew that Theresa would not have abandoned me, or her cause, willingly, so I wasn't surprised when I found out she had been cursed and was now living in a facility."

"And Wanda was able to blame the curse on Erebus," I said.

"And probably on me too," Circe said, nodding. "For a long time, I couldn't figure out why Wanda had cursed Theresa. Why not just accuse her of Red Magic and erase her memory? Then it hit me: Wanda needed something that only Theresa knew. Wanda never got her talisman back, and only Theresa knew where it was." Circe paused here. "I visited Theresa a few times over the years, wanting to see if I could communicate with her, but I never had any luck. Then, when Cassandra got cursed, I was desperate, so I decided to try again. I was so distraught that I wasn't paying attention, and when I was on my way to see her, I ran into Tom. Yada, yada, long story short, they kidnapped me, stole my talismans, and now here we are."

I sat there in silence. "Why did you think finding the talisman would help Cassandra?" I asked.

"If it was a talisman created by Wanda, then it would be powerful enough to break a curse created by Wanda," she said.

"A curse like my mom's," I said.

"Yes," she said, "a curse like your mom's."

My mind started to frantically try to fit the pieces of this puzzle together. "So, with this talisman, you wouldn't need Erebus or Wanda or any Red Magician to break the curse," I said. "Anyone who had the talisman could do it." Circe must have known what I was getting at, but she didn't say anything. She just nodded.

"And my mom stole it," I said.

Circe nodded again. "And hid it," she said. "And no one has been able to find it since. Not even Wanda."

"I think the band is looking for it too," I said. "I don't know how they even know about it."

Circe groaned, and it seemed like she deflated a little bit. "I do," she said. "They stole my notebook."

"So," I said, "they read your diary?"

She nodded. "They never knew what happened to Erebus," she said. "He had convinced them all that they were going to use magic to become very successful. Then when he and

I disappeared, they thought we'd sold out on them. They've been mad for fifteen years, and I guess this is all part of their revenge."

"How many talismans do they have?" I asked.

"I was down to six," she said. "Though, if they're using them haphazardly, they'll run out quickly."

I let this information wash over me, and it felt like waking up from a dream. For the first time, things were starting to make sense, but I was also starting to panic. I couldn't just sit there, wasting time and waiting for someone to come save me. "Circe," I said, "we have to get the eff out of this storage unit."

"You're telling me," she said. "It's spelled. That door is like concrete, and I've screamed my head off every time there's been anyone outside, but no one has heard a thing."

I was still wearing my purse, and I pulled it onto my lap and clicked it open. I gasped when I saw that they hadn't taken my phone, but the joy was short-lived. There was no service in the storage unit. It was almost ten, which meant I'd been in there for at least an hour.

Even if Amirah, Ji-A, and Janis were still in the throes of band euphoria, Brian would have noticed I was gone immediately, so undoubtedly he was out there looking for me. But what about Cassandra, Ruby, and Mallory? Or Adrian?

"Ugh," I said. "There are five other Sitters out there right now. Unfortunately, two drank the Superfüd Kool-Aid."

"Kool-Aid makes super-food flavors now?" Circe asked.

"Legit question," I said, "but no. The band is called 'Superfüd' now, and they spiked the punch at our school dance. Now everyone, including all my friends, think those guys are the best band in the world."

"Even Cassandra?" Circe asked.

"No," I said. "She wasn't there. She went to look for you." In the darkness, I could see Circe's eyes widen, and I gave her a brief rundown of what had happened earlier in the night, omitting the fact that I couldn't get ahold of Cassandra. I didn't want Circe to worry any more than she already was. I took a few deep breaths, which only succeeded in sucking a few more bits of coffee grounds up into my nostrils. My head felt like the inside of a pillow, and I really needed to wake up. I wondered if it was possible to absorb caffeine through your sinuses. Or maybe I should just eat some spoonfuls?

"Can I see the coffee? That you shoved up my nose?"

Her eyes got wide with concern, and she got up, grabbed a canister, and passed it to me. "It's not burning, is it?" she said.

"No, no, it's fine," I assured her. I twisted the lid and took a deep inhale. Then I squinted at it, so that I could make out what the label said. This was instant coffee, the kind that was supposed to dissolve in hot water. Normally the worst kind, but right now the best.

I was quiet as I picked up my bottle of purple sports drink and held it between my knees.

"Esme? Esme?" I looked up to see Circe staring at me, a look of concern on her face. "You okay?"

"Yeah, yeah," I said, refocusing my attention on the task at hand. "Circe," I said, "don't judge. These are desperate times and they call for desperate measures." I tipped the canister and dumped a whole bunch of instant coffee crystals into the purple drink. Then I screwed the lid back onto the bottle and gave it a long, hard shake. I held the bottle up to the light from the lava lamp, and could see that only about half of the coffee had dissolved. There was a layer of brown sludge on the bottom, but the sports drink itself was now the color of a muddy river. It would have to do. I unscrewed the cap, tipped it to my lips, and gulped down the mud.

Circe had been watching me, silently, the entire time. "I worked in coffee shops for years, and I never . . . ," she started, then trailed off. "Well, how's it taste?"

"Disgusting." I grimaced as I finished it.

"Esme, has it ever occurred to you that you might have a caffeine problem?" she asked.

"I really don't consider it a problem," I said, standing up and popping my knuckles. "Now let's get out of here."

CHAPTER 19

I was worried that Cassandra might be in trouble, which seemed silly, considering that being kidnapped and dumped into a storage unit might make some people think that I was the one in trouble. I guess we were both in trouble, which was nothing new, but normally we were in trouble together.

I pulled out my phone and looked at it again, trying to will it into service. Still nothing. I walked over until I was standing a few feet from the door. I held up my hands, then tried to push the door with my kinesis, but my powers hit the door and died. Then, in the silence, I heard a dog bark.

I strained to listen. I could hear the sounds of the traffic nearby, the whoosh and rhythmic thud of cars. I strained for something else but got nothing. The sound of the cars told me we were by the highway, probably in a strip of town that was home to storage units, tire shops, and not much else. Not exactly the kind of place where someone would take their dog out for a walk at ten p.m. on a Saturday night. I was about to turn back toward Circe when I heard it again, and closer this time.

A dog barking. Not just any dog but Pig. Pig rarely barked, but when she did, it was like something out of a cartoon—"ra-rar-rar-ra-ra"—like she was a crooner in the moonlight, belting out love songs over red roses and ravioli. I'd recognize that bark anywhere, and it was here now.

"What is it?" Circe asked.

"I think they're here," I said.

"The band?" she said. We were both whispering, even though we knew no one could hear us.

"No," I said, "my friends. My friends are here." And then I heard a car door slam. It was hard to hear through the storage unit's metal door, but it seemed like the car wasn't that far away. Not right outside, but no more than a few doors down. Circe raised her eyebrows, and wordlessly walked over to stand next to me.

Silence, and we waited. Then we heard it. People. Specifically, Janis and Brian, arguing. And someone—it sounded like Ji-A—still singing about camping. Janis and Brian appeared to be arguing about an after-party, one that Janis thought Brian was trying to keep her from attending.

"It's not fair that Esme gets to hang out with them just because she's a Sitter and I'm not," she was saying. "It was my idea to book them for the dance in the first place."

"Jackson," Brian said, "if I could assign detention simply because a student annoyed me, you would never see the light of the lunchroom again."

"Coach," Janis interrupted, "you really need to get a new threat. Detention's kind of tired. Nobody's scared of detention these days." I couldn't see him at that moment, but I imagined Brian rolling his eyes.

"Like I said, Esme is *not* hanging out with Superfüd. They kidnapped her, and we need to find her. We are here to try to find her." The singing was still going on in the background. "Ji-A, Amirah," Brian said, "get over here. One of these units belongs to Superfüd. See if you can figure out which one."

"Oooohhhh," Amirah said, "is this where they live? Apartment buildings look so different here in Kansas. We don't have anything like this in New York."

"This isn't where they live," Brian said, sounding exasperated. "It's their storage unit, where they keep the stuff they don't use anymore."

"Oh," Amirah said. "So they don't just keep their old stuff in the apartment downstairs?"

"Not everyone owns two floors, Amirah," Ji-A said, ever the voice of reason. Then, "Do you think they have any extra boxes of T-shirts?"

"Who cares about the T-shirts? Esme might be in there somewhere." This voice was male, and it took me a second to place. It was Adrian. What was he doing with them? Had he outed himself to them, for me?

Then, without being able to stop myself, I screamed his name. "Adrian! Adrian!" Then I screamed for Brian as well, and even pounded on the door a few times.

They didn't hear a thing.

"You don't know which one it is?" Brian said, and I couldn't hear Adrian's response.

Then Janis's voice, carrying over the concrete in the cold. "If you think Esme is here, just yell for her!" she said, and then she proceeded to do just that. What followed was a great deal of shushing, it seemed, from Adrian and Brian, but Ji-A, Amirah, and Pig joined in, a chorus of girls singing my name.

"Did you get their autographs?" Ji-A yelled. "I want Tom to sign my copy of *The Catcher in the Rye*!" I couldn't help but be momentarily distracted. Why in the world would she want that? And why did Ji-A have a copy of *The Catcher in the Rye*?

"We're not supposed to be here. It's closed." Adrian's voice sounded stressed. "There are hundreds of units here," he continued. "This place is huge. We're never going to find her. Wait. Amirah, you can walk through walls. Go through these doors to see if you can find Esme."

I couldn't hear her answer, but there was silence, then Adrian's voice again. "I know it's dark in there. It's a storage unit. And we're not looking for the band; we're looking for Esme." A beat. "Okay, we're looking for the band, and Esme might be with them. Try again, try that one." Two beats. Three. "I'm sorry it stinks in there. The next one will be better, only about a hundred and fifty more to go."

It got quiet again, and then Brian's voice: "Okay, please don't cry. We're going to find her. I mean, we'll find them. Come on."

Then a sharp yelp, and Adrian's voice. "Jeez, she's strong."

I groaned. I needed—we all needed—Ji-A and Janis and Amirah to stop being useless five minutes ago. "If Amirah or Ji-A would just come here, they could feel the door and know that something is wrong," I said to Circe.

"Maybe not," Circe said. "If the band took extra precautions, the spells might not be detectable from the outside because they wouldn't want anything that would arouse suspicions." I sat down on a box labeled "protein powder," and it dented slightly under my weight.

"I can't believe we're right here, and they're right there, and there's nothing we can do," I said, feeling hopeless. "And Cassandra and Ruby and Mallory aren't with them." I looked up at Circe, and then something just beyond her head caught my eye. A fire alarm. The one that had gone off in the gym hadn't done us any favors when it had come to quelling the chaos, but maybe this one might actually save our lives.

I jumped back to my feet, and Circe must have known what I was thinking. "It's hooked up," she said, "but I went through all the boxes and couldn't find anything to set a fire."

I looked at Circe, and then up at the fire alarm, and felt a twinge pierce through me. I'd felt it earlier tonight, when I had opened the door to the gym and found the Spring River student body about to explode in a Superfüd frenzy. Something was missing: Cassandra, normally my right hand, was now my phantom limb.

In all the time I had been a Sitter, I had never felt hopeless, and now I was starting to see why. I was always with Cassandra. Even Wanda—who had decades of magic on our paltry few months—couldn't keep us down. And why? Because no matter what we were in, we were in it together. If we were defeated by Superfüd, it wouldn't be a victory that they had earned. It would be one we handed to them, the minute we decided to split up for the evening.

Cassandra could set off a fire alarm in her sleep. She'd done it several times. And now I was here with her mom, and neither of us could conjure so much as a waft of smoke. After all, why bother learning fire spells when the other half of your tag team is pyrokinetic?

I stood in the middle of the storage unit for a second, listening with every cell in my body, and heard nothing but the rush of traffic and the whoosh of the wind. Then, voices again, muffled but coming closer. Brian and Adrian were talking, and Brian was urging everyone to get back into the car.

"We can't just leave her here," Adrian said.

"I know," Brian answered, "but we don't know for sure that she's here. They could have taken her back to their house, and we know that the others are there. We've lost so much time already. You yourself said you saw them pull in, and then just saw them leave. What happened in the meantime?"

"There was a flock . . . I was getting bullied . . . It's not important. If you don't think she's here, then we need to go," Adrian said.

Go? *No*, they couldn't go. They couldn't just leave us here. I looked frantically around the room and racked my brain. The fire alarm was our only possible connection to the world outside the concrete garage box. I had to know a spell that would trigger it. I could move things with my mind, make plants grow, make animals talk. I could make things popular, clean up messes, make a steak appear out of thin air . . .

Wait, steak? My meat manipulation had once gone horribly wrong, and I'd conjured a live chicken. After that, I'd concentrated really hard on conjuring something that was cooked. But what about overcooked? Like, burned to a crisp. Smoking hot.

"You look like you just had an idea," Circe said, but I didn't have time to answer her. This was going to be tricky, because I was going to have to use my kinesis and cast a spell at the same time. I needed to conjure a sizzling steak, and have it hovering just slightly below the ceiling.

It was an absolutely ridiculous idea.

Outside, I could hear Adrian and Brian sounding more and more urgent as they tried to herd everyone into the car. I turned and focused my attention on the fire alarm, specifically a space just a few inches below it. "Kréakinesis," I said, holding out my hands. The air wavered a bit, and then, there it was. A giant ribeye, like something out of a cartoon, and it was still sizzling, practically starting a grease fire in the storage unit, and the temperature started to rise instantly.

And then, success. It was an earsplitting screech, and instantly I bolted to the door. Behind me, the still cooking steak fell through the air and landed with a thud right on the floor. Over the racket of the alarm, I could no longer hear voices outside, but then one lone sound cut through the alarm's screeching. Pig was howling from the other side of the door. Then I heard an engine revving, loud and close. I had just enough time to turn around and knock Circe to the ground, and out of the way before Brian's Ford Explorer came crashing through the door.

CHAPTER 20

Apparently, the way to defeat Red Magic was with an SUV. The force of the collision had caused the door to bend in like a baseball glove, the metal crumpling and crunching against the Ford's hood. This divot pulled the door away from the floor and the sides, and I could feel the spells break around me, the magic rushing out like the storage unit was exhaling, as the alarm continued to wail.

"What the what?" Circe said as I rolled off her and we disentangled our limbs, the crunch of the door having stopped just mere inches from totally dismembering our feet. There was a groan of gears and then another *vroom*, and I scrambled to my feet, pushing boxes out of the way, as the Explorer started to back up.

"There are people in here!" I screamed through the crack at the side of the door. Then I grabbed the door with my kinesis and pulled as hard as I could. I managed to wench it enough that I could then squeeze my arms through at least, and I waved wildly. "Stop the car!" I yelled. "Stop the car!" All

I could see through the gap were the headlights, bright enough to blind. My attempt to cook a steak had set off the fire alarm for the entire property, not just our unit. It was a shrill shriek, with lights that strobed like a camera flash. After tonight, I never wanted to see or hear another fire alarm again.

Then, in the split second between the shrieks, I heard someone yell my name. Adrian. The next thing I knew, I couldn't even count the number of hands that had grabbed on to me and were trying to pull me out through a hole that was way, way too small.

"Stop! Stop!" I screamed again. "I can get the door open! I just wanted to make sure you didn't hit it with a car again."

"Stand back!" Brian yelled, and then everyone disengaged. There was a weird hiss behind me, and I spun to see that Circe and I were no longer alone. Amirah, looking like she'd been to hell and back—or just to a school dance—was standing in front of me, wringing her hands and looking around, distressed.

"Superfüd's not in here," she said. "Brian lied to us!" And then, with that, she walked right back out through the middle of the bent metal door.

"Well, that was definitely a Sitter, of some sort," Circe said, almost sounding amused.

"That's Amirah," I said. "She's from New York, and she's also under Superfüd's spell."

"Clearly," Circe said. "Now, please, get us the heck out of here." I nodded, then turned and focused again on the door. I raised my hands and used my kinesis, making the door groan and creak as I managed to make a little progress with the hole on the right side. Not a ton, but it looked big enough for us to crawl through.

"By all means, you first," Circe said.

I stepped back to examine it, and nodded, and then used my kinesis to move some boxes, and climbed up and shoved myself through. Brian and Adrian were waiting on the other side and grabbed me and helped pull me out so that I wouldn't just fall and tumble into a pile on the asphalt. As soon as my feet hit the ground, the Explorer's horn honked. I looked up, peering past the headlights, into the driver's seat. Janis was at the wheel, her face illuminated every few seconds by the blinding strobe of the alarm. Pig came bounding over, then stopped to howl, the shrill alarm no doubt murdering her ears. I pushed myself up, ran over to her, and clamped my hands down over her ears and she tried to cover me in kisses.

"Esme!" Janis screamed at me. "Did I do good?"

"Very good," I yelled back at her. "You're an excellent driver!" I turned to see Adrian and Brian helping Circe around the crumpled door.

"Brian," I shouted to him over the alarm, "this is Circe, Cassandra's mom. Where is Cassandra?"

"We don't know," Brian said, "but we need to get out of here, fast. The last thing I need tonight is to have to explain something to the fire department, again." I turned to see Amirah materialize out of another storage unit, apparently still trying to find Superfüd.

"Esme," Ji-A said, running over to me. "Did you hang out with them? Did you get their autographs?"

"No," I said, "but we're going to go meet them right now!" There was a chance this was not a lie. "Amirah, Ji-A, get in the car right now! Janis, you are not driving."

"What?" Janis shouted back. "You just told me I did good!"

"This is not your car," Brian yelled. "Into the backseat." Janis started to protest, but then obliged, joining Ji-A and Amirah as they climbed into the car. I used my kinesis to pick Pig up, and deposited her on the floor in front of them, and then climbed in as well. Four people and a dog were kind of tight, but then Brian got in the front seat, and Circe and Adrian squeezed in shotgun.

Brian put the car in reverse and started to maneuver what no doubt would be a seventeen-point turn to get the car pointed in the right direction. The fire alarm was still screaming, and I put one hand over Pig's ear and one hand over my own. Everyone else in the car was doing all they could to block out the sound, except for Brian, who kept his hands on the wheel at ten and two as he pointed the car in the direction of the exit and started to drive away.

The sound of the alarm didn't start to fade until we had pulled out of the parking lot, driven down the street, and crossed an intersection into the next block. Then I could hear sirens in the distance. Brian drove extra carefully, and his mouth was set in a grim line. Adrian also seemed nervous. As did Circe. The backseat, however, was absorbed in a conversation about which member of Superfüd was the cutest.

"I just really like what Todd does with his hair gel," Janis said.

"Gross," I said. "Janis, he's old enough to be your dad." She ignored me.

"I think Tom's facial hair is really creative," Amirah said. "What do you even call that kind of beard anyway?" Of all the things that I had endured tonight, overhearing this conversation might have been the worst. Then I suddenly had an idea.

"Brian!" I hissed, turning away from them so that I was facing him. "We need a soundtrack!"

"You're kidding me, right?" he said, and I shook my head, frantically digging for my phone.

"I doubt we can break the spell," I said, "but what if we can hurry it along? I don't know what the rest of this night is going to bring, but we need them." I motioned toward my seat mates. Janis was bobbing her head to a song that no one else could hear, Ji-A was tracing something on her thigh over and over, and Amirah looked like she might cry. "I want to play some good music, actual good music, and maybe we can push Superfüd out of their heads."

"Oooh," Ji-A piped up. "If you have any Superfüd, put that on." Her fellow backseat inhabitants nodded enthusiastically, but the front seat ignored this suggestion.

Brian leaned toward the stereo. "I have some Maroon 5 in here," he said.

"No!" Adrian and I yelled at the same time.

"Here," I said, passing my phone up to Adrian, "go into my playlists. There's one called 'Epic.' Put that on." Adrian plugged in the USB cord and hit a few buttons, and a second later, the first few beats of "Hypnotize" by the Notorious B.I.G. kicked in. Brian had surprisingly good speakers, and I could see Adrian start to smile as he scrolled the track listing.

"Wow," he said, looking back at me. "This playlist is definitely epic."

"Thanks," I said, looking down before I could blush.

Brian was intensely focused as he piloted us down the street, but I swear I could see him doing the most minute, almost invisible head bob.

"Wow," Circe said. "You kids still listen to this? I remember dancing to this at my prom."

A few bars passed and the car was silent. Brian turned off the main street onto a side street as the chorus started. "Oooh," Amirah said, "I like this song." Everyone who wasn't under Superfüd's spell held their breath.

"Dang," Janis said, "Biggie was the best." By the end of the block, the whole backseat was dancing and rapping along, and I felt like I could finally exhale.

"Way to go, Esme," Adrian said, turning around. "I'm so glad you're okay. If you *are* okay. Are you okay?"

I nodded. "What happened?" I asked. "Where are Cassandra and the others? Where are we going?"

"We don't know where they are," Brian said. "We haven't been able to get ahold of them."

"I flew over there to check on them like you asked," Adrian explained. "Their van was parked outside the band's house, but there was no sign of them. So I flew back to meet you, and I got there right as four guys shoved you into the back of their car. I followed them to the storage lot but got ambushed by a big flock right when the car turned in, so I didn't see where they put you. Then I flew back and found Brian, so he drove us over here. We were getting ready to leave. Then right before the fire alarm started to go off, Pig began to sniff this one particular unit, and wouldn't stop."

"Oh God," I said, reaching over to grab her wrinkles and give her a hug. "She smelled the steak! I'm sorry, girl. I should have brought it with me."

"Where did you get a steak in a storage unit?" Adrian asked.

"I panicked," I said. "Meat manipulation hasn't failed

me before. Or wait, it has failed me, but not because it didn't work . . ."

Adrian gave a quick glance past me into the backseat and lowered his voice. "Janis jumped into the driver's seat when Brian wasn't looking." He gave a mock grimace that made me giggle.

"Sadly, wrecking his car is not the worst thing we've ever done to Brian," I whispered back. "Fortunately, I think I can find a spell that'll fix that bumper."

Adrian swallowed, and I couldn't help but think he looked nervous, and then I suddenly remembered why.

"He's not going to turn you in," I said. "At least not in a bad way. Brian's not like that." Adrian swallowed again, his eyes flicking back to Brian, who was asking Circe a million questions. She kept assuring him that she was fine, that she didn't need a hospital, a doctor, or even a shower, and that she just wanted to find her daughter.

"So you didn't see them at the house?" I asked, turning back to Adrian and the most pressing problem, my missing partner.

"No, but there was a broken window in the back of the house," he said, then suddenly smacked himself in the forehead. "I should have looked in it. Or gone in. I don't know why I didn't."

"Don't worry," Circe said, leaning over and patting him on the knee. "The house is spelled to keep people away."

"I still don't understand what is going on here," Brian said. "Why now? Where have these guys been all these years? Even if we weren't trained to watch out for Red Magic, I can't believe that they never showed up on our radar."

"They didn't have magic until two months ago," I said.

"What?" Brian asked, flipping on his turn signal about a block before we needed to hang a left. I had also noticed that he was driving about two miles under the speed limit, no doubt being extra careful because we were seven people and one dog in a car built for four. "How did they get magic two months ago?"

"They stole it from me," Circe said.

A beat passed. "Oh," Brian said. He pulled to a stop at a yellow light, and I stifled a groan. I understood that Brian didn't want to get pulled over, but this was getting ridiculous.

"Brian, you have to go faster," I said.

"I am going as fast as I can," he replied, which was patently untrue.

I turned back to Circe. "So, if we can just steal the talismans back, will their powers go away?"

"Not necessarily," she said. "Judging by the number, and the intensity, of spells they've cast so far, I think the talismans are probably about to run out. However, there's always a possibility that the guys have figured out how to make new talismans. We'll have to completely strip them of all magic. Your mother and I learned the ritual. We were planning to use it on Erebus, but then we never got the chance."

"You remember what you need for it, though?" I asked, and she nodded. "Brian, do you have paper and a pen?"

"Yes," he said. "In the glove compartment." Circe popped it open, and out fell a stack of parking tickets.

"Brian!" I said, shocked. "I never figured you for the type!"

"I have a friend at city hall who takes care of them," he said, then cleared his throat. "Being head football coach does have a few, small privileges in this town, and I figure I might as well use them."

I turned toward Circe, who was already using the back of one of the tickets to write out a list. "Okay, so here's what we're going to do," I started. "You guys are going to drop Circe and me at the band's house so we can see if we can find Cassandra, Ruby, and Mallory. Then you guys take these three to round up these ingredients."

Brian nodded, and Adrian looked to the backseat and then back at me. "Do you think they can handle it?"

"It's shopping," I said. "These three could handle shopping in their sleep."

"What about Pig?" Brian asked.

"She can wait in the car," I said. "And, Brian?"

"Yes?"

"Can't you drive any faster?"

I had been trying hard to stay calm, but I was beginning to freak out. Cassandra going dark on text? Completely on brand. Cassandra going MIA in the midst of a rescue mission for her own mother? Not like her at all. If she wasn't letting us know where she was, it meant she couldn't.

"There's no way we can beat them back to their house," Brian said. "Even if I drove like Janis. They had a huge head start. If they are going back to their house, they would have been there at least fifteen minutes ago." We were approaching an intersection, and the light changed to yellow. Now I groaned out loud as Brian once again hit the brakes, bringing the Explorer to a stop instead of gunning it to speed through.

Suddenly Adrian grabbed my hand and squeezed my fingers so hard that my knuckles crushed together. "Unless they stopped on the way," he said, his voice low and barely a whisper. Then he jerked his head toward the window. Brian, Circe, and I followed his eyes, straining to see what he was talking about.

And there it was, in the bright neon glow of a Sonic drive-in: a purple PT Cruiser, drum kit in the back and four losers in the front.

"No way," I said.

"Way," Circe said, and this time, when the light turned green, Brian gunned it, leaving the smell of burning rubber behind us.

CHAPTER 21

I gave him directions, and Brian drove like a bottle rocket, careening around corners and blasting through yellow lights, and all the while the backseat sang along to "No Diggity" like they were high on Pixy Stix and on their way to a house party. No one even mentioned the S word. I thought my epic playlist was working. We all did.

Then we turned onto the band's block.

"Hey," Janis said, leaning forward and punching me in the shoulder, "I recognize this street." Oh no, oh no, oh no. Then she squealed, "This is where Superfüd lives!"

Amirah pressed her nose against the window, Ji-A clapped, and Pig started to croon. Shoot me now. Or, don't shoot me. Shoot them. Or shoot somebody. This was definitely one of those occasions when somebody needed to be shot.

Adrian leaned forward and turned down the music, and Brian slowed the car to a crawl. The block was dark and lit only by the moon, which was almost full. All of the streetlights seemed to be out, and I doubted that was a coincidence. We made one pass by the house, and then Brian stopped the Explorer down the street, next to the van.

"That's Dion's," Circe said. "He spent so much time fixing it up." It was like she was talking to herself, and for a second I wondered how she knew. Then I remembered that she'd said she'd been checking up on them. It seemed she'd kept a closer eye on her children than they, or anyone, had ever guessed.

Brian stopped the car, and Adrian hopped out, peered into the windows of the van, and then quickly came back. "It's still empty," he said. "And it hasn't moved from when I was here before."

"Lemme out, lemme out!" Ji-A cried. "I need to have Superfüd sign my dress!"

"Stay in the car," I hissed at her. "That dress is Valentino, and no one is going anywhere near it with a Sharpie."

"Esme, you're so mean," she said with a pout. "I don't understand why you hate Superfüd so much."

"I hate them because they kidnapped Cassandra's mom, kidnapped me, and used a spell on all my friends," I said. "I also hate them because they have a stupid name and they make bad music."

"It's like you don't even have a good reason," Ji-A responded, her voice sounding small and wounded. Brian looked at me, and we rolled our eyes in unison, a unified gesture that made me wonder if I was becoming more like him or if he was becoming more like me. Neither was a welcome thought.

"Okay," I said, "Circe and I will go look for Cassandra and the others." I turned and addressed Janis personally. "Janis, we would be remiss in showing Amirah and Ji-A a good ole Spring River time if we did not take them on at least one late-night Target run."

"Oooh," Janis said eagerly. "I love Target. It's a whole vibe."

"I know," I said, nodding vigorously, "and Circe put together a list of things that Superfüd likes. It's their rider for the after-party, so we need you guys to go get everything on the list and then bring it here. And hurry." I passed the list back to Janis, and she started reading it.

"Greek yogurt, calamine lotion, lavender oil, sleep masks, a mouse skull . . ." Her head jerked up sharply, and she narrowed her eyes at me. "What kind of after-party are you planning for them?"

"Think of it as a little going-away thing," I said.

"Target does not have mouse skulls," she said, raising an eyebrow. "At least not this time of year."

"I know where we can get one," Adrian said, making us both look at him.

"Okay," I said, smiling. "Have fun, and see you soon!" Then Circe and I climbed out of the car. I realized I'd left my phone in the car when I could hear strains of "Wonderwall" drift out the window as they turned the corner and drove away.

Circe and I turned and started toward Superfüd's house. If their neighbors had been barbecuing earlier, there was no sign of it now. In fact, the whole street seemed dead. We were still a few houses away when Circe stopped suddenly.

"Do you feel that?" she said, and I did. There was something in the air that made my jaw tighten and my fists clench. I felt hot, but cold, breaking out simultaneously in beads of sweat and goose bumps. The spells that Superfüd had cast on their house were now screaming. I started to rub my arms, trying to keep them warm, but touching my own skin made me start to itch. My gums had that swollen, just-flossed feeling, and I had to fight the urge to pick at my cuticles.

By the time we were standing in Superfüd's yard, it was unbearable. My skin felt like it was on fire, and there was a high-pitched shriek in my ears. I had trouble concentrating and had to fully focus to even get a sentence out.

"Wh-what is g-going on?" I asked, stuttered. I tried to clamp my hands over my ears, but that didn't help at all.

"The protection spells know they've been violated," Circe said. "They're on the attack now." I nodded and started to follow her. I felt like a skeleton, each step making my bones knock together, and the shrieking wouldn't stop. It felt like my body was going to vibrate apart from the inside out. We made it a few yards before we triggered the motion lights. I clamped my eyes shut against the blinding brightness of the lights. The Red Magic was overwhelming. If Cassandra and the others were still here, how could they stand it?

I opened my eyes, squinting to see that Circe was in front of me, and she was talking, but her voice sounded like an echo coming to me from a million miles away. I tried to look at her, but her face swam in my vision, all of her features rearranging themselves. "Focus, Esme. Focus." Her words finally made it to my brain, and I could feel her hands on my arms, moving me around like I was a bendable doll. "We need to turn these lights out now." She held my arms in front of me, and flexed my wrists. "Oscurokinesis," she said, but nothing happened.

"Crap, crap, crap," she said, starting to dig in her pocket.

"Where's your purse?" All I could do was shake my head. "Take this," she said, pressing something small and soft into my hand. "Put it in your shoe or in your bra, someplace where you won't drop it." I looked down. It was a tiny pink bear, a Beanie Baby key chain, and as I looked at it, I felt like myself again.

"It's the last Red Magic I've got," Circe said. "The band overlooked it. It's not very powerful, but it should at least make it so you can stand to be here."

I nodded, and shoved it down my dress and into my bra, giving myself one lumpy boob that was significantly bigger than the other. The shrieking died down, until it was a tolerable buzz, and my burning skin soothed. The lights were still too bright, but in an ordinary and not supernatural way. I raised my hands on my own now, pointed my palms at the lights, and repeated the spell. We were instantly plunged back into the darkness. I took a few gulps of cool, fresh air.

"The talisman should give you some immunity," she said. "The Red Magic is reacting with your Sitter magic, so you feel it more than I do. We have to hurry, though, because if Cassandra and the other girls are in the house, the Red Magic is probably unbearable for them."

I nodded, then kept nodding. "The talisman's working!" I said. "And it's not just that the spells aren't bothering me. I feel great." Circe was quiet. I tried to look at her but couldn't read the expression on her face in the dark.

We were close enough to the house now to step onto the porch. I was still aware of the Red Magic and could tell that it was popping and fizzing and felt like it was going to explode, but it didn't affect me as much. I tried to look in the door, but could see nothing, and the large tapestry still covered the front window completely. With Circe close behind me, I crept back off the porch and around to the side of the house.

The cold February air moved around us, smelling like cold concrete and slush piles. Except for the sound of the frozen, dead grass crunching under our feet, and the bare tree branches rubbing against each other, the night was silent. I could hear Circe's breathing behind me. As soon as this was over, I was going to have to talk to her and find out more about this talisman. I felt like running a race, or maybe just busting out in a dance routine. I wanted to talk to my friends, all of them, right now, because I was the most charming person I had ever met, and I was sure that wherever my friends were right now, they missed me.

"What we should really do," I whispered to Circe, "is just push that PT Cruiser off a cliff, with all of them in it. Too bad we're in Kansas and I don't know where there are any cliffs, but I bet an overpass would do, especially if we could make sure that the purple pustule landed on its roof." I chuckled, as I was pretty pleased with myself for coming up with the phrase "purple pustule" on the spot right then.

"Esme," Circe said, completely missing the poetry of my words, her voice dripping with parent, "those guys are going to be back any minute, and we need to find Cassandra and the other girls so that we can get them out of here and away from this."

"Sure, sure," I said, nodding and reminding myself to focus, focus, focus. We finished crunching around the side of the house, and I was totally focused on the task at hand, and was wondering if Amirah and Ji-A would be willing to trade all of the clothes that they'd brought with them for one Super-füd T-shirt. We were at the band's house, after all, so I could probably just steal one, and then give it to Amirah and she'd be so grateful to get rid of that YSL dress that she seemed to hate, and I would wear it and love it like it deserved to be worn and . . .

We turned around to the back of the house, and I stopped dead in my tracks at the sight of a white billowing "Ghost!" my brain mentally shrieked at first, equal parts terrified and thrilled, since I had always been somewhat offended by the fact that I, of all people, had never seen a ghost. But it wasn't a ghost. It was a curtain, or rather a sheet being used as a curtain, sneaking out into the night through an open window. A broken window.

So much for sneaking in, I thought. "Cassandra," I said to Circe, and she nodded. "But if they climbed in to get in, why can't they just climb out?"

"That might just be it," she said. "Maybe they can't get out."

"Okay," I said. "Then I'll just go in." I held up my palm toward the window and broke the rest of the glass off the bottom of the pane. As soon as I did it, the shrieking in my head made a little *woomba-woomba-woomba* sound. "Ooooh," I said, turning to Circe, "it didn't like that." I wiggled my eyebrows. "It's mad." I turned back to the window and now flicked the last remaining piece of glass with the tip of my finger. It made a light tinkle as it hit the frame, and the shrieking quivered again. I giggled. "I'll be right back." I turned and was starting to climb through the window, when Circe grabbed me.

"Esme, listen to me," she said, turning me around to face her. "Look me in the eyes as I am speaking," she said. "Do not look away from my eyes." I did as she said, and for a second, it felt like I was staring at Cassandra. The same dark brown irises, laced with fire someplace deep inside.

"Okay," I said.

"The talisman will keep you from being overwhelmed by the Red Magic because it is Red Magic," she said. "It will protect you and make you more powerful, but it will also make you forget what and who you really are. So listen to me when I say this: Your power comes from being a Sitter. It comes from your heart. Your biggest power is that you care, and that makes you vulnerable, because anyone who cares about anything or anyone other than themselves is going to be vulnerable. Red Magic makes you feel invincible because it makes you not care about anything but yourself. And no matter how powerful you are, if you don't care, you're never going to be able to help your friends. My daughter. So, when you go in that window, don't forget who you are. Don't get distracted." I nodded. "And hurry."

She let me go, and I turned around and climbed in. The inside of the house was even darker than it had been outside, not even a glowing clock. I stood still for a minute to get my bearings. I was in someone's bedroom. Two someones' bedroom, it looked like, since there were bunk beds. For grown men. Whatever.

The bedroom was empty, so I moved on, out into the hallway. Even with Circe's talisman, it felt like I was moving through chaos and static. "Focus, Esme, focus," I told myself.

I took small steps, feeling around as I walked, and came to an abrupt halt when my foot hit something on the floor. Something soft. I started to step over it, but realized that it was bigger than I thought. It wasn't a piece of clothing or a stuffed animal (which wouldn't have surprised me, considering the bunk beds). Even though I was squeamish, my Sitter sense told me that I needed to know what it was, so I crouched down and put my fingers out to feel it. I reached forward in the darkness and felt my fingers find flesh. A foot. That was attached to a leg. That was attached to a person.

Oh my God. Their pant leg was hitched up, revealing a stretch of calf above their sock, and that was what I had first touched. I'd never felt a dead person before, but even so, I was pretty sure that this person didn't feel dead. In fact, if I were very still, throughout all the frizzled energy in the house, I could hear them breathing. I worked my hands up the leg, feeling denim, and then the fuzz of a sweater, a furry knit with bits of metallic. It felt like a sweater I owned. It was my sweater. It was Mallory. I gasped.

She was lying facedown, and I grabbed her by the arm and shoulder and rolled her onto her back. Still not knowing who was in the house, I shook her and whispered her name. Then again. Nothing. I put my head down next to her face and could feel her warm breath on my cheek. She took long, slow breaths, like she was in a deep, deep sleep. "Mallory, we have to get out of here," I said, trying to pull her to her feet, but her body was like a bag of sand. Crap. I could pick her up with my kinesis, but I was scared to use my powers, since there was no telling what they might trigger the Red Magic to do. Feeling panic, I looked around me, but could still just barely make out where walls ended and doors began.

"I'll be right back," I whispered, finding Mallory's hand and giving it a squeeze. "Don't move." Telling an unconscious person not to move made one half of my brain giggle, and the other half tell it to shut up.

I crept down the hall, and at the end, I got to what I thought must be the kitchen. My knee hit something and knocked it over, and I nearly jumped out of my skin at the metal clangs it made as it rolled across the floor. I bent down and touched the part of it that was nearest me. It was metal and round, like a cup. Lightweight and hollow, with paper wrapped around the outside. It was a soup can. I had knocked over a grocery bag full of empty soup cans. I was toeing the cans out of my way, when my foot hit something soft again, and now I wasted no time in figuring out what, or who, it was.

I felt the soft fuzz of a buzzed head, and I could tell it was Ruby. She was slumped up against the wall, her legs sprawled out in front of her and the top half of her body curled in on itself so that one of her shoulders was almost touching the floor, and she was in the same state as Mallory. Breathing steadily and deeply, but 100 percent out.

What had happened to them? I stood up quickly, and resumed feeling my way through the kitchen, and finally made it to what I assumed, by the presence of a couch, was the living room. I bumped around until I found the third person I was looking for. Cassandra was lying half on and half off the couch, like she'd been crawling on the floor when the spell had finally overtaken her, and she'd collapsed there.

"Cassandra," I whispered, frantically shaking her. "You have to wake up. We have to get out of here. They're going to be back any minute." Nothing. I looked around the room and could just barely make out the shapes of the furniture, and the front door. It wasn't that far away, so maybe I could open it and drag her?

I crawled to the door, not wanting to think about the decades of spilled soup lurking in the carpet, then felt up until I found the doorknob. I turned the knob and pulled, but of course nothing happened. I continued to feel upward, looking for a lock, but there was only a keyhole. A door that could only be opened from the inside with a key? Yeah, nothing creepy at all about that. I turned and crawled back to Cassandra, trying to mentally run through my options. I could drag them out one by one, physically, but that would take forever. Even if I could use my kinesis without triggering some sort of further attack from the Red Magic, that would also take forever, because I'd have to move as slowly as possible to keep from banging my friends' heads on every doorway and corner we passed.

The Red Magic in the house had overwhelmed all three of them, and there could only be one reason why it wasn't overtaking me: the talisman. I reached down into my bra and pulled out the bear. Then I bit the head off, ripping the threads with my teeth, and shoved it into Cassandra's pocket.

As soon as I did, the static sounds around me got louder, and I could feel my face get heavier, that kind of artificial, I-could-sleep-here tired, like the time I accidentally took NyQuil first thing in the morning. I forced my eyes to open wider, and gave Cassandra a shake again, and this time she stirred.

"Cass," I hissed, "get up! Superfüd will be back in a

minute." She groaned and rolled onto her back, and then slid down to the floor.

"Blooper dude?" she mumbled. I had forgotten that she didn't know what the band's name was tonight.

"No . . . ," I started, then stopped myself from correcting her. "Blooper Dude" was a name that really captured what the band was all about. "Yes," I said, "and they're going to be here soon." I stood up and pulled her to her feet, and then shook her again. "Come on, shake it off. Your mom is outside."

"What?" Cassandra said, her voice suddenly back to normal. "You're kidding."

"I'm not," I said. "I'll tell you the whole story, but right now we have to get out of here, and fast. Ruby and Mallory are out cold, and I'm worried that if I use my kinesis to carry them out, that will trigger the house even more."

"I can just . . . ," she started to say, and all of a sudden, I saw a small flame flare up, momentarily lighting up the living room with glowing orange. I immediately slapped my hand over hers, extinguishing the flame and sending a searing pain through my palm.

"No," I said, but it was already clear that my fear had been right. The noise from the currents of Red Magic instantly got louder, progressing from a static buzz to a full-on shriek. Cassandra and I both clapped our hands over our ears, and I felt like I wanted to crawl right out of my skin. My eyeballs were bulging, I couldn't keep my tongue in my mouth, and I couldn't decide if I wanted to jump up and down and do backflips or lie down and sleep for the rest of my life. I couldn't do backflips, so sleep it would—

"Stop it, Esme! Stop it!" My conscience in the form of

Circe's voice was yelling at me. "Go, leave now!" I grabbed Cassandra by the arm and started to pull her. Using my free hand, I raised my palm and said, "Luxikinesis." A soft, glowing orb appeared, hovering about a foot in front of us. Since the alarm had already been triggered, I figured we should at least be able to see.

I started to run, and Cassandra stumbled after me. In the kitchen, she caught sight of Ruby and was at her side in two steps, shaking her and calling her name. "She won't wake up," I said. "Just grab her and go."

Cassandra looked confused, no doubt the Red Magic messing with her mind and energy, but she nodded and leaned down, grabbing Ruby under her armpits. I stepped over them into the hall, and Cassandra followed, dragging Ruby on the ground behind her. When I found Mallory, I bent, scooped her up, and knocked soup cans out of the way as I pulled her down the hall. "Follow me," I said to Cass, not sure if the words actually came out or if I just thought them, but she still managed to follow me, the little glowing orb hovering just above us.

We made it back into the bedroom, and I sat Mallory down on the floor. I felt dizzy and out of breath, but stumbled over to the window and shoved the curtain aside. Cassandra was also breathing heavily, and she kept squinting, like she was trying to focus. "Are they going to be okay?" she asked.

"I think so," I said. "You were like that when I found you."

"How'd you wake me up?" she said.

"A Red Magic talisman your mom gave me. Its head is in your pocket," I said, and from the look Cassandra gave me, I might as well have told her that I'd used bananas from Mars.

"I'll explain outside," I said. "Or she'll explain outside, but we need to go."

She nodded, picked Ruby up, and then walked her over to the window and set her down gently right beneath it. With much less grace, I dragged Mallory over.

"You go first," Cassandra said, "and then maybe you can use your powers to pull them through from the other side." I nodded, then put my hands on the windowsill and hoisted myself up and over. A gazelle I was not, and I landed on the ground outside with a thud, my dress stretched up behind me, the skirt caught on a snag of wood. I yanked it down, ripping the fabric and leaving a shred of pink behind me. The inside of my brain still felt like a tornado, but now that I was at least outside the house, it was easier to ignore the Red Magic noise. Cassandra appeared in the window, holding Ruby like a rag doll, and I was as careful as I could be as I lifted her with my kinesis and guided her out the window.

It was a team effort, and Cassandra helped, placing Ruby's arms on top of her body so that they didn't bang on anything, and then holding on to Ruby's feet so that they went right through the center. I kept my palms up and did my best to focus, and was grateful for the help, even though it felt kind of like we were two handlers and Ruby was our Thanksgiving parade balloon.

As soon as she was through the window, I set her down on the grass, and Cassandra readied Mallory, doing the same to make sure that none of her limbs, and especially her head, hit or scraped the windowsill. Once we'd cleared the window, I set Mallory down next to Ruby, who was already starting to stir, though she still had her eyes closed like she was asleep. Cassandra jumped through the window quickly, landed quietly, and then shook her head and blinked her eyes.

"We have to get away from this sound, or whatever it is," she said, then stopped. "Wait, you said my mom's here?"

"Yeah," I said. "They kidnapped us both and put us in a storage unit."

"Then where the heck is everybody?" she asked, bending down over Ruby. "Why are you a solo rescue mission?"

"They're shopping," I said.

"Now?" she said, sounding pissed. "I mean, come on. I know you guys are into clothes, but priorities, people!"

"No," I said, "not shopping like that. For ritual stuff. Your mom knows a ritual that will strip the band of their powers, so we want to do it tonight, and get this over with." I ran down the driveway and looked up and down the street, but there was no sign of Brian's car. Crap. I ran back to where Cassandra was bent over Mallory, and almost screamed when a dark blur tackled Cassandra. I raised my hands, ready to fling them off, when I realized that it was Circe, and that the tackle was actually a hug.

"I'm sorry," she said, "but I'm just so happy to see you—to finally, really, truly see you." She pulled back, and Cassandra seemed stunned. No doubt staring into a face that looked so much like hers was a shock. "But now we have to hurry! We need to get them someplace safe to wait for the spell to wear off," Circe added. Cassandra nodded, and swallowed. "There are some bushes a few houses down, if we can get them there until Brian gets back . . ." Circe stopped, and we all froze, as we heard the sound of tires crunching in the driveway. Superfüd was home.

And they were fighting.

A car door slammed, and an angry voice carried through the night. ". . . trying to pay at Sonic with a five-hundred-dollar bill? They brought the freaking manager out, dude!"

"Are you, or are you not, enjoying that cherry limeade?"

"Yeah, it's delicious, but that's not the point."

"What is the point?"

"The point is that, for the last two months, whenever any of us wants to do something fun, you get on this soapbox about lying low. But when you just have to have a Nerd Slush . . ."

Circe, Cassandra, and I exchanged looks. The driveway as exit route was now out of the question, which meant we had to go away from the street, farther into their backyard, which meant still more time in the Red Magic. Cassandra caught my eye and nodded, and I held out my hands and scooped Ruby and Mallory up, lifting them each to a few feet off the ground. Mallory's hair trailed down behind her, and they both looked like possessed children levitating off their beds. With Circe in front of us, leading the way, and Cassandra behind me, I kept my attention focused on the floating bodies in front of me, and it felt like we were making good progress. A small chain-link fence separated the backyard from the alley that ran behind all the houses, and once we got over that, it would be easy to get Ruby and Mallory back to Dion's van.

Ha, right. Wishful thinking.

"Shut up, both of you!" A voice rose up over the two that were arguing. "It feels like someone was here." In a split second, Superfüd's backyard lit up like a stadium. In front of us, there was the fence, still very far away. Behind us, four black silhouettes against the light, staring straight at us.

"You two, go!" Cassandra hissed. "I'll distract them." I nodded, and then Circe and I turned and ran, all the while zooming Ruby and Mallory along like they were on a zip line. We got to the back fence, and Circe jumped it neatly. I started to scramble over it, then heard something. A hiss, a crackle, a rush of air. I turned, and saw that Superfüd's house had gone up in flames, the blinding bright lights of their backyard now tinted with a flickering orange. Cassandra stood there with her hands out.

Oh no. This was a distraction all right, but not a subtle one. I quickly set Ruby and Mallory down in the alley, almost too roughly, and then ran back for Cassandra.

I reached her in a few steps, and then grabbed her by the arm and started to yank her back toward the alley. "They ran away," she crowed. "They just turned and ran away!"

"Good," I said, "because we need to get out of here."

The house, the grass, the clothes that hung on the clothesline were all on fire, and up and down the block, house lights were starting to come on and voices were beginning to shout.

In the middle of it, Cassandra seemed to be having a grand old time. In fact, in the disco glow of the inferno, I could see that she was smiling. I had never seen her so happy. And then it hit me. She still had half of the talisman in her pocket. No wonder she was having so much fun. She was loving this chaos and destruction.

I stuck my hand down into my bra, and started to feel around for the other half, but it was gone, probably having fallen out somewhere along the way. I panicked for a second, but then felt a wave of relief. Since I was no longer under the influence of Red Magic, I could trust my decisions again.

"We have to leave," I said, now yanking Cassandra with both my arms and my kinesis. "We won," I said. "We got your mom and nobody got hurt. We will deal with them later." Orange and yellow light danced across Cassandra's face, and beads of sweat were starting to form on her forehead. I was sweating too, because it was hot. In the distance, I heard sirens wailing. Tonight was turning out to be quite the night for the Spring River fire department. "Cass," I said, and then she nodded and we both started to run.

We jumped the fence, and in the alley, Mallory and Ruby were where I had set them down, and Circe was crouching over them. Ruby was awake, but still groggy.

"Oh my God," Cassandra said, falling to her knees and throwing her arms around Ruby.

Ruby hugged her back, but weakly. "Where are we?" she asked. "What happened? Why do I feel so awful?"

"The house spelled you," I said as Cassandra and Circe helped Ruby to her feet and started to pull her down the alley. I picked up Mallory and stayed close behind them.

"You look familiar," Ruby said, looking at Circe with a mixture of recognition and confusion.

Cassandra cleared her throat. "Um, this is my mom," she said. Ruby's eyes widened, and then she looked back and forth between the two of them.

"Nice to meet you," Circe said, smiling at Ruby and instantly picking up on the fact that this was someone very important to her daughter.

"So, we found you?" Ruby said, stumbling briefly as her foot hit a rock.

"Not exactly," I said. "But it's still mission accomplished, and we're going home. We have to get out of here while we still can."

"Where's Ma—" Ruby started, and then gasped when she turned around and saw me with my hands out, and her partner floating next to me.

"She's just asleep," Circe explained, quickly assuring Ruby and trying to keep her moving forward. "We just need to get her someplace safe so she can sleep it off."

I glanced back and saw nothing but shadows in the alley. Every second that Superfüd wasn't in my sight made me more and more nervous. "We need everyone back from that Target run, now," I said.

The sound of sirens was growing louder and louder, and I could hear people shouting. I glanced up and down the alley, but still no sight of Superfüd. Maybe they were back at the house, trying to save their home with a garden hose on full blast. But no matter where they were, we couldn't walk, or run, down the street with a girl floating in midair.

Cassandra seemed to sense my worry. "Stay here," she said. "I'll go and get the van."

"No," I said back, more forcefully than I had meant to. "We're not splitting up again."

"Well, we can't leave them here alone," Cassandra said, gesturing to Ruby, Circe, and Mallory.

"Then we're all going together," I answered. "Slower, but stronger."

Cassandra hesitated, looked behind her, and then turned back to me and nodded.

"I can walk," Ruby said. "I'm fine." Then she took a step forward and her knees buckled beneath her. Circe was quick and managed to grab Ruby before she hit the ground. My kinetic grip on Mallory momentarily slipped, and she gave a little snore as she dipped, before I hoisted her back up. "She's always been a heavy sleeper," Ruby said.

I shifted Mallory so that I was carrying her upright, and together the five of us were moving as quickly as we could, just another group of teenagers (and one party mom) out having too much fun.

We turned the corner, and Dion's van was in sight. Fortunately, when they had arrived, Cassandra hadn't parked too close to the house, but we could still see the flames. The street was dotted with people standing on their front porches and yelling about calling the fire department, and I hoped that none of them would notice that Mallory's feet weren't touching the ground. We didn't have time to zap a bunch of brains right then.

At the van, Cassandra pulled the door open, and she and Circe helped Ruby inside, and then turned to take Mallory from me. As I released my kinesis, I looked down the block. Superfüd were still nowhere in sight.

"Cass," I said, "I don't like this." Circe climbed into the back, and Cassandra shut the door behind her. Then I climbed in shotgun as Cass ran around to get behind the wheel. "Where are they?" I turned, craning my neck and squinting as I peered up and down the block, and there was no sign of them. "What are they doing?"

Cassandra turned the key, and nothing happened. "Oh, come on," she said. "Now is not that time. She banged her hand on the steering wheel and took a deep breath, then did a complicated routine of key turns and foot pumps that seemed just as religious as it did mechanical. I think Circe and I were also holding our breath, and we all exhaled as the van finally whined to life. Cassandra cranked the wheel and started to do a U-turn. The van had no power steering, and it felt like we were moving in slow motion. After one final reversal, we were finally facing the opposite direction, and Cassandra floored it. Ruby got up on her knees and leaned forward between our seats.

"Hey," she said, her voice unsteady, "something's about to happen, but I don't really understand what."

Then a guitar came flying through the air and smashed into the van's windshield.

Everyone in the van screamed, and Cassandra slammed on the brakes, sending us all tumbling forward. The guitar had hit hard, leaving the windshield spiderwebbed, and I gasped as it picked itself up and swung through the air again. This time when it collided, the windshield shattered. I threw my arm up over my face and squeezed my eyes shut, and when I opened them, my pink dress was covered with glass.

"What the heck was that?" Cassandra screamed.

I was scrambling to unhook my seat belt when something crashed into the van from the side, denting the metal and sending the van skidding down the street. I grabbed the door handle and held on as time seemed to momentarily slow. I looked up just in time to see that the van was heading straight toward a telephone pole, so I raised my hands and gave the hardest kinetic shove I'd ever given anything and sent the van skidding back in the other direction. The van turned in a half circle before it came to a stop in the middle of the street, facing the opposite direction. Circe and Ruby screamed, and Mallory woke up as she collided with the side of the van. Cassandra got her door open before me, and started to climb out.

"Oh my God," she yelled, diving back in and pulling the door shut behind her, a split second before something smashed into the van again, making the experience feel like the worst amusement park ride I'd ever been on. I now had whiplash in both directions. I managed to unhook my seat belt and get my door open. "Stay in the car," Cassandra yelled, so I pulled the door shut again. "No, not you!" she yelled again. "We have to distract it, or it will smash this van to bits."

"Okay," I yelled back. I jumped out, and the broken glass from my lap cascaded down my skirt onto the street. "But what is it?" I asked, dazed, but I saw it as my feet hit the pavement.

It was a hard-rock monster.

I couldn't think of any other way to describe it. It stood two stories tall. Its arms were mic stands, and its fingers, what had just broken our windshield, were guitars. Its body was a bass drum, its head an amp. One leg was a bass guitar, the length of a short school bus, and the other was a keyboard. Every time it moved, the instruments that made up its limbs gave off sounds that reverberated down the street. Distorted guitar string twangs that made my ears ache. In any other circumstances, I would have laughed. But it was held together by a red, fuzzing energy, glowing in its joints, and it was gearing up to take another swipe at the van.

Cassandra sprinted at it. "Over here, you big poser!" she yelled. Then she threw out her hands, sending two streams of fire right down the middle of the street toward it. The monster stopped and turned to her, its hand splayed flat like it was about ready to give a high five, the energy that held the guitar fingers together sparking red, and then it swung at her.

I held out my hand and was able to use my kinesis to lift her up into the air and out of the way, but the guitars swung so close to her that they cast a red light onto her cheek. I set her down, and the monster momentarily forgot about her because it was now focused entirely on me. It ducked Cassandra's streams of fire and took a step closer to me.

Out of the corner of my eye, I could see Cassandra raise her hands and sweep them in a circle, and a ring of fire burst up around the monster, the flames taller than me. The monster howled, which sounded like someone falling and grabbing on to a keyboard to try to steady themselves, and then the monster began to grow. Up, up, and up it stretched until it was three stories high, and it stepped over Cassandra's ring of fire.

"Oh crap!" I heard her yell as the monster roared again and prepared to hit me.

I held out my hands and directed the full force of my kinesis at its swinging arm, but when my powers hit it, I felt like I was plunging into a tidal wave. I struggled to find my breath, and heard something far off. I dropped my hands, pulling my kinesis back to me, and realized what the sound was: it was voices, specifically Cassandra, Circe, and Ruby, screaming at me to run.

So that was what I did. The monster was big, and I wasn't fast, so just like I had seen prey do on nature documentaries, I zigzagged back and forth. I jumped a curb, ran around a tree, and then darted between two cars as I sprinted back out into the street. I raced across it and into someone's yard, skirting an icy birdbath. All the people who had piled onto their porches to watch Superfüd's house go up in flames had gotten more than they'd bargained for, and now people were screaming and running back inside at the sight of the monster.

And, no doubt, at the sight of things everywhere spontaneously bursting into flames as Cassandra tried desperately to get the monster off my trail. I ran past a blazing tree and a station wagon that was on fire. The monster, unfortunately, seemed to have figured out my game, and as I ran into yet another yard, it didn't even follow me. It just waited in the middle of the street for me to come back.

As I scrambled through a front yard, I used my kinesis to grab whatever I could and throw it. A wheelbarrow, an old tire, a heavy cement garden gnome. The monster just swatted everything away like they were gnats. Behind me, I could hear Cassandra screaming at me, but what she was actually saying was drowned out by all the sounds—the monster itself, the fire, the sirens, the people, everything.

Before I knew it, I was almost back to Superfüd's house, the fire Cassandra had set now glowing brighter and closer. I could see that at the top of the monster's head was the very cymbal, now enlarged twenty times, that the band had been arguing about when I'd been in the back of their car. In the light from the fire, I could see that the grass blackened every place where the monster stepped, and at its passing, a pine tree shuddered and dropped all its needles.

I kept throwing whatever I could at it, which slowed it down a little, but I was running out of lawn ornaments. Also, I had a feeling that there was nothing I could do that would stop this thing. To stop it, we had to stop Superfüd.

At their house, I turned up the driveway and then stepped into a hole, twisting my ankle with a searing spray of pain. I hit the ground hard, embedding rocks into my palms as I tried to catch myself with my hands. But a tiny bit of fuzz caught my eye. The teddy-bear-turned-talisman. Or at least its head. I grabbed it and then rolled over onto my back. I saw the monster for a split second, and then my vision went black and there was hair in my eyes.

"Get up, get up, get up!" Cassandra shouted as she pulled me to my feet. "I don't know how to stop it," she said. "It's not a demon." As I put weight on my ankle, I was aware of the pain but distanced from it, and I felt a buzz through my entire body, like I'd just slammed an iced Venti and was going back for a refill.

"Torch that Beetle!" I shouted at Cass, pointing at a nearby Volkswagen. Without asking questions or hesitating a second, she held out her hands and did it. The car went up in flames.

"Sorry, bug," I said as I used my kinesis to grab it, and then I hurled it, with surprising accuracy and force, at the top of the monster. The flaming bug collided with the amp that made up the monster's head, and in a shower of flames, sheared the head straight off. The amp sailed through the air and landed with a skid in the middle of the street, shrinking back down to normal size as it did so. Decapitation did not stop the monster, though. Instead it just seemed to make the creature madder, and now that Cassandra and I had basically trapped ourselves between a rock and a hard place—between a burning building and a three-story music monster—we couldn't run anymore. The monster, it seemed, was trying to slap us, swinging left and right, its guitar fingers splayed out.

"Split up!" Cassandra shouted at me, before taking off to one side of the yard. As I ran to the other side, I saw the monster swipe at her. She dove to the ground and flattened herself, but as she did so, she held out her hand, and a Mitsubishi Eclipse went up in flames. Instantly I grabbed it and threw it, just as I had before, and this time it severed the guitar fingers and sent them flying in all different directions. The Mitsubishi Eclipse crashed into the neighbor's house and took out their front porch. My bad.

The monster glowed an even brighter red and swung at Cassandra with its other hand. Cassandra pushed herself up off the ground and then darted right between the monster legs. The PT Cruiser was only a few feet from me, and it went up in flames. The sight of it roasting like a purple marshmallow made me giggle, and then I picked it up and chucked it, this time aiming right at the base drum that made up the monster's body.

Bad choice. I'd been trying to hit it where it would hurt, but the car just crashed right through the center of the drum, leaving the metal circle intact, with a singed PT Cruiser–sized hole right in the middle. The car hit the pavement and skidded to a stop, upside down in a front yard, and knocked down a mailbox. I winced. I was pretty sure this was a federal crime.

None of this distracted the monster, though, and it seemed dead set on getting Cassandra. She sprinted to behind a tree, which the monster uprooted with one swing of its one arm.

I started to spin in a circle, not sure what to do next, since flaming automobiles didn't seem to be doing all that much good. And then I saw them, a little behind the house, previously blocked from view by the car.

Superfüd, standing in a circle, absolutely motionless, their heads all tilted back toward the sky, their arms to their sides, palms forward. It was like they were worshipping something, and then, in the center, I saw that they were. It was a pile of Beanie Babies. I wasn't even surprised.

Clearly they were in the middle of channeling whatever was controlling this monster. Maybe this was going to be easy. Disrupt the channel, disrupt the monster. I raised my hands, ready to give all the guys a shove hard enough to knock them onto their butts. And then something hit me, plowing me into the ground. My body screamed in pain as I scraped into a bush.

It was a giant guitar. It felt like I'd been run over by a truck. My head was ringing, my vision was blurry, and I couldn't tell which way was up. I had a feeling that the guitar wasn't going to stop at just one smack. It wanted to squash me. Cassandra screamed my name as the monster reared back for another swing. I used my kinesis to grab a nearby outdoor lamp from someone's front yard and yanked it out of the ground. As the monster swung an arm toward me, I swung the lamp toward it, and managed to hit the mic stand with the lamp before it hit me, sending a clang ringing out. I didn't have time to breathe before the monster lashed out again, and I did the same, this time catching it on the other side.

Cassandra came running toward me, and the monster turned to her and kicked at her. She dove out of the way and rolled under a bush, but then with one fell swoop, the monster ripped the bush right out from over her. The monster now had no head, one arm, and a hole in the middle of its body, but it continued to glow red where its limbs had been. It was energy, pure Red Magic, and as it loomed over Cassandra, I realized it was unstoppable. In that second, I had to make a choice, and I decided that right then, at least for the next fifteen seconds, Cassandra could fend for herself.

I turned and ran back toward the band, and when I was about twenty feet away, I held up my hands and shot my powers their way. But they didn't even budge. It felt like I was reaching out into a void. My kinesis felt like it was being pulled out, and out, and out from me. Cassandra started to scream, and I turned to see that the monster had momentarily forgotten about her and was just standing there. But it was getting bigger. I gasped, and then looked back at Superfüd. My kinesis hadn't stopped them. Instead it had made them stronger, mixing my own innate magic with their acquired powers.

I felt a vibration in the air, and the ground beneath my feet started to shake. Across the street, a tree was ripped from the ground, a massive oak, and it zoomed through the air until it connected with the monster's body, replacing the missing arm.

Cassandra had been fighting for her life when I'd tried to use my kinesis to stop Superfüd, and now that she had a break, she seized her moment, running toward them with her hands out. "Cass, no!" I screamed as flames started to lick up their pants legs. The monster let out a howl like a thunderclap. From down the street, a garden shed rose up and flew through the air, and joined everything else as a replacement head.

"What is going on here?" Cassandra screamed, watching in horror as her fire sputtered out.

"Magic won't stop them," I yelled back. "It just makes them stronger." Cassandra's hands dropped to her sides, and for a second, we both just stood there, two girls who had barely escaped death by guitar and now had no idea what to do next. There had been no sign of Mallory or Ruby, and I had to hope that Circe had somehow hidden them and kept them safe.

The monster, now apparently feeling itself, was no longer just content to destroy me and Cassandra, and with a swipe of its new tree arm, it leveled the house two doors down from Superfüd, leaving it looking like a mobile home that had just been through a tornado. "Those neighbors must have called the cops on band practice," Cassandra said, and I couldn't help it. I laughed.

"I'm glad you're back," I said, and she shot me a weird look.

"What are you talking about, weirdo?" she said. "I never left."

Down the street, the monster picked up a swing set and hurled it at us. Instantly Cassandra broke left and I broke right, and the swing set shattered as it hit the ground, except for the slide, which spun until it came to a stop just a few feet from me. If we couldn't stop the monster, then we had to at least get it away from there before someone got hurt.

Then I heard screaming from behind me, a male voice screaming my name. I turned to see that while Cassandra and I had been looking at the monster, the rest of our crew had returned from their Target run. The person screaming my name was Adrian, and he was outside the Explorer, trying valiantly to hold the door closed as the rest of the passengers fought him, trying to get out.

"What are you doing?" I screamed at him. "Cassandra and I need all the help we can get!"

"They don't want to fight the . . . ," he yelled back, dodging an arm that was trying to hit him out the window, "whatever that is! They want to get an autograph from the band!"

As I ran toward the car, I noticed it was rocking back and forth. I could barely see through the flames reflecting in the windshield, but I could see that Brian was similarly under siege, and that he was gripping the steering wheel and holding on for dear life with both hands.

"Drive away! Get out of here!" I yelled at him.

"Jackson took the keys!" he screamed back. Suddenly Amirah appeared outside the car, standing on the street right next to Adrian, and this startled him so much that he let go of his grip on the door. This split second was all Janis and Ji-A needed. They pushed the car door open, flinging it into Adrian and knocking him to the ground. Pig was right on their tail as they clambered from the car. Amirah had gotten a head start, and, shrieking, they took off after her as she ran straight toward Superfüd.

"Janis! Stop! Pig, come back here!" I screamed at them, but if they heard me, it didn't slow their roll one bit. I pulled Adrian to his feet, and we took off after them. Cassandra joined in the chase.

"Amirah! Wait!" I screamed. "They're not just bad musicians! They're evil! This is dangerous!"

"I'm going to get a lock of what's-his-name's hair!" Ji-A screamed, the epaulets of her glorious green dress billowing out behind her. "He's an Aquarius just like me!" I had no idea how she could know his sign if she didn't even know his name.

The band didn't see them coming.

Pig launched herself at Brad. Her paws hit his chest and she knocked him to the ground, and then proceeded to cover his face with kisses. At the same time, Ji-A looped her hands into Chad's hair, yanking his head down like she was about to knee him in the face. Instead she held him there and screamed for someone to bring her some scissors. No one did, because Janis was busy trying to rip the shirt off Tom's back, and Amirah was going after Todd.

"Do not run away from me!" Amirah screamed. "My dad will pay you to play my birthday party! He will pay you a lot of money!" Then she dove at him from behind, pitching him forward so roughly that his forehead bounced off the ground when he hit.

Adrian stood motionless beside me, and Brian skidded to a stop beside him. Then a tremendous crash caused us all to spin around with a jolt.

The crash was the sound of a metal storage pod dropping to the street from three stories up, followed a second later by the tree, and then everything else as the monster fell apart until it was nothing but a pile of debris on a flaming block that looked like it had been hit by seven natural disasters at once.

Cassandra and I looked at each other, then back at the band, who were still under assault from their fans. She cocked an eyebrow. "I never thought of tackling as a viable option," she said.

"Oh, you know us," I replied. "We always make things too complicated."

"I have tackles who couldn't bring down a guy like that," Brian said, looking at Amirah with admiration in his eyes.

"It must be her kickboxing lessons," I said.

"Should someone stop this?" Adrian asked.

"Someone should," Cassandra said, but none of us moved

an inch, momentarily handing over responsibility so that we could catch our breath.

"Okaaayyyyyyy," I said, drawing the word out and speaking as slowly as I could, "Inter . . . vene . . . ing . . . now."

It took all four of us to break it up, though Superfüd appeared to be in some sort of fugue state left over from their ritual and didn't put up much resistance to anything. Adrian and I took charge of the fans, who were only placated after Adrian scribbled some pretend autographs on a piece of paper, while Cassandra and Brian decided what to do about the band.

It was agreed upon that they needed to be knocked out until we could do the ritual that would strip them of their powers, but the point of contention was how to knock them out. Brian said spells, while Cassandra was in favor of what she called "good old-fashioned punching." They finally agreed on spells, with the concession that Cassandra could punch anyone who woke up.

We decided to split up. Ruby, Cassandra, Circe, and I would take care of the band and perform the ritual. Brian was staying behind to start to clean up the mess, and Adrian and Mallory were in charge of getting Janis, Pig, Amirah, and Ji-A home and into bed. Thankfully, the spell seemed to be wearing off.

"They just weren't that impressive up close," Janis said, and Ji-A quickly agreed.

"Yeah, they're huge now," Ji-A said, "but I have doubts about their staying power."

"Totally," Amirah said. "One-hit wonder."

Mallory ordered a car, and I gave Adrian the addresses.

"Where are you going to stay?" I asked him.

"I don't know." He shrugged. "I'll figure something out." We stood there looking at each other for a second, and then I heard Cassandra yelling at me that it was time to go. Quickly I reached out, grabbed his hand, and gave it a squeeze.

"Thanks," I said, "for everything." Then, before I could overthink it, I leaned in and gave him a kiss, then I turned and ran toward the van.

I helped Cassandra load the band into the van. Whatever combo of spells and punching Brian and Cassandra had used had left them stiff and catatonic, so we piled them into the back like a bunch of rolled-up carpets. Ruby and I squeezed in so that we were close to Cassandra and Circe in the front and as far away from the band as possible.

Circe sat in the passenger seat, and I think she and Cassandra were both still kind of in a state of disbelief. "I've spent so much time looking at this van," Circe said at one point. "I can't believe I'm actually in it now." But other than that, the tasks at hand prevented them from getting too much into a reunion, and Circe explained the Red Magic ritual as Cassandra drove.

"Hey, Cass," I said, leaning forward. "Where are we going to do this, anyway?" She'd just turned onto a road that would take us out of town.

"There's a little spot in the woods I know about," she said.

"Well, that doesn't sound creepy at all," I said.

"I go there to think sometimes, Esme," she said, and that shut me up, considering I'd always just assumed that whenever

Cassandra didn't come to school, she was at home doing boot camp workouts on YouTube.

She finally stopped the van a little ways down a dirt road. As we climbed out, I could see a dark tree line a few yards away. It sounded like there was a creek nearby, and it was indeed a very pretty spot. It had been a long time since I'd been out of the city at night, and the amount of stars overhead was almost shocking.

"Whoa," Ruby said, looking up at the sky as her breath puffed out in front of her. "The only other time I've seen this many stars was when they were projected onto the ceiling at the planetarium."

This made Circe laugh. "If I ever left Kansas, I'd miss the sky the most," she said. "I can't handle that small sky that other states have. It makes me claustrophobic."

"Yeah," Ruby said, rubbing her arms, "I think I might be more of a summertime stargazer, but this is really pretty, even if it is cold AF out here."

As we started to unload everything for the ritual, I turned to Cassandra. "Are you sure you want to poison the vibes of your meditation spot?" I asked, gesturing at the pile of Superfüd in the back of the van, but she just nodded.

"Ninety percent of the thinking I did here was about my mom," she said. "So I think it's the perfect place to take care of at least some of the people who took her from me."

"You guys have a lot of catching up to do," I said, and Cassandra smiled.

"I'm sorry, Es," she said.

"Why?" I asked. "You didn't do anything."

"I know," she said. "I just meant that we'll get your mom back too."

I stood there, quiet for a moment, the cold rushing right through my dress. "Yeah, I know," I said. "Now come on. Let's go finish these losers once and for all."

CHAPTER 22

It was well after midnight by the time we got the ritual set up, and I'm sure if anyone had seen us, we would have looked like the world's worst nightmare of witches. Four women in a clearing in the woods, working under a full moon to strip a group of men of the power they had cheated, lied, and manipulated to get.

Cassandra hovered, fists at the ready should they wake up, but they remained unconscious throughout the entire thing. We could tell the ritual worked, because as soon as we were finished, the guys aged right there, sprouting gray hairs and paunchy bellies and under-eye wrinkles.

"What do we do with them now?" Ruby asked.

"Leave them here," Cassandra said as chirpy as a cheerleader, "and when they wake up, if they remember where they live, they can walk home and find out their house burned down."

Ruby was shivering, and Cassandra put her arms around her and pulled her close. "I think," Ruby said, "that I could use a hot chocolate. With lots of whipped cream."

In the dark, I could see shock register on Cassandra's face. "You know that whipped cream is full of corn syrup, right?"

"I do know that," Ruby said. "How do you know that?"

"Because you told me!" Cassandra said as we turned and headed back toward the van.

"Not to be the third wheel in this convo," I said, "but I'm pretty sure that the corn syrup is what makes it so good."

It was only a few hours before sunrise when Cassandra dropped me back at my house. I let myself in, and found Pig and Mallory cuddling, completely passed out on the couch. I went into the kitchen and chugged a glass of water, then went down the hall to my room. I kicked off my shoes but was too tired to get undressed, so I flopped into bed, and that was how I slept, still in my pink, beat-to-hell prom dress, facedown in a pile of Amirah's designer clothes.

The next thing I knew, Mallory was shaking me. "Esme," she said. "It's after noon, and my flight leaves in an hour! Ruby and Cassandra are on their way to pick me up!"

I jolted out of bed and looked at my phone, which was flooded with group texts and missed calls. Then I followed Mallory back out to the living room. She'd already packed up her stuff. Pig's tail was wagging and she looked much happier than she had the night before.

It seemed like it was two seconds later when Cassandra honked the horn outside. To my surprise, she had Ji-A and Amirah in the van with her and Ruby. We walked out to the van, and I pulled open the back door to see Ji-A, who had dark circles under her eyes, and Amirah, wearing sunglasses that were about the size of party plates.

"I feel like holy hell," Amirah said, "but I had a lot of fun."

"Me too," Ji-A said. "I can't wait to come back."

"Same," Mallory said as she climbed in, "though maybe in the summer."

"Yeah," I said. "In the summer, we have mosquitoes. You're gonna love it."

"Ooh, exotic," Amirah said.

"Hey," I said, "where's Janis?"

"Oh," Amirah said with a grimace. "Janis is grounded."

Ji-A nodded. "Like, really, really grounded," she said. "Her parents were waiting up for us at home. She had to lie and say that we were at a bonfire, because we all smelled like smoke."

"It was kinda awkward this morning," Amirah said, and I nodded, making a mental note to text Janis and offer to make a coffee and doughnut delivery as soon as I could. Then I gave everyone hugs and stood on the sidewalk in my pajamas, waving to the back of Cassandra's van as it drove away. As I did, my phone dinged.

I figured it would be the group text with an update on everyone's flights out of town, but instead it was a number I didn't recognize. I clicked through to read the text.

Hey, it's Adrian. I got my phone back on and Brian gave me your number.

My eyes widened and my heart started to race. I had no thoughts of playing it cool, and wrote back immediately.

> Brian???

Yeah, he let me stay here last night too. He's been pretty cool about this whole thing.

> Awesome. Brian is kind of the best.

He seems like it. He's gonna take me shopping too, so I don't have to wear the same clothes to school tomorrow.

I read the text again, then stood there and let it sink in.

> School? You mean . . .

Ha, Spring River. So I guess I'll see you tomorrow?

> Not if I see you first!

Before I even had time to second-guess such a cheesy text, Adrian had already responded with a crazy-eyed emoji, and I could feel myself grinning as I walked back into the house. For the first time in as long as I could remember, I had something to look forward to at school.

Dad must have been at the gym or out running errands, so Pig and I had the house to ourselves. She was still snoozing in the living room, and I desperately needed a shower. I went into the bathroom and cranked the water as hot as it would go, then climbed in. I grabbed my shower pouf, soaked it in coconut body wash, and gave myself a good scrubbing. I hoped that Janis's parents hadn't gotten too close to her, or else they might have picked up on the fact that the "bonfire" she had been at smelled a lot like a burning house.

When I was done, I rinsed and stepped out of the shower. I wrapped my hair in a towel and then walked back to my room, still dripping. My clothes from the night before were piled in a corner, now looking like the remnants of a Halloween costume, and I dug through the ripped and torn pink to find a bit of fuzz. I picked out the tiny bear head and sat it on my desk.

Red Magic had almost killed us the night before, but it had also saved our lives. Red Magic was the reason Mom was cursed, but it was also probably the only thing that would ever, could ever, break that curse and free Mom once and for all. There was a whole world of Red Magic out there, and I was going to find it. Maybe not that day, maybe not the next, maybe not even the next weekend. But soon. Very, very soon.

Pig was sitting there, staring at me as I towel-dried my hair. I looked at her, and she looked back like she wanted something that, for once, wasn't breakfast.

I pulled on my sweats, and then dropped down onto the floor, so that I was sitting cross-legged, and looked her straight in the eye. "Okay," I said. "We're going to figure this out once and for all."

Back when Cassandra and I had first discovered Circe's spell book, I had used a spell to make Pig talk in words that I could understand, and I had been both disappointed and totally freaked out by the results. All Pig had wanted to talk about was dog food, and it turned out that hearing a human voice come out of your dog's mouth was less "Oh, cute!" and more "Oh God, no. . . ."

But now I was prepared, and I raised my hand, aiming my palm at her face. When her lips started to move, it looked like when she was trying to eat a rock, but then she spoke.

"It's okay," she said. Her voice didn't sound like it had before, which was like it had been being dragged out of her with a rusty fish hook. Now it sounded normal. "You don't have to force me."

I dropped my hand back into my lap, and she raised a hind foot to scratch an itch behind her ear. "Who are you?" I asked.

"It's me, dear," she said. "Abigail." The name sounded familiar, but I couldn't immediately place it. Still, I knew I'd heard it before. Pig cocked her head to the side. "Your grand-mother," she said.

That was where I had heard the name.

"Though I had always imagined that you would call me Nana," she continued, "because that's what Theresa called my mother."

I was sitting there, dumbfounded, and I had no idea what to say. My grandmother was my dog, or my dog was my grand-mother? "Wait, what?" I said finally, the only words that I could manage to get out. "I thought you were dead, but this whole time, you were a dog? My dog?"

"It's a long story," she said, cocking her ears.

"Well, I've got time! Like, all the time in the world. Does Mom know?"

"I think she was beginning to suspect," she said, and her eyes looked as sad as they did when we were out of dog food. "And I think that me showing up here again last week might have been the trigger on her curse."

Ruby's words came back to me, and I was sure that Mom did know that her mom was a dog. "She was happy to see you," I said. "It was everyone she loved in one house. That was what ramped her curse up."

Pig/my grandmother nodded, the tags on her collar jin-gling against each other with the movement. "I don't think she knew when we saw each other on Halloween," she said. "There was a lot going on that night, and she was so focused on you." My eyes started to get warm and fill with tears. "But I think she did know it was me this time. She's aware of so much."

I nodded, and now the tears spilled over onto my cheeks. Abigail/Pig took a step forward, and licked the tears off my cheeks, her rough pink tongue as familiar and slobbery as ever. "Stop," I said, pushing her away. "Now that I know you're my grandma, that's too weird."

"Sorry," she said, sitting back down. "Old habits die hard."

"I thought you died when Mom was young," I said. "Dad said there was some sort of accident, and he never met you."

"Oh no, no," she said. "That must have just been what Theresa told him. I'm very much alive and well."

I looked at her, confused. "But you're a dog," I said, not quite sure how that constituted "well."

"Oh yes," she said, "but I haven't always been a dog. I was a cat for a while, and a flying squirrel, a bunny, and I even spent a few weeks as a mountain lion." At this, she seemed to give a little shudder. "Didn't enjoy that one bit," she said. "I don't want to have to chase my food down. I prefer having it dumped into a bowl for me. Speaking of . . ."

"You already had breakfast," I said.

"Oh yes, of course," she said, "but I figured it never hurts to ask. So yes, being a dog suits me the best, and it allowed me to be close to you, my granddaughter."

I was starting to think that every person involved in the Sitterhood had no idea how to craft a narrative and told stories that were lacking more info than they contained. "But how?"

"Oh, there was an accident, all right," she said, "but I didn't die. I just got separated from my body. I had nowhere to go for a while, but then I figured out that I could share."

"Share?" I asked, and she nodded, then licked her nose.

"Yes, share," she said. "I don't completely take over, because our mission is to protect the innocent, not possess them. So there's still a dog in here, and we just switch off. Sometimes she drives, and sometimes it's me."

"The night of Halloween, when we did the ritual to help open the Portal . . . ," I started.

"That was me," she said. "But the farting, that's all her."

"Glad you, uh, cleared the air on that," I said, "but what happened at the Summit? When Wanda threw you off the roof?"

"That was a little bit of both of us," she said. "She took the initiative. Dogs have a lot of intuition, you know, and when she saw Wanda up there, she just snapped. She really does love you, which isn't surprising, since we've been here five years."

I nodded. "I love her—I mean, you—I mean, you both—too," I said.

"I took over once we were actually flying off the roof," she said. "I tell you, that was about the scariest thing I have ever experienced in all my lives. I would have peed my pants if I'd been wearing any. I didn't think we were going to survive."

"How did you?" I said.

"We landed on something soft," she said. "A Sebring."

"A what?"

"A Chrysler Sebring," she repeated. "A convertible."

I sat there in silence for a second, dumbfounded. One of my favorite episodes of *The Office* was where Michael Scott demands a Chrysler Sebring as his company car, and now I was hearing that one had saved the life of my grandmother—who was actually my dog.

"Like the one Michael Scott drives?" I said in disbelief.

"I don't know him," Pig said. "But the car broke our fall." I thought back to running down to the parking lot. Everything was hazy and there had been plenty else going on, so even if I had seen a Sebring with a dog-sized dent, nothing about it would have stood out to me.

"But where have you been?" I asked. "I put signs up everywhere for you."

"I don't know where she went, dear," she said, settling back down on the ground and putting her head on my knee. "The impact knocked me right out of her, and I had to grab on to the first being I could find who was willing to share. By the time I got my bearings, she was gone. She was injured pretty bad from the fall and scared to death. I think that someone must have picked her up and taken her home."

"What were you?" I asked. "Where were you?"

"A cardinal," she said. "Truth be told, I didn't mind it. Cardinals are pretty birds, though I'm not much for heights. But it made it easier to look for her, and I was flying along just last week, and there she was, padding down the street. I think she was happy for us to be back together, and we both wanted to come home."

"That's nuts," I said. "I mean, that doesn't just happen. Dogs don't just run away and come back several months later." I stroked her ears. They were as velveteen as ever.

She sighed. "Sure they do," she said. "Don't tell me you started believing in magic and stopped believing in miracles."

"No," I said, "not at all." I sat there for a minute, stroking her ears. "I have to break Mom's curse," I said. "I have to find that talisman she stole from Wanda. You don't know where it is, do you?"

"I don't," she said, "but I've got a pretty good idea of where to start our search."

"The backyard," I said.

"Righty-o," she answered. "And lucky for you, your grandmother happens to have four feet and be very good at digging."

I smiled as I gave her one more pat and stood up. She was right. I was a very lucky girl.

ACKNOWLEDGMENTS

First and foremost, always and forever, Krista Marino. You are like a book fairy who skips around, making stories sparkle by sprinkling gemstones of twists, turns, wisdom and insight every which way. Thank you for your humor, your expertise, and your understanding. I'm so glad we're friends. Also, thank you for your Instagram—my mom really enjoys it (and so do I).

Kerry Sparks, I feel so fortunate to have an agent who kicks ass at her job and who is also a wonderful person. Words cannot express how happy I am to be one of your authors, as you have truly built a coven of talented, supportive writers. I don't know if "Kerry's Girls" is a thing, but if it isn't, I'm starting it now and ordering us jackets. Thank you to everyone at Levine Greenberg Rostan as well.

Beverly Horowitz, fearless publisher, for leading us through 2020 and other disasters, and everyone at Delacorte Press. There's no place else I'd rather be.

Regina Flath and Rik Lee—I still can't get over the gorgeous cover illustrations and the fact that my books have pentagrams on them. Thank you for turning these books into objects of magic.

Copy editors Bara MacNeill and Colleen Fellingham—thank you for catching all the little things and for laughing at my jokes. I live for a copy-editor note that says "Funny!"

To Daria, Kourtney and Taylour, my trio of IRL baby-sitters.

To Amy and Joe, for being such cheerleaders and distribut-ing the Coven to all the age-appropriate family members.

To Rosie, for being a good girl and protecting the house from the people who need to get into it for legit reasons.

To the House on Pearl Street, for providing sunshine, bougainvillea, bird of paradise, and a place to write by a window.

To Lawrence, for welcoming us with open arms.

To our new house, for giving us a home.

To Star, I miss you every day.

To Carolyn—if twenty-three years of best-friendship isn't magic, then I don't know what is.

To Molly, Zack, and Poppy—family over everything. Thank you for being our favorite person's favorite people.

To Joe and Diane, for making me the person that I am today, and for being such awesome grandparents.

And to the Baby Penguin and the Daddy Penguin—it's a very special thing to wake up to your two favorite people every day. Remember that time we drove halfway across the country in a pandemic with raw dog food and a bunch of children's Dramamine? I never want to do it again, but I sure am happy we did it once. I love you both more than anything.

And lastly, to Esme, Janis, and Cassandra. The three of you

have gotten me through some pretty tough times over the last few years, and I am so grateful that it was my head you decided to pop into. It has been a joy to spend so much time with you, and while this may very well be our last book together, I have no doubt that you three will continue to live on, in forms and ways I haven't even imagined yet.

Heart emojis all around.

ABOUT THE AUTHOR

Kate Williams has written for *Seventeen, NYLON, Cosmopolitan, Bustle,* Vans, Calvin Klein, Urban Outfitters, and many other brands and magazines. She is the author of the Babysitters Coven trilogy: *The Babysitters Coven, For Better or Cursed,* and *Spells Like Teen Spirit.* Kate lives in Kansas. To learn more about Kate and her books, go to heykatewilliams.com or follow @heykatewilliams on TikTok and Instagram.